Dedication

For my love of writing, nature, art, and so much more.
And for my mom for always being my dutiful loving editor and my constant support.

Author's Note

Hello everyone! My name is Leyna Warrior (well, my pen name anyway, my real name is Anna Barill). Surprise, surprise, I love making stories. I have so many ideas it's a bit scary really, (over 50, I swear!) but I thoroughly enjoy all of them! As such, it is my life's mission to make sure all of these stories get written, no matter what. But why the name Leyna Warrior? Well, the reason is simple. You know that saying "the pen is mightier than the sword"? Well, I prefer the saying "the pen is my sword". I'm not just writing stories for the fun of it, there's a very powerful reason behind why I write. I want to show you worlds that people don't often consider, societies people don't think could ever be real, and situations that are outside of your standard fantasy fight for the throne. I'm here to make a difference through the words I write and that is why I chose the name I did.

The Mystics Reborn is actually a re-write of my first publication of the series under the name *The Mystics* back in 2015. Then, the book was published by Word Branch Publishing which, regretfully, went out of business. As such, I decided to re-write the series and titled it *The Mystics Reborn* to commemorate not only the rebirth and re-imagining of the story, but also represent the transformation that Rosey and her world has to go through in the series. Also, at the time, Word Branch did not allow me to publish under my preferred pen name so I had to go by Leyna Barill, a combination of my preferred pen name, Leyna Warrior, and my real name, Anna Barill.

I wasn't thrilled with it, but I was willing to comply so that I could get the story published. Now, I am committed to being known by the name I've always wanted to write under, Leyna Warrior.

This story is my first. I have many others and intend to keep writing for as long as I have ideas. I love animal characters, blending their wild nature with the human psyche, so you can always expect animals in each story. Being an environmentalist and spiritual person, nature is also a huge factor. Humans have grown apart from nature and it's vital that we reconnect. I'm a proud feminist, so women play major and inspirational roles in each story. An individual's character is not reliant on gender, so I don't see men and women as different from one and I don't treat them differently either.

For each of my stories I have what I call a patron song, a piece of music that I feel completely embodies the story as a whole. I'm not a music writer or composer so none of the songs I choose are mine; however, they're the work of artists from almost every genre. For *The Mystics Reborn*, I have chosen the song *Corchen- The Goddess and the Serpent* by Peter Grundy. Rosey's patron song is *Human* by Christina Perri because it adequately portrays the struggle that Rosey will face in this series. Check the Author's Note in each book to see what other patron songs I add as new characters emerge throughout the story.

Check out more amazing trivia and information about The Mystics Reborn on the story's blog **themysticsreborn.blogspot.com**. You can also check out my blog **leynawarrior.blogspot.com** for more information about me, the worlds I write, and the books I make. Finally, check out my website at **sites.google.com/view/leyna-warrior/home** to see all the newest books series I'm working on.

I hope you enjoy this first installment in *The Mystics Reborn* series and remember the power of the elements is always with you!

Gallery of Characters

Rosey Mystic

Rochelle Calling

Alex Crane

Contents

CHAPTER ONE

Something Amiss

Rosey gasped awake as heat spread through her body. Her chest tightened as it intensified and she kicked the covers off. She tried to remain calm for this wasn't the first time this happened. To be specific, it was the third time this week she'd awoke in a panicked sweat and experience told her to lie still and remain calm.

Eventually she felt her chest loosen and her breath come easier. She relaxed slightly, moving against the uncomfortable feeling of sweat-soaked pajamas. She licked her lips, her throat felt swollen and sore. Reaching over to her nightstand she took a sip of the water she'd made sure to go to bed with every night. It was much better than her uncle catching her struggling to the kitchen for a glass of water every morning she experienced a night terror. She took a long swig of the cool liquid and sighed.

Finally feeling like herself again, she got up and paced around the room, pushing her semi-wet hair out of her face. The night terrors started a few weeks ago and she had no idea why. She hadn't been through any trauma to warrant them, and her recent health checkup had assured her she was healthy and fit as always.

She paused in her pacing at a sudden thought. A vision of a late-night campfire surrounded by her uncle and closest friends, listening to the stories of the great heroine's Esperanza and Maharen as they battled the fearsome Raptor Demon, flashed before her mind's eye.

It couldn't be from my uncle's stories. I've been listening to them ever since I was little!? It couldn't possibly be fear of a history she didn't even remember.

The story of the Raptor Demon was ingrained deep within her. About twenty years ago a demonic evil had threatened their world, working its way onto the planet and devastating millions of people. It was devious and cunning, able to manipulate anything to its will and used powers that were foreign to them. Many thought it was the end, but the legendary warrior Maharen rose to the challenge. She was a powerful elemental warrior who'd trained in the Navy for years. Her courage and bravery earned her the title of Commander of Eyelamenta's Navy, leading a vast army of War Ships of her specific design into battle. Maharen carved the way for the Keeper, Esperanza, to strike the final blow.

Rosey shivered at the thought of the beautiful woman she'd heard so much about. Esperanza, the black haired, blue eyed, earth elemental had been chosen by the great Addina to save their world. As the Keeper, she was able to use the twelve mighty elements to slay the Raptor Demon. And slay she did. Esperanza gathered each of the twelve elements and vanquished the Raptor Demon forever.

SOOOOO there's no reason to be afraid anymore, Rosey soothed herself. *There's no Raptor Demon and no terrible monster waiting beyond Neran's walls. I'm safe...we're all safe.*

She went to her bedroom window and pushed open the wooden shutters to gaze into one of Neran's many courtyards below. Already vendors were opening their stalls for the morning market, the sweet aromas of puff pastries, pies, cooked meats, and delicious fermenting spices wafted toward her on the early fall breeze. She sighed, letting the familiar smells calm her.

See, there's no reason to fear. Not anymore. Her gaze settled on the wooden walls that still surrounded Neran and her brows furrowed. *Okay, maybe there's still* some *reason to fear.*

The Raptor Demon may be gone, but it had left behind its hordes of Raptor and Blood Goron armies. The reason behind the Raptor Demon's name were the foul gruesome beasts it had created called Raptors. Tragically formed using a poison the people called the New Copy Disease, or

NCD, the disease infected a human subject, slowly mutating them into a ten-foot-tall monstrosity with no will of its own, just an insatiable hunger for blood.

Rosey shuddered, rubbing her arms. *Of course, they're just foot soldiers, it's the Blood Gorons that are the real threat.* The four-foot-tall creatures might be small but they made up for it in smarts being almost as devious as the Raptor Demon was. They were quick and cunning, usually remaining well-hidden and resorting to guerilla tactics at every available opportunity.

A lot of effort had gone into hunting down the last dregs of the Raptor Demon's army without success. The Gorons cleverly took over leadership in their master's stead, easily re-organizing the Raptors and dictating their movements to evade extermination. Even today, Neran guards posted warnings about Goron activity and Raptor movements. How many times had Rosey heard about some assault on a seemingly safe village, built for the first time outside the walled cities? People thought they could live in peace with the Raptor Demon gone, but until the Gorons and Raptors were eradicated, they were better off remaining inside.

That's what my uncle has always said, Rosey thought, frowning. *That's why he refused to move us to the country like he'd always wanted. It's still too dangerous to live without a wall.* Thus, her uncle had resigned himself to living within the walls, stealing all his dreams of being a Research Magikin.

It also stole my parents...

The thought sliced through her heart and she rested her arms on the windowsill, gazing at the distant mountain range. Her father had been born here, in Neran. He'd been a water elemental who'd joined the guard. Brave and loyal, he'd married Rosey's mother, none other than the Keeper herself, Esperanza. Rosey closed her eyes; overcome by the conflicting emotions she felt every time she reminded herself that she was Esperanza's daughter.

Rosey blinked, thinking of her mother's journey as the Keeper. She'd become pregnant with Rosey near the end of her journey. After giving birth, Esperanza had returned to the task at hand, leaving Rosey in the care of her uncle who'd left the front lines to raise her, creating spells behind the lines to aid the fight. Rosey's father had been slaughtered by Raptors in the final battle. Esperanza had died shortly after defeating the Raptor Demon, too worn down from the terrible struggle the fierce battle had placed on her and the loss of her lifemate. Had Rosey's uncle, John, continued to fight...she might have lost him as well.

Rosey closed her eyes tight, a different kind of pain gripping her heart. *I wish...I wish I had gotten to know them, even a little.* She opened her eyes and sighed, shivering as a cool gust of wind blew the sweet smells of fall past her face. Freshly baked goods and hot wispy fires accompanied the scents. She started for a moment, surprised. The goods were already baked?!

It must be well past noon! She looked at the clock near her bed and gasped.

"One o'clock! Seriously?" She stuttered, surprised. *No wonder Hazel and Noly aren't here*! she thought, looking for her usual bed companions, a marbled collie and diluted tortoiseshell cat. The two loudmouths were noticeably missing. They'd probably snuck off to let her sleep soundly.

She smiled. *I'm pleasantly surprised at their manners for a change...but I can't believe my uncle let me sleep in this late! Heck, I can't believe I slept in this late!* She was typically an early riser on account of her warrior training regimen. *These damn night terrors are getting in the way of my sleep schedule!* What did they mean? It was as if something was nagging at her consciousness, but she couldn't figure out what. Something was there...calling out to her...something bad.

Quickly she drew the blinds closed and left the window, tossing off her pajamas on the way to the bathroom. *Though, its only Friday, it's not like I have to be anywhere.* School days were Monday through Thursday while Fridays were reserved for independent warrior, elemental, and magikin training. She was just a warrior, so she didn't need quite the extensive training as magikins or elementals did.

The thought made her stop midstride to the bathroom. Unlike her talented elemental parents, Rosey was neither elemental nor magikin, making her one of the rare Potentials, a person without power. The term referred to the fact that everyone was born with an element, however, for whatever reason, a Potential was unable to use their elemental power. Rosey was one of them. She'd never been able to use her elemental power, no matter how hard she'd tried. To make matters worse, no one seemed able to *identify* what element she had. She'd no idea if it was water, earth, or maybe some other element from her family line. Learning she'd been potential had been one thing, but then learning she was also unable to use magic took the cake. She was powerless and it stung even more with the Keeper's vast legacy on her shoulders.

She pushed the thought away and entered the bathroom to brush her teeth and wash her face. She then went to her closet to don her hard leather training gear. Pausing briefly, she admired her hard muscled frame in the long mirror on her wall. She ran her hand over her abs and flexed her biceps, impressed by the muscles bulging her skin. *Maybe it wasn't all bad.* To make up for her lack of power, she'd become quite the warrior, training with her friends and uncle at every opportunity. She'd quickly become a talented swordswoman, sparing with local guards and travelers alike to glen as many new techniques as possible.

She'd better hurry, by now her friends and uncle would already be at the training ground practicing. *Given how quiet it is in the house, Noly and Hazel are probably with them.* Her stomach growled. *Though, I'd better get something to eat first.*

Grabbing her mother's sword, Andraste, she strapped it onto her back and hurried downstairs. Her uncle was missing but a plate of food was left near the fire for her. She didn't see Noly or Hazel, confirming her suspicions they'd already gone. She greedily consumed the eggs and bacon her uncle had left, then washed it down with milk before heading out. Going to the barn she swung open the door to find her friend, a Frisian mare called Sarabie, waiting for her.

Sarabie's eyes lit up when she saw her. "Well, about time someone decided to join the living," the black beauty nickered to her, amused.

Rosey went for the grooming kit nearby, embarrassed. "It's not my fault my uncle let me sleep in. There's nothing stopping him, Noly, or Hazel from waking me."

Sarabie tossed her mane, the horse equivalent of rolling one's eyes. "Oh please, little lady, it's not like you need the practice. You're already a top-notch warrior."

Rosey walked into Sarabie's room putting the grooming kit down. It was a spacious area, complete with food bin, water trough, and a large red pillow in the corner to sleep on. "Oh contraire, my beautiful one, a warrior can always use more practice."

"And that's why he let you sleep in," Sarabie countered, whipping Rosey playfully with her long black tail as she walked up to her. "You get hair-brained ideas like that and forget to take a break."

"You didn't have to wait for me," Rosey said, butting her head into Sarabie's neck.

"What kind of partner would I be if I hadn't?" Sarabie softly answered. "Besides...I have a terrible patch of mud on my rump that I need you to groom out, also my mane has a burr in it..."

Rosey pushed the horse gently, laughing. Sarabie whinnied amused while Rosey worked on the horse's long thick mane. Sarabie sighed contentedly when Rosey moved next to her glossy coat, brushing out the offending muddy patch and any other dirt. As Rosey finished her hooves, Sarabie nibbled Rosey's long black hair and Rosey laughed, hugging her neck.

Sarabie was the closest thing to a mother Rosey had ever had. She was a gentle giant, easily standing over eighteen hands with delicate black eyes and a firm but understanding personality. She was the middle ground in Rosey's world, acting as a solid anchor whenever she needed comfort or just someone to talk to. Hazel and Noly were too silly for serious conversation and her uncle would just try to solve her problem. Sarabie listened, and sometimes that's all Rosey needed.

"I've been having night terrors," Rosey confessed to her suddenly. She left Sarabie's side and opened the barn doors. Sarabie bobbed her head as she considered Rosey's words, joining her as they walked out into the daylight.

Afternoon rays dappled them as they took to the stone covered streets. People nodded to her as she passed them, issuing greetings and small talk. Rosey waved and Sarabie bobbed her head to them. In a walled city, there weren't too many faces you didn't know. A long moment passed between them before Sarabie finally spoke.

"I know...we *all* know."

Rosey's gaze shifted to Sarabie shocked, but she nodded. She wasn't too surprised, as her most beloved companions, Hazel and Noly spent almost every second of every day with her, including when she slept. No doubt they'd caught her tossing and turning at night or early in the morning. Then again, she'd yet to have an awkward waking moment with them. Perhaps they'd pretended not to notice? Or had turned away whenever she'd woken? She caught the eye of a passersby as they waved to her. She waved back.

"I don't know why I keep having them," she said, sighing. "It's not like I've got anything to be afraid of."

Sarabie considered for a moment. "Sometimes our subconscious is just trying to tell us something...or warn us that something is coming."

Rosey gave her a skeptical glance. "Really? Like what?"

Sarabie's ears flicked. "How should I know?"

Rosey laughed and Sarabie nickered good-naturedly, her hooves making comforting clopping sounds as they walked. A few moments later they arrived at the training arena. Rosey gave an awkward smile. Arena was a strong word for what was essentially a cleared grassy patch left open for the public to do with as they saw fit. Some days it was the perfect place for school recess, sometimes it served as the festival grounds, most often it was the training arena.

Rosey sighed and stretched, feeling her muscles pull contentedly. As she entered the arena, she spied several familiar warriors sparring. Golden armored men, women, and animals from the Neran Guard practiced alongside regular warriors, elementals, and magikins from town. The air was filled with the clash of weapons and elements and spells ricocheting around them. Rosey and Sarabie carefully maneuvered around them, greeting a few they recognized as they went.

Finally, Rosey spotted her uncle's shoulder-blade length black hair, beyond him were her friends Rochelle Calling and Alex Crane. The two were sparring near a line of trees while her exhausted uncle watched them with Noly and Hazel near his feet. The two fluff balls were playing, chasing each other around the stump her uncle sat on. When they saw her, they stopped and came running, excitedly talking up a storm.

"There she is!" Hazel purred, tail high. "We thought we'd lost you to dream land, girly. Way to make an entrance!" She winked at her with a devious cat grin.

Noly skidded to a stop beside her, panting. "Rosey, Rosey, Rosey, Rosey!" she chanted, tongue lolling. "I didn't want to leave without you but they *made* me." She pointed her nose at John and her friends. "Believe me, I swear, I'd *never* leave you of my own free will...but uncle said I'd disrupt you cause I'm too loud and talk too much...which is kind of true... so I left for good reason...."

Sarabie tossed her mane again and neighed something unintelligible to Hazel who meowed back. Noly barked at them but Hazel just snickered.

"Hey, no talking in languages I can't understand," Rosey chided, smiling. "After all, you're in trouble for leaving me behind!" She then cocked her head teasingly as if contemplating whether to be mad at them. "All right, I'll forgive you this once." She then bent down and hugged them both, letting Hazel jump onto her shoulders before joining her uncle.

"Breakfast was delicious," she said, smiling at him thankfully.

"You're welcome," he answered warmly, not taking his eyes off Rochelle or Alex.

Rosey followed his gaze while she pulled her long thick black hair into a braid. Rochelle was hoovering a few feet above ground, flinging swirling mini tornadoes at Alex who blocked with a shield spell then chanted a counterattack spell at her. She dodged the white spell that slithered at her. Air whipped her brown hair about her face, her pale silver eyes alight with giddy abandon.

"You'll have to do better than that to get me, Alex!" Rochelle taunted him, smiling.

Suddenly she screamed as the tree behind her bent and a branch wrapped around her leg, pulling her to the ground in a rush. Leaping at Rochelle, Alex quickly pulled out his long dagger and had it hovering near her neck by the time she recovered.

"And you should be more observant of your surroundings, air elemental," he chided. "My spells aren't always aimed *at* you." He glanced up at the tree that was un-animating itself back into its original solid state.

"Wow," Rosey whispered to her uncle, "Alex finally got that animation spell down, I wonder if it works on more than just trees?"

John shrugged. "Why don't you challenge him next and we'll see. Come on, you could use some magikin training time." He inclined his head to Alex but Rosey gulped, fighting magikins and elementals wasn't easy. She may be a great warrior, but physical strength could only go so far. Still, the challenge couldn't go unanswered and her clever uncle knew it.

She pursed her lips at him. "Fine, I will."

John winked at her and Hazel jumped from Rosey's shoulders as she walked over to her friends. Suddenly Alex fell backwards as Rochelle threw a powerful gust of wind right into his face. He coughed and gasped on the ground, his short light brown hair a mess after Rochelle's whirlwind. A stray breeze swept over Rosey's face, making her sputter as the oxygen was almost ripped form her lungs. *Damn Rochelle!*

"And you, little magikin, should know better than to get close to an air elemental!" Rochelle finished with a victorious smile, getting to her feet.

Rosey grinned. "Okay you two, if you kill each other, I'll have no one to spar with!"

"Hey!?" her uncle shouted, raising his arms as if insulted.

Rosey waved to him.

Alex sputtered and looked at her with kind green eyes, titling his head back from his position on the ground. "Well, early bird gets the worm I hear...you should have been up," he teased. "The legendary daughter of Esperanza, sleeping in, how dreadful!"

"Har Har, I've heard that all day, get something better, dude," Rosey said extending her hand to him.

He smiled taking her hand as she easily lifted him back to his feet. As a magikin, he wasn't as heavily muscled as most warriors or elementals were, but years of sparring with them had toned him into an attractive young man. It wasn't often that a magikin trained in both magic and warrior arts, but Alex couldn't ignore the benefits of it, even if just from a fitness perspective.

Rochelle suddenly hugged Rosey from behind in a tight embrace. At six feet tall, Rochelle nearly lifted Rosey off the ground with bulging muscular arms. "Those that sleep in are doomed to smell my elemental musk!" Rochelle chanted, pushing Rosey's head into her underarm. "Breathe the sweet smell of victory!" she went on triumphantly, her pony tail smacking Rosey in the face.

Alex laughed as Rosey sputtered. Stopping dead, Rosey drew Rochelle to a halt and escaped her grip, then ducked behind her and grabbed the brunette's long lengthy body lifting her off the ground and throwing her down.

Rochelle landed with a humph and coughed, "Oh, and the mighty warrior has humbled the elemental, but I'm used to this kind of abuse. You'll have to do better than that!" She rolled onto her back and jumped up quickly.

Rochelle's gleaming silvery eyes were hypnotic and delicate, a drastic contrast to the many scars covering her body from the numerous times she'd fallen while learning to fly as a child. Flying using the air element was the hardest technique an air elemental could learn and Rochelle hadn't given up till she'd mastered it. Now, she could fly or hover for hours on end without rest.

Rosey backed away from her, smiling. She lifted Andraste from her back, assuming a fighter's stance to face Rochelle and Alex. Both were decked out in their tough leather training gear. From the dirt on then, they'd already been at it for hours. She'd really been late.

"Let's go, my daring foes. Fight like warriors!" She taunted them, excitedly.

Rochelle titled her head at Alex questioningly. "Why would we ever want to do that?"

Alex shrugged then the two of them rushed Rosey in a quick coordinated attack. Rosey started, backing away. *They planned this? Those traitors!* But she was fast and she was well trained. She quickly used Andraste to block a burst of air sent her way from Rochelle on her left, cutting the breeze in half so it went around her harmlessly. Then turned around just in time to expertly dodge a magically made net forming from the tip of Alex's wand, its yellow energy pulsated as it ensnared Rochelle instead of Rosey.

Rochelle sputtered as the magic net wrapped around her, pushing her arms to her sides and her legs together in a tight hold. To her credit, she didn't let herself fall, using blasts of air from her hands to maintain an upright position...though a comical one. Rochelle cursed angrily as she fought to release herself, leaving Rosey free to deal with Alex.

Rosey knew, from her years of practice, that the best way for a warrior to beat a magikin was to either knock them out before they could cast anymore spells or separate them from their wand. While magikins could still cast spells without a wand, the item helped supply the magic needed to create more advanced spells, so taking the wand away limited them significantly. Most importantly though, speed was key. Spells took time and the more advanced a spell, the longer it took, so the best opening for counterattack was the time in between spells.

She advanced on Alex quickly. The shock of hitting Rochelle instead of Rosey had distracted him enough to make him slow to recover. Rosey was beside him in a moment, using the hilt of her sword, she knocked his wand from his left hand, kicked the still falling wand away from him, and grabbed his dominant left hand with her free arm, twisting it behind his back. She then forced him to the ground with a soft kick to the knee while yanking his left arm and torso back towards her, unbalancing him. He toppled easily, overwhelmed by the ferocity of her counterattack.

She held him to the ground with her left knee in his back and pinned his right hand to the ground with her pommel. If she'd been serious, she'd have pushed the pommel and her knee in deep, causing pain, but this was only practice and she didn't want to hurt him. She looked up, only to see Rochelle escaping the bonds of the magic net. The spunky brunette called forth a whirlwind of air around herself that she then sent hurtling outwards at impossible speeds, tearing the magic net apart. The force was so strong that it hit Rosey in the chest, pushing her off Alex and onto her back.

She coughed as she hit the ground hard, but rolled with it, jumping back to her feet quickly. Thankfully, she'd kept ahold of Andraste. Alex was an exceptional magikin, but Rochelle was an even better elemental. Rosey knew there was only one thing she could do. When facing elementals, the best counterattack was a warrior's *element* of surprise and distraction. Rosey quickly, purposefully, threw Andraste straight at Rochelle in a perfect arch.

Rochelle's eyes went wide and she yelped comically as the sword sliced toward her. She stopped whatever wind attack she'd been about to unleash on Rosey as she now formed a defensive maneuver to deflect the sword. Only, Andraste was no longer slicing toward her, instead, it was now imbedded in the ground right in front of Rochelle, exactly as Rosey had wanted. With Rochelle's eyes on the sword, she didn't see Rosey rushing towards her at breakneck speed.

Alex was trying to get up from the ground. As Rosey passed him, she pushed him back into the ground and grabbed his wand from the ground as she went. She then yanked Andraste from the ground, grabbed Rochelle from behind with her left arm, pinning her arms to her sides again and held Andraste at Rochelle's throat. Rochelle stilled herself, but Rosey wasn't done. Moving Andraste, she then shoved Rochelle into Alex right as he got to his feet. The two of them collapsed to the ground, a mess of tangled limbs.

John burst out laughing and started clapping, the fight over. "Well done, Rosey!" He praised, "That was flawless, I knew you could do it."

Rosey gasped for breath, the adrenaline of the moment wearing off. Noly, Hazel, and Sarabie were staring at her in awe, impressed.

She laughed and sheathed Andraste. "I'm shocked myself..." She really was. That was the first time she'd won against both Rochelle and Alex at the same time. Memories of her past losses flashed through her mind. She'd felt far more prepared and focused this time than ever before...almost as if...she was on edge. She shook herself, instead saying, "It's easier to do knowing you're there to make sure no one gets hurt, uncle."

John nodded. Rosey's biggest hurdle with training was that she'd always feared hurting the people she was sparring against, whether it be her friends, uncle, or a stranger. The only things she wanted to hurt were the Raptors and Blood Gorons. And there was no way to truly gain experience and practice correctly if they weren't using real swords, real elements, and real magic. So, in every practice session, one of their group would solely focus on protecting the others from serious injury, stepping in if the fight got out of hand or a mistake was made, leaving them open to train unrestrained.

It wasn't that foreign of an idea, lots of practice groups used referees to help keep watch over the sparring sessions. In fact, in some cities, there was a designated referee in charge of the practice arena whose job was to maintain the arena and protect the lives of those that used it. Neran was too small to have an official referee, it was 'spar at your own risk' here, but those that did use the arena/field had done the same as Rosey's group did.

By now, Alex and Rochelle had sorted themselves out and were gazing at Rosey, half amazed, half embarrassed.

"Dang girl...you had me thinking you were actually going to cut my head off..." Rochelle said, pouting as she rubbed her neck, sweat beaded her brow.

Rosey rolled her eyes.

"At least you got an attack in, I was constantly on the ground today...four times!" he said. His face was now spattered with dirt, it didn't do much to diminish his handsome features.

"You both don't fare well with close quarter physical attacks," John said, considering them. "We'll need to work on that."

Rochelle stuck her tongue out at him while Alex said, "Yeah, yeah...we've always been better long-range fighters, we know."

Rosey smiled at them, giving Alex back his wand, then offering both her hands to pull them to their feet. "Don't worry, I'll help you get better."

A wicked grin spread across both of their faces suddenly and Rosey knew she'd made a fatal mistake. Rochelle and Alex grabbed her offered hands and yanked her to the ground with them. Rosey laughed as they then started a very childish play wrestle in the middle of the practice arena.

Alex tried to wiggle away and she quickly grabbed him, tickling his sides.

"Rosey!" he chided, giving her an annoyed look. "You said you'd stop doing that!"

She and Rochelle giggled as they all got to their feet.

"Seems you all don't take the Raptors and Gorons too seriously, do you?"

The voice split the three friends from each other like a cold bucket of water. Those who'd stopped to watch their crazy banter gasped and backed away. The Golden armored Neran Guards took a knee, bowing low, their heads downcast.

Standing a few yards away was the Golden Goddess. The woman pursed her golden lips while golden eyes surveyed them. Long, thick black hair was wrapped in golden tassels and a simple gold headband rested on her forehead. She wore a gold Neranian outfit with golden plated armor along the left side of her body under her left breast, ending at her left thigh. She eyed them with a gaze like daggers, her expression hardened by years of battle. A silver wand scabbard hung on her left hip, elegantly decorated unlike the wooden one Alex wore.

All three friends gulped and bowed their heads as she approached them, her right hand draped across the scabbard of her golden saber resting on her right thigh.

"I'm sorry, my lady Goddess," Rosey answered her. "We didn't mean to make light of the situation."

The Goddess paused beside her, looking her over. She then smiled. "I know."

The three relaxed, smiling as the Goddess moved to John's side. He bowed his head to her before offering her the stump he was sitting on. She bowed back but waved away the offered seat, preferring to stand. Onlookers went back to their sparring.

"For crying out loud, my lady, do you have to go scaring everyone like that?" Rochelle asked, crossing her arms.

"Well, I've got to hold onto some respect, don't I?" she answered elegantly, her voice rich like honey. "But in all seriousness, things aren't all fluff and bunny rabbits beyond those walls." She inclined her head to the tall 20-foot barrier surrounding them. "We've got to stay vigilant."

Rosey gulped. Of all the warriors and leaders who'd fought the Raptor Demon's hordes, no one knew more about the danger of the Gorons and Raptors than the Golden Goddess. She was one of the many World Leaders and Neran's main leader. She'd fought long and hard in the war against the Raptor Demon as a captain of one of Maharen's War Ships. She'd slayed hundreds of the brutes and still her job wasn't over. She went out almost every day to hunt down the remaining army, determined to kill them all.

The term Goddess wasn't used loosely, in fact, no one deserved it more. Elementals and Magikins were classified into three levels of power. The lowest level was called witch or wizard for magikins and apparition for elementals. The middle level was called god and goddess for both magikins and elementals while the last and most powerful level was called queen or king for elementals and mage for magikins.

Rosey's gaze settled on the golden-clad woman. Being the most powerful magikin alive, it would seem strange that she was only a goddess level, but no one had ever achieved the mage level...not since the last great mage that lived over three hundred years ago. According to Alex a magikin became a mage when their wand transformed into a staff. Until then, the god/goddess level was as high as they could go. For now, the Goddess's wand had stubbornly remained a wand.

"Did you come to help us spar, Golden Goddess?" Alex asked her hopefully, twirling his wand playfully with a wide grin.

Always looking for a chance to hone those skills, Rosey beamed at him. It wasn't too often the Goddess joined the morning spar. She was far too powerful to spar with the citizens so she usually trained alone within the safety of her Golden Palace. If she did join the citizens, it was usually for warrior training, not magikin practice. *Humph, tell that to Alex.*

The Goddess looked at him, her eyes distant. "I'm afraid not children, I'm making my rounds through Neran with an announcement."

Her golden gaze, normally filled with kind humor and understanding, suddenly hardened making Rosey frown. John tilted his head at her and Sarabie looked up from the grass she was nibbling. Noly and Hazel became quiet, giving the Goddess concerned looks.

They all waited, but the Goddess turned away from them, directing her attention to all the gathered warriors in the arena. Taking out her wand she issued a quick spell that amplified the sound of her voice. Speaking into the tip, she said, "Tonight, Addina will call a meeting at Central Square. All will need to attend, for it is of the utmost importance. Please, don't delay. The meeting will be held at 7pm sharp. That is all!" She put her wand away as the onlookers whispered to each other.

Rochelle wasn't so quiet. "Seriously! *The* great Addina, the one and only!?" she asked, her mouth hanging open.

"Rochelle, close your mouth. You look like a gaping fish," John advised teasingly and Rochelle obliged.

The Goddess turned back to them, nodding. "Indeed, that's what she told me." She lifted her hand quickly as Rochelle made to ask more. "Please, I don't know any more than I've already stated. Addina approached me this morning and asked I prepare the people for her announcement tonight, that is all."

For a moment her gaze rested on Rosey before settling on her mother's sword, Andraste. There was something hidden in the woman's expression that Rosey couldn't read. Rosey's brows furrowed but before she could say anything the Goddess turned away from them, her golden sash swishing as she left. She waved over her shoulder.

"Happy training, I've got a lot of city left to cover. I'll see you at the announcement tonight."

She paused beside John who bowed to her. Something seemed to pass between them before she kept walking. For a moment Rosey thought she saw her uncle fidget worriedly as if something was wrong.

Her chest tightened suddenly...just like it did with her night terrors. She started coughing, then she bent over as pain sliced through her chest and heat bubbled in the pit of her stomach. She heard Rochelle gasp and Alex call out her name. John came rushing over, his gentle hands grabbing her as she fell. She was sure she heard Noly yip, Hazel meow, and Sarabie neigh alarmed, but the darkness of pain clouded her vision. Fear gripped her and she swore she heard something calling out, something dark and twisted. A terrible cloud of black hate seemed to ooze over her consciousness and all she could see were shadows. Pain...fear...hatred...so much hatred...it bubbled over her like a poison. She gasped and her world went black.

CHAPTER TWO

Rude Awakening

"Are you sure you're feeling all right?" Rochelle asked for what seemed like the hundredth time.

Rosey almost rolled her eyes but stopped herself, Rochelle was just worried. They all were. Her uncle stood by the water basin, carefully washing the dishes from their dinner. Out of all of the worried faces staring at her, his seemed the most unconcerned, as if he'd expected this. Rosey's gaze watched him as she spoke.

"I assure you, I'm fine. The night terrors are just that, terrors that come and go," she answered.

"Yeah, but night terrors tend to happen at 'night'," Alex emphasized, sitting down on the couch next to her. He'd washed his face and magicked away the dirt from his and Richelle's clothes while she'd been out.

He and Rochelle hung out at her house all the time. Normally they'd eat dinner at their own homes with their own families, but Rosey's odd episode had left them worried enough to stay behind and keep an eye on her. A warrior healer had been practicing at the arena that day and took a look at her while there. Apparently, she was right as rain, physically at least, so they'd brought her back home to rest.

"I know," Rosey said, looking at her hands. "I don't know what's going on! I thought it was just nightmares at first, but this time was different.

All I know is something doesn't feel right and it ends up manifesting in this...terror..." she trailed off, unsure of what she was trying to say.

Rochelle and Alex exchanged glances as if they knew something she didn't. For a moment, their eyes locked with John's at the basin before breaking away. Rosey frowned at them knowing what they were thinking but was too exhausted to say anything. Given her heritage, some looked to her as a shining relic of her mother's legacy, and that often-carried superstitions with it. As the daughter of the Keeper, if the planet did something, all eyes usually went to her for an explanation as if she was some planet whisperer. But what her chest pains had to do with it, she had no idea. She took a swig of her uncle's hot tea, enjoying the orange flavor.

Hazel rubbed against her left arm, purring loudly. "I was so worried...especially when you fell." she meowed.

Noly nodded nearby as she lapped up bread scraps that had fallen on the floor from dinner. "It was..." crunch "...really scary..." crunch "...I couldn't..." crunch "...help you" she said between chews, licking her face. She swallowed then pushed her nose under Rosey's arm and Rosey patted her head.

"Suck-up," Hazel whispered and Noly nipped at her playfully.

"Yeah, yeah, I love you both," Rosey said, petting them. She suddenly felt very exhausted, even after consuming her uncle's luscious chicken stew. She fell against the pillows, sighing. "Come on guys, the healer said I was okay, right?"

"True," Sarabie whinnied sticking her head in through the window connecting her barn room to the interior of the house. "But she also said the terrors could be a subconscious portrayal of your inner fear about not having any elemental or magical powers," she went on softly.

Her dark gaze burrowed into Rosey questioningly and Rosey stiffened, looking away. Could that really be the reason? Was she afraid, afraid of being powerless?

"That's hard to believe," Alex said, making Rosey want to hug him. "After what Rosey did today, she's anything but powerless."

"Yeah," Rochelle said, stretching exaggeratedly. "I'm gonna' be sore tomorrow."

"I admit, Rosey's performance today was exemplary," Sarabie agreed, "but that's the first time she's won against the two of you. Her ability may be improving but I worry it is born of fear instead of confidence."

Geesh, Sarabie! Rosey's brain screamed silently. *She's always been brutally honest.* "Please guys...I'm right here, have a little tact," Rosey said, eyeing them.

Rochelle wrapped her arms around Rosey in a big bear hug. "Sorry, Rosey, we're just worried about you!" she insisted.

"Come on, now, the healer said Rosey's all right and I have no reason not to believe her," John said, finishing the dishes. He sat them to the side to dry. Rosey would put them away later. Normally she was the dishwasher but her episode today had made him insist she take it easy. He walked over to them, leaning against the kitchen counter. "The terrors will pass in time as Rosey grows as a warrior. Everything will be all right." The stern but gentle assuredness of his voice calmed them. He looked at the magically powered clock. "Oh, we better get going, the announcement will be made soon."

Rosey started. She'd almost forgotten about Addina's announcement! She swallowed a wave of nervous energy that had nothing to do with her terrors. "Wow...Addina...do you all really think she's...you know...a winged unicorn?" Rosey asked no one in particular, but she saw Rochelle and Alex shiver excitedly.

"I don't know...that's what they say at least," Alex answered. "I've read she rules the Settled Valley, you know, where the unicorns and pegasi make their home. But no one's ever really seen or spoken with her much. Those that have are usually the World Leaders like the Golden Goddess. *Addina* comes to *them*, not the other way around."

"Do you think she's going to appear to us in person!" Rochelle wondered; her eyes large with awe.

Noly yipped excitedly, tail wagging. "I hope so! I've heard she's magnificent! And big, really, really big!"

"Yeah, I heard...when she appears, it's like light is shining all around you and you can barely breathe..." Hazel murmured, lost in thought. Rosey patted her fur comfortingly.

"Sarabie, you're a horse," Rosey said, turning to the black beauty. "What's the horse 101 on Addina?"

Sarabie smiled before huffing. "There's about as much similarity between horses and Addina as there is between a spoon and running water, my child! I know absolutely nothing about Addina nor the unicorns and pegasi of the Settled Valley, only that they live there and stick to themselves."

"Well, she's got to be nice, right? She's our Immortal, after all," Rosey said, confidently.

Alex shrugged and Rosey fiddled with the end of her hair, remembering what she'd been taught. Immortals were planetary caretakers, they looked after all the life on a planet from the smallest insect to the largest dragon, they were in charge of it all. They certainly weren't invincible, but they had a lot of power and their very life force was connected to the planet they protected.

Immortals could either be well known by their planet's citizens or unknown, hiding in the shadows, always watching. Addina was neither hidden nor really out there. She mostly kept to herself and her Settled Valley, only usually seen by the World Leaders. Some said she dedicated her time to hunting down the Raptor Demon's armies, while others said she was busy righting the world after the war...but there were too many rumors to know the truth. Most everyone knew she was a winged unicorn, and the only one of her kind on their planet.

From what Alex has been able to find in his books, Immortals can be any species...heck...they can even be a species the planet has never seen before. At least in Addina's case we have unicorns and pegasi, so she's not that unusual. Rosey briefly wondered what other Immortals from other planets might look like.

"Let's just go to the meeting and we'll see for ourselves, okay?" John urged them on.

Rochelle and Alex nodded, getting up. Hazel climbed onto Rosey's shoulders, draping across her neck as the trio followed her uncle out the door. Outside, they joined Sarabie as she opened the barn door by stepping on a magically constructed blue pad with a paw print on it. Rosey had always thought they were cute looking.

They took to the streets drawing into an already thickening crowd. Eventually they made it into the Central Square, the largest courtyard in Neran. Vendor's booths were already put away for the evening due to the meeting, leaving ample room for the numerous citizens. The nearest shops and restaurants remained open on the perimeter, allowing seating and serving refreshments as needed.

Rochelle and Alex called out to their parents and went to greet them. Rosey waved them on but was distracted by the sight of the Golden Goddess who waited patiently in the middle of the Central Square. She was pacing at the base of a magically made golden platform, something the Goddess conjured whenever making announcements. This one was much larger than those she'd conjured for herself in the past...winged unicorn sized perhaps? The Goddess herself looked unsure and Rosey couldn't blame her. It wasn't every day that Addina said she was making an announcement and if she was coming in person, then it had to be important.

Rosey fidgeted as she waited in the crowd with her uncle. She leaned against Sarabie's giant frame, rubbing her neck. Hazel, in turn, rubbed her head against Rosey's cheek sensing her unease.

"I can't see..." Noly complained. "Hey, sky-tower," she said to Sarabie, "let me up, please?" She grinned a fang-filled grin and Sarabie tossed her mane.

"Fine, but no claws or I'll buck you off," Sarabie relented, lowering herself by bending her left leg.

Noly barked happily then leaped onto Sarabie's back, balancing expertly.

Rosey paid them little mind as people gathered closer, their eyes trained on the pacing Goddess. She looked at the sky. It was just starting to darken as the sun set in the horizon, its rays casting shadows over the crowd. Rosey sighed feeling uncomfortable all of a sudden as if the walls surrounding Neran were closing in around her heart. She took a breath and let it out slowly. Her uncle stood on her other side and craned his neck to see over a gryphon in front of him. The brown and tan beast titled her head and wings toward her body as she sat down and his view cleared.

"I wonder if she really will appear to us...*physically*," John wondered.

Rosey looked for Rochelle and Alex, but they'd become lost in the crowd. A few dogs went running by between the people's legs and Noly barked at them. Two other horses drew close and Rosey smiled, recognizing them. It was Bronzo and Filla, Alex and Rochelle's partners. She hadn't seen them at the arena that morning so they must have been off grazing. They greeted each other warmly then made room for the two horses.

Bronzo titled his buckskin body towards Sarabie. "Hey Sarabie, still letting Noly ride you huh?" he teased swishing his tail at Noly. Noly just grinned.

"Don't start, mustang or I'll bite ya," Sarabie shot back, annoyed. She was much bigger than either of them and they knew it.

Filla chuckled on Bronzo's other side. "Good to see you still have your sense of humor," she commented, tossing her mane. "How're you doing Rosey?" the palomino thoroughbred asked with concern.

"Yeah, Alex told me you weren't feeling well earlier," Bronzo added. "He was really concerned. We all were."

"I'm fine, really," Rosey said, embarrassed. She was starting to hate all this attention. "It's nothing that won't go away with time."

Bronzo's ears went horizontal to the ground, the equivalent of a human furrowing their brows. "If you say so. I'm sure it's nothing."

"We would have come sooner but we figured we'd see you today at the meeting," Filla explained.

Rosey nodded to them and was about to ask if they'd seen Rochelle and Alex but suddenly the Goddess spoke up, now standing on the platform.

"Citizens of Neran," she said, her voice amplified by her wand, "I want to thank you for coming tonight. Very soon, Addina will make her announcement. Please be patient. But first, I want to clarify something. This announcement is not just limited to Neran. No, in fact, it's being issued all over the world!"

Rosey gulped as a shocked hush fell over the crowd. She really shouldn't be surprised, after all, if it was important enough for one town, it had to be important enough for them all. Still, what could be so important that it required Addina to address the entire world?

She shivered suddenly, a chill running up her spine. *Could it have anything to do...with the Raptor Demon? Oh, Almighty One, I hope not!* She rubbed her arms together, feeling cold all of a sudden as if her life's energy had been sucked from her body.

"I don't know what she's going to say," the Goddess went on, "but know that I am here for you as I have always been. Whatever the announcement, we will not falter. We shall never falter!"

A resounding triumphant cheer went up from the crowd. Animal and human voices alike crying out, their eyes ablaze with determination. Elemental's elements seemed to sizzle and wrap around them while magikin's wands hummed with life. Rosey swore she felt Andraste, her sword, ringing on her back. There was no doubt the people had come a long way in this battle and they'd never give up their hard-won victory, not now, not ever. The thought filled Rosey's heart with bravado and chased away the cold surrounding her. She straightened and her uncle smiled beside her, resting his hand on his wand's scabbard.

They didn't have long to wait, almost as soon as the Goddess stopped talking a bright light suddenly enveloped the square. Rosey shielded her eyes from the blast and felt a rush of energy slam into her. It wasn't strong enough to knock her back, but it left her almost out of breath and momentarily stunned. She wobbled where she stood, balancing against Sarabie's large frame. Noly whimpered, probably now regretting her high seat, while Hazel ducked behind Rosey's long black hair, cursing. Rosey peeked past her arm and gasped.

Standing in the middle of the square was Addina. There was no one else it could be for there was no other winged unicorns besides Addina and the creature before them was most certainly a winged unicorn. Shimmering light radiated from her silky, cream-colored body, highlighted as if from the inside by golden tendrils. A long golden mane and tail fell elegantly along her thick, muscled body, reminding Rosey of the Percheron horse. A crystalline horn of alabaster white glowed on her forehead with pupil-less and iris-less white eyes, outlined in gold and silver dapples. A spray of dappled colors ran along her rump flowing into muted multicolored wings, so large they were twice her size. She was huge, by Rosey's measure, she had to have been well over twenty-five hands tall, if not taller. She was magnificent, purely magnificent. Rosey was too captivated to speak or do anything more than stare and she wasn't the only one, all eyes were locked on the majestic creature.

The Goddess, however, was not so undone. "You've finally made your appearance, Addina. It's good to see you." She bowed low at the waist; her eyes downcast.

The sophisticated part of Rosey's brain thought the Goddess sounded far too informal when addressing their planet's Immortal.

Addina turned her elegant head to her, a smile touching her lips. "What, am I late?" Her voice was deep and powerful.

"Of course not, but we've all been holding our breath to see what you have to say. And, I admit, I wasn't expecting you to appear to us so...physically," the Goddess explained, voicing everyone's thoughts.

Addina laughed and Rosey almost flinched, surprised by how normal it sounded. "Indeed, but what I have to say is far too important for just my voice to pass along." The elegant creature became solemn suddenly, her eyes downcast as if pained by what she was about to say.

Rosey's brows furrowed concerned and she felt her uncle shift uncomfortably beside her. For some reason the Goddess's eyes rested on his and Rosey looked between them, taken aback. What was it with those two?! But what Addina said suddenly struck her. *Wow! If she's here physically with us, does that mean she's also* physically *present at the other towns around the world?*

Addina turned to the crowd, her mane billowing around her. "Listen all. What I'm going to say won't be easy to hear. But you deserve to know. You...my beloved citizens...have been through so much." Her voice broke and she bowed her head to them suddenly. "You deserve my most humble respect, and it is for that reason that I approach you now." She was silent for a moment but finally lifted her gaze to theirs and Rosey could swear she was looking right at her. "The Raptor Demon is gone, that is true, however, it left something behind."

A gasp of fear and dread spread through the crowd and Rosey felt her chest tighten.

"While we fought to destroy the demon that threatened us, it was busy poisoning our world. Slowly but surely, it tainted the very life force that flows through this planet and allows it to live. Like a disease, it has spread and soon it will devastate the world."

Rosey swallowed a wave of panic in her chest. People and animals shifted all around her, whispering harsh exclamations but they fell silent as Addina went on.

"The fault is mine, my citizens!" Addina confessed, once again bowing her head. "I was so focused on helping Maharen and Esperanza...so focused on preparing the Shanobie Crystal for the elements that I...I let the Raptor Demon's poison slip by my attention."

The Shanobie Crystal, Rosey thought, her mind led astray as if to avoid the devastating truth. *Created from the tip of Addina's own horn, it served as a way for Esperanza to collect all twelve of our world's elemental powers and use them in battle.* The Shanobie Crystal had allowed Esperanza to control each of the world's twelve elemental powers, including her own earth element, at the highest level possible, Queen. Using those elements Rosey's mother had vanquished the Raptor Demon...but what did it matter if the beast had poisoned their planet!

Suddenly, her brows furrowed with realization. "Of course," she whispered under her breath, "the best way to defeat an elemental is misdirection." All of her mother's efforts...her life...spent on the demon's *distraction*! Anger flared in her heart as Addina spoke. She clenched her fists, fighting the urge to scream, to grab Andraste from its sheath and start hacking at something...anything! Just so long as she could *do* something! Her parents...all those who had died...had it all been for nothing?

She suddenly felt her uncle's right arm wrapping around her shoulders, pulling her into him, and drawing her back to the present. His gaze was locked on Addina worriedly, but his familial action had saved her from the dark vision she'd been drowning in. She blinked gratefully at him before turning her gaze back to the platform.

The Goddess's eyes widened worriedly. "The poison, Addina, how far has it extended?" She took a step toward her. "Please don't tell me...the Energy Flows?"

Rosey shivered and everyone strained to hear, holding their breath for Addina's answer.

"Rest assured, so far, the poison has not reached the Energy Flows."

At this, a noticeable sigh of relief washed over the crowd. The Energy Flows were large tubes of energy running throughout the world. They were like the DNA strands of the planet itself, housing every single piece of biological information that made the planet what it was. This not only included the elemental powers people had access to but the magical ones as well. If the poison were to taint them, it wouldn't be long before people lost their powers and soon after...their lives. Without Energy Flows, a planet was nothing and there'd be no way they could help either since most Energy Flows were hidden from sight and only the Immortal could see them. Their planet was no exception.

Rosey gulped but Addina bowed her head. "Please, forgive me!" She bowed lower, her horn almost touching the ground. "I have let you down! But I swear to you...I have not come just to bring you this bad news. I also come with a plan!"

The Goddess's gaze sharpened suddenly and she crossed her arms, her gaze focused on Addina.

"There's not a single person on this world that doesn't know about Esperanza and the twelve elements. It is my belief that, just as the Keeper destroyed the Raptor Demon, so too might another Keeper be strong enough to eradicate its poison."

"Another Keeper?" The phrase was whispered all around Rosey like a promise.

John stiffened beside her, his grip tightening on her shoulders. She shivered, amazed at the idea. *Could it be possible? Another Keeper?!* Another warrior to take up the Shanobie Crystal and collect the twelve elements from the Elemental Mothers? *There's twelve Mother's, right? Six were pegasi and six were unicorns...*if she remembered correctly. They watched over the twelve elements, protecting the Elemental Wells where vast energy gathered. The Wells were fed from the Energy Flows and gave the world's elementals the ability to control their elements. Without the Wells they'd be powerless. *Just like me.* She shook her head. Who in the world could take the place of Esperanza!?

"Citizens, let me assure you," Addina spoke up, distracting Rosey from her thoughts, "I've looked long and hard into this and a new Keeper may be the only way to save the planet. Instead of facing the Raptor Demon, this Keeper will be eradicating its disease! The results should be the same."

Should? You don't know? Rosey wanted to scream but she dared not utter a sound.

"It's true, I cannot guarantee anything, but this is the only way. The new Keeper will once again collect the twelve elements from the Elemental Wells, then she or he will purify the planet of the poison. Only then shall we be free of its hate...of its terror. Please, do not lose hope. We fought this once before and won, we can win again! I know I can never undo what has been done, I can only promise to be there for you and stand beside you. I ask for your trust, please."

Addina went to lower her head again but the Goddess stopped her, lifting the great beasts head to her gaze. "Please my lady, Addina, I don't think there's a single person here who blames you." She looked out to the crowd and everyone cheered in agreement, raising their arms to wave proudly.

Rosey and John's voices joined them. Rosey didn't know much, but her uncle had told her that Addina was horrifically weakened after the battle against the Raptor Demon. She'd returned from the final conflict, bleeding and bruised, with a barely alive Esperanza on her back. Despite a master healer's expert care, Esperanza had died from her ordeal and Addina had returned to the Settled Valley, falling into a five-year slumber. It was obvious the fight had exhausted and pushed them all to their limits...there was no way any of them blamed Addina.

"If you say another Keeper is necessary then we believe you, at least Neran does," The Goddess added, smiling. "I can't speak for the other leaders, but I'm certain we're all with you. Now, the real question is, who's this new Keeper going to be?"

Addina was silent for a moment, her gaze wide and surprised. Rosey was almost shocked by how innocent and uncertain she looked. When she thought of her Immortal, she'd never assumed she'd be a regular person...filled with doubts and worry.

Finally, Addina spoke. "Thank you...but, it's not up to me. Only the Shanobie Crystal can chose its next master. And we won't have to wait long. With the world's permission, I wish to initiate the ceremony now." She turned to the Golden clad woman before her expectantly.

The Goddess smiled and bowed to her. "Don't let me hold you back. The sooner the better."

Addina bowed her head. "Very well, when the world has spoken, I shall begin."

They waited for a few moments as Addina stood perfectly still, her eyes closed in concentration. *She's asking all the World Leaders if she can choose a new Keeper! Amazing!* Rosey beamed. How powerful must Addina be to do something like this?

She hopped from foot to foot anxiously, wondering who the next Keeper would be. *What if it's Rochelle?!* Her brows furrowed. *We'd all be doomed!* She shook her head. *Who am I kidding? It'll probably be someone all the way across the world. Someone I don't even know. I wonder if it'll be another woman...or...maybe it will be an animal this time? What element will they have? Will they even be a warrior?* Rosey knew there were no requirements for Keeper other than being an elemental. It was all left up to the Shanobie Crystal and its decision was indubitable.

Another thought crossed her mind and it startled her so much she almost laughed. *What about...No!* She shook her head. There was no way it could be her. She might be Esperanza's daughter but she was a Potential. There was no way a Potential could ever be a Keeper. The solid weight of that truth made her feel suddenly insignificant, but she wasn't the only one thinking it. People were already giving her slight nods, peering at her from the corner of their eyes and whispering possibilities under their breath. Yet, moments later they'd shake their heads, no doubt coming to the same conclusion she had. She sighed, momentarily disappointed before lifting her head proudly. Whoever the next Keeper was, she had no doubt they would do Esperanza's legacy proud.

Rosey fidgeted anxiously, the minutes drawing out like years. Finally, Addina perked up and Rosey caught her breath.

"All have given their consent. It's time," Addina declared.

A hush fell over the crowd as they waited. Addina closed her eyes, her body suddenly humming with energy as light flowed from her horn, lifting her mane and tail into a dance. Her great wings, perfectly arched to either side in an elegant display, casting luminous light around the square. Slowly, the tip of Addina's horn detached itself and floated before her. Addina took a shuddering breath, her body quivering.

"By the power flowing through me and the planet, chose your new master," the Immortal commanded.

In a flash, the crystal was gone, disappearing into nothingness as if it had never been there. Rosey flinched, half expecting some loud noise to erupt around her but it was eerily quiet. She waited, her gaze flicking between the people nearest her and the distant crowd, searching their faces for the slightest bit of surprise. Any one of them could be chosen. Hazel stiffened on her shoulders, her paws kneading anxiously. Noly's ears perked forward, alert, observing everyone while the horses fidgeted. Rosey swallowed a rising wave of apprehension as the silence went on.

Then she felt something. At first, she thought it was just her imagination, but the feeling didn't go away, it intensified. She gasped and looked down at her chest, surprised to find something glowing *inside* her heart!

People suddenly gasped at her, including the gryphon in front of them who whipped around and gave out a startled squawk. "It *is* Rosey!" she shouted.

And just like that, all eyes were suddenly on her, including her uncle's. His gaze bulged and he shook his head. "It is you...no..." he whispered under his breath.

Rosey was too stunned to comment, but her mind raced a mile a minute. *What do you mean it's me?! It is!? How can it be me!?* But there was no denying the crystal worming its way out of her chest. Her skin seemed to melt back from the crystal, producing a flawless white gem that left behind no evidence it had been there. It floated before her, bobbing innocently as if it hadn't done anything odd.

She suddenly felt lightheaded and wobbled on her feet. For the second time that day, her uncle caught her, cradling her close. She didn't lose consciousness but her mind was fuzzy, her energy low, like something had sucked it from her. Some inner instinct made her reach out and grab the glowing gem that waited for her. The light pouring from it suddenly diminished and it warmed at her touch, as if welcoming her.

"It's good to be with you again, Rosey."

The unknown but strangely familiar voice echoed in her mind suddenly and she tensed, unsure of what she'd just heard but she was too disoriented to be shocked. Maybe she was going crazy?

Sarabie neighed worriedly next to her and Noly was barking something she couldn't understand. Hazel pawed at her shoulders, but remained quiet.

"Just like her mother," the gryphon before her whispered, eyes wide.

Someone in the crowd, Rosey wasn't sure who, responded. "But how can it be, she's a Potential!"

The crowd suddenly started talking all at once, their voices echoing sorrow and dread as this realization spread. The gryphon gasped and put a paw to her beak. People's moving shapes closed in around them.

Rosey's brows furrowed, but she barely had the energy to comment, though the sting of truth was nonetheless crushing. Andraste hummed against her back as if feeling her confusion, her mother's sword had always been weird like that.

Suddenly the crowd parted and the Golden Goddess was standing before her, brows furrowed but not with confusion or shock...no...it was...as if she expected this.

"John, we're bringing her to the palace," the Goddess stated bluntly. "Rochelle, Alex, come along too, I know you will anyway!" she shouted to the crowd.

Without further explanation she turned on her heel and indicated for them to follow. Golden clad Neran Guards joined the Goddesses side, ushering people aside as John gently followed her, hugging Rosey against

him. She blindly followed, too shocked to resist. She was sure she heard
Sarabie and the other horses' hooves behind her. She was also sure she
heard Alex and Rochelle calling out to her, but her voice felt thick suddenly
and she couldn't move or say anything other than to follow her uncle's
guidance.

As they passed the main square, Rosey's eyes searched for Addina but
she didn't find her. The giant was gone. Rosey swallowed, feeling nauseous
and her grip tightened on the crystal. *How can this be?!*

CHAPTER THREE

The Truth Hurts

This wasn't the first time Rosey had been to the Goddess's Palace. Like any citizen, she and her friends were free to come and go as they pleased and had done so many times before to visit or train with the guards. The palace was a wealth of information, including a huge library on magical lore alongside elemental techniques written by masters of old. But Rosey had had another more personal reason for visiting the palace, it was where her mother Esperanza had spent most of her time.

As well as being instrumental in the war, Esperanza, John, and the Goddess had all been very good friends and though John did his best, he was still quite sore on the subject of his sister. So, the Goddess had helped Rosey fill in the gaps of Esperanza's story. Rosey's mother had lived at the Goddess's palace for much of the war, there were a lot of things there that had belonged to Esperanza. Hallways she'd walked, objects she'd touched, and elements she'd used. It was the place Esperanza had stayed while pregnant, the place she'd given birth, and the place she'd been brought to after the battle and thus it was also the place where she'd died. To Rosey it was both a place of comfort and sorrow.

Built into the side of the Upper Ridge Mountain, a random hillock of tall cliffs and white mountain peaks near Handan's southern tip, one had to take a windy trail at an incline to get there. To make haste, they mounted the horses who'd kindly offered to carry them. John rode with Rosey on

Sarabie, while Bronzo offered his back to both the Goddess and Alex. Filla had Rochelle and Hazel to carry. Quickly they took to the immaculately gardened trail leading to the Goddess's Palace at the top.

Rounding a bend, the grand three-story castle came into view. A great golden wall surrounded it, immaculate doors with the image of Addina and the Keeper engraved on them opened to let them pass. Guards bowed as they entered and the gates shut behind them.

The mulch beneath became fine white gravel paths that led to the front entrance, a large double door of golden designs and reliefs depicting dragons and Addina with the Keeper astride her back. Rosey's hazy vision rested on her mother's regal image, hefting Andraste above her head in a symbol of triumph.

The castle was well hidden, surrounded by giant evergreen trees flowing with purple pinecones and delicate deciduous trees with red branches, their smell made Rosey sneeze.

As the horses drew to a stop, castle staff came running to attend them. John helped Rosey dismount. The ride up had given Rosey time to catch her breath and compose herself, but she was still a bit wobbly from the connection forged between her and the crystal so John stuck close, supporting her with one arm around her shoulders.

Not pausing for a moment, the horses and her friends hurried into the pristine palace. Inside there were golden tiled floors with silver designs, tall golden walls inlaid with murals and carvings, and immaculately carved wooden columns and moldings to offset all the gold. Across from the castle's foyer was an intricate wooden staircase. Directly to the left of the grand entrance was the large common room where the Goddess would meet with guests and correspondence, no matter the occasion. Many times, Rosey and her friends had sat in that very room, talking the day away. The familiarity of it made her feel sleepy.

Her uncle shook her gently with one arm. "Oh no you don't. Stay awake, honey. We need to talk a bit," he said softly.

She groaned slightly, wishing they'd all just leave her alone to sleep it off. Maybe if she did, she'd wake up to find it had all been a dream. "How can this be?" Rosey whispered to herself as her uncle helped her to one of the common room's pristine couches.

Her left hand still clutched the crystal and she looked at it, examining its very delicate yet fairly normal looking diamond shape. She frowned; it certainly didn't seem like the powerful object the Keeper would use to save their world.

The Goddess waited for her friends and the horses to enter, holding the double doors open before closing them behind Noly who entered last. The room was lavish, covered by a high ceiling with four alabaster statues of Addina in each corner. Shelves lined with books occupied the walls with numerous red embroidered couches resting on golden tiled flooring.

Her friends sat down across from her on one of the couches. The horses stood nearest their partners, Sarabie taking up a position behind Rosey's couch to gently nuzzle her head. Her uncle sat down next to her on her right as attendants brought in tea and spoke to the Goddess in hushed whispers. Rosey barely paid them any mind. She wasn't sure what to think but clearly something had gone wrong. There could be no way that she was the new Keeper!

Finally, they were alone. The Goddess chose to remain standing.

"Soooooo...Rosey was just chosen...to be the next Keeper? Was that...supposed to happen?" Noly said, sitting down in front of Rosey's legs to lean into her.

Hazel settled next to Rosey's left on the couch, whiskers twitching. "Not that we're not proud but..." She paused and looked between Rosey and the others awkwardly. "Well...we all know Rosey's a Potential so something's not right...right? And what happened to Addina?"

All eyes turned to the Goddess who shook her head before crossing her arms, looking exasperated. "I don't know, Addina has a habit of appearing and disappearing whenever she wants. She's...." She stopped, then chuckled under her breath. "Oh well, she obviously didn't want to stick around for the complicated part."

Hazel twitched the tip of her tail, unsure how to respond to that. Her friend's faces held an awkward twist of concern and understanding as if they still expected this to happen despite Rosey's missing elemental power.

"It can't be me," Rosey said as if trying to convince herself. "I'm powerless!" She looked at the crystal and it glowed a slight pink color as if reflecting the color of her skin. "I'm not an elemental...heck, I'm not even a magikin...not that that would help."

"Rosey's right," Rochelle finally spoke up. "I know her bloodline is the reason she was chosen, but does her lack of element mean anything?"

The Goddess shrugged. "The Keeper is an oddity. No one's ever supposed to have more than one element at once, but the Keeper has all twelve. Obviously if it did mean anything, Rosey *wouldn't* be holding the crystal." She inclined her head to the white crystal in Rosey's hand, her gaze sharp as if analyzing the situation. "Questioning it will get us nowhere," she declared with finality, "we must accept that Rosey is the new Keeper and must take on the same challenge Esperanza faced."

"She traveled to each of the Twelve Elemental Wells, right?" Rosey asked, her gaze still locked on the crystal, fingering it as if looking for an answer in its design. "The Wells...guarded and maintained by the great Elemental Mothers." Her brows furrowed. "Is it true that they are six unicorns and six pegasi?"

The Goddess nodded, "I didn't accompany Esperanza on her journey, so I can only tell you what she told me and according to her, that's true. There are six unicorns and six pegasi that are chosen from the Settled Valley by Addina herself. They watch over and protect the Wells, maintaining them until they are unable. They were doing that long before the Keeper was chosen." Her gaze softened suddenly as it rested on Rosey. "Of course, you'll see for yourself eventually."

The room was silent with that humbling thought. Rosey's world had suddenly collapsed all around her. Her family, her dreams...everything seemed so far away now and she was left in the middle grasping at the leftover reality she was faced with. Everyone's eyes were on her, hanging by a thread of doubt and apprehension. One word from her would make or break what they did next. But how could she respond? She wasn't even sure she understood it herself.

She took a deep breath. "Okay...so I'm the new Keeper...is there anything else I need to know?"

She'd meant it as a joke, but John and the Goddess exchanged glances. Something in her uncle's demeanor changed, his eyes glistened as if begging the Goddess not to say anything.

Rosey frowned at them. "What is it!?"

The Goddess set her jaw and shot John a look. "Rosey deserves to know," she said solemnly. "We cannot keep this from her, not when so much is riding on her as the new Keeper. It's time...no matter how much it may hurt."

Rosey sat up from the couch's plush cushions, her grip on the crystal tightening. "What are you talking about?" Rosey demanded. Thankfully her friends seemed just as confused, they didn't know either.

"It's about your mother," the Goddess said. "It's about the way she died."

"What do you mean? She died from her injures in battle against the Raptor Demon?" Rosey said.

The Goddess's eyes glistened suddenly as if emotions ran rampant beneath her calm exterior. She swallowed, "Yes, she did...but there's more to it than that."

Rosey shuddered. "Tell me."

"We'd *all* like to know," Alex added, giving the Goddess a questioning stare. "In fact, I'm pretty sure that *no one* really understands how the most powerful woman in the world suddenly lost her life but won us the war."

"We know the stories...we know a master healer accompanied Esperanza on her journey. He should have easily been able to revive Esperanza no matter how badly she'd been hurt," Bronzo murmured in support of his friend. "It's hard to believe he'd have failed her."

Noly looked from Rosey to Bronzo worriedly as if picturing Rosey's dead body after a terrible drawn-out battle. Rosey shuddered at the thought. *But that's not likely to happen this time. I'm not fighting the Raptor Demon I'm just purifying the planet...right?*

The Goddess looked away and Rosey got the feeling she wasn't too thrilled about what she was about to say. Finally, she began. "During the final battle, Esperanza and Addina faced the Raptor Demon together. I and the other leaders led the army on the ground which included your father Matthew, and Esperanza's team. Maharen led the assault at sea."

The Golden woman finally sat down in an armchair to their right, her face filled with sorrow. "After we were half way through the battle, I suddenly sensed another presence, something that was neither Raptor nor Goron...but I couldn't tell who or what they were. They were going for Matthew and Esperanza's team. I tried to get to them, but I was too late. I saw the assassin...a black cloaked figure, humanoid, standing amongst a sea of black corpses; Matthew was one of them." Her eyes glistened as if she was reliving the memory. "Before I could attack, the killer vanished."

She paused for a moment to gather herself before going on. "Addina told me what happened after that. At a critical moment, when Addina and Esperanza were locked in combat with the Raptor Demon, their powers ripping into one another, the assassin suddenly appeared. They stabbed Esperanza through the heart from behind, taking advantage of their fight. Then, just as quickly, they were gone. Esperanza didn't stop...she used the last of her life energy and power to exercise the demon from our world. Addina tried to save her but no amount of healing could heal her wound or the poison killing her. Just like Matthew, her body turned black."

The Goddess took a shuddering breath, tears running down her face. John was silent beside Rosey. "Only a few people know about the assassin. And we've been trying to hunt them down ever since...to no avail. So, you see Rosey, there's something or someone out there still and I'm sure they'll be coming for you now."

There was shock and fear expressed on every face. Noly whined and Hazel pushed her little body against Rosey's shivering form. Rosey swallowed, her hands suddenly shaking.

Alex broke the silence first. "It sounds like a powerful poison was used on..." he hesitated from saying their names but the Goddess understood.

"That's what it seems like, and I know what you're thinking. It's the same thought I had when Addina made her announcement."

John spoke for the first time. "The same poison that killed my sister and her husband is probably the same poison now slowly killing our planet."

"Either that, or it's a new and improved version," the Goddess agreed, looking forlorn.

"What is this poison?" Rochelle asked, she looked at the Goddess. "If it was used on Esper...the Keeper...then wouldn't your team have been studying it all this time? Haven't you figured anything out?" She looked hopeful, Rochelle was always optimistic, sometimes to a fault.

"I'm afraid not," The Goddess answered. "It's true, after what happened, a team of my most trusted healers and magikins worked on trying to figure out what was ultimately used to kill Esperanza, Mathew, and several others. People from around the world, even some dragons, did the same. Despite their best efforts, no one has been able to figure anything out."

"So, no antidote then?" Bronzo concluded.

The Goddess shook her head. "To make an antidote, you have to understand the poison, and we don't."

"But...Addina believes the Keeper's power will be strong enough to eradicate it?" Sarabie asked.

"Perhaps, there's no way of knowing till we try," the Goddess said. "In fact, Addina believed that if Esperanza hadn't been fighting the Raptor Demon that day, she might have been able to eradicate the poison that infected her and so many others. And I trust Addina's judgement."

"What did Addina do?!" Rosey shouted suddenly and everyone went silent, eyes on her. Rosey's sadness fell away to burning anger and she stood up. "According to what I know, she slunk back to the Settled Valley and took a nap for five years while an assassin went free and a poison ate at our planet!"

"Rosey," John said with a gritty voice, "If Addina had gone after that assassin she might be dead now and we'd be left without our Immortal. As it is, she was barely strong enough to bring Esperanza's body back to us. We're lucky the assassin didn't kill Addina along with Esperanza that day. She helped with the search efforts after she awoke, but she didn't find the assassin either."

Rosey let out the breath she'd been holding as John's rational words sank in. She clenched her fists, knowing he was right. Suddenly the crystal in her clenched fist started to grow warm, it soothed her and she brought it up close to her heart.

She turned back to the Goddess and the regal woman straightened. Rosey saw her tear-stained face and the pain in her eyes and Rosey's anger faded.

"Addina really didn't notice our planet being poisoned till recently?" Rosey asked gently and the Goddess nodded.

"She's..." the Goddess sighed, looking exhausted suddenly. "She's not been herself since that day. Not in power, nor in confidence...but I still...I still believe in her."

The sudden spark of passion in the Goddess's eyes moved Rosey and she smiled slightly.

"It's reasonable to assume then that the assassin was the one who most likely poisoned our planet. If that's the case, who knows when that actually took place," Alex reasoned. "I'd assume that poisoning a planet is different from poisoning a person, it could have taken years to prepare. Addina may have only caught on recently because it just happened recently. Not to mention that this assassin seems to be pretty good at hiding, stands to reason they'd be skilled enough to hide their poisoning." He tapped his index finger on the sleeve of his folded arms, something he did while thinking. "The assassin is cunning; they took advantage of Addina's weakened state and our mourning to infect the planet with their deadly poison."

"Whoever this assassin is, they're pretty good," Rosey admitted. Swiftly she reached behind her and drew Andraste from its sheath, positioning it before her with the grip over her heart. "But I'm better," she stated cockily.

Alex smiled and Rochelle jumped up excitedly.

"Yeah, you are!" she said, holding up her fists, bursts of air circled them with explosive energy making the tea cups rattle. One fell over, spilling tea everywhere. Rochelle made an 'eek' sound and hurriedly went to clean it up with the napkins, but the air currents still swirling around her fists made it worse, flinging napkins into the air with the tea cups and sending drops of tea flying.

Everyone burst out laughing as they dodged flying tea and napkins. One hit the Goddess in the face and Noly decided to add to the chaos by jumping up onto the table and promptly laying down on everything.

"Rochelle, turn your air off!" Alex shouted half annoyed, half amused.

"I'm sorry!" Rochelle said, "It's kinda' involuntary sometimes."

"Ha! Sounds like Bronzo when he gets gassy," Filla said, snorting.

Bronzo nipped at her playfully. "I eat some unusual grass *one* day and you never let it go."

"Like you did?" Sarabie teased, sticking her tongue out at him.

Rochelle finally got herself under control, the air stilling, but not before several guards followed by some staff members burst into the room. They'd drawn weapons and wands, expecting some kind of attack only to find the mess the group had made.

"Are you all right, my Lady Goddess?" one of the guards asked, smiling at them. She was a tall human woman decked out in the guard's golden armor. She sheathed her blade as the Goddess nodded to her.

"Thank you, Hasi, we're perfectly fine. Just a little accident. Please, don't trouble yourselves."

"I take it you all were listening outside the door then?" John asked, giving them a smile.

"Yes, sir," Hasi admitted, shrugging.

"Well, go back into the hallway and listen again, okay?"

Seeing all was well, Hasi bowed and excused herself and the guards and staff members left them.

The Goddess and Alex put everything right, whipping out their wands and correcting anything broken, spilled, or soiled in a matter of seconds. Even Noly's fur was left clean of any tea.

For a few moments they all stared at each other before laughing again. Rosey sheathed Andraste and sat back down.

"Thanks Rochelle...for being...you," she said.

Rochelle winked at her. "Anytime."

"Rosey," the Goddess said, growing serious. "The whole world is behind you. We will do everything in our power to make you victorious. All you need to focus on is collecting the elements, a task I fully intend to help you with. I'll arrange for my finest and most trusted ship to take you anywhere you need. I'll also put together an escort of my strongest warriors to protect you. No matter what, your safety will be the highest priority."

"We're going too," Rochelle and Alex said at the same time.

"Don't even try to convince us otherwise," Alex added for good measure.

"And that includes us," Sarabie nickered, and Filla and Bronzo whinnied agreement.

"And us," Hazel said.

Noly nodded, licking Rosey's hand.

Rosey looked around the room, seeing the faces of her family and friends staring back at her. If a new Keeper didn't purify the planet of the Raptor Demon's poison, then that was it, they'd all be dead...and they'd have lost the battle. *My parents will have died for nothing!* The last thought made her twinge determinedly and she looked again at the crystal she still held in her left hand.

"Okay," she declared, lifting the crystal for all to see. "I accept."

Right before their eyes, a single tassel of intricately woven white fibers materialized and attached itself directly into the crystal, forming a necklace. Getting the message, Rosey put the Shanobie Crystal around her neck.

Chapter Four

The Assassin

Rosey dived behind a boulder as Rochelle let lose a volley of miniature whirlwinds in her direction. She coughed from the dust and debris whipped up by the wind. She covered her mouth and closed her eyes, but the boulder did its part. The whirl winds slammed into it and it shook violently at the encounter, cracking slightly but holding.

"Good use of the terrain, Rosey! Remember, on the real battlefield you'll have elements of your own to use," the Goddess shouted to her from the nearby bleachers.

If it had been any other day Rosey would have thought herself lucky to be receiving a personalized training regimen overseen by the Golden Goddess herself, but this training wasn't for just any battle. It was to fine hone her skills as a warrior and prepare her to be the next Keeper. To accomplish that she was using the Goddess's personalized, indoor training arena that could be magically altered to represent different biomes depending on the Goddess's fancy. For the last hour Rosey had run, hid, and scraped through about ten different scenarios and terrains. The Goddess had saved the arid and dry landscape for last.

I wish I had an element right now! Rosey thought, giving Rochelle a dirty look. She dived out from behind the boulders and hid herself in the resulting debris cloud form the earlier collision. Coming in fast, she rounded behind Rochelle and grabbed her from behind, locking her arms in at her sides, an air elemental's weak point. Kicking gently, she pulled Rochelle off her feet and onto the ground, pinning her.

The Goddess clapped. "Well done, your reputation proceeds you." She winked at her and Rosey helped Rochelle to her feet.

"Yeah, I have the bruises to prove it," Rochelle chirped, rubbing her sore muscles.

"Really, come on, you got me four times out of ten!" Rosey gave her a semi angry smile.

Rochelle grinned. "So what, you still won against an elemental with wit and cunning, that's something to be proud of." She turned away. "Isn't it Alex's turn yet?"

"I sent Alex to train with John this morning," the Goddess answered. She wore a simple white and gold training tunic with brown leather pants, her saber and wand scabbard hung at her sides. "It's important you two get as much training as you can if you're going to protect Rosey sufficiently. If I wasn't the leader of Neran I'd be going myself, but that's out of the question."

Rosey's brows furrowed as she dabbed at the sweat beading her temples. "Are you *sure* you guys should go?" she asked Rochelle, giving her a worried glance but the brunette turned to her with a smile on her face.

"Of course!" she said, matter of factly.

Rosey stared at Rochelle. It made perfect sense for her friends to be going with her, they were fellow warriors after all, but the possible dangers raced through her mind and she stuttered, "But...I...I don't want you...to get hurt."

"And neither do *we* want *you* to get hurt," Rochelle responded. "Girl, we've stuck with you since day one and we're not going back on that now. We're coming and that's final."

Rosey stared at her for a few moments then sighed. She knew that look. Once Rochelle had decided something there was no talking her out of it, nor Alex for that matter.

The crystal flashed at her chest and she reached up to touch it. According to the Goddess, the woven thread that had appeared to firm the necklace was actually a gift from Addina. It had been braided from Addina's mane.

Rosey wasn't sure what to think about that, but the Goddess said it might be a way for Addina to stay in touch with her. Why she hadn't delivered it in person still struck Rosey as odd, but she was an Immortal and with the poison threatening their planet, she had other priorities. Rosey looked at the crystal. It looked so innocent now, as if it hadn't burrowed its way out of her just the day before.

"Come on, that's enough training for today. Let's get breakfast," the Goddess called, waving them over.

"Yay! After I shower for a year," Rochelle chuckled. She stretched, cacking her knuckles. "All this training has left me dirty as a mudfalpper! My element's been worn thin, I'll be lucky to conjure a breeze after all that!"

Considering just how mud-covered the swamp-dwelling mudfalpper was, Rosey thought Rochelle was stretching the comparison a bit. "At least you've got an element, I'm a Keeper with no power," she grumbled walking beside her.

Rochelle gave her a sideways glance. "Hey, not for long," she responded grinning.

Rosey managed to smile back but she couldn't ignore the fact that she was a powerless Keeper. Until she made it to the first Well, she'd have no powers at all. *Come to think of it, what element will I be getting first? I think it's fire? Where are these Wells? How will I know where to go?* Suddenly her mind was filled with questions...questions that seemed a lot more important now. She just couldn't escape the feeling of being underqualified.

"Rosey, come on, we're hungry!" Noly called out from the bleachers, wagging her tail. She hopped from paw to paw excitedly. She and Hazel had opted to wait to have breakfast till Rosey and the others were ready to eat, something they didn't always do.

A warrior always trains every morning, Rosey thought, remembering her uncle's words and those of other warriors she'd met over the years. *Training is never-ending. A good workout every morning sets the body up for success.* Rosey wasn't so sure about that, but like most warriors she'd fallen victim to the rigorous routine that had chiseled her into a pristine warrior. *But will that help me be a good elemental? It certainly can't make me worse.*

"Hold on, we're coming," Rosey called back. Hazel sat next to Noly, flicking her tail impatiently. "You're not the ones sweating out here on the battlefield! And if you're dead set on coming with me you should probably start your own training," she finished.

Hazel and Noly exchanged glances. "We're good," Hazel chimed, yawning. "After all, how hard is it for a feline to scratch something's eyes out?"

"Or me to bite a few bones?" Noly agreed.

"Incredibly difficult actually!" came a sharp replay.

Rosey flinched and Rochelle halted beside her, looking around for the voice. Both Hazel and Noly turned suddenly to see a black, six-foot-tall wolf standing near the top of the bleachers, glowering at them. Red eyes seemed to glare into their souls while thick black fur rose along his hackles. Golden armor, plated evenly across thick muscles glistened in the light. He growled low in his throat.

"Commander Wolvereen, you've returned," the Goddess said pausing before him on her way up to the training room's entrance. "I wasn't expecting you till tomorrow, did your mission go well?"

Wolvereen drew his glowering gaze from Noly and Hazel, they softened with respect as he beheld the Goddess. "Yes, Lady Goddess," he said, bowing his head to her. "We tracked down the Raptors and slaughtered the entire group. It was small, only about thirty. All my warriors survived."

The Goddess smiled, bowing her head to him. "I'm not surprised. You always deliver quick results, that's why you're my Commander. Keep up the good work, but for now take a rest." Her gaze rested on Rosey who flinched as the black beasts' eyes followed the Goddess'. "I've got a new mission for you, so be ready," the Goddess finished. "Take your showers quickly, girls, breakfast will be served in thirty minutes."

Rosey swallowed a wave of apprehension as she gazed at Wolvereen. She'd only ever seen the giant Commander of the Golden Guards at a distance so most of what she knew about him came from the Guards she'd trained with. As the Commander, he was usually out on missions and rarely ever trained with rookie warriors due to his large size and power. Most all the wolves in the Goddess's Guards were like that, silent and silky beasts that hid in the shadows, using guerrilla tactics. They could be gone for months at a time, tracking down the Gorons and Raptors. They were ruthless killers and with the Raptors being ten feet tall, six-foot-tall hunters such as the wolf guards were ideal opponents. As far as Rosey knew, Wolvereen wasn't an elemental or a magikin, he was just as powerless as she was, but for some reason, he seemed far stronger.

She swallowed as his gaze rested on her blue eyes. For a moment their will's clashed like daggers but, eventually, he bowed his head to her and Rosey released the breath she was holding.

"It's an honor to meet you, Rosey Mystic," Wolvereen said, his voice even, tail parallel to the ground.

The girls took the stairs and came to a stop before him, bowing in return. Rosey almost flinched away at how large he was, standing before her his head was twice the size of hers and rose at least a foot above her, if not more.

His white fangs flashed as he spoke. "I've been informed about Addina's announcement and I want you to know that I take the matter very seriously. I will do everything in my power to assist in any way I can, especially if it means training those that would make light of your...situation," he finished, his gaze resting on Hazel and Noly who cringed slightly under his gaze.

Rosey stepped between them protectively. "I appreciate that, Commander, really, but I can assure you they were just keeping light for my sake." She cringed inwardly. *Great, I just admitted I'm scared! Whatever, it's not like I've got anything to prove...to him anyway.*

The wolf's brows furrowed as he watched her. Rosey couldn't read his gaze but she hoped he wasn't looking down on her.

"Very well, I look forward to working with you," he stated simply, turning to leave. "By the way, you can address me as Wolvereen if you wish, my Keeper."

Rosey started for a moment at the title. It was the first time she'd been addressed that way and she wasn't sure how she felt about it.

Noly and Hazel joined Rosey's side and Hazel jumped onto Noly's back, her fur on end. "Well, isn't he the social butterfly," she teased, sticking her tongue out at him.

Noly whipped her tail from side to side aggravated, ears parallel with the ground. "Yeah...annoying too. He might be fun to mess with." She grinned wickedly, panting.

"Don't you dare!" Rosey chided. "Stay out of his way, he's the Commander of the Golden Guards, we don't want to be a nuisance."

"Aweeee! Okay," Noly relented, lowering her tail.

Rochelle giggled. "Okay, *my Keeper*," she teased, making Rosey blush. "Let's go. I'm starved!"

"Tell me again how you got Alex flipped upside down and floating around in the air," Rochelle asked John again, smiling from ear to ear.

Alex gave her an annoyed look, cheeks bright red. "I told you I was preparing a counter spell, but he was just a fraction of a second faster, okay! It won't happen again!"

John chuckled from his seat. "Alex did splendidly as always, it's not his fault I've got more experience than he does."

Rochelle kept laughing. "Oh, too good. Too good! Rosey, we need to make sure we watch the next time those two duel, okay?"

Rosey smiled but gave Alex an apologetic look. "Come on Rochelle, cut it out. I know of a certain *someone* who was held to the ground about six times today by a *non-elemental*, after all," she said raising her brow at the cocky brunette.

Rochelle smiled sheepishly. "Well, ahem...yeah, so...uh...when will Rosey be going on her journey?"

Rosey rolled her eyes at the brunette's subject change and took a bite of her eggs, enjoying their rich heavy flavor. Her eyes wandered over the ornate dining room setting, amazed that she was a guest at the Goddess's lavish estate. Never in a million years did she ever suspect she'd be trained by the Goddess, welcomed into her home, or get to meet some of the most powerful warriors. Of course...she'd also never assumed she'd be chosen as the world's newest Keeper either.

"Rosey will set forth as soon as my ship makes dock," The Goddess answered. "They were a far ways' from here when I scryed them about their new assignment with the Keeper," she explained. "I'm sorry for the delay but I admit it's a good thing in the long run. After all, there are some things I need to explain to you before you can truly take your first steps as the Keeper."

Rosey put down her utensils and took a swig of milk. "Actually, there are some questions I have, like where I'm going and how I collect the elements from the Wells," she said voicing her earlier thoughts.

"I know...don't worry, I'll tell you as much as I can. Esperanza shared a lot with me while she was traveling. There are a lot of things I can pass onto you that will be helpful, including things Esperanza had to discover on her own while she was the Keeper." She paused and took a sip of her tea before continuing. "However, I want you to understand that you'll be your *own* Keeper."

Rosey's brows furrowed and Hazel and Noly exchanged glances. They sat at the table as sophisticatedly as possible, on their best behavior with the Goddess around. They sat across from Rosey with John near the end and Rochelle and Alex sitting on either side of her, as they usually did.

"What do you mean?" Rosey asked, fiddling with the napkin in her lap.

"I just don't want you to assume you'll be exactly like your mother," the Goddess explained gently. "From what I understand, the Keeper's power and even their outward appearance is all derived from the individual. You're your mother's daughter, but you're still your own person, so you may handle the elements differently than she did. Be yourself, that's the best advice I can give you."

"That's good advice for *any* elemental, actually," Rochelle chimed in. "I know lots of other wind elementals who fight with air much differently than I do. There's no right or wrong way to be an elemental, you just go with your gut. We can guide you, but it's ultimately up to you to make your own style." She winked at Rosey.

"With magic, it's the exact opposite," Alex added, looking at his empty plate. The light of the chandelier overhead reflected off the left-over syrup from his pancakes. "We have to speak spells in the Fracture Language, the Angensile Language spoken backwards, and if we mess it up, the results could be catastrophic."

They were all silent for a moment before Rochelle final broke the peace. "Nice way to suck the humor right out of us, huh Alex," she stated simply.

Alex shrugged. "It's just the truth."

Rosey sighed. "Well, at least Esperanza *was* an elemental before she became the Keeper, I don't even have that going for me."

"Oh please," Rochelle said, giving her an exasperated look. "You just admitted yourself that you held me down six times out of ten today! Obviously, you're strong."

"Yeah, but, as we know, it only takes one time to kill me," Rosey finished bluntly, silencing them all. The story of Esperanza sizzled in the tense atmosphere.

"Okay," John said, raising his hands as the silence lapsed between them. "Let's all take a deep breath. Rosey, you're only going to be without an element for, what…maybe a week at the most, depending on where the first Well is located. I'm sure we can more than handle your protection in that time, and you're underestimating yourself." She met his gaze. "You've been training for a long time now. As soon as you could wield your mother's sword you were out there taking charge. Remember, the Raptor Demon's gone now…all you have to do is outmaneuver the Raptors and Blood Gorons and that's not that difficult to do."

"For sure," Rochelle added, punching the air as if attacking an imaginary enemy. "We'll keep em' on the run, no doubt!"

"You can count on us," Alex agreed, patting her shoulder comfortingly.

Rosey looked down, apprehension gripping her like knives. "What about the assassin?" She saw everyone tense up. "Neither you, nor anyone else, including Addina, have been able to find any trace of them? That means they're still out there somewhere."

Alex nodded, clearing his throat. "Yes, we've all been thinking a lot about your tale of the assassin. We need to clarify some things with you, Lady Goddess. If we may?"

"Of course," the Goddess said. "I figured you all might have some follow up questions after that particular revelation."

Did they ever. Alex, Rosey, and Rochelle hadn't done much after Rosey had accepted her position as Keeper other than be shown to their rooms to go to bed. Not only had it been pretty late, but the Goddess had wanted them to consider what she'd told them and approach with questions later.

The Goddess sighed. "Let's go to my study and we'll talk, okay?"

Rosey nodded and the others called out agreement. There was no time to waste, every moment that ticked by was another moment the world remained poisoned and Rosey had no intention of letting it continue.

The group thanked the chef before following the Goddess to her study, a golden, high-ceilinged room nestled comfortably in the corner of the building. The horses were waiting for them as they entered.

"Sarabie," Rosey called out, happily. "How was your morning run?" She ran over and embraced the giant mare, feeling at home all of a sudden in her warm shadow.

"It was good. As usual I beat Filla and Bronzo back," the black beauty stated haughtily, swishing her tail with bravado.

Rosey grinned. It wasn't the first time Sarabie had outrun the others, she was wickedly fast for so large a horse and the others knew it too. *But they still insist on racing her,* she thought amused.

While Rosey and her friends trained, the horses had done their own training. They'd expertly aimed their kicks at targets and improved their stamina. It was the most they could do considering that the trio were just as non-elemental as Rosey was and just as equally non-magical.

"I'm sorry I wasn't there this morning," she said guiltily. She usually always groomed her but from Sarabie's pristinely brushed coat, it was obvious a groom in the Goddess's stables had seen to that.

"Don't concern yourself Rosey, we're getting the royal treatment here," Sarabie nickered respectfully, bowing her head to the Goddess as she passed them. The Goddess bowed back. "Besides, you've been through a lot, I think you're allowed to be a little hair-brained every now and then."

"Hey, I wouldn't go that far," Rosey smiled and ruffled Sarabie's forelock.

Sarabie twisted her head away gently before pushing Rosey with her large nose. "Come on, let's get some things answered already, we're dying to know ourselves."

"That's for sure," Filla added as Rochelle braided her long mane from her seat before the Goddess' desk. Rosey joined her in another seat, Sarabie standing comfortably behind her. "We're more than curious," Filla finished, adjusting her stance behind Rochelle's seat so she could finish the braid.

Alex sat down on Rosey's left side, patting Bronzo's muzzle behind him as he did. Noly and Hazel settled down beside Rochelle to her right in another seat, eyes fixed on the Goddess. John sat down on the other end near Alex, his face drawn as if he knew what was going to happen and didn't like it. Rosey gulped.

"Can I get seats for you, Bronzo, Sarabie, Filla?" the Goddess asked, extending her hand to them. All three horses thanked her but declined. She nodded. "Then in that case, let's begin."

Rosey took a deep breath; everyone was waiting for her to start. "The assassin, what specifically do you know about this being? Anything?"

The Goddess sighed, looking very disappointed. "Unfortunately, other than the fact that this assassin killed Esperanza and many others...we know nothing else. We have several *theories,* of course, but nothing concrete. In fact, if Addina hadn't also seen them, I would have thought I was hallucinating that day," she admitted, her eyes growing distant. "It was so fast, the blink of an eye...one moment there, the next...gone. Their image has haunted my dreams ever since."

"You said they were humanoid though, right?" Rochelle asked and the Goddess nodded.

"Yes, they stood up right on two legs. The general figure was humanoid," she explained.

"But...who in the world would assist the Raptor Demon...willingly? Rochelle asked incredulously.

"That's very unlikely," Alex said, his arms were folded, his index finger tapping away. "As I see it, there's only a few possibilities here. This assassin is a willing participant – which is *very very* unlikely – they have been manipulated in some way, or they're not actually...real."

Even John gave him a questioning stare at that one. "Explain," he said, intrigued.

"Well...I mean that it might be something like with the Raptors. Raptors are biological anomalies created by the Raptor Demon manipulating the NCD. The assassin could be something along those lines...but worse. Or more deadly, something the Raptor Demon was finalizing before its defeat."

"We considered that," The Goddess admitted. "It's a likely scenario, especially since we can't *find* the assassin no matter what we do. I, and others," she glanced at John, "have cast countless spells...we are masters in our field, yet we've turned up nothing. Not to mention the number of hunts and investigations launched by other nations and friends of Esperanza also yielding no results." The Goddess clasped her hands before her, exasperated. "It's so frustrating! We have so much power, yet this *thing* took the most important person from us in a heart beat," her voice broke at the end and she glanced away.

John immediately reached out and took her hands. She nodded to him giving him a smile before composing herself. Rosey just stared at them, more amazed by her uncle's reaction than the Goddess's rare show of emotion.

"You know as well as I do that demonic cloaking is *very* powerful," John said gently. "It's the reason the Raptors, Gorons, and, most likely, the assassin can remain so well hidden."

Rosey's brows furrowed at this sympathetically. Her friends had talked with many warriors at the Neran training arena over the years and had learned a few things about demonic cloaking. The Raptor Demon had imbued the Raptors and the Blood Gorons it had made with its demonic energy. That energy could very well be used to cloak their presence when needed, effectively hiding them. It could also taint others that got too close. A healer or a purification spell could remove the taint since such demonic energy was too weak to result in actual possession, but the experience of coming into contact with that taint was often horrific. If not cleansed in time, those exposed to it could lose their minds or experience horrible pain.

Directly after the war, many had wanted to track down the Raptor Demon's remaining army, but their cloaking had proved to be too effective and the Gorons stealthily maneuvered the Raptors to keep them alive. At the time, the people were far more concerned with rebuilding than they were with hunting down an army that didn't want to be found. Unless the horrifying beats attacked and drew attention, it was decided they'd be, temporarily, left alone. *It's only been in the last ten years that warriors have actively gone out to try hunting them down now that the world is mostly back on its feet,* Rosey thought. *And now...this happens.*

"The warriors have done the best they can. *Everyone* has," Rosey said aloud, drawing the Goddess and John's attention. "No one could ask for more."

Everyone sounded their agreement and the Goddess smiled ever so slightly, warmed by their support. John did too, nodding to Rosey gratefully. His expression then grew somber.

"There's something else the assassin could be...something worse," he added, sitting back in his seat and reluctantly releasing the Goddess's hands. "This being could be *a part* of the Raptor Demon itself."

Noly's mouth fell open and Hazel's ears went back against her head.

"We don't mean to scare you," the Goddess said quickly, "but you're the Keeper now, and her friends, we *have* to be honest with you."

"We appreciate that," Rosey said. "Please explain more."

"Demons are terrifying entities, beings that dwell in the Realm of the Dead created by the sorrowful, hateful, and angry emotions of those who *lived and died* in pain and terror. Once demons gather enough power, they're able to manifest in the world of the living," John explained. "Once among the living, they use the natural world around them to cause mayhem and destruction."

"The NCD." Sarabie whispered.

"Correct," John said. "The demon used the NCD to create the Raptors. It also created the Gorons, how it did that *exactly* is still unknown, though most evidence points to them being another mutation forged from the NCD. Anyway, one thing powerful demons *can* do, is split their power apart from themselves. In fact, they do this to *diminish* the power they have so they're less detectable by the planet they've manifested on. It also gives them 'allies' they can utilize while they're initiating their attack. These split beings can be and look like anything that the demon desires or needs for their overall plan. We believe," he gestured to the Goddess, "that the assassin might be one of these beings. It's possible, the Raptor Demon split this assassin off from itself and gave it the sole purpose of creating the poison that killed Esperanza and now threatens our planet. While we were all busy dealing with the Raptors and Gorons, the assassin was creating the poison, only revealing themselves at the end once said poison was refined."

"After Addina made her announcement, it became clear that *this* theory is the most likely scenario," The Goddess finished. "Though, as I said, we have no concrete facts, just theories.

"Doesn't that mean that the assassin might be almost as strong as the Raptor Demon was?" Hazel asked.

"Not exactly," The Goddess said, "these split beings can either be as strong or as weak as needed to perform the demon's designated task. They can be as powerful as a dragon or as weak as a fly. However, given that the assassin was strong enough to kill Esperanza, Matthew, and several of their warriors, I'd say they're at least as strong as either John or myself."

This last made them all shudder, the Goddess was considered one of the most powerful warriors on Eyelamenta. She could probably hold her own against a dragon in a duel. It was a humbling thought, considering that dragons were the most powerful creatures on their planet, one step below Addina herself.

"One thing is clear though," the Goddess said with finality, "this assassin, whoever they are, is not nearly as powerful as the Raptor Demon was. If they were, they wouldn't have come and gone as they did."

"Like we said before," John reminded them, "if Esperanza hadn't been so focused on destroying the demon, she'd probably have survived the attack. So, it's safe to say this assassin isn't demon level."

"Question," Rochelle said. "If the assassin is a split being from the Raptor Demon, then could they have been destroyed when the demon was destroyed?"

"That *is* a possibility," the Goddess agreed, "but these split beings are often not linked to the original that created them. They are, by design, meant to be self-sustaining so that they can continue the battle if the demon should be defeated."

"The sole purpose of any demon is to destroy the planet they manifest on, causing the citizens as much pain, suffering, anger, and sorrow as they can," John explained. "When those besieged people die, they take those negative emotions with them into death which then feeds the creation of more demons, and the cycle continues. For the Raptor Demon, creating a planet-killing poison and sustaining a war was the best way to get results which meant that Esperanza, the power behind our world's salvation, had to die. I wouldn't be surprised if it had always planned on sacrificing itself so that the assassin would have the opportune time to strike," John finished, vehemently.

"I should also clarify something," the Goddess said. "Rochelle, you'd asked earlier if it was humanoid. Yes, it was...at the time. If this assassin is indeed a split being from the Raptor Demon, then it's possible it can change its shape."

"So...it might not be a humanoid anymore?" Bronzo asked.

"Since it was witnessed by both myself and Addina, the smartest thing would be to change shape. But that would only be possible if it *has* the ability to change shape," the Goddess explained. "If it doesn't then its probably disguised itself as best it can."

"The most important thing to take from that," John said, "is that it could be anything or anyone."

"Okay," Rosey said, taking a deep breath to clear the tension in the air. "So, its very likely that there is a shapeshifting piece of the Raptor Demon still out there somewhere, along with numerous Raptors and Gorons that we still haven't hunted down, plus a mysterious deadly poison." She took another breath. "What else do I need to know?"

Chapter Five

To Be the Keeper

The Goddess chuckled a bit, impressed by her resolve. "Tell me, Rosey, how much do you know about the Elemental Wells on our world?" she asked, putting her hair in a messy but elegant bun, stray strands hung pleasingly around her face.

Rosey blinked, thinking back over her history lessons and what her uncle had taught her. "There are twelve, one for each element. The Wells are the source of an elemental's power, without the Wells an elemental wouldn't be able to work their element."

"That's right. The Wells are direct links to our planet's Energy Flows, acting as a conduit from which the power of elemental control is granted to an elemental, like Rochelle. What about the Energy Flows, what do you know about them?"

"The Energy Flows contain all the vital scientific, biological, and spiritual details about a planet, as such, every world has them, even ones that do not host intelligent life," Rosey recited, feeling like she was back in school reading from a textbook. "Due to their all-encompassing nature, demons and other evil creatures like to target Energy Flows as a way to devastate a planet, often its their first method of attack. As such, the Energy Flows are protected and monitored by the planet's Immortal or other powerful creatures. The flows themselves can look like anything but are usually invisible to the naked eye and typically buried deep beneath the earth."

"Excellent, I'm glad to know your education was so thorough," the Goddess praised.

Rosey shrugged. "When your mother was the Keeper...you hang onto every detail that involved her."

There was silence for a moment before Alex said, "Our Energy Flows even regulate Eyelamenta's magic levels. There are Wells for magic use too, right?"

"Yes," the Goddess confirmed, looking at him gratefully. "Most planets have something like the Wells from which the citizens can draw out their powers, though they may call them by another name. Now, as you already know, Rosey will be traveling to each of these Wells and collecting the elemental power there. So, the first thing you need to know is that the locations of the Wells change. That means that the places Esperanza went to won't be the same places you'll be going to now," she explained.

"So...how will I know *where* to *go*?" Rosey asked.

The Goddess fingered a pencil on her desk. "That's a bit more complicated to explain." Her gaze rested on the crystal Rosey wore. "The answer is in the Shanobie Crystal. What do you know about it?"

Rosey shrugged. "Not much, just that its where all twelve of the elements reside when the Keeper collects them from the Wells."

"Indeed," the Goddess agreed, "but there's more to it than that. The Shanobie Crystal acts as a collection jar for the elements so that the Keeper can access them without causing harm to themself. Normally an individual would be torn to shreds if she or he were to contain different elements inside their body all at once, nevertheless twelve. The crystal allows the elements to be connected but remain at a safe distance from their power." She paused for a moment. "But that's not all. Now...keep in mind I only know what Esperanza told me but, supposedly, the crystal has some kind of spirit residing inside of it. Sort of like...a ghost."

Rosey's brows shot up intrigued and Noly whined.

"Esperanza called her the White Witch, a spiritual entity that gave her the location of each Elemental Well. Without her guidance, there'd be no way to know where each Well was located. Thus, to answer your question, the Witch will be your guide."

Rosey cocked her head, intrigued. "How will I meet her?"

The Goddess almost snorted. "I have no idea, but Esperanza said she often met her in her dreams. 'She's a tall woman clad in white robes with porcelain white skin, cream colored lips, delicate eyes, and a sharp tone,'" the Goddess mimicked, smiling. "That's how Esperanza described her. As the Keeper, you will be the only one to *ever* see her. I guess you can ask her who and what she is when that time finally comes."

"But...I didn't dream or meet any Witch person last night," Rosey stated. "What if I never see her or she never appears?"

The Goddess considered this but John was the one that answered.

"Esperanza didn't see the Witch for the first time till several days after she was chosen. I'd say just give it time. I doubt the Witch *won't* appear."

"And if she doesn't, we can always seek council from Addina on the matter," the Goddess added.

"Speaking of Addina, isn't she going to help Rosey like she did her mother? Where is she?" Alex asked. "I know you said she hasn't been the same...and I can understand her wanting to give the world and Rosey some time to adjust...but still."

"Ah, yes. I'm glad you mentioned that as it brings me to something else I need to discuss with you," the Goddess responded, leaning forward onto her desk. "I actually had a scrying meeting with Addina and the other World Leaders this morning to discuss the situation. Addina answered a lot of questions and explained a few things. As such, I have news to pass along."

Everyone straightened at this, leaning forward intrigued.

"Firstly, Addina will not be joining Rosey on her journey," The Goddess announced.

Rosey shivered, sudden apprehension and fear worming their way into her. She'd been pretty confident up until that moment. She'd just assumed Addina would be by her side to protect her. With an assassin still unaccounted for and hundreds of Raptors and Gorons around, the last thing she'd expected was to be without Addina's protection! Even John looked perturbed by this.

"What!?" Rochelle asked incredulously, voicing everyone's thoughts. "You can't be serious? What else does she have to do?!"

"Let me explain," the Goddess said with such force that Rochelle slunk down in her seat a bit.

Rosey patted her hand as thanks for her support and nodded for the Goddess to continue.

The Goddess sighed. "I understand your anger. Addina was *highly* involved in Esperanza's journey. So, I'm not surprised you find her missing status odd. But, back then, things were different. Esperanza's life was the only thing that mattered, so Addina dedicated herself to protecting her. If something happened to her, there was no way to know if another Keeper would even be possible or if they would have the time to take over what Esperanza started."

Her gaze settled on Rosey. "Understand, my dear, Addina is aware of your importance, however the poison consuming this world is strong and we're racing against the clock." Everyone tensed up. "Addina is going to be dedicating all her energy and power to holding this planet together. By giving so much time and effort to Esperanza during the war, she neglected the planet's safety and now it's on the brink of rotting from the inside out, a fact she takes very *personally*. Addina's risking life, limb, and all the strength she has to keep it from falling apart, giving *you* the time you need to be the Keeper."

She stopped for a moment, folding her hands before her and fixing her gaze on Rochelle. "Now, is that good enough for you?"

She, Rosey, and Alex all nodded, unable to respond. John smiled slightly, amused.

"Anyway," the Goddess went on, relaxing. "Addina asked that, in her stead, I and John mentor the Keeper. Given our background with Esperanza and you, we were the obvious choice. There aren't many who know as much about being the Keeper as we do. However, since she can't be there with you in person, she wanted me to assure you that she'll be sending someone else to help you. One of her best warriors. She wouldn't elaborate on who but you can be assured he or she will be the best Addina has to offer."

Rosey brightened at this, feeling less apprehensive.

"Remember, Rosey," the Goddess went on, "even if she's not by your side. Addina is always watching." Her gaze rested on the crystal's necklace and Rosey fingered it. "Thanks to that necklace, she can get to you whenever you need. Just call out her name and I'm certain she'll come running. Though she may be far away she'll never truly take her eye off you. You can be certain of that," the Goddess promised, smiling.

Rosey's brows rose and Rochelle smirked mischievously, grinning like a child. "Ooooooo she's always watching you," she taunted in a ghostly voice, giggling.

"That actually goes for *all* of you, really," the Goddess commented with a sly grin.

Rochelle stopped and slumped in her seat; her bravado lost.

"But...how? We don't have a hair necklace like Rosey does?" Alex asked, looking bewildered.

"Not that you can see," the Goddess stated.

Alex waited for her to elaborate but she didn't and Rochelle and Noly both started looking themselves over, searching for whatever it was Addina was using to watch them with. Rosey smiled, amused and John laughed.

"Okay, Goddess, stop teasing them," he said. "Addina can pretty much monitor anyone she wants, it's like scrying, but different. The necklace just makes it easier and allows Addina a more in-depth review of Rosey's current condition. As an Immortal she has a kind of third eye that links her to the citizens and another that links her to the planet...so, four eyes maybe."

The Goddess laughed. "Oh, John, you were always bad at explanations," she said teasingly.

"That's why I usually let you do all the talking," he agreed, winking at her.

The awkward but cute moment was broken by Hazel's sharp meow.

"Well, one of those eyes missed the poison somehow." The feline stated bluntly. "Did Addina happen to mention anything about that in her report to you, Lady Goddess?"

Rosey had to hand it to Hazel, she had a way with words.

The Goddess blinked at her, but her voice was even. "I admit, I asked about that myself. She said that she noticed the poison a month ago."

Everyone's eyes went wide, incredulously, even John's brows furrowed, concerned.

The Goddess held up her hand as if to physically block the confusion coming her way. "She'd explained that once aware, she'd immediately investigated the situation and determined the next course of action. But doing so required time to get the Shanobie Crystal ready for another Keeper, hence the month long wait before her announcement."

"Does she know just how much damage the poison has caused already?" John asked.

The Goddess nodded. "It's not good, she said about fifteen percent of our world is infected. Currently, she's using all the power she has to stop it from spreading to the Energy Flows and more. A battle that will exhaust her more than it did fighting the Raptor Demon."

Rosey's gaze fell and she fiddled with the end of her long black hair, deeply concerned.

The Goddess tsked at Rosey's subdued look. "Come now child, we have no time for wallowing." She winked at her. "Addina is counting on you and so is the rest of the world. Now, what questions do you have so far?"

"Well, considering the severity of the situation, my biggest question would be why do I have to collect the elements from each Well?" Rosey asked, fingering the crystal. "That could take months or years depending on how well I do. Why can't I just...have the elements already inside the crystal?"

The Goddess sighed. "Believe me, I wish that were so. But I'll tell you what Addina told me...told all of us. In order for the Keeper to be the true master of the elements she must be tested by each Well. You see, unlike a normal elemental, the Keeper will be accessing elements she wasn't born into. In this case, you were born with none of them." Rosey flinched slightly but the Goddess kept going. "Thus, to use them, you must prove you're *worthy* to use them. The Elemental Mothers, those six pegasi and unicorns, are meant to test you on the element's behalf and judge your worth. If they find you unworthy, have no doubt, they will fail you."

Rosey stiffened and Rochelle stuttered, "What does that mean?"

"If Rosey fails a Mother's test, the Well will not grant her its element."

Rochelle's mouth fell open and Alex's leg slipped making his chair creak loudly in the stunned silence. "Are you serious! Even knowing what's on the line?!" he stuttered incredulously.

"Even then." The Goddess said firmly, her eyes hard. "The Wells are there to guard the immense power each element holds. Unlike the power of a regular elemental, the elemental power the *Keeper* is offered is *unlimited*! Rosey's power will be unlike anything you've ever seen. If that kind of power were in the wrong hands, it could rip the planet apart including the very fabric of reality. Instead of one single planet, the whole universe would be at stake!"

The severity of her tone made Alex's face go white, eyes wide. He nodded slowly and Rosey gulped.

The Goddess sighed, calming herself. "I'm sorry, but you must trust this process."

"Why...." Rosey breathed softly before she realized she'd said it. She was so shocked she put a hand to her mouth.

But the Goddess didn't look surprised. She nodded and closed her eyes, considering something. Finally, she opened them. "What I'm going to tell you is known only to the World Leaders." John's eyes widened. "Yes, even you don't know about this, John." She took a breath, and whispered her next words, as if afraid someone was listening in. "The whole Keeper process, collecting the elements from the Wells, the creation of the Shanobie Crystal and the Elemental Mothers...all of it was the brainchild of...Valley Elathos."

Now John's mouth fell open. Everyone was silent and Rosey was sure no one breathed. *Valley Elathos...the Valley Elathos!* It couldn't be?! The legendary...the powerful...the holiest of holies. The Valley traveled from planet to planet offering its vast knowledge and guidance. To any planet that was in dire need, the Valley was the ultimate sign of hope. It offered much needed help, locating and assisting its chosen planet in whatever terrible assault it faced. Rosey really shouldn't be surprised. Usually, the

Valley assisted those accosted by demonic beings, beings of ultimate evil. *The Raptor Demon most definitely fits that description.*

Finally, Rosey took a breath and whispered back, "Is it still here?"

The Goddess shrugged knowing she meant the Valley.

If the stories were to be believed, when Valley Elathos helped a planet, it usually settled into a natural valley formation somewhere on the planet, blending in as if nothing had changed. From there, the Valley would communicate with a chosen few, helping them as secretly as possible. The secrecy not only protected the Valley from potential evil, but also kept the rest of the world safe from getting too closely involved in something far beyond their comprehension. Rosey assumed that if the Keeper process was being reinstated, then most likely the Valley was still on Eyelamenta...or had returned in response to the poison.

"Addina told the World Leaders about the Valley when it first appeared some twenty years ago," the Goddess explained. "Only *she* ever entered the Valley and communicated with it personally. It directed her on the best path to defeating the Raptor Demon. I have no idea if it's still here and Addina has not said anything, though we did ask. Obviously, she's only told us what's necessary so, no, I can't tell you anything more about it," she finished.

They sat for a while thinking, shocked. Rosey wasn't too surprised that Addina was being tight lipped about the Valley. Given the assassin and the poison in their planet, it would behoove them to keep particulars to a minimum.

"All right then, that's enough for me," Rosey stated firmly.

Everyone nodded, all manner of doubt gone from their faces. If the Valley had orchestrated the Keeper's creation and the elemental collection process, then there was nothing left to question.

"Good, I'm happy to hear it. Now that that's out of the way. We need to discuss the Raptors and Gorons," the Goddess said, pulling them back to the matter at hand. "Tell me what you do know."

Rosey's gaze widened and she shuddered. "I mean, besides what was taught in school, about the NCD and such...nothing else," she answered simply.

The Goddess knew the Gorons and Raptors had never gotten past the walls and she also knew that Rosey and friends had never roamed outside the barricade. They'd seen images of the vile beasts, heard the warnings, and listened to countless stories told by warriors; all of which had gone a long way to keeping them from trying to get past Neran's gates, but they'd never actually seen the Gorons and Raptors. Rosey's plan to join the Golden Guards after graduation this year obviously meant she might eventually have to fight the evil brutes, but the likelihood of an attack was pretty low. Typically, only those that went *looking* for them actually fought them as they stayed away from most well defended cities and towns. But, as the Keeper, there was no doubt she'd be fighting them now.

The Goddess' voice broke into her thoughts. "There's no way we can send you all outside the walls without having more information about the Raptors and Gorons. Hearing about them is one thing, seeing them is another. You're in luck. My sister just so happens to have one of the largest and most detailed archives about the Raptors and Blood Gorons in all of Eyelamenta," she stated proudly. "She's agreed to let you see it to your heart's content and I highly recommend you do."

Rosey's mouth hung slightly open. "Your...sister," she stuttered, astonished.

"You mean...," Alex almost leaped out of his seat, leaning forward excitedly. "The Silver Goddess?!"

The Golden Goddess smiled innocently but nodded. "Well of course, who else?"

"*The* Silver Goddess, the one no one ever sees!? Leader of the Stealth Operations Task Force and Caretaker of the War Archives!?" Alex emphasized; eyes wide.

The Goddess chuckled. "That's the one. Although, don't let her hear you say that, she'd turn bright pink. She's a bit shy that way."

"Don't tell me we're going to meet her?!"

"All right then, I won't."

"Almighty One, yes!" Alex got up and started to pace.

John shook his head and grabbed his arm. "Come on, Alex, settle down. She's not that amazing," he commented rolling his eyes.

Everyone present, including the Goddess, looked at him sharply. The Goddess looked irked but the others just looked surprised.

"*You've met her*?" Alex said slowly, stunned. He advanced on John so fast that he leaned back in his seat.

"Well...ah...a few times...." John stuttered, rubbing the back of his head.

Alex sat back down, shaking his head in wonder.

"*Who* are you?" Rosey asked comically, eyes wide and Rochelle and the horses all snorted.

Rosey had meant it as a joke, but when she thought about it. What did she really know about her uncle? He was a magikin, almost on the same level as both of the Goddesses and knew them personally due to being Esperanza's brother. But...what else? Where had he learned magic? Who was his magic teacher? Had he ever had a crush? Besides the information related to Esperanza, there wasn't really much else she knew about him personally. From the moment she could remember, he'd simply encouraged her to learn, train, and focus on school. He'd dedicated himself to bringing her up, and though she'd tried to worm her way into his past, it had mostly been to ask about her mother, not him. It didn't help any that he'd been pretty closed off about it due to the pain of losing his sister. She'd barely been able to get it out of him what happened to her parents...in fact, she was pretty sure that he'd had the Golden Goddess help with that part. *He wasn't exaggerating when he said he let the Goddess do all the talking!*

The Goddess waved her hands. "All right, listen up, my sister is...well...a touchy subject and John knows why." She shot him a look and he looked away. "But she's no different than me and any other World Leader. Her operations keep her busy that's all. Without her we wouldn't know half of what we know about the Raptors and Gorons." She was silent for a moment as if she realized she was comparing herself to her. "She's the other half of war, the unseen half."

Rochelle inched closer; eyes wide. "Why is she so secretive? Why do we never see her?"

Noly wagged her tail, tongue lolling with excitement. "Yeah, there are so many rumors! Which are true? Like...is she *really* afraid of society, you know like deadly afraid...irrationally so. Or does she have some terribly humorous thing that...ow!"

Rosey pinched Noly's tail, giving her a shut-your-mouth look as the Goddess's eyes glowered with irritation. Noly smiled awkwardly as Hazel chuckled.

"You can't blame them for being curious, can you?" John commented, giving her a look only the Goddess seemed to understand.

Rosey looked between them as the Goddess's gaze suddenly softened despite her irritation. "No, I suppose not," she answered, "but I can begrudge loud mouthed dogs who don't know when to..." she trailed off as John's brows furrowed. "...when to *behave*," she finished.

Noly whined and lowered her snout.

"The only thing I can really tell you is that she has her reasons and that's that. You must respect my word on this matter and drop it, understood?" The seriousness of her voice silenced them and they nodded, defeated.

Alex gave John a sly look. "You'll tell us, won't you?" he begged.

For the second time all eyes, besides the Goddess's, settled on John.

"You're so going to spill the beans!" Rochelle added but John was already shaking his head.

"Sorry, I'm sworn to secrecy and so was Esperanza. Unless the Silver Goddess decides to tell you herself, I'm taking it to the grave." He nodded to the Goddess who smiled.

"All right, we've gotten off topic," the Goddess said, seriousness lacing her voice. "Rosey, my sister and I will be sharing with you all the information we've gathered over the years. We need to be sure you're prepared. Likewise, my library will be available to you at all hours, night or day. You need only ask and it will be done. That being said, your training is about to take on a whole new regimen." Her eyes darkened mischievously and Rosey swallowed nervously. "From now on, you'll be sparring with *me* and a few, handpicked weapon masters, elementals, and magikins. By the time you leave here, any holes in your education will be quite thoroughly filled."

The gleam in her eye told Rosey she was dead serious, not that she should be surprised, the Raptors and Blood Gorons were nothing to laugh at and they were still out there, waiting for the chance to kill. Not to mention the assassin. But for the Goddess to take her training on personally? She shivered; it was enough to make her sweat.

"I accept the challenge," Rosey stated firmly, feigning confidence. "How long will I be training with you?"

"Until I deem you strong enough to leave," she said with finality and Rosey grimaced.

"Well, the planet's doomed," Rochelle scoffed and everyone looked at her sharply. She rolled her eyes, "Oh come on! I just mean that there's no way any of us would be strong enough to beat the Goddess so we'll be stuck here forever."

"*I* defeated her one time," John stated proudly.

"I let you win," the Goddess admitted guiltily at the same time Alex shouted, "No way!"

John's mouth dropped and he went to say more, but the Goddess spoke first. "Rosey doesn't have to defeat me!" She looked at Rosey kindly, "Sorry dear, but until you have twelve elements at your fingertips, defeating me will be pretty much impossible."

Rosey deflated, throwing her hands up.

"However, you don't have to defeat me, you just have to survive what's waiting for you out there," the Goddess finished, gesturing to the world outside the office window. "I have full faith that you're strong enough to accomplish the task, I just want you to be as prepared as possible."

"I have a question," Sarabie said, startling Rosey. Despite the large horse's size and black hide, she was pretty good at blending in. "Do the Raptors and Gorons possibly know about Rosey? Does the assassin?"

Everyone went silent at this, their gaze back on the Goddess whose brows furrowed.

"We're not sure," she said delicately, "As far as we know, they know nothing about the current efforts being made to eradicate the assassin's poison. Hell, we don't even know if the Raptors and Gorons are aware of the assassin and its poison! Most likely they are, but there's always the possibility they were kept in the dark should we ever interrogate them." She folded her hands before her, her face a dark calm. She cocked her head. "You could say this is another reason for Addina keeping her distance.

If she were covering Rosey with protection, it would undoubtedly draw attention. Even with Esperanza, Addina mostly focused on keeping the tides *away from* her so she could do her job. This time around, we want to be sure they don't know about Rosey so secrecy is of the utmost importance." She inclined her head to the crystal. "Keep *that* hidden when you're traveling and don't talk too loudly, we don't want to *give* them a reason to start coming after you. We also don't want to let them know their master has created a poison *if* they're unaware, so keep that tight-lipped as well, understood?"

"What about the announcement Addina made?" Alex asked, eyes wide.

"Don't worry, Addina had all of the towns and cities cast soundproofing spells before the announcement was made. Only someone on the inside would know what's going on," The Goddess assured him.

They all nodded solemnly, locked in by the Goddess's powerful words.

Rosey felt sudden goosebumps rise along her arms and legs. *This is really happening, isn't it? I'm the new Keeper! The planet's last hope.* She shuddered. *Will I be anywhere near as good as Esperanza was? Esperanza....my mother.* The position of Keeper had always seemed so foreign to her despite her heritage. It didn't seem real. She was too used to being the girl without parents, the girl raised by her uncle. That life seemed so far away now.

"When will we be seeing your sister?" Alex asked eagerly and Rosey rolled her eyes at him, amused. He'd always been a fan boy when it came to the Goddesses.

"That's to be decided by her, unfortunately," the Goddess answered him, sighing. "She will send word when she has the time to meet you. In the meantime, Rosey and I will begin our training." She fixed her gaze on Rosey with a determined look.

"I have one last question," Rosey said and the Goddess inclined her head for her to continue. "When I've finished collecting the elements, how do I purify the world of the poison?"

"I'll tell you what Addina told me. *When* you finish, you'll set sail for Scorched Mountain." At this an apprehensive shiver shot through them but the Goddess didn't pause. "As you know that is also where Esperanza defeated the Raptor Demon. It's far from here to the north and even today the mountain is torched black from the touch of the Raptor Demon. Most stay away, afraid of being poisoned themselves should they get too close. I'm sure you're not confused as to why you'd go there?"

Rosey shook her head and grasped the crystal. It glowed slightly at her touch, growing warm. "That's where the Raptor Demon resided during the war. It buried itself deep into the mountain, hiding behind rock and earth while orchestrating its hordes of Raptors and Gorons from afar. The siege on it when Esperanza finished her journey was...brutal," Rosey recounted from her history lessons.

The Goddess's eyes darkened, shadowed memories flashing before them. "Indeed," she agreed, looking away. "Almost all the World Leaders aided in the Scorched Siege, Esperanza wanted to lead the assault but she agreed to stay behind the lines, protected by Addina. They watched from afar as countless warriors were cut down to make way for them. Maharen and her ships came from the sea while the rest of us attacked by land. The Leaders lead the charge. We thinned the tides, then Esperanza on Addina came in from behind, two fully-powered warriors who sliced through and went right for the Raptor Demon. We won the battle, but at a terrible loss."

There wasn't a single Eyelamenta citizen that didn't know about the Scorched Siege, the battle that ended it all. Rosey couldn't imagine how much self-control Esperanza and Addina had to have had to sit by while people died for them. At the same time, if Addina hadn't protected Esperanza, she'd have been vulnerable and if she'd been killed, their efforts would have been wasted. Rosey closed her eyes against the image, her grip tightening on the crystal.

"It's also from Scorched Mountain that Addina believes the assassin created the poison and injected it into our world." Everyone's gaze was back on the Goddess. "There are hundreds of tunnels and cave systems in that mountain and they stretch for miles deep and through. It also has an underground river." She shook her head. "It wasn't just a strategical decision but a planned way to thoroughly infect the planet. In fact, Addina is now certain that the poisoning of our world was the Raptor Demon's true intention all along. Killing us is one thing, we can come back, rebuild, repopulate, and, eventually, all of this would disappear into history. But a poison buried deep inside our planet would put us to an ultimate end."

Everyone shivered, unraveled by her words but also filled with anger. She could feel everyone's resolve radiating around her. Rosey had never turned away from a challenge and it wasn't happening today. She was determined to win.

Rosey stood up sharply. "I'm ready to get started whenever you are," she said firmly.

The Goddess's eyes lit up, impressed. "Of course....my Keeper."

Chapter Six

The Past

Rosey awoke the next morning feeling strange...like something just wasn't right. She'd assured the Goddess she was ready to be the Keeper but, in all honesty, she didn't really know how she felt. It didn't seem real. It still felt like, at any moment, she'd wake up in her little bed at her uncle's house inside Neran's quiet barricaded walls...like it had all been a dream.

She sighed and flopped out of her plush bed to start getting dressed, rousing Noly and Hazel who yawned. One thing hadn't changed: training. She was due to start her new intense Keeper exercises today. The thought had her stuck somewhere between giddy excitement and nervous energy.

"I'm happy to see you slept peacefully," Hazel murmured sleepily.

"Night terrors...gone?" Noly asked, yawning again.

Rosey paused as she strapped her training gear on. It was different than the one she usually wore and specially made for members of the Guard. It had been waiting for her in her room last night.

"For now," she said. "Sometimes days go by between...episodes."

She hoped they'd stay away but something in the back of her mind told her they weren't finished with her yet.

Noly and Hazel nodded, then stretched and jumped from her bed, shaking themselves awake as Rosey finished dressing. She grabbed Andraste, strapping the sword into place, then the trio headed to the dinning room, picking up Alex and Rochelle along the way.

After breakfast and exchanging pleasantries with her friends and uncle she, Noly, and Hazel made their way to the training room for practice. The Goddess hadn't been present at breakfast, apparently, she'd had to catch up on some business for Neran that she'd neglected because of the current situation. Rosey frowned, wondering who would train her then. Alex and Rochelle hadn't said anything nor accompanied her, and her uncle had quickly scurried off to attend to something he'd neglected to mention.

Pacing into the arena she spied Wolvereen waiting for her, golden armor gleaming.

She paused, mouth agape. "You're my teacher today?" she asked him, unsure.

He tilted his giant black head. "Indeed, young Keeper. As you should know most of your opponents, if any, will be Raptors and Gorons, thus you'll need to know how to fight an animal."

He growled menacingly and Rosey flinched, swallowing. She hid her apprehension by stretching. The giant wolf paced around her. When she was done, he stopped in front of her, red eyes gleaming. Noly and Hazel took to the bleachers, their eyes wide.

"So...how do I do this...do I...." Rosey began, but cut off as Wolvereen lunged for her.

It was so sudden she almost cried out as she dove out of the way. His fangs flashed, barely missing her arm as she rolled. When she came to a stand, she slid Andraste from its sheath, the blade ringing, cursing as she fixed her gaze on him. But he was back again, snapping at the air above her head as she twirled away. She slashed Andraste toward him hesitantly, not intent on hurting him, and he ducked easily, snapping at her legs under the arch of her sword. She danced away, startled by the ferocity of his attack.

Is he trying *to bite me?!* She backed away as best she could, keeping him in her sights, but his large bulk was surprisingly fast and in one solid leap he sailed over her, landing behind her in a spray of dust that made her cough. With one giant paw, he slammed her to the ground, face first, Andraste clattering to the ground as she dropped it.

She felt the air knocked out of her and she coughed, sputtering for breath, but Wolvereen did not remove his paw. It dug into her back, the claws just barely pricking her skin despite the armor.

"Is this all you have, pup?" Wolvereen taunted, disappointedly. "You're in worse shape than I thought." He huffed as she glared at him from the corner of her eye.

He let her up, moving to stand in front of her as she hefted Andraste. "Well, if you're so smart, why don't you teach me instead of torment me!" she accused him, bitterness stinging her pride.

His brows arched expectantly and he laughed. "You trained well against two legged humanoids, mind you, but an animal is a far different opponent." His ears flicked. "Come now, I thought you'd fought against animals before?"

She had, but none like Wolvereen. Most of the animals she'd fought in Neran's training grounds had been regular citizens, honing their skills like her in case of Raptor or Goron attacks. They weren't the Commander of the Golden Guards, and none had been wolves. They'd usually been smaller than her too, no larger than a small horse or a dog, but Wolvereen was six feet tall, towering over her.

She told him as much and he bristled, ears going flat against his head. "And that's an excuse!? Remember the Raptors are even bigger than me, little one." He drew close, making her take a step back. "They're *ten* feet tall, and even faster than me...on occasion. Now, straighten your stand and watch me closely," he instructed, stepping away from her.

Her eyes followed him as he moved, still stung by his harsh rebuttal but determined to conquer it.

"Remember, the most important thing you can do as a human is make use of your upright position. Animals are larger than you and stronger than you, so using brute strength on your part would be a death sentence." He fixed his red gaze on her. "*Don't* do that. Instead, use your head and never attack first." Her brows furrowed and he went on. "If you know *how* an animal is going to attack, you can counter it. Never take your eyes off them. Focus on defense instead of offence. Wait for an opening, then take it. I'll show you." He paced before her. "When I jump, move out of the way, then attack," he instructed.

"How?"

"My back will be turned. You could lure me in, let me lunge at you, then dodge and score your blade down my side, however, that would most likely make me angry rather than stop me. Instead, you should raise the blade and slice through my back, attacking the spinal cord, or you could go low and chop off a limb, immobilizing me."

She grimaced at the image but nodded and took up a stance. He came more slowly, lunging for her, she moved aside as instructed and raised the blade, making to ram it into his back but of course it clanged against his armor, leaving him unfazed. These moves would only be used against the Raptors and Gorons and they didn't wear armor for some reason, perhaps it made them too slow?

For the next hour or so Wolvereen showed her different techniques for fighting all manner of creatures, not just Raptors and Gorons. She was surprised by how complex some of the moves were but the world's animals could be just as dangerous as any Raptor or Goron.

"Why do I need to know how to fight so many different animals," she said between breaths. They'd paused for a moment to rest, Wolvereen sitting nearby. "Won't I just be facing Gorons and Raptors?"

He huffed. "When I fought in the war, I thought the same thing." His red eyes flashed suddenly as if he saw something she couldn't. "The Raptor Demon found many ways to manipulate people, Rosey, not just humanoids but also animals. Some were coerced into aiding it, believe it or not."

Her brows rose, surprised. "No...you mean...someone actually *assisted* the Raptor Demon?" Her mind went back to the assassin.

He shifted uncomfortably. "It wasn't by choice, believe me."

Rosey nodded, remembering suddenly what the Goddess said about the assassin perhaps having the ability to shapeshift. That meant it could become anyone or anything. Knowing how to defeat multiple kinds of enemies was imperative.

"Was anyone ever...saved?"

Wolvereen's gaze hardened and he stared at the floor, lost in thought. "Yes and no, I have countless horror stories...but it was never willingly, and they usually didn't survive the experience."

Rosey's brows furrowed. She wanted to say more but Wolvereen's ears pricked in the direction of Noly and Hazel, playing on the bleachers. From the looks of it they were playing hide and go seek with Hazel stealthily flitting between the bleachers and Noly tracking her.

Wolvereen frowned. "You know, I'm curious, how did you come to be so close to Hazel and Noly?" He indicated the two. "I know smaller animals do sometimes leave their packs and make friends with humans, but it's rare to see them actually lodging with them?" He shook his head. "You know, it's even odder when I consider Sarabie, Bronzo, and Filla? Why are they not with their herd?"

He titled his head perplexed and Rosey smiled, hefting Andraste to study the blade. "You should know, Wolvereen, it was you that assigned them to us...or, I should say my uncle and Rochelle and Alex's parents," Rosey answered.

He shot her a confused look, tilting his head. "I beg your pardon?"

She grinned and paced to the bleachers, taking a seat to begin cleaning her sword. Wolvereen followed her intrigued. "It was seventeen years ago, before I was born," she explained. "At that time, the war was nearing its end and, per my uncle, there were three villages that laid just outside Neran's border, perhaps a mile or so away. Neran was absorbing all of them for safety purposes, so of course there was a huge influx of refugees. Noly and Hazel happened to be among them."

She paused for a moment thinking. "I believe the village was called Connolly. It was a farming village that hosted a local dog pack and cat clan. Both had contracts with the humans. The cats for mice control with the grain the humans grew and the dogs kept out unintelligent pigs from the crops. Noly and Hazel worked closely with one another and became friends. Of course...when the war started, a lot of the dogs and cats left to serve but Hazel and Noly were too young, so they had to remain behind. Their families didn't return."

Wolvereen's brows furrowed, eyes glazing with sorrow and she continued. "To accommodate the refugees, it was agreed that they'd bunk with locals in Neran's border till it was safe to leave. My uncle and Rochelle and Alex's parents were among the few who happened to have barns and living space suitable for animals. You were there the day the refugees were being assigned and just happened to assign Hazel and Noly, who'd requested to remain together, to my uncle's house. A year later, I came along."

"And what of the horses?" Wolvereen asked.

Rosey glanced at him from Andraste, she'd finished cleaning it to a glowing shine. Sweat from their training had long ago dried, cooling her. "It's much the same story, really, but they came to Neran before Noly and Hazel did," she answered. "Sarabie, Bronzo, and Filla came from the horse herd Black Hoof."

Wolvereen's ears pricked and he raised his head. "I remember that herd. Didn't they roam the grasslands along Neran's eastern coast, behind the mountain?"

Rosey paused and thought for a moment, picturing a map in her mind. Neran was nestled into the base of the Upper Ridge Mountain, slightly hovering in its shadow. Behind the tall peaks was a large stretch of chaparral grasslands trailing right to the beach.

She nodded. "Yep, they were a pretty large herd. Sarabie told me they were about sixty strong? Maybe a little more? Sarabie's parents were the Herd Mother and Father, two giant black beauties, wise and loving." She sheathed Andraste. "At the beginning of the war, the herd only produced three young foals that year, Sarabie, Bronzo, and Filla. When the war started, almost all the herd went to fight except the old, pregnant, and young. They went to live in Neran, joining other refugee animals and humanoids seeking safety behind barricaded walls. My uncle, and Rochelle and Alex's family took most of them in."

"I remember now," Wolvereen said, eyes distant. He turned to her sharply. "I believe I actually met Sarabie's parents. Their herd was one of the first to offer their services to the war efforts. The herd joined the Golden Guards in many battles." His voice got soft as the memories flashed before him.

Rosey blinked, realizing this all happened twenty years ago. Wolvereen had been the Commander for five years prior to the war's start. He'd been a regular Golden Guard for at least ten years before that. The horses were twenty years old and Rosey hoped they'd outlive her as their kind should.

"What of the others you spoke of, the pregnant mares and elderly?" Wolvereen asked, curiously.

Rosey frowned. "My uncle housed the elderly: a mare and two stallions. The pregnant mares were with Rochelle and Alex's families. When the war was done, the elderly, mothers, and their newborn foals all left to join another herd far from here. I was a baby still when they left." She shrugged. "Sarabie, Bronzo, and Filla could have left with them, but they stayed behind and I'm happy they did, or me, Rochelle, and Alex would have never met them. In the end, they'd come to love Neran and the families that had taken care of them."

"Even Hazel and Noly?" Wolvereen huffed

Rosey gave him a look. "Yes, even them."

"Did any of their herd return?" he asked.

"Actually, some did, but Sarabie said they were so weary and devastated they hadn't the heart to reform the herd. Most of the herd was lost...including Sarabie's parents. They went to other herds or retired in Neran."

Wolvereen nodded. "I see, once the Herd Mother and Father go it's pretty difficult to get the herd back together. Did Sarabie have no desire to lead them?"

"No," Rosey said, shaking her head. "She did at first. Apparently, my uncle said she'd check in on the herd members at Rochelle and Alex's place to see how they were doing. Like they were her responsibility with her parents gone. But...I think, doing so reminded her too much of the parents she lost."

Wolvereen sniffed, scuffing his paws on the arena's mulch floor. "I figured they must have been refugees but I had no idea how deeply their ties went." His gaze fixed on Hazel and Noly who still chased each other around the bleachers above their heads. "They're older than I thought they were. From the way they act, I thought they'd be quite young."

Rosey laughed. "Well, they say cats and dogs don't mature till they're in their thirties. Noly and Hazel have about ten more years to go before they mellow out...then again, I don't expect much."

"Indeed, it seems I owe you an apology then," he stated firmly, dipping his head.

"What do you mean? Why?"

He titled black ears to the two fluff balls. "For assigning them to you. Almighty One knows what you have to put up with." He shook his head but Rosey just smiled and swatted at him playfully.

"Well, *I* happen to adore them and hope they live to the ripe old age of 100, like my uncle's friend Dustick. He was a grey dog that used to live with my mom and uncle when they were little. He died before my mom and uncle came to Neran. I believe my uncle said he was 110 years old."

Wolvereen's brows rose. "Wow, quite a feat. Was he annoying as well?"

Rosey batted at him again and he danced away smiling. As he turned back to her, she regarded him. Thoughts turning in her head.

"Did you know my parents?" She asked suddenly, surprising herself.

He stopped and sat down, looking quite regal in his armored glory.

"Yes," he said, "but not in the way you hope. I rarely saw them and when I did, it was mostly from afar or at a war meeting where politics and strategies consumed our attention. Often, I was off leading a battle somewhere else." He looked at her apologetically, ears low. "I'm sorry, there's nothing much I can tell you about them, other than that I admired them greatly."

"What about my father? Wasn't he one of your guards?" She asked hopefully.

She had asked other guards about her parents countless times. They'd all had stories to share, but she'd never asked the Commander.

"Yes...Matthew Kingsley," Wolvereen sighed. "Before he became involved with Esperanza Mystic, he was just a regular guard. A native Neranian, he was an excellent spearman dedicated to his art. I remember when I'd see him practicing water techniques with his spear, longer than any other warrior trained. He also carried a large shield he called Sturdy."

Rosey blinked, taken aback. "Sturdy?" she repeated, smiling. She'd known he'd carried a shield, but she'd not heard much else about it.

"He wasn't that good at naming things," Wolvereen agreed. "I believe he named his spear Slicer?"

"Yep," Rosey said, "that's what I heard."

"I believe Matthew did a lot of things out of jest," he admitted. "I remember a lot of my guards spoke of him as the 'life of the party'. He didn't take himself too seriously." The wolf's eyes met Rosey's. "I believe that's what Esperanza liked most about him, his ability to make people smile. No matter the danger or the stress."

"Yeah, well. 'Slicer' and 'Sturdy' aren't nearly as powerful names as my mother's Andraste," Rosey said, expertly pulling the gleaming sword from its sheath and holding it before her in a balanced pose.

Wolvereen's gaze settled on Rosey's sword.

"So Andraste stayed, but Slicer and Sturdy did not," he concluded.

Rosey nodded. Typically, when a warrior died, specialized weapons vanished with them, dying as they died. There was one exception, some weapons would continue to exist if there was an heir to inherit them. Despite this, the passing of a weapon was completely up to the weapon and how much of a relationship the wielder and weapon had forged.

"When my parents died, my father's spear and shield dissipated with him, but my mother's blade remained. It was given to my uncle for him to pass onto me," she explained, studying the sword as it reflected the light. "My uncle said that Andraste probably stayed because my mother had wielded it while pregnant with me. Slicer and Sturdy didn't have as much of a connection."

"Well, considering the power in that blade, I wouldn't be surprised if Andraste *knew* you'd need her one day," Wolvereen said solemnly.

Rosey smiled slightly, remembering that the word 'Andraste' meant 'unconquerable'. Then, she shivered, mentally exhausted all of a sudden. "True but...I would trade my blade any day for its wielder," she admitted, sheathing the sword.

She saw Wolvereen's ears go back against his head, eyes downcast. He got up and stretched, the armor clinking to life.

"Let's go, we've got some more work to do before I give you my seal of approval," he said, tail high.

Rosey groaned.

"Come on, little Keeper, the Raptors and Gorons won't wait around for you to catch your breath. You need to be in top shape." He paced to the center of the arena and Rosey followed more slowly, drawing Andraste again but Wolvereen shook his head. "Sheathe your blade, my Keeper. I'm going to show you how to fight an animal with your hands."

Her brows rose, curiosity overtaking her aching muscles. As she walked, she heard Noly bark loudly and turned to them. Noly backed Hazel into a corner and Hazel hissed before swiping at her. When Noly backed away, Hazel darted around her and Noly took off after her, chasing her through the bleachers. She managed to catch up and cut the cat off, but Hazel jumped down the bleachers a way, causing Noly to follow more slowly. Rosey watched for a second, perplexed. Hazel dove and hid, swatting at Noly with sheathed claws whenever she got too close. Noly would also hide, waiting as Hazel sought her out. To anyone watching, including the giant wolf Commander, it would look like they were playing, but Rosey had seen them play.

They're training, she thought suddenly, smiling.

CHAPTER SEVEN

Magic

The next few weeks seemed to fly by for Rosey. Most of it was taken by hours of endless training and trips to the Goddess's lavish library. Rosey knew it was important that she quickly learn as much as possible, but it was beginning to weigh on her. Her friends could tell and tried to keep the atmosphere light and energetic. Despite the information overload, it helped that it came from her friends who knew exactly how not to overwhelm her.

Given how busy the Goddess could be, she assigned Rosey a Weapons Master called Durag to take over her training when she couldn't. He was a gruff man with thin blond hair and deep grey eyes, he was kind but socially awkward and usually very quiet. The Goddess explained he'd been her master when she was little and there was no better teacher. Rosey agreed. She'd seen him many times training the Golden Guards in Neran's practice field, overlooking them with sharp eyes. He was stern but gentle.

As Rosey's confidence grew, she found herself matching the Goddess and Durag step for step with the sword, fueling her drive to become better. She was even getting better against Wolvereen and some of the other animal guards he occasionally enlisted to help. She got so good that Durag changed things up a bit, teaching her how to use different kinds of weapons from maces to staffs to spears. He even littered the training arena with several objects, giving her the challenge of making a weapon out of an everyday chair or a piece of wood. If she could lift it, throw it, or wield it, she trained with it. He also instructed her in hand-to-hand combat, enhancing her flexibility and maneuverability. He even had Rosey train with her non-dominant left arm and leg, pushing her body to the extreme.

If the weapon and martial arts training weren't enough, her friends had their own agendas. She regularly attended elemental training with Rochelle and other expert elementals from among the Guards who taught her all sorts of elemental techniques. To Rosey, it reminded her of a delicate dance, only the partner was one's element. Still, without Rosey's own element there was little she could do but mimic the moves.

The last thing Rosey learned about was magic. As the Keeper, magic mattered little, but it was important that she understand it should it ever become an obstacle. The Goddess only had so much time to train Rosey and most of that was taken by the sword and hand to hand training, thus Alex was her magic teacher.

One day, after a particularly hard sword lesson with both the Goddess and Durag, Rosey showered then tracked down Alex for her first magic lecture. They sat in one of the Golden Palace's many common rooms surrounded by the four statues of Addina at the corners and books lining the walls. As they settled down on a long red couch, an attendant brought them refreshments and sandwiches which they greedily consumed. Their appetite satisfied; Alex wasted no time.

"So, magic!" Alex stated, brows raised.

"Yes...also known as: the lecture I've been dreading," she admitted.

"Oh, come on," Alex said, "It's not that difficult to wrap your head around, at least as a concept. Magic is making the impossible possible by only using words! There are all sorts of things you can..."

He trailed off as Rosey feigned falling asleep. He huffed and threw a pillow at her face. What followed was a mini pillow fight until Alex held up his hands in defeat.

"Okay, all right, you win, so...let's get back to my lesson, please?"

He raised a brow at her like a teacher begging his student to behave. She smiled wickedly, then put her half-raised pillow down, hugging it to her chest as she leaned back into the couch.

"Fine, I surrender. Go on with your lecture, Sir Magikin," she relented.

"Thank you. So, as you know, magic is controlled by speaking spells in the Fracture Language. Doing this keeps magic from taking a hold of its master or running amuck. We owe the Fracture Language's discovery to a masterful magikin called Elorina Dorsava," He began.

"She wrote the Book of Magic, right?" Rosey asked, remembering her teachings.

Alex nodded. "Yes, *and* she was the first to think of magic as a biological form like a mineral, gas, or energy that floats all around us, invisible to the eye but capable of being used. It requires no energy on the part of the magikin. It just needs a command to follow. The larger and more complex the spell the more magic is needed to achieve the result."

Rosey cocked her head. "I believe you said once that the Fracture Language is our Angensilian Language spoken backwards?"

Alex nodded, impressed. "Yes, there are a few exceptions but that's for only really advanced spells. For standard situations, Z stands for A, and Y is for B, and so on." He then sighed, looking away. "However, it's also for this reason that controlling magic is hard. Unlike the elements, magic is a free power that isn't a part of a living thing like the elements are. That's why magikins need spells to control their magic. Otherwise, the dangers could be unspeakable. The wrong words could cause a spell to backfire or create an alternate affect. It could even rebound onto the caster."

Rosey's brows furrowed; she'd heard some of the horror stories about magic gone wrong. Untrained magikins working spells could do all sorts of damage. Those who were magically talented where always watched carefully and schooled as soon as they were able to avoid accidents.

Alex held up four fingers. "There are four different types of powered individuals," he said. "There is a person who is just an elemental and they have no magical talent. There is just a magikin, someone who is born with a magical ability and their element is Potential. There is someone who's a Potential elemental, like you, who's element will never activate and has no magical talent." She looked away at this and he smiled apologetically. "Then there's those who are born with an element *and* a magical talent."

Alex sighed and looked away suddenly as if he had a confession to make. "I am one of those rare people," he admitted and her eyes went wide. "When you have both talents, you must decide which you wish to pursue, for you can't be both, and I, of course, chose magic."

Rosey blinked, amazed. She'd known Alex her whole life, but he'd never told her that.

"Since I chose magic, I have no idea what my element is," he went on. "It's better not to know since the knowledge could tempt me to use my element and my magical talent would fight against it." He sighed, leaning into the couch. "It's like you've entered into a contract. Once you make that decision, there's no going back, and if you try," he shrugged "you could end up losing your magical ability forever. Simply put: a magikin can never become an elemental and an elemental can never become a magikin."

Rosey's brows furrowed, concerned. "So, this works both ways?" she asked.

Alex nodded. "If someone has both talents and decides to be an elemental instead of a magikin, then, one day, tries to use magic as well, they could lose their elemental power and become a Potential."

Rosey shook her head, flabbergasted. "Why?"

"Because, the two powers are just too different, one cannot exist while the other is around. Your initial decision determines which one will be on the chopping block should you be tempted to use the other. So, I prefer not to know."

"Would that person be able to continue training in magic now that their element is gone?"

"Yes," Alex confirmed. If a person has both powers, but trained as an elemental first, then decided to start using magic, they could continue training as a magikin but they'd never be able to use their element again. And vice versa."

Rosey thought about what her uncle had told her. When someone was born, they were always seen by a healer who assessed the child, reporting what powers they had or didn't have. That's how he'd learned she was a Potential.

In that way, the parents can best prepare for their child's upbringing and keep them from making dangerous mistakes at a young age.

She voiced her thoughts and Alex agreed. "It also helps that for the first eight to ten years of a person's life, their powers, whether magical or elemental, are exceptionally weak. So, if they did accidentally do anything, the likelihood of it causing harm is very small," he explained. "With magic, it's imperative it's done right or it could be disastrous. Restraint is the first lesson any magikin learns but it's not like that for elementals. They *rely* on their feelings to fuel their power and that power is determined by their stamina, not their knowledge. Magical talent has to be fine-tuned with years of practice and study. Elemental power is...felt."

Rosey gave him a sly grin. "What are you saying? Elementals don't work as hard?"

"You know I don't mean it that way," Alex said pointedly, "it's just different is all."

"Tell me more," she urged.

He smiled and explained that the training process for magikins was very different from elementals. The only thing that was the same between them was the age that training started. Age ten was when most powered people's abilities started to manifest in full. Though, elemental powers could blossom earlier if their ability was strong enough.

Since elemental technique was so keyed to a person's individuality, most young elementals were encouraged to train themselves or with family members, allowing them the freedom to develop mentally and physically with their power. Once they'd reached a certain point in their training, they could then seek out an Elemental Master if they wanted to enhance their techniques or level.

On the other hand, training for a magikin started no earlier than ten years old. Some particularly adept students might start intellectual studies before ten, but no actual magic was worked till at least ten years of age. They'd be sent to a magikin academy where they'd stay for as long as needed but no shorter than four years. After graduation from the academy, the magikin could seek out an apprenticeship with a Magikin Master to become stronger or advance in a particular magical niche.

"I remember when you attended your magikin academy," Rosay reminisced. "You were gone for four years. Rochelle and I missed you a lot then." She gave him a mock pouty face. "We had no one to tease."

A pillow hit her in the face again and the pillow fight restarted briefly before settling down.

"What did you do at that *'oh so amazing academy'*?" she asked dramatically.

"Well, I'd tell you if you'd stop interrupting," he chided teasingly.

"Okay, okay!" She made a motion as if locking her lips together and tossing away the key.

He waited for a few brief moments before going on. "At the academy, magikins spend most of our first two years studying and reciting phrases and words in the Fracture Language. The spells are useless till we get our wands so there's no danger in it. Around the age of twelve or thirteen, once we've mastered the Fracture language and most basic spells, our training becomes one on one with a specially chosen mentor. Only when the mentor gives us the go ahead will they assist us in creating our wand."

He drew his mahogany wand from its scabbard. It was about as long as his arm and traced with interlaid red and gold designs. Rosey had seen it many times before, her eyes inspected its delicate patterns as he spoke.

"The magikin choses a branch from a tree or plant that they have a connection with, even if that connection is as simple as chopping it for a fire. They then recite the Wand Creation spell while meditating. During which the 'stick' transforms into a wand. The process can take hours or minutes depending on the magikin. Believe it or not, my wand took me three hours to finish!"

Rosey gave him a skeptical look. "Three hours? Almighty One, I wouldn't have the patience for that."

"Neither would I," Alex confessed and she gave him a confused look. "The meditation makes it so the time passes by in a split second. I was barley aware of when it started and when it ended."

"How long has one ever taken to make?"

"Elorina Dorsava's wand took the longest. According to her author's note in the Book of Magic, her wand took a day and a half to finish."

"Poor her!" Rosey gasped, imagining how hungry she'd be after such an experience.

Alex shook his head. "Not so…I bet it was the most amazing experience of her life."

Alex's eyes seemed to gloss over as he looked at the wand. There was something powerful there that Rosey wasn't sure she understood but guessed it was probably a lot like the light in Rochelle's eyes whenever she used her element.

I wonder if I'll ever feel like that one day? Rosey frowned. *It just seems so odd, though. A relationship with something that isn't alive?*

"Once we successfully make our wand, we graduate from the academy," Alex went on, escaping whatever 'spell' he'd been under. "The mentor that helped us can either continue to train us if we want, or we can go it alone from there, seeking a mentorship with another master somewhere else. Typically, most continue to train with their mentors."

"It would seem counterproductive to not train with that mentor," Rosey agreed.

Alex shrugged. "Depends on the magikin, but I know what you mean. The mentors are specifically chosen to work with their chosen student so they know them inside and out, probably better than most know themselves. Since everyone learns differently, each mentor trains in unique ways, geared towards their student's specific needs. Some require them to live away from home for a number of years. Others require them to take on various tasks or go to various places and solve problems."

"So, do the mentors leave the academy with their student if the student wishes to keep training under them?" Rosey asked. "Or does the student have to remain at the academy?"

"Glad you asked," Alex beamed. "It depends on the mentor and the student's needs really, but one of several things could happen. If a student wants to continue training with their mentor, the mentor can leave the academy with their student and teach them as they travel, taking them to specific places that would best suit their continued education.

If the mentor is a permanent resident of the academy, they can request that the student remain at the academy to continue training. It's perfectly fine for a mentor to have more than one student at a time, though, typically, the best results occur one on one.

Lastly, some mentors continue to train their apprentices from afar through a physical and telepathic projection spell called Astral Connection. The spell allows the mentor to appear before the student as a ghostly figure of themselves that can answer questions or guide their student when in need from anywhere in the world. If the student does not need visual aid, they can also just communicate telepathically through a spell called Telepathic Link," Alex explained.

"Why not just scry one another?" Rosey asked.

"They can, but scrying requires a preconstructed reflective surface and those are typically located in designated areas, areas that might be limited depending on the time of day or their location. Astral Connection and Telepathic Link are advanced spells that are more personal and allow instant connection between two individuals regardless of location or distance, it's the most convenient way to communicate," he explained, rolling his wand between two fingers. "It's also the most effective when an individual needs to be trained. Scrying is better used if you just need to talk face to face."

Rosey inched forward in her seat suddenly, realizing something. "Was what Addina did during her announcement a bit like Astral Connection?" she asked. "What we saw at Neran was actually a projected image of herself that she was sending to every city and town on the planet from her location."

Alex's brows furrowed. "That's a pretty good example of what Astral Connection is, but it's not usually able to be spanned across multiple locations at a time like Addina did. Astral Connection is only for communication with one individual or location."

"Huh...does that mean Addina can use magic?" Rosey asked rhetorically, knowing Alex would not be able to answer.

He shrugged. "Addina is an Immortal, I think only she can answer that question."

Rosey shook her head apologetically; she'd gotten them off topic. "Anyway, your mentor, which option did you chose?" she asked.

"Oh, right, I opted for the last option, mostly because...well, I like training on my own...plus, your uncle and the Goddess had promised to continue my training if I wanted to *and I really wanted to*. He and the Goddesses are legends of the magikin world. They've both made good on their promise so far."

Rosey agreed, he'd been through several training sessions with them both in the last three years since he'd returned from the academy.

"Still, I wanted to be able to get my mentor's help should I ever need it."

"So, who is this mentor of yours?" Rosey asked.

"Her name is Thera and she's a Golftriden, one of the toughest and strongest mentors the academy has. She's still there now, raining terror on the students," he said jokingly. He then straightened, becoming serious again. "Once she determines I'm ready, she'll terminate my mentorship and tell me my level."

Rosey's mouth fell open and this time John wasn't around to tell her to close it. She'd only ever seen images of Golftridens, they were a lion bodied creature with a bird's head, four long dragon horns, and two sets of giant feathered wings. It was a cousin to the gryphon but much bigger at eight feet tall and hooved front legs with a lion's back legs.

"Your mentor is a Golftriden!" She leaned forward and whispered, "Are they really eight feet tall? And have two sets of wings?"

He nodded. "They're incredible...I was scared shitless the first time I met her," he admitted and they both started laughing.

"I can't imagine *how* you trained with a Golftriden! Training with Wolvereen has been hell, and he's not as big as she'd be."

"It's not easy, but magic isn't as hands on as what you're doing with Wolvereen. She was mostly instructing me in spells, not making me avoid snapping fang-filled jaws."

He gave her a pointed look. "You know, a lot of training is done in Dream Worlds. Have you seen yours yet?" he asked.

Rosey glared at him. The subject of Dream Worlds was an ongoing dispute between Rosey and her friends. It was supposedly were someone's subconsciousness went when a person slept. There they'd often train or meditate with their element or magical power, becoming stronger without expending energy or fearing injury. Rosey had never seen her Dream World. Powered or not, everyone had one, but she didn't really give into all the hype. She preferred her mistakes to actually hurt, made her learn faster.

Alex saw her face and guessed what she was thinking.

"Dream Worlds are pretty great. Once you see yours, you'll know what I mean," he assured her, winking.

She was determined not to but didn't say so. "I guess...it's one way to train," she said instead.

"It's affective," Alex agreed, "and it's one of the best ways people learn without hurting themselves. The Book of Magic talks about it a lot."

"So, how'd you meet Thera?" Rosey asked, seeking a new topic.

Alex took the bait. "I met her the first day I arrived at the academy, she scolded me for trying to read something I shouldn't have at that age."

"Bad boy," Rosey taunted.

Alex rolled his eyes. "It wasn't like that! You try arriving at one of the most prestigious magikin academies in the world and *not* try to read a restricted spell book!" he insisted but she giggled despite herself, earning her another pillow whack on her arm.

Alex rearranged himself on the couch to a cross-legged position. "So, now you know about how magikins learn and train, let's talk wands."

He lifted his and twirled it in his right hand before pointing it at her.

Rosey gasped and put a hand to her forehead in mock terror. "No! Not wands!" She mocked, then straightened, confused. "Wait, I thought we already talked about wands?"

"There's more."

"There's more?"

"There's always more," he whispered dramatically with a smile.

Rosey squirmed. "Ugh...can I go train with Rochelle now?"

She made to get up and leave and he reached out and gently pulled her back. "Sit down, it's worth it, I swear," he insisted.

"No, it's not."

"Rosey."

"Honestly, I'll face Rochelle, the Goddess, *and* Durag...."

"Don't make me test you later."

"...at the same time," she whispered lastly and he gave her a look.

She shut her mouth and indicated for him to continue.

"Thank you." He straightened. "As I was saying, these things mean more than you could imagine to a magikin." He tapped the wand. "Without a wand we're defenseless. You see, magic is all around us, even though you can't see it, it's still there. The wand draws the magic to it like a beacon. Then, when a spell is spoken, it releases it and the magic performs the spell. The spell is an *order* that the magic is *obliged* to carry out. As long as there's magic around a magikin can cast as many spells as needed."

"What happens if there's not enough magic in the area to perform the spell?" Rosey asked, intrigued despite herself.

"Then the spell won't work. There's either enough or not enough. Now, even if all the magic is used up in the area, it'll eventually return. It can take days or years for the levels to return to normal depending on the spell and how effective the area is at replenishing its magic."

Rosey pursed her lips. "What about animals? I doubt they carry or operate wands without opposable thumbs," she said while lifting her hands to show off the humanoid appendage.

Alex grinned. "No indeed, instead they make stones or gems that they wear around their necks. They make them in the same way we make our wands, they just start off with a rock or mineral instead of a stick. After some careful meditation...poof! The stone becomes a gem...or geode...it depends on the magikin."

"The magikins can't choose what it becomes? Both for wands or stones?"

Alex shook his head. "Unfortunately, not." He lifted his wand to the light, studying it. "The design we get is completely random, derived from the meditation we go through. The shape, color, and so on could be absolutely anything. My wand could have just as easily shaped itself into the image of a feather. You know, a cat I went to school with, her stone took the shape of a beetle! A ruby beetle!? Of all things...to this day she still has no idea why."

He laughed and Rosey frowned, her mind reeling. "Sounds like a lot more work than what Rochelle and I have been practicing."

Alex nodded. "Learning magic can be a pain in the butt if you don't have patience," he agreed. "It's like math, some people are good at it and some aren't. Most people will decide to ignore their magical talent even if they're a Potential. My decision to ignore my elemental power and work with magic is *very* uncommon. If given the option between their magic or their element, most people would always go for their element because it's the easiest to learn."

"That's why elementals far outnumber magikins, isn't it?" Rosey finished.

"That and everyone is born with an element. Even Potential elementals like you have an element, you just can't use it. But you aren't always born with a magical talent. You could speak the Fracture Language fluidly, without error, and never make magic react."

Rosey studied Alex, seeing the proud magikin that she'd missed before. She'd watched Alex and her uncle's training sessions many times before and respected what they did, but she'd never truly understood it.

I was too busy feeling sorry for my powerless self. She admitted.

"Another reason why some people chose not to be magikins is this whole mage business," Alex said sounding slightly annoyed and Rosey cocked her head at him. "The last mage alive was three hundred years ago. There hasn't been one since and that frightens people. They think it's a dying art. The Goddesses especially worry everyone. They're so powerful, they *should* be mages! But they aren't and...it scares people." He shook his head. "It's like there's something preventing magikins from getting stronger."

Rosey rarely saw Alex get like this. She reached out and patted his arm and he squeezed her hand gratefully, giving her a smile.

She bit her lip, suddenly realizing something. "Alex," she said softly and he looked at her. "Why did you never tell me or Rochelle about this before now? All of this?" She looked away, unsure. "I know I was joking around before but, did you really think I wouldn't care?"

Alex looked away. "I tried...when I came back from the academy for the first time..." he paused, his gaze locked with hers. "You were both really excited to see me and asked me all sorts of questions, but both of you fell asleep halfway through...so I didn't bother to finish."

Rosey's mouth fell open and her hand covered her mouth in horror, actual horror this time. "Are you serious!?"

He smiled. "Dead serious."

"Oh, Alex, I'm soooooo sorry...I..." she started, livid, but he shook his head.

"Rosey, it's all right," he insisted. "Both of you had spent the day training hard. You were exhausted and...its true, magic is *very* boring to elementals and warriors. Honestly, it was kinda nice to be back at a place where no one was hounding me about magic every second of the day."

"It's no excuse Alex!" Rosey exclaimed firmly, sitting up on the couch. "That's not how this works between us. We tell each other everything. You, me, Uncle, Rochelle, the horses...even Noly and Hazel. No one's left out!"

He nodded, laughing at how insistent she was.

"I'm serious! Tell me next time, okay? Wake my ass up no matter how many times I fall asleep!" I'm serious, Alex!" she reached over and shook his shoulder determinedly and he nodded. "And...and I'll do better too. I could have asked about this a long time ago and I didn't...I really am sorry."

He saw her sad expression and shook his head. "Nope, I'm fine, you're fine. We're all fine."

He tossed the pillow at her, but she caught it putting it out of his reach. "You better tell me everything from now on...or I'll have Noly lick you all over," she threatened with a sly smile. Alex hated it when Noly tried to slobber him.

He shivered at the idea. "Okay...but please, anything but that."

They laughed but started as the common room doors opened suddenly behind them. Her uncle walked in, followed closely by Noly and Hazel.

"Well, has Alex bored you to tears yet?" her uncle asked, smiling knowingly.

Rosey straightened and said proudly, "Absolutely not! He's intrigued me in every way possible. Highly interesting stuff over here."

Rosey and Alex's eyes met and they both started laughing.

She made room as Noly and Hazel rushed between them. Noly yipped excitedly and licked Rosey's cheek in the way Alex hated but she loved.

"Where have you two been hiding?" Rosey asked, patting Noly.

"We were practicing, of course," Hazel explained, rubbing against Rosey's arms for a scratch behind the ears which Rosey supplied. "As the big bad wolf said earlier, we have to start taking our involvement more seriously if we're to do our jobs as responsible protectors."

"Yeah, what she said," Noly added, tongue lolling.

"Good to hear," Rosey said, impressed.

Alex grabbed at Noly's swishing tail swatting him continuously. He then sputtered as her tail suddenly flipped across his mouth.

"Pft! Okay, time to go," he said getting up and Rosey joined him.

"Good, I came to get you for dinner anyway," John said, indicating the open door.

They filed out and John hugged Rosey close to him, whispering in her ear as they walked, "Let's go before Alex tells you about how the unicorns are masters of magic and that wands are actually made to mimic their horns."

Rosey's mouth widened. "Now that might be interesting to hear!"

"Well, there's not much to tell, that's about it really..."

He winked at her and she swatted him playfully. Alex followed behind them, chatting with Noly and Hazel who were gossiping about the night's dinner choices.

"Say, where have you been all week?" she asked her uncle curiously. "I know everyone's been training like crazy and I just assumed you were too, but...I rarely see you at the practice arena?"

He coughed and looked anywhere but at her, her que he was avoiding the subject.

"Out with it," she demanded.

He sighed and ran a hand through his short jet-black hair. "It's no secret, really. I've been working closely with the Goddesses on a spell. We've actually been working with *a lot* of magikins over the past few days, exchanging information and organizing people."

"A spell? What for?"

"The Scorched Mountain," he answered. "Addina advised that it might be worth a shot to see if the magikins can't gather their resources and create a seal that might prevent the poison from spreading for a while."

Rosey pulled away from him shocked. "Are you kidding, that's great news! That would give me time to collect the elements from the Wells. Why'd you keep it from me?"

She frowned and stopped in her tracts suddenly. Alex overheard them and paused with Noly and Hazel going silent.

"What's going on?" Rosey demanded, fixing John with a hard stare.

John swallowed; his eyes filled with guilt. "The spell takes a lot of time, effort, and attention hun...it means...well. It means I won't be going with you on your journey. In fact, me and a bunch of other magikins will be leaving for the Scorched Mountain soon."

Rosey was shocked to silence. Her gaze shot to Alex who looked as taken aback. Noly and Hazel exchanged flabbergasted looks.

"You're leaving Rosey!?" Noly spoke first, breaking the silence.

That was all it took. John went to say more but Rosey was already running down the hallway.

"Rosey, wait!" her uncle called after her, but she barely heard him. She wiped away angry tears, more ashamed of crying than of her uncle's confession. In all but a few moments she'd lost her appetite.

CHAPTER EIGHT

The White Witch

Rosey burst into the Golden Goddess's office; her manners forgotten in her blind rage. She sought out the tall, golden-clad woman standing at her desk rifling through some papers as she barged into the room, fuming from head to toe.

"HOW COULD YOU DO THIS TO ME!" Rosey shouted, utterly betrayed. She slammed her hands down on the Goddess's desk, making it rattle.

The Goddess glared at her, her expression a mix of confusion and distaste at Rosey's tone. "What are you talking about, child?"

"How could you...take my..." her voice broke as emotion bubbled over and she hated herself for it. "Uncle..." she managed to murmur.

The Goddess's eyes widened and her gaze softened with understanding. "I see, he told you."

Rosey was shaking. She wanted to say so much more but if she tried to speak, her voice would break again and she knew she'd start crying and that was something she was too proud to let happen. Andraste hummed against her back as if sharing her pain. Wordlessly her hand flew to the Shanobie Crystal around her neck and it instantly grew warm at her touch, soothing her.

"Rosey...I'm sorry," the Goddess began. "Addina just suggested the idea a day ago and John and I were discussing how best to tell you." Her gaze met Rosey's and they stared each other down for a few moments. "Please, Rosey. I understand you're upset, but I'd never ask John to leave you if it wasn't very important. You know that."

Something in the Goddess's voice quelled Rosey's anger. As fast as the fire had come, it was snuffed out and Rosey felt herself relax into cold understanding. She straightened a pencil holder on the Goddess's desk that had tipped over.

John burst into the room, finally catching up with her. Rosey glared at him, but he didn't falter.

"Young lady, I realize this is upsetting news, but do you think I *like* the idea of leaving you behind?" he said as he drew near. "I said no, at first...but apparently, *I'm* the only one for the job." His gaze flitted to the Goddess.

"You know you are," The Goddess agreed sternly. She walked over to him and gripped his shoulder. "Go onto dinner John, I'll talk to her," she insisted.

He nodded and looked back at Rosey, his eyes glistened with pain and whatever anger Rosey still had dissipated. "I'm sorry, Rosey," he said before turning and walking out the office doors.

Rosey watched him go, quelling the sudden urge to run after him. She needed to hear what the Goddess had to say.

The Goddess sighed, turning to her. "Addina's plan is simple: magic may help slow the poison down long enough for you to complete your journey. But the spell to hold it back will require a tremendous amount of magic and magikins to work it." She crossed her arms. "You could call it the first ever Collaborative Spell that's ever been written. I can't even begin to fathom what kind of effort will go into it."

"Are you and the Silver Goddess attending?" Rosey asked.

The Goddess shook her head. "No, our work is far too important here, I am the sole protector of most of Hondan's citizens and my sister handles its stealth operations. As far as Addina is concerned, we've been officially assigned to you as your back up just as we were with your mother. Most of the World Leaders are, to be honest." Rosey's gaze shot to her astonished and the Goddess smiled. "That's right, little Keeper, you're now considered one of the World Leaders, second only to Addina herself in the line of command."

Rosey felt her jaw drop and she plopped into one of the chairs before the desk. In a few short days she'd gone from Rosey, a citizen of Neran, to Rosey, the Keeper, World Leader.

"Though my sister and I are powerful magikins," the Goddess continued, walking around her desk to lean against it, "we are also World Leaders and thus we maintain a Leader's responsibilities. We can't just up and leave our posts."

Rosey crossed her arms, giving the Goddess a knowing look. "I think we both know you go wherever you want. You led one of Maharen's War Ships while still being a World Leader, remember?"

"That was temporary for an emergency situation and I was *brilliant* at it," the Goddess admitted teasingly. "Anyway," she leaned in, "the strongest and most powerful magikins were considered for this Spell, your uncle happens to be one of them. In fact, he was the first they considered for the Scorched Spell Collaboration. So, be proud."

Rosey nodded and her cheeks reddened suddenly at her childishness. No matter if she was sixteen, it was time to start acting like the Keeper! She wiped away whatever tears were left and stood up.

"I'm sorry for barging in, I was just...upset," she offered as explanation though it sounded like an excuse.

The Goddess waved a golden hand dismissively. "Forget it, my Keeper. Given the situation, we understand."

Rosey cocked her head confused. *We?* Turning, her eyes went wide as she spied grim-faced Wolvereen siting to the right of the desk and next to him was another tall wolf with thin white fur wearing silver armor. Her blue gaze held Rosey's for a moment and Rosey blinked, surprised by their kindness. At the same time, she shivered for the wolf's gleaming armor against her white fur made her appear ghostly, like a phantom lingering in mist.

Rosey's cheeks reddened as Wolvereen's gaze narrowed at her, his red eyes hard. *I can't believe I didn't notice them here! And they saw all that!* It was enough to make her want to run away. Instead, she bowed her head to them in greeting.

"Ahem," the Goddess coughed, smiling at Rosey's embarrassment. "My Keeper, this is Nagura, Commander of the Silver Goddess's Silver Guards." She indicated the flawless six-foot-tall white wolf and Rosey inclined her head to her. She bowed elegantly in return.

"It's nice to meet you, my Keeper," the wolf greeted her kindly. Her voice was so soft Rosey marveled it came from a wolf's throat.

"You too, Commander Nagura," Rosey said. "I'm sorry you had to witness that."

Nagura smiled warmly and chuckled. "It's not a problem, dear. Things can get difficult when it comes to family."

Something in her voice hardened at the end and Wolvereen shifted uncomfortably next to her, ears going back slightly. Rosey's brow rose, intrigued to see the hard and stoic Wolvereen suddenly looking more like a puppy then the Commander of the Golden Guards.

"Nagura, Wolvereen, and I were discussing security measures. It seems my sister may have a plan but we have yet to come to an agreement," the Goddess said.

"Plan?" Rosey asked intrigued.

"I'm afraid I can't go into any details just yet. As soon as I know more, I'll update you. Now, I was going to hold off on giving you this till after dinner but it seems you've made your own schedule." The Goddess tilted her head to her knowingly and Rosey looked away.

The Golden woman turned around and picked up an elegantly carved silver dagger from her desk. At the same time Nagura moved around Wolvereen and stood face to face with Rosey, her gentle blue eyes like sapphire diamonds. "My Keeper, please take this dagger as a token of the Silver Goddess's kindness. It's called Silver Knight."

The Golden Goddess paused beside Nagura and extended the dagger to Rosey. Andraste hummed jealously but Rosey ignored it. Amazed she reached out and took the dagger, gingerly admiring its ornate design. The hilt and scabbard were both a shining silver decorated in exquisite patterning. She removed the blade from the sheath, testing the grip and twirling the long dagger through the air. She smiled at it, surprised by how nimble it felt in her grasp. Not wasting a moment, she strapped it on. It fit snugly around her waist.

She turned to Nagura beaming. "Please give the Silver Goddess my utmost thanks. The dagger is just amazing, a fine weapon." She bowed and Nagura bowed back, silver armor clinking.

"I'm pleased you like it, the Silver Goddess worked tirelessly on it since you were chosen," Nagura explained. "She wanted you to be well protected."

"Nagura will be here for some time," the Goddess explained. "She's visiting Wolvereen for a while before she heads back to my sister's services. Of course, she's also here to discuss my sister's plan, thus, feel free to pester her as much as you like. I'm sure you have many questions."

Rosey nodded. "You bet I do; I had no idea the Silver Goddess had her own set of Guards! I mean, it makes sense and all, but no one's ever said anything about it...wait...why are you visiting Wolvereen?" She looked between the white beast and the red-eyed brute astonished, remembering what had transpired earlier between them.

"He's my mate," Nagura explained, tilting her head with a dainty laugh. "I'm here to make sure he isn't becoming too introverted while I'm away."

Her soft gaze lingered on him and his ears went level with the floor.

"What's wrong with being introverted?" he sulked.

Rosey was happy Noly and Hazel weren't here, they would have sputtered aloud or said something obnoxious. She could already hear Noly running around shouting "OPPOSITES ATTRACT!" at the top of her voice.

The Goddess clapped her hands, distracting Rosey from the image. "Now, shall we go to dinner, we're already late and..."

Suddenly they heard wingbeats approaching and Rosey looked up sharply to see a giant creature approaching the Goddess's window. To her surprise, the beast easily pushed open the eloquent stained-glass structure and burst into the room on long dragon-like wings. She tensed and pulled both Andraste and Silver Knight from their sheaths, positioning Andraste in her right hand before her and Silver Knight in her left hand behind her. Thanks to her extensive weapons training, she knew how to wield the dagger while also wielding her sword. She looked around for the creature, but lost sight of anything as she was suddenly surrounded by armor.

In a flash, Wolvereen and Nagura were on either side of Rosey, so fast she barely noticed they'd moved. Their large frames sheltered her protectively as the beast flew through the air overhead. Rosey tried to peek around the wolves' large bodies but was unsuccessful. Suddenly she heard the clip clop of hooves that must have been the beast landing. Wolvereen sighed and relaxed while Nagura laughed slightly.

"Honestly, Argno!" Rosey heard the Goddess shout. "How many times do I have to tell you to stop using my windows when you deliver a message!? Next time use the front door!"

Sheathing her blades, Rosey elbowed her way out from the Wolves' sandwiched, protective positions, grabbing the armor to help hoist herself free. Finally, her eyes settled on a creature she'd only ever read about in books. It was a Dragnagor, a creature with the body of a horse but the tail, head and wings of a dragon.

Argno smiled at the Goddess, tilting his head at her criticism. "Sorry, my lady. I just love to go fast...you know that. Stopping to come in through the door for a flying creature is like well...weird...." He stopped, putting the tip of one wing to his chin as if confused. He shook his head. "Anyway, I come bearing good news, you want to hear it, right?"

Rosey approached amazed, looking him up and down with interest. A blue stone hung around his neck, bobbing against his chest on a golden chain. He was a magnificent dappled gray beast with a red mane and brilliant orange-red scales on his legs and wings. Perched on his forehead and arching along his neck was a single, long green and yellow feather. Bordering it were two arched black horns.

The Goddess put her hands on her hips, exasperated. "Of course, I want to hear it, but next time use the front door or I'll *magically* escort you back out that window and *make* you use the door instead!"

Argno smiled at her as if he didn't believe her. "Okay, misses grumpy Goddess."

He laughed and she threw up her hands, defeated. "You better be happy you're the best messenger my sister and I have, or I'd have replaced you long ago."

"I love you, too," Argno said in a sing song voice, waving one wing at her bashfully.

The Goddess huffed at him annoyed, though she hid a slight smile.

Argno finally noticed Rosey and beamed at her. "Ah, you must be Rosey Mystic, the new Keeper?" he guessed cheerfully, though Rosey doubted he didn't know who she was. "I'm Argno, the official messenger for the Silver and Golden Goddesses. I'll also be delivering messages to you while you're on the Hondan Continent, my Keeper." He bowed and winked at her, white fangs gleaming as he smiled.

Rosey bowed back. "Pleased to meet you. Wow, you're a...Dragnagor," she said, pausing before him. Her eyes kept tracing the elegant curve of his horns and the long exquisite bend of his wings. "I've...never seen a Dragnagor before," she admitted.

Argno chuckled. "Want to touch?" he offered, extending one long dragon's wing to her.

Smiling like a child she gently touched the scaled skin, marveling at the way the light caught each scale. Dragnagors weren't related to dragons in any way, but had earned their name due to the dragon-like characteristics they had. They were actually a part of the *Gor* animal family, a group of species whose title ended in 'gor'. She was just happy to be this close to anything remotely dragon related.

"Okay, the petting zoo is closed," Wolvereen said, barging in to glare at the Dragnagor. The two were equally sized, but somehow Wolvereen's poofy black fur and gleaming armor made him seem larger. "What message do you have for the Goddess, Argno?"

Argno folded his wings elegantly to his sides and paced around Wolvereen. "Of course! My Keeper and my Goddess, your ship has arrived at dock. Captain Marine is ready to depart whenever the Keeper is," he announced elegantly.

The Goddess beamed. "Good! Finally, Marine's here. I was getting worried." Rosey looked at her concerned and the Goddess waved her hand.

"Don't fret Rosey, it's just that the seas can be a bit tricky this time of year, that's all."

Having never sailed before, Rosey would have to take her word for it, though she'd heard some tales about the fall season bringing bad sailing weather.

The Goddess went to her desk and riffled through one of the drawers. Finding what looked like an envelope she walked over to Argno and presented it to him.

"Argo, report to my sister what you've told me, then deliver this to Marine. Let him know what's going on," she ordered, firmly.

Argno bowed, one long wing extending before his body like an arm. "Of course, my lady Goddess." With the same winged arm, he tapped the blue stone on his chest. With a flash the envelope disappeared into the stone.

Rosey studied the stone intrigued. She then brightened, realizing the stone was one of the magikin stones Alex told her about. *Argno must be a magikin then!*

Turning, Argno bowed to Rosey. "It was nice seeing you, my Keeper. Farewell, and good luck!" With that he turned and leaped for the window.

"Would you please use the..." the Goddess started, but it was too late. The long winged Dragnagor flew out the window just as quickly as he's appeared. Just to add insult to injury, he flicked his tail expertly as he left and shut the window gently behind him.

The Goddess and Wolvereen muttered annoyed but Nagura just smiled.

Rosey's eyes widened, only just then comprehending what Argno had said.

"Wait...the ship is at dock?!" She paused and the Goddess turned to her. "Does that mean...I'll be leaving soon?"

"That depends on you, my dear," she answered. "In order for you to leave, you must first know *where* you're going. Have you seen the White Witch yet?" the Golden woman asked.

Rosey looked away. "No..." she answered slowly. "Not yet, and I've never once dreamed of the Dream World Alex and Rochelle talk about all the time."

The Goddess was silent for a moment then shook her head. "It' doesn't matter, Rosey. When the White Witch is ready, she'll come to you..."

The Goddess's words started to dull suddenly, as if her hearing was going out. Rosey cupped her ears but the sound phased out into white noise. She started and backed away, unbalanced. Her chest tightened suddenly and she fell to one knee.

Rosey gasped, aware of Wolvereen and Nagura rushing to her side and the Goddess calling out with alarm, but Rosey knew what was happening. It had been weeks since the last night terror attack, but now it was back with a vengeance. Some part of her had hoped the attacks were gone for good, but clearly, she'd been wrong. She coughed, sputtering and gasping for breath as her vision blurred. Pain, hot and searing, ripped through her chest and a darkness swam before her, black creeping smoke swarming like vines at the edges of her vision. She buckled into unconsciousness as the black vines rushed her.

Rosey opened her eyes to darkness. No, it wasn't completely dark. There was some kind of light, soft and dim. She lifted herself up and looked around startled. She was in a room, but one she'd never seen before. She was wearing a simple white shirt and pants, lying on an incredibly comfortable bed with soft, plush white linens. The room seemed to be lit with bright brilliant lights, yet it was so dim and dull looking. Not nearly as bright as it should have been given how brilliantly the lamps were glowing. It seemed...depressing.

A single closed white door was on her left and two-night stand tables were on either side of the bed. Across from her was a simple desk and on the right wall was a large dresser that reached the ceiling and a door leading into a bathroom. The last thing Rosey saw was a single rounded mirror stretching from floor to ceiling with an elegant border resting in the left-hand corner of the room.

Where was she? It certainly wasn't her room at the Golden Palace. She tried to remember what had happened last. *Another terror attack! That's right...I was with the Goddess in her office when the attack came!*

She took a deep steady breath. Her gaze rested on the mirror again, her blue eyes staring back at her like radiant sapphires. Mindlessly she got off the bed and walked over to it, as if caught in a trance. She eyed her reflection. She was a tall, well-muscled young woman with a thin figure, long legs, and the crisp white skin of her mother's Hayralian blood. The people of Hayral, a large mountainous continent across the sea, were black haired people with monolid eyes and skin so pale it was almost white. The lack of color stemmed from living their lives inside vast mountain cities. They were tall, thin, and incredibly beautiful. Rosey had adopted all of their features except the eyes, she had the rounded eyes of her father's Neranian trait. It was odd, she'd always been amazed that her mixed heritage hadn't given her a darker skin tone matching that of the nut brown Neranian race, but her mother's dominant traits had prevailed. She'd been told by many a boy, including Alex, how beautiful she was.

She started suddenly. The Shanobie Crystal was missing from her neck. She turned to look for it, a million things zooming through her mind, but stopped dead.

Standing in the middle of the room was a tall white-haired woman clad in white robes. Her eyes were a gentle purple cream color like silken violets and her lips were painted white. She smiled at Rosey and extended her hand to her chest as she bowed.

"Greetings, young Keeper, I am the White Witch," she said elegantly, her voice smooth and rich.

Rosey faltered, halting. "The White Witch?" she repeated. Her brows furrowed. "That means...is this my..." she looked around startled.

"Indeed, Keeper. This is your Dream World," the Witch answered for her, smiling kindly.

Rosey immediately felt apprehensive. She knew this place was off.

The Witch stared at her as her gaze flitted about with uncertainty. "You seem on edge, what ails you?" she asked gently.

Rosey sighed. "What *doesn't* ail me, you mean," she shivered. "Dream Worlds are new for me. I've never been in mine before. The whole idea of them kinda creeps me out really." She shook her head and took another calming breath. "I wasn't sure how you'd be showing yourself to me, but meeting inside my Dream World makes sense, I guess."

"I see. Well, there's nothing to be afraid of. Though, I admit," she looked around them at the dull dimness of the room, "the ambiance is leaving much to be desired. But *I* have no control of that, you do."

Rosey twisted a strand of hair around her finger awkwardly. *I get what she's saying, this place looks like this because my perception of it has always been negative. That's probably why I'm here without my armor or my weapons, I'm defenseless, keeping in line with it reflecting my distrust of this place. I guess I need to work on that, figure out how to master it now that I have it.*

"So...I guess I decided to dream myself as powerless, I'm even missing the Shanobie Crystal," she stated, hopping back onto the bed. For some reason it felt safe, like a location that no one could enter without her say so.

Inside a Dream World, anything was possible. She could go to sleep and dream herself naked into her Dream World, or battle a terrifying made up foe, or climb a huge ice capped mountain with no mind for the bitter cold. Nothing was real, it was all just a fake reality made by the dreamer to serve whatever purpose they desired.

"Not exactly," the Witch answered. "Actually, it's because *I* am here. You can't wear me and I be around your neck at the same time."

Rosey cocked her head at her, confused. Then her brows lifted and her mouth dropped open.

"You're....you're...the..." Rosey stuttered, her hand motioning to her chest where the crystal normally rested.

The White Witch chuckled. "Yes dear, I am the Shanobie Crystal personified. I can only appear to you like this in your Dream World."

"Oh wow," Rosey managed to say. She put her hand to her mouth, as if she could pull more words from her throat, but all she said was. "Wow...I...um...hum."

The Witches' smile broadened warmly. "I know, Esperanza was just as shocked to realize that I had my own...well..."

"Mind...personality..." Rosey offered, finally getting her voice to work. "So...just how aware are you? I mean, in the real world, as the crystal are you able to...I guess...*see* what I'm seeing. Perceive the world as I do?"

Her mind almost immediately went to all the times she'd undressed while wearing the crystal. Sure, she did that all the time with Noly and Hazel, but undressing around animals or even a powerful crystal was different from undressing in front of another human.

"Yes, I can perceive the world as you do. I also monitor your health and safety. How else do you think Addina keeps tabs on you?"

That makes sense, Rosey admitted. Still, internally her mind was screaming at the awkwardness of it, but it was too late now.

"Wait, so why do you go by the White Witch and not the Shanobie Crystal then?" Rosey asked her.

The Witch considered for a moment, formulating her answer. Finally, she said, "In order to manifest myself, I have to choose a form to personify. I could have chosen anything or anyone that can communicate, but I decided to copy a famous magikin who'd earned herself the title of White Witch."

"Really?" Rosey's brows furrowed confused. "If that's the case, why wouldn't any of us have known about her? The Goddess even spoke of the White Witch as a mystery."

"That's because the White Witch lived thousands of years ago, long before the war. She was one of the first magikins to walk this world."

Again, Rosey's mouth dropped. "Alex is gonna lose his mind when I tell him this."

"I imagine he will," the Witch agreed.

"So, why did you take on her persona? What was so special about her, was it just her abilities?"

At this, the Witch's gaze became incredibly soft. "No, it was because she was a dear, close friend to Addina...and thus...to me."

Rosey blinked. *Of course, the Shanobie Crystal is literally the tip of Addina's horn. Strange...you'd think she'd have taken on Addina's form instead of the White Witch's?*

She voiced her thought, but the Witch laughed. "I'm afraid most of us would not want to personify ourselves. We are our own harshest critic after all."

"Ah, I understand," Rosey agreed, remembering how much *she'd* always belittle herself for a lack of elemental or magical power. She sighed and straightened up. "Well then, White Witch, please tell me. Where's the first Well?"

"Yes, my Keeper," the White Witch inclined her head to her. "Your first destination is the Molt Volcano, here on Hondan."

Rosey's gaze widened. "Really, that's about a four-hour horse ride from here," she said happily. "Why so close?"

The Witch shrugged. "That's just where it is this time around. You're lucky." She clasped her hands before her. "Is there anything else I can help you with before I take my leave, my Keeper?"

Rosey considered, then nodded. "Yes...could you...tell me more about my mother?"

Many people had always been willing to talk about her mother should she ever ask but, for some reason, the White Witch seemed more personal, like she was the door to Esperanza's inner life, the part no one else had been able to see.

The Witch's eyes softened, genuine sadness outlining her delicate features. "That depends on what questions you have. I met her as I am meeting you now, briefly. Besides that, I know little else."

Rosey considered for a moment. "What was her dream world like?"

The Witch brightened at this. "Ah, yes. It was different every time we met, but one thing was the same: it was always a well-maintained garden, bursting with life. I'd usually find her tending to the plants with gentle care, she'd usually keep tending them while we talked."

Rosey rubbed her chest, feeling an odd sense of loss and longing, remembering what her uncle had told her. Esperanza had wanted to be a landscape architect before being chosen as Keeper. She'd kept up her training while on her journey and had even designed the gardens in the Golden Palace, using her earth element to it's greatest potential. She'd been able to grow some of the rarest plants in the world with minimal effort.

Rosey wanted to ask more, but she knew there was nothing else she could ask of the Witch. Rosey felt herself deflate; her chest heavy.

The Witch must have seen her despair for she said, "I'll tell you this, Rosey. She was the gentlest woman I'd ever met."

Rosey nodded feeling more confused than sad. The weight on her chest tightened and she coughed suddenly, sputtering. She took a long shallow breath.

"No way..." she managed to say, "...even here....night terrors...."

The Witch's gaze looked her over, uncertain. "As for the new question flying through your mind. I have no idea what these 'night terrors' are...you will have to figure that out on your own."

Rosey took a shuddering breath and gripped her chest but the warm crystal that gave her comfort was gone. Instead, she felt the White Witch's arms wrap around her in a warm embrace and Rosey latched onto her, closing her eyes tight against the darkness closing in.

Rosey opened her eyes to her room at the Golden Goddess's castle. Lifting herself out of bed, her chest untightened and she took a shuddering breath. The pain was very suddenly gone and her hand found the crystal resting on her neck peacefully. She gripped it, the warmth spreading over her like a fine blanket. She reached for the glass of water at her bedside and stared into the Golden Goddess's eyes. She started, flinching away.

"How are you feeling?" the Goddess asked in a low gentle voice. She was sitting in a golden chair at Rosey's bed side, staring at her with a worried expression. Her uncle was sitting in another chair next to hers, he was slumped over asleep. They'd been holding hands.

Rosey didn't answer. Instead, she took the water and took a long swig. Thankfully it was ice cold. The Goddess repeated her question and Rosey leaned back against her pillows. She was wearing her blue night clothes and it was dark outside. She'd slept through dinner. Her stomach growled and she took another sip of water.

"I'm as well as I can be. I thought...I hoped that these stupid terrors had left me alone," Rosey said softly.

"Yes," the Goddess agreed. "We'd all hoped that."

"I assume my uncle told you about the terrors then?"

The Goddess took a sip of water from her own glass siting on the bedside table. "I witnessed it at the training ground weeks ago, remember, but yes, John explained more the day you were chosen as Keeper. I have been concerned about them ever since."

"So, you know then that I've already been looked over by a healer. Nothing's wrong with me...as least as far as *they* know."

The Goddess sighed. "Honestly, what are we going to do about this? What if this happens in the middle of battle or during a Mother's trial?"

Rosey's grip on the glass of water tightened, her eyes glistening with tears. "I'm sorry Goddess...I just...don't know what to say to that."

The Goddess's gaze softened and she got up. To Rosey's amazement she wrapped her in a sudden warm embrace. It was so fast that Rosey was startled for a moment. She'd never thought in a million years that the one and only Golden Goddess would hug her, yet here she was gently wrapped in the woman's arms.

She pulled away and held Rosey at arm's length. "Are you hungry? I can have the chef whip something up for you."

Rosey glanced around noticing the others were missing. With her having an attack, she'd have expected them to be waiting over her worriedly. How long was she out?

"Where are the others?"

"Noly and Hazel were far too worried, they kept barking, meowing, and making a fuss so I shooed them into another room so you could get some rest. John refused to turn in, but the others agreed to go to bed. None of us ate very well at dinner with you out like a light." She was silent for a moment. "My healer told me the same thing, that there was no sign of any health issues and once you'd lost consciousness you appeared to be sleeping normally. He suggested the terrors could be stress-induced."

"Maybe....I don't know." Rosey looked at the glass of water in her hands and twisted it about, wiping away the water beading the sides. She gave the Goddess a weak smile. "Thanks for the offer, but no food. I'll just go back to sleep and eat a big breakfast tomorrow."

The Goddess nodded and turned to wake her uncle, her own golden and silver night clothes fluttered about her frame perfectly.

"Oh right!" Rosey said, smiling. "The night terrors knocking me out isn't all bad."

The Goddess's brows furrowed. "What do you mean?" she asked as she shook John's shoulder.

"I just saw the White Witch. Looks like we're going to the Molt Volcano."

Chapter Nine

Departure

Balra worked her way through the underbrush, mindlessly pushing away fall greenery and shrubs. Her breath billowed in the cold air. She paused and looked to the pale sky, clouds gathering thickly overhead. Her brows furrowed. Winter was on its way but Hondan was still grasping at summer's last warmth. She smiled wickedly, soon it wouldn't matter anymore.

She went on, her long black cape billowing out behind her as she leaped over sharp rocks and scraggly bushes. She wasn't on a road of any kind, so the going was rough, but she didn't care, she had a mission to fulfill. She could feel it, the poison deep within the earth beating strong with power, the same poison that rushed through her veins. Her and the Master had worked the poison through the world magnificently. All had turned out just as the demon had promised. Now, she had only to ensure the poison completed its job.

I cannot let the Master's hard work be undone! Never! She thought doggedly, but the poison hadn't gone unnoticed for long. Addina, that damned winged beast, had discovered the poison sooner than expected. *I need more time...I need help!* She certainly couldn't stop Addina on her own, she wasn't strong enough to face an Immortal nor was she going to let herself be found. She'd taken enough of a risk revealing herself during the war sixteen years ago, a risk that had ended in the successful assassination of

Esperanza, her lifemate, and most of her friends. But at a cost. Balra's brief revelation had put a target on her back which meant she'd had to go into hiding, effectively ending her surface involvement in the Raptor Demon's affairs. So, covertly, she'd dedicated herself to the poison's care, nurturing and feeding it so that it spread at a rapid rate. She smiled slightly. *I will lead the charge from the shadows still...but now with the Gorons and Raptors at my beck and call.*

She felt the black stone embedded in her chest vibrate slightly and she paused, looking into the forest. She'd approached a rocky bluff layered with numerous large boulders and thick winter-resistant greenery. Nearby she felt the air shift and the rocks tremble slightly. Small stones scattered in the distance and she turned to the noise sharply. As fast as lighting a Blood Goron attacked her, flying in on dragon-like wings, it's spiked tail lashing as it slashed at her throat. She dodged, just as equally fast, and outmaneuvered it, grabbing its tail as it aimed for her head. Pulling back hard, she yanked it from the air and brought her arm down expertly over the beast's throat, pinning it to the ground. The beast writhed in her grasp, snapping at her with long fangs dripping saliva, but she spoke one solid word and the beast stopped. Its spiked tail hovering inches from her neck.

Carefully she let the Goron go and it got to its paws, its four-foot body relaxing into a submissive position as it beheld her and the glowing black stone in her chest. Slowly it bowed.

"Apologies, ma'am...I was unaware you were on our side," he said with a surprisingly even voice.

Balra nodded, unamused. "I'm not sure how much Master told you, but I was its right hand during the war. I killed Esperanza and her friends, and I helped make the poison that's killing this world." She knelt down and lifted the beast's head to her face, whispering, "I know more about the Master than you could ever possibly know."

She let his head fall and he backed away, folding his wings at his sides. His black scales flashed menacingly and red eyes regarded her with uncertainty.

"What do you command, my lady?" he asked.

"You've been acting on your own for too long, Goron. It's time you were moved into position." She turned away and sat down on a nearby boulder, crossing her legs. "Addina has discovered our Master's poison and is working to stop it." The Goron hissed hatefully as Balra spoke, clicking its fangs. "We have to stop her...or at least slow her down long enough for the poison to do its bidding."

The poison was perfection, there was nothing else like it! The perfect mix of magic and power, she just had to see it through to the end!

The Goron chuckled, gnashing its jaws and kneading the ground excitedly, tearing up clumps of dirt. "Of course, my lady! Command us! What do you want us to do?"

Balra thought for a moment, her mind going back to Addina's announcement in Neran. She smiled slightly. It had been so simple to spy on the world, even while in hiding all those years. Concealing herself wasn't difficult, not with the power of the black stone in her chest cloaking the demonic aura surrounding her. To anyone who saw or met her, she'd seem like a normal human woman. She'd hid in plain sight for years, mostly living alone in remote areas, but close enough to a city or town to keep up with local news, keeping a sharp eye out for anything that could threaten the poison. For the last few months, she'd been living near Neran, and Addina's announcement had meant she'd visited the city to see it with her own eyes...including the new Keeper that had been chosen.

"The Immortal has chosen a new Keeper to be her champion," she announced.

The Goron hissed, its ears flat against its head and its eyes bulging with rage. "Keeper! The damned one! The hated one! That wretched creature!" he spat, tail lashing.

"Indeed," Balra agreed. "*That* woman, Esperanza, put an end to our Master, despite the hole I put through her chest...however, a new Keeper means that the poison may be threatened. I cannot let that happen. Your mission now, dear one," she said, gently patting the Goron's head, "is to kill the new Keeper."

The Goron licked its lips, smiling with giddy abandon. "New orders...new blood to spill...yes...give us war, give us death!"

Balra smiled warmly, the black stone in her chest beating a steady rhythm with the beat of her heart. "Of course, Goron, you will taste her blood eventually. For now, you must be patient." The Goron growled, eyes narrowing. "She's with the Golden Goddess, a fortress for which even I'd have little chance of infiltrating. We must wait for the opportune moment, am I clear?" She gripped his snout roughly and the Goron squirmed slightly.

"Of course, my lady, of course....we'll wait your command," he murmured around her iron grip.

She nodded then released his snout and placed her hand on his head. "Now, stay still while I share her identity with you," Balra ordered.

The Goron closed his eyes and Balra did the same, her other hand touched the black stone on her chest and she imagined the image of the new Keeper in her mind. The stone vibrated in her chest as the image was then passed to the Goron who shared not only in her image but her name and her heritage as well.

"Rosey Mystic..." the Goron growled angrily as it opened its eyes.

"Yes, the horrid spawn of the first Keeper, Esperanza," Balra agreed, her own annoyance radiating from her.

How many times had she spied the young woman in Neran learning to fight with fellow warriors in the training grounds. How many times had she looked at her and considered that she might need to die? But making a move on Rosey would mean revealing herself...and that would leave the poison vulnerable. Still, Balra had watched her and even sparred against Rosey one day in the training grounds, just to see how strong she was. Balra hadn't been impressed, determining that Rosey was just Esperanza's daughter and nothing more, so there'd been no reason to act against her. Till now.

"Make sure you share her image and identity with the others," Balra ordered the Goron and he nodded. She then got up, removing her hand from his head and he backed away but waited for her to dismiss him. "From this moment on, the Gorons and the Raptors will answer to me. Gather those in the area, but be discreet about it, and meet me in a day's time near Neran's border. Whatever you do, don't be seen." She fixed her sharp red gaze on him. "And don't worry about contacting me, little Goron." She touched the black stone in her chest. "This little gift from Master will lead me to you every time. No matter how far you are, I can always find you."

Her gaze hardened and the Goron backed away even more, eyes glinting. She flicked her chin at him and he took off, flying stealthily through the trees. Despite how nervous he must have been he didn't make a sound and she couldn't see him anymore. She had to give the Gorons credit, they were crafty and very good at disappearing. *Which is why most of them are still alive, though I can't say the same about the Raptors.* The brutes were stupid compared to the Gorons and hopelessly too animalistic. It made them great for battle but terrible for strategy. *Oh well, that's what I'm here for. But I have to be careful, too much sudden strategy will cause people to wonder what's going on. I have to make it seem like the Gorons are behind this, not a warrior like myself.*

She walked swiftly till she found a trail leading back to Neran. Nearing the city, she stopped suddenly and straightened her cape to cover the black stone. If anyone saw that, they'd no doubt have many questions. She shielded her eyes against the morning sun lighting the mountain range in the distance and warming the misty air. She took a long breath before continuing on, clenching her fists as she walked.

She hated the idea of getting the Gorons and Raptors involved when it would be easier to assassinate the Keeper herself. She would have loved to do it the night of the announcement, but it would have been suicide to attempt such a venture surrounded by an entire city of warriors, not to mention the Goddess and Addina, for Balra had no doubt Addina could have been there in an instant if Rosey were in danger. And the Goddess's palace had closed its doors to unannounced, uninvited, and unfamiliar visitors whilst the Keeper was staying there. With so many now involved with Rosey's protection it was better to have a plan.

Once she leaves the palace, I'll use the Gorons and Raptors to distract everyone, then go in for the kill. She smiled. *Eventually, Rosey will be gone and there'll be nothing left to stop my and my Master's perfect poison. Nothing!*

"The Molt Volcano!?" Wolvereen repeated incredulously as Rosey hungrily gobbled down a plate full of eggs, toast, and bacon. The Goddess had called him into the dinning room to give him the update, as well as announce it to the others.

She was only half listening, her attention too focused on stuffing her face. Explaining her encounter with the Witch to her uncle and the Goddess had kept her up most of the night, which meant she'd barely gotten any sleep and the excitement had made her limited sleep restless. The experience had left her starved and exhausted that morning.

"Out of all the places, that damned Volcano is the *most* unpredictable," Wolvereen went on, giving the Goddess a pleading look. "Are you sure this is our first destination?"

"Don't ask me, Wolvereen, I'm not the one who dreams of Witches." She winked at Rosey who downed a delicious sausage. "Anyway, you should count your blessings, my Commander. The Molt Volcano is located *in* Hondan, a few days ride from the palace. Would you rather it be some far-off Volcano that could take weeks or sea travel to get to?"

She cocked her head at him expectantly and he put his ears back awkwardly. "Of course not...it just seems so..." he faltered and Rosey couldn't blame him.

Growing up but a few miles away from the volcano had made her all but an expert on it. It was the most fascinating landmark in all of Hondan, and its biggest tourist attraction. The land beneath the volcano was layered with pristine caves formed from magma flows and dappled with thick layers of magic. So much magic that the place was pocketed with naturally occurring wild spells, a spell that was not created by a magikin. According to Alex, wild spells only occurred in areas with abnormally high levels of magic and could continue on or evolve into new wild spells years later. She'd heard several stories from travelers about what kinds of wild spells existed at the volcano. One person had found themselves walking up invisible stairs while another had thrown something that had come back at them.

Due to the unpredictable nature of the wild spells, only the most experienced magikins and warriors were allowed to get near the volcano and magikins were not allowed to cast new spells near it. If they did, there would be a serious danger of overlaying a spell with a wild spell, a big no no in the magikin community. Overlayed spells could either work, phase out, or do the opposite of what the spell intended which could have disastrous consequences.

Bottom line, the volcano was unbalanced, always in an active state, but never going up with a bang. However, it also begged the question of why such a magically enriched site was the location of an Elemental Well? Wouldn't the two powers clash?

She'd asked the Goddess that question the night before and her response had been, "The Molt Volcano isn't any less of a volcano just because it's steeped in magic. If that were the case, then there would be pockets of the world where a magikin could work their spells but an elemental couldn't use their element. The restrictions between magical and elemental use apply to people *only*. In nature, the two overlap each other quite regularly."

Rosey dabbed her mouth as she finished her breakfast, comfortably stuffed. "I understand it's not the most attractive destination," she added, making Wolvereen turn to her, "but I assure you, the Witch was not mistaken when she spoke. She very clearly said the Molt Volcano and I only know of one such volcano."

Wolvereen sighed, defeated. "Understood, my Keeper, Goddess. I'll begin preparations for our departure." He bowed to them both before exiting the dining room.

"I can't believe we're going to the Molt Volcano," Alex said next to Rosey. He, Rochelle, John, Noly and Hazel had long ago finished eating. Rosey was the only one making up for a missed meal. "I mean...we're going to be the envy of everyone at school when they find out."

He smiled and Rochelle giggled from across the table. "I know, I might just fly over the city later today and write it across the sky in cloud letters to taunt them!"

She laughed but the Goddess slammed her hand on the table. "You'll do no such thing!" she shouted making them all start. John shot her a look and her expression softened. "Ahem, I mean...I can imagine your enthusiasm Rochelle, but you must remember your first priority is Rosey's safety and we don't know how much the Raptors, Gorons, or the *assassin* knows.

So, we certainly don't want to advertise any clues to Rosey's location." She raised an eyebrow at Rochelle and the brunette winced, stung.

"Of course, I promise I was just joking," Rochelle insisted awkwardly, exchanging glances with Alex.

Something seemed to pass between them as if some invisible switch had been flipped on. Rosey twisted her napkin in her lap, self-consciously. *Out with the old and in with the new.* Her gaze shot between them. *Will things still be the same once this really gets started?*

"Now, Rosey," the Goddess said and she perked up, "Captain Marine will be updated promptly of the situation. He'll await your arrival as soon as you get a location off-Hondan, which I expect won't be too long from now. In the meantime, I want to update you about the plan I was talking about the other day with Nagura. Now that we know about the Volcano, we can reach an agreement."

They all turned as Nagura entered the dining room, her silver armor gleaming. Her giant frame settled neatly near the end of the table, her ears elegantly poised and blue eyes sharp. Rosey inhaled, breathlessly taken by the wolf's beauty.

"Nagura will explain from here," the Goddess finished inclining her head to the wolf.

Nagura bowed respectfully. "My Keeper and Goddess, the Silver Goddess has offered her Crystal Caverns as your personal *road* to the Volcano. The caverns are the safest place in all of Hondan and offer the most secure route to the Volcano as well as the docks where your ship is waiting. You will be escorted by her finest warriors led by myself. Is this to your liking?"

Her gaze settled on Rosey but Alex answered. "*The* Crystal Caverns! We're going to be walking through the Silver Goddess' *personal Crystal Caverns*!?"

Rosey smiled at him. "I think that's your answer, Nagura. We'd be honored to take the Caverns. Give the Silver Goddess my thanks, will you?"

Nagura dipped her muzzle, amused. "Of course, my Keeper."

Alex was at a loss for words, so Rosey took over. "What was all the discussion about, Goddess?" she asked the Golden Woman. "The Caverns sound like a splendid idea. I know from what Alex has told me the Silver

Goddess is rumored to have made the caverns herself. Surely, they're the safest place for me to be, even if I was only being escorted to the ship?"

The Goddess sighed. "I have no argument there, Rosey. The problem wasn't your safety it was the use of the Crystal Caverns at all. They're not only my sister's personal domain but they're also the home of Neran's stealth force. I was concerned about having you *and* them in such close proximity given how important you *both* are..." she trailed off, then shook her head. "But my sister is right, the Caverns are the safest and most discreet route to the volcano *and* the docks are but a few hours ride away from the Volcano. This course should make it easier for you to slip by fairly unnoticed."

Rosey swallowed, suddenly apprehensive. She should get used to this, calculating every single move she made and constantly hiding, surrounded by guards. She thought back to when Argno had barged in and how quickly Wolvereen and Nagura had moved to defend her, literally using their bodies as shields. How quickly she'd drawn her weapons. Her gaze flashed to Alex and Rochelle.

Just how much danger will they face...for me?

"So, when are we departing?" Noly asked, looking excited. "I can't wait to go! This place is beautiful, but the high life can only keep you occupied for so long." She grinned, tongue lolling while Hazel rolled her eyes.

The Goddess smiled amused. "I believe the escort will be here tomorrow morning, correct, Nagura?" The giant wolf nodded. "Then there you have it." Her gaze shot to Rosey. "You'll take your first steps as Keeper tomorrow, Rosey. So, get packed and ready to go."

"What about the friend Addina was supposed to send?" John asked. "Should we wait for them? I'd imagine they'll be quite powerful?"

The Goddess considered. "I agree they will be exceptional, whoever she's sending, but we cannot afford to wait. Every second here is another moment Rosey is without an element. The Crystal Caverns escort should be more than enough to keep her safe until Addina's friend can arrive. I will contact her to update her on the situation," she promised.

Rosey nodded and they all got up from their seats. John joined Rosey as she fell into step with her friends, Hazel on her shoulders and Noly at their heels. The Goddess went to her office, no doubt to contact Addina.

"This is going to be so much fun," Noly said, prancing around them. "Are you excited Rosey!? We get to go see the world!" She hopped between them giddily and Rosey smiled, knowing she was just trying to distract her from what that *actually* meant.

Rosey frowned, despite how long she'd been at the palace, everything seemed to be moving too fast. She took a deep breath and stopped. Alex, Rochelle, and John paused, giving her concerned looks. Hazel meowed from her shoulder, rubbing cheeks with her, while Noly whined, coming to a stop.

"Is everything all right, Rosey?" John and Alex asked at the same time, brows furrowed.

Rochelle rushed to her side. "Is it your chest?"

Rosey shook her head. "I just...can't believe this is happening...I..." She reached up and gripped the crystal. It grew warm and Andraste hummed on her back.

"Yeah, I can't believe it either," Alex agreed. "To think, days ago we were just three regular citizens...our only possible fear locked safely away behind giant wooden walls." He shrugged and clasped her shoulder. "But, what have we been training for? Sure, we had no idea the Keeper would be needed again, but that doesn't mean we're not ready."

"Remember, we're coming with you and we'll be here to help you through this," Rochelle added.

"What about your families?" Rosey asked, sudden shock rippling through her. She'd been so distracted by her training at the palace that she'd forgotten Alex and Rochelle's parents! She hadn't seen them in weeks. How must they be feeling about their only children going off on some adventure with a new Keeper? Did they know about the assassin?!

Alex and Rochelle exchanged looks but John answered. "They're aware of what's going on, of course, and they know the risks involved...we all do. To protect them, they're being moved to a secure location which only the

Goddess knows of, they haven't even told Rochelle or Alex where they're going."

Her gaze widened, amazed, but she shouldn't have been surprised. As her friends accompanying her, any direct family would be a prime target for the Raptors, Gorons, and assassin. Though they could stay with the Goddess, her palace served as the Keeper's base of operations, which meant it would also be a prime target for their enemies. Discreetly spiriting away Rochelle and Alex's parents to a secure location was the best option. Still…what must her friends be going through, separated from their parents like this.

"To be honest, I'd have thought they'd demand to come with us?" Rosey said.

"They considered it," John agreed, "but they realized that their presence might be more detrimental then helpful. If they were in danger, Alex and Rochelle might have to choose between saving their Keeper or their parents."

Rosey's mouth fell open and Rochelle and Alex looked away, concerned at even the idea of making such a choice. For that matter, the same could be said of her and John…would she neglect her duties as Keeper to protect her uncle? Of course she would! Though her uncle had a valid reason for leaving her, perhaps it was for the best after all?

"Rochelle…Alex…I'm sorry." Rosey looked down, ashamed of herself. "I've been a terrible friend, I never stopped to ask what was going on with you guys through all this."

Rochelle patted her back soothingly. "Girl, please! Are you kidding me? *You're* the one who's the new Keeper, we're just along for the ride."

Alex nodded. "Out of all of us, you've got the most to contend with. Don't worry about us. Our families are more than on board with our decision and we're okay with ours. This isn't about us, it's about you."

"*You* focus on being the Keeper, let us worry about all the rest," John insisted.

"I promise to keep you laughing," Noly said, licking her hand. "So don't worry so much."

"Do as your told, my Keeper," Hazel ordered bluntly, winking at her.

Rosey couldn't help but smile. To an unspoken queue forged from years of friendship, the three embraced. Hazel purred and Noly leaned into them. John smiled, eyes bright with emotion and pride for the little family he'd helped raise. Rosey's gaze met with her uncle's and she reached her hand out to him. He took it with both hands.

"All right, I understand. Thank you...all of you. I promise...I won't let you down," Rosey breathed out determinedly. "Now let's get packed so we can go tell the horses, I'm sure they'll be back from their morning run by now."

They broke apart, smiling. Noly yipped happily as they started talking a mile a minute about the Volcano. Old stories told at school and rumors about the world outside Neran's walls met John's ears as he followed the five friends. What Rosey didn't see was how his eyes glistened and for a brief moment, John saw not the little niece he'd raised but the confident and talented sister he'd adored.

CHAPTER TEN

The Crystal Caverns

Rosey pulled at Sarabie's riding gear, setting some last-minute adjustments. Part of her was doing it for practicality, the other part did it to lengthen the inevitable. After these long hard weeks of training, she was finally starting her journey and it couldn't be more bittersweet.

The cold air caught her long black hair and she inhaled the crisp breeze. It stung her lungs but she barely felt it, her mind was too conflicted over the goodbye she'd been dreading ever since John announced he'd be joining the other magikins at the Scorched Mountain. She swallowed back the pain in her heart, biting her lower lip. It wasn't like she'd never see him again, but it felt that way. Everything was changing and she was stuck in the middle, unable to alter the course chosen for her. She could either go with the flow or resist but with the whole world counting on her, resisting wasn't an option.

Behind her John and the Goddess were talking in low voices. From the way their eyes met and how they held hands, she could guess what the topic of conversation was.

Sarabie nickered softly and butted her head into Rosey's arm as she pulled the seat strap tighter.

"Not too tight, little missy," Sarabie nickered playfully, pulling Rosey from her stupor. "Horses have to breathe, too."

"Oh gosh, sorry Sarabie!" Rosey apologized, loosening the strap.

She'd be riding bareback if it wasn't for the gear the horses had agreed to carry. As her partner, Sarabie would help her carry her weapons, food, and other survival necessities needed for proper travel. Being the Keeper, Rosey wouldn't need to carry nearly as much as most traveling warriors and their partners did, but her needs were significant enough to require minimal travel gear.

Rosey's eyes examined the newest item of Sarabie's gear; her armor. It was extremely lightweight, made with the same magically enhanced material the Golden and Silver Goddess's Guards wore. It consisted of a helmet that covered her snout and forehead, a neckband which protected the back and sides of her neck, leg bracelets, breastplate, and finished with back, shoulder, and rumpcovers. The spectacle was pretty intimidating especially since she'd decided to have it decorated to look like dragon scales. The helmet even resembled a dragon's gaping mouth, fangs protruding along Sarabie's snout with two long curved horns. It was all decked out in crimson red and brilliant gold, made to Sarabie's specifications. During the long weeks they'd stayed here, the horses had each requested armor be made for them. Filla had green and gold armor, while Bronzo had blue and gold; and both had decided to adopt the same dragon design that Sarabie had.

The horses weren't the only ones with new gear, Rosey and her friends also had new wardrobes. They'd all flat out refused any elaborate armor set up, but had agreed to magically enhanced leather armor. It was the armor they'd grown up with, the brown woven leather style of the Neranians. Underneath it they wore heavy winter trousers and a thick white winter shirt. The Goddess understood that Rosey and her friends liked the lightweight versatility of minimal armor wear and agreed to their decision, having done the spells herself on their armor. It was a bit more extensive than their training gear, including a full-length leather breastplate that wrapped around the chest and abdomen, leather gloves that extended up to their biceps, and leather boots that extended up to their thighs. Attached to the back of their breastplates was a large thick hood that could be pulled on to cover the head. All spelled to repel almost any kind of attack, weather, or grime. The horse's armor was equally as spelled.

The only ones who had opted out of armor of any kind, even light-weight, was Noly and Hazel.

Hazel had stated, "I'm small, so I make up for it in my speed. I don't need armor slowing me down."

And Noly had said, "My thick fur and armor, trust me, it won't mix well."

Rosey couldn't let that slide though. It was very likely that they'd all face danger at one point, so she had begged them to compromise.

Eventually they'd agreed to wear easily removeable bracelets on their right legs that were spelled to cast a sort of protective shield around them, able to repel attacks, weather, and grime.

Rosey was both impressed and saddened by their new get ups, it truly marked the beginning of the battles to come. She really shouldn't be too shocked, when Rosey had decided long ago to join the Golden Guards, Sarabie had said she'd be joining Rosey as her partner, and that meant she and Sarabie would both have to have armor just like this. Though Rochelle and Alex hadn't fully decided yet on their futures, they'd all shared a common goal: to help eradicate the Gorons and Raptors. That's why they'd all been training so hard for so long...only now it was all too real.

Sensing her unease, Sarabie flicked her forelock to the others. "Chin up there, we don't want Rochelle and Alex thinking they have to lighten the mood for ya?"

Rosey eyed them talking to Bronzo and Filla as they loaded the last of their traveling supplies into their riding gear. They looked remarkably calm, a clear opposite to Rosey's hammering heart and clammy hands. She swallowed the lump in her throat and managed to smile.

"Of course not, we've got to keep smiling," she whispered, gently fingering a lock of Sarabie's mane between her fingers.

"CUT IT OUT NOW!" Wolvereen shouted angrily.

Rosey looked at him sharply in time to see Noly and Hazel chasing each other in and out of the guard's legs. The best of the Silver and Golden Goddess's Guards had been chosen to escort Rosey to the Crystal Caverns and they included all manner of species Noly and Hazel had only dreamed of seeing. In their excitement, they'd done a fabulous job of annoying everyone...though Rosey suspected it was mostly just to annoy Wolvereen.

"Would you two calm down and get over here!" Rosey called out, giving Wolvereen an apologetic look.

Noly and Hazel yipped some more last-minute questions to a few of the Silver Guards before rushing over to Rosey's side, laughing.

Wolvereen's black fur was on end, his tail held high with annoyance. "Rosey," he growled, "keep them in line or *I* will!"

Rosey smiled sweetly. "Of course, Wolvereen, I'll talk to them," she promised, shooting them a warning look and they lowered their heads.

"But...but Rosey, one of the guards is a Fleeting Carasak..." Hazel murmured, innocently. Light caught the gold of her bracelet in the early morning sunlight. "Can you even begin to comprehend how rare they are?"

Hazel's little eyes glazed, transfixed and Rosey started. Turning she spotted a white and black dappled, four-foot-tall, armored cat with long blue fangs grooming a clawed paw amongst the guards. Rosey felt her jaw drop slightly, impressed. The Fleeting Carasaks were so named because one could rarely hope to catch sight of one. They weren't even native to Hondan! She'd seen the chosen guards gathering, but her mind had been way too occupied with her coming departure to notice their individual species.

"Well, as amazing as that is," she admitted, "you still need to be respectful. They've got an important job to do remember? We don't want to get in the way."

Noly and Hazel pouted but nodded nonetheless. They walked back towards the guards but this time kept a respectful distance.

"They're going to be a handful," John observed, joining Rosey's side suddenly.

Rosey started for a moment, resisting the sudden urge to turn and run away from what was about to happen. Instead, she looked away, murmuring, "Yeah."

Sarabie pivoted from hoof to hoof as the silence loomed between them. Finally, she blew out a deep breath. "I'm gonna go keep an eye on Noly and Hazel," she said, trotting over to them.

Rosey watched her go, then gripped the crystal. As always, it sent warmth trough her limbs but the cold lingered despite it. Her gear might be spelled, but only in the worst of conditions when her life might be in danger. The spell had the ability to turn itself on and off so the magic imbued in it wouldn't be used up too quickly and need replenishing. It did this by keeping track of her vital signs, she hoped her sudden racing heart wouldn't activate it.

They turned to each other at the same time, shocked, they both laughed. Then John wrapped Rosey in a warm embrace, this time the warmth felt real.

Pulling back, he cupped her hands. "Remember, it's not for forever. I'll just be in another part of the world, cheering you on...and I can always be reached by scrying. You're strong Rosey, you can do this without me. I know you can." His eyes glistened. "If you're anything like her, and I know you are, you'll be a natural."

Rosey looked away, brows furrowing. "I don't know about that...without a natural element, I'm not sure how good I'll be." Even after watching Rochelle and other masterful elementals showcase their talents to her in the Goddess's arena, she still had no idea about how an elemental operated. Until she had her first element, she probably never would.

John patted her back. "Come on now, I've never known you to give up without a fight. The crystal wouldn't have chosen you if you weren't the right choice. So, stop worrying!" He patted her head teasingly and she pulled away, laughing.

He straightened and became serious suddenly, making her pause. Reaching into a back pocket he pulled out a silver locket and presented it to her. She took it, examining it curiously. It was the kind that could be clipped onto a desired item of clothing or belonging. Opening it, on one side she found an image of her parents Esperanza and Matthew while the other side had an image of John. She gasped softly and looked at her uncle, shocked.

"I had that made for you while we were here," he explained. "I wanted you to have a little part of them with you since I wasn't going to be there.

I know they're looking over you, Rosey, watching you always. The image of me is to remind you to behave."

He winked at her and Rosey rushed forward to grip him close. His great arms enveloped her and she choked back tears. How long would it be till he hugged her again?

"Uncle," she said, stepping back. "I'm sorry..." John blinked at her confused, but she held up her hand to stop him from saying anything. "I realized something all the time I was here...there's a lot about you and my friends that I seem to have neglected and...I need to make right on that. I was going to use this journey to help bridge the gaps I'd made, and that included the gaps with you too. So," she suddenly held him at arm's length, fixing him with a hard stare, "you have to promise to be here when I get back, you understand!" Her grip tightened on his shoulders. "Don't you dare die on that mountain too..." she whispered the last bit and saw his eyes go wide with understanding.

John's composure seemed to snap then and he closed his eyes briefly against the tears she knew were gathering. What was he seeing in that moment? Her or her mother? Maybe both.

He lifted his eyes to hers and nodded. "I promise," he said with genuine resolve.

His gaze was hard and unwavering, she knew that look and it made her smile.

"Also," she added, leaning in, "get with the Golden Goddess already! It's so obvious you too are in love, I honestly don't know why you're holding back?"

John sputtered, going bright red. His mouth opened and closed as if trying to decide what best to say, Rosey enjoyed the spectacle, but he finally stopped and crossed his arms.

Rosey's brows furrowed; she knew that stance. She sighed and stopped him before he could utter words she knew weren't true. "Don't you dare try and make excuses! *Nothing* is complicated about this. You are both of the same mind here, so stop wasting time...before it's too late."

She lifted the locket he'd given her and his eyes went wide, her message clear. Her parents had had five wonderful years together, but that was it.

If they'd waited for after the war, they'd have never enjoyed the love they'd had.

John sighed, putting his hands on his hips. "Well, per usual, you've bested me," he relented. His gaze then looked past her and over to where the Goddess was. She and Wolvereen were discussing things with Nagura. The silver wolf would be leading them to the Silver Goddess, no doubt they wanted to be sure everything was ready before they departed.

Rosey's gaze went to Rochelle and Alex who were conversing with the Silver Guards, their backs to them out of respect. Earlier, their parents had visited the palace and made their own farewells, offering Rosey their best before they too departed for their secret hideout. She couldn't imagine what they were going through.

Her eyes left them to linger on Filla, Bronzo, and Sarabie who were gently nibbling some winter grasses nearby, corralling Noly and Hazel between them while they waited.

Rosey sighed and clipped the locket onto her shirt, safely tucking it underneath the leather armor she wore. "Okay uncle, let's not keep them waiting."

He nodded and together they joined the Goddess and Wolvereen.

The giant black wolf turned to Rosey, bowing his head. "We've checked the way ahead, my Keeper. It's thoroughly safe."

"If you're satisfied, we can leave whenever you're ready," Nagara agreed, bowing as well. "We'll await your command."

Rosey thanked them and inclined her head as they turned to the group of warriors standing watch, their armor glimmering in the early morning sunlight. Rosey shivered and pulled her coat tighter against the coming winter. She could feel the fall weather preparing for snow and wondered what it would be like sailing this time of year instead of preparing for winter celebrations as she normally did? She closed her eyes against a rush of insecurity, hating how different things had become so suddenly.

"Rosey," the Goddess said, distracting her. "I'll be in touch. All you need do is ask Alex and he can scry me or John in an instant. If you need anything or simply need to talk, don't hesitate to do so," she urged, her gaze serious.

Rosey smiled. "I appreciate all you've done Goddess. I can't imagine how things would have fared without your guidance." Her gaze shot to her uncle, he was saying his farewells to Rochell and Alex nearby. "Just promise me one thing." She hesitated, gripping the edges of her coat. "Please, watch after my uncle...okay?"

Rosey's gaze held the Goddess's for a long moment, hoping more than just her earnest request would get across. After a moment, the Goddess's eyes widened slightly with understanding. She smiled and bowed her head, something someone of her standing rarely ever did. Rosey almost started, but she'd have to start getting used to it, she was the Keeper, after all.

"Yes, my Keeper," the Goddess answered with sincerity.

Neran had two walls. One wall was directly surrounding the city and a few crop-filled acres. The second exterior wall was twice the size and thickness of the inner wall and housed inside of it a two-acre perimeter of thick forest called the Barrier Forest. Rosey's escort was currently inside the Barrier Forest following a path that only the Golden and Silver Guards ever used when tracking back and forth between the Crystal Caverns and the Golden Palace.

It had been thirty minutes since they'd left the palace. Rosey patted Hazel's head and the tortoiseshell licked her fingers from her perch on Rosey's shoulders, huddling against her neck for warmth. Behind her, Alex rode Bronzo, keeping his gaze alert for danger while his hand rested on his wand's scabbard. Before her, Rochelle rode Filla, happily chatting away with one of the Silver Guards that surrounded them.

Suddenly she felt a cold snowflake land on her nose. Glancing up she smiled slightly as it started to snow fat intricate snowflakes on her and the escort. *The first snowfall!* she thought and Sarabie snorted as if in agreement. Rosey held out her hand to catch the flakes, watching them melt in her palm.

"Yay! Snow!" Noly yipped excitedly from Sarabie's left. She took off, happily biting at the flakes, tail wagging.

Wolvereen huffed at her as she zigzagged between him and Nagura. The two wolves were leading the escort, but it was Nagura they were following, she knew where the entrance was.

Rosey fiddled with Sarabie's mane; her mind suddenly taken by the Silver Goddess. *What will she be like? Will she be anything like her sister...probably.* Her eyes wandered over the towering pine trees that surrounded them on either side, their red-tinted pine cones peeking at her between long limbs. *Who knew the Silver Goddess was this close?* They'd all heard rumors about her Crystal Caverns but they'd never known where they were. *How many times did Rochelle, Alex, and I gossip about the Goddesses?* Memories came rushing back of her uncle's stories, gathered around campfires and singing songs. The thought of John twisted her heart and she shook her head.

"Nagura, how much farther is it?" she asked, trying to leave the assaulting memories behind.

Nagura peeked a look at her, dark blue eyes soft with kindness. "We'll be there shortly, my Keeper. Do not worry."

Rosey nodded but bit her lower lip, her gaze lingering on the warriors surrounding them. *Is it always going to be like this? Am I always going to be protected and watched?* The thought unnerved her for some reason.

After another half hour they came to a large clearing. Tall evergreen trees, spaced three yards away from each other, bordered the edges, looking like soldiers on watch. Rosey's eyes went wide as she spied a massive evergreen tree at the center of the clearing. It was so large she couldn't even see around it! Its roots stretched in either direction, covering the ground with looping interwoven strands that dug deep into the earth.

As they passed through the border of smaller evergreens, Rosey felt a strange zap of energy sizzle around her like static electricity. Sarabie snorted and stopped, feeling it too.

"A magic barrier," Alex explained, seeing Rosey's confusion and Sarabie's hesitation.

Of course, the barrier probably protects from any unwanted guests finding or entering this place, Rosey reasoned.

Despite the barrier's protection, once inside, the guards dispersed to evaluate their surroundings. Rosey paid them no mind; her eyes were glued on the gigantic tree. *It must be hundreds of years old!*

Wolvereen paced the perimeter with the other Guards, ears pricked and eyes alert while Nagura jumped from giant root to giant root easily. Her armor was as silent as she was.

Rosey and the others came to a halt, watching as Nagura stopped before the tree's base and bowed low. She then leaned forward and whispered something to the tree as if it could hear her. Suddenly the ground under the evergreen began to shake and the earth fell away, revealing a large hole. Rosey gasped as the giant roots lifted from the ground framing a small but adequate path leading into the hole. The tree stayed aloft on top of the opening while the roots ran down the sides, acting as supporting beams. Rosey stared wide-eyed into what was now a cave entrance. It must have been about eight feet high and two yards wide. The tunnel slanted at an awkward but manageable hypotenuse, straight down into pitch darkness.

She turned to Nagura excitedly. "Let me guess, home sweet home?" she asked, inclining her head to the hole.

Nagura gave her a soft smile, nodding. The other guards rejoined them, not in the least bit stunned by the spectacle before them.

Rosey couldn't help being impressed and, thankfully, Alex and Rochelle looked just as amazed. It was all so thrilling for them. This was the kind of thing they'd only ever *talked* about and here they were experiencing it! She took a deep breath and dismounted, the others following her example. The tunnel was way too small for them to ride so they'd have to walk.

"Why is the passage so small?" Rochelle asked as she stepped up beside Rosey, Alex close behind with Filla and Bronzo at their sides.

"Too small for Raptors but perfect for most other species within the Guards," Nagura explained.

Alex opened his mouth as if to say something then shut it fast. Rosey smiled. *He was probably going to point out that the entrance is perfectly big enough to let Gorons in.*

"It's easy to get lost down there, so I'll go first," Nagura instructed kindly. "Rosey, you and your friends come in behind me. Horses after them and Noly, you come in behind them. Wolvereen will take up the rear." She then stepped forward and bowed to the rest of the guards. "From here on out your services are no longer needed. Well done, and thank you for your help."

They bowed their heads, honorably. Wolvereen stepped forward. "Exceptional work team, dismissed!" he praised, his voice gruff.

They nodded and bowed again. "Yes Commanders!" they chorused, before turning and disappearing silently into the forest. Rosey wished them well.

"Follow me and don't be frightened of the dark, it will get light soon," Nagura soothed, indicating the cave entrance.

They all nodded. Once Wolvereen's tail had cleared the entrance behind them, the roots and rocks tumbled over the opening, closing up behind them. Rosey and her friends flinched at the sudden darkness but remained calm. Slowly, soft light began to penetrate the darkness from pulsating crystals buried within the walls on either side. Rosey looked at the wall of rock and roots behind Wolvereen. There was literally no turning back. She shivered but turned to Nagura who had paused expectantly, waiting for them. The Wolf smiled then turned and headed down the tunnel. Rosey followed but slowly as the path started to gradually angle down, focusing on her footing so as not to slip on the rocky floor.

As promised, the glowing crystals she'd seen earlier became larger and more numerous, allowing for ample light. After a few minutes she found herself getting warmer the deeper they got, her full winter coat becoming stiflingly hot in the cave's constant comfortable temperature, but it was too narrow to stop so they kept going. Eventually they left the magically made tunnel and entered a natural cave system. Cave crickets chirped and strange centipedes ran over the walls. A four-winged bat was huddled in a corner, sleeping. She smiled, enchanted. She'd always loved caves.

After a few minutes, they entered a large wide chamber, brown ceilings stretching high above them covered in elegant stalagmites and stalactites. Several tunnels branched off from this chamber, leading deeper underground. Nagara paused to give them a short rest. As her eyes wandered,

Rosey and her friends took off their coats and stuffed them in their travel bags.

Noly raced by Rosey's legs, barking. "This is amazing!" she shouted, tongue lolling. "I've always wanted to see a cave, yes yes yes!" She paused, hopping on her back legs and pointing her nose to the ceiling. "Ooooo, is that a stalag...ah....tighty wighty...thing?" she looked at Rosey who snickered.

"Yes, that's a *stalactite*, they hang onto the ceiling *tightly*," Rosey instructed.

Wolvereen paused beside her, ears flicking. "She isn't going to be asking about everything the *entire* way there, is she?" He gave her an exasperated look.

Rosey sighed. "Most likely, let's just be thankful caves don't have that much to talk about."

Hazel rolled her eyes from Rosey's shoulders. "I wouldn't be so sure. She's always got something to say."

Sarabie snickered behind Rosey, pawing the ground. "What's not to talk about? This place *is* magnificent."

Filla and Bronzo whispered agreement and Alex nodded. "Indeed, remember we're in the largest cave system on Hondan. It stretches all over the continent. Most of the passages," he pointed to a patch of black rock nearby, "were hollowed out by the Molt Volcano's underground magma flows."

Rochelle frowned at this, concerned. "This might sound like a dumb question but, are we safe?"

Alex waved his hand as he walked over to the black rock which Rosey guessed was hardened lava. "Oh yeah, the magma is long gone by now." He tapped the black stone as if in confirmation. "The Volcano is active, but it's not as active as it used to be."

"Indeed," Nagura agreed, her silver armor and white fur clashing with the brown surroundings "Have no fear young ones, the Silver Goddess and her Stealth Force have been operating down here for years, long before you were born. Trust me, there's no safer place." She angled her head to the passage ahead. "Come now. There's a way to go before we reach the main chamber."

Rosey nodded and her friends joined her, Wolvereen bringing up the rear. For a few minutes they walked in relative awed silence, except for the occasional instruction from Rosey whenever Noly asked a question. After a while, even she fell silent, her nose twitching as she took in the cave's odd smells.

As they rounded a sharp corner, Rosey gasped as the cave went from brown to an unbelievable shade of blue-violet covered from top to bottom in numerous glowing crystals. She started and took a step back, her senses assaulted by the sudden shift. Some of the crystals were as large around and as tall as buildings while others were miniscule, no larger than her finger. It was like walking into a crystal palace! Large crystals hung from the ceiling like daggers, shedding fragments of dazzling brilliance across a crystal covered walkway. Rosey frowned at it worried about her footing but found it wasn't the least bit slippery.

"This can't be crystal, can it?! How did it get down here?" she asked, bending down to touch it.

"My dear, nothing is impossible with a little magic," Nagura answered charmingly.

"I guess we know why these are called the 'Crystal Caverns,'" Rochelle stated, gazing about her dumfounded.

"All of this is from the Silver Goddess, isn't it?" Alex asked beside Rosey, indicating their surroundings.

They gave Nagura expectant looks but she just cocked her head. "Perhaps." But said nothing more.

Rochelle crossed her arms. "Always with the secrets, huh?"

"That is how the Silver Goddess works," Alex reasoned. "We should just be happy we even *get* to meet her."

They continued on, transfixed. Small fountains poured water down the sides of crystal carvings, flowing into springs on either side of the passage. Blues, pinks and magentas bathed the walls in iridescent designs. They were so transfixed, they followed Nagura hypnotically, walking in silence.

Even Wolvereen was awestruck, a thoughtful look on his scared face as he followed at the rear. For a change, Noly was silent, her eyes wide.

Alex's voice broke the stillness. "Where are the Silver Goddess's guards?"

"Oh, they're around, hidden and well out of sight I'd think," Wolvereen said softly, his eyes still wandering. He glanced at Nagura worriedly and she nodded but said nothing.

After about twenty yards the corridor opened into a large chamber. It continued in either direction as if a fast-flooding river had come in and carved it out within minutes. The crystal pathway they'd been walking on suddenly rose into a slight incline bridging a huge chasm before them. Looking over the railing Rosey saw a large ravine below them. At the bottom she spied large crystals sticking straight out of the ground like white daggers. It had to have been a good 300-foot drop. She squinted, there seemed to be another bridge below. The image of the other bridge rippled and she started, realizing she was staring at the glassy surface of a lake, not a chasm. The large crystals were really there however, breaking the water only slightly. She cast her gaze upward and more spiked crystals jutted from the ceiling in menacing points of captivating beauty. She gulped and kept walking.

The bridge was wide enough to ensure a safe passage of about twenty people standing shoulder to shoulder and led up to a platform where the path continued along the wall into an opening that led deeper into the cave. They took to the path, following Nagura carefully.

Finally, they entered a large circular room lit by the same elegant glowing crystals. Chairs and couches of various sizes and shapes rested on crystal frames. A crystal table adorned a side wall with an assortment of beverages and snacks. A small, silver, rat-like creature sat next to it attentively. When it spotted them, it raced over to greet them, bowing. Rosey looked it up and down, unsure. It looked like a silver gelatin carved to resemble a rat.

"Alex..." Rosey said wearily, looking to him.

He smiled upon seeing it. "Don't worry, it's a classic magic spell, a charm on a jell known as flub and then carved with a wand. I used to make them all the time." He shrugged and bent down to pat the rat's head. "They're a low-level spell that lots of young magikins love to practice with."

Rosey smiled at the rat and bent down to its level. "We're here to see the Silver Goddess, my name is Rosey Mystic...the new Keeper," she introduced herself.

The rat bowed and offered them seats. They relaxed into the soft furniture, grateful for the rest after the long walk. As they settled, the rat creature ran back to the table and started serving refreshments. Rosey accepted a glass of water and a plate of fruit then gave Nagura a concerned look.

"Where's the Goddess, is she coming?"

"Don't worry, she knows we're here. She'll come when she's ready." The white wolf settled onto a plush seat, Wolvereen sitting beside her. He licked her neck and she smiled at him.

Rosey glanced away and fiddled with the tip of Silver Knight's hilt as she waited. After they'd finished a few refreshments, Rosey heard the sound of footsteps approaching. Looking to a far passageway in the wall, the Silver Goddess entered. As one, the group rose to their feet respectfully.

Like her sister, the Silver Goddess was dressed in intricate silver robes and armor. She even had the same metal armor under her breast but hers was under her *left* breast instead of the right. Her long black hair was woven with silver strands and silver coated her lips and the tops of her eyes. A simple silver headband encircled her head and a golden saber hung at her side next to a silver wand scabbard. She was shorter than the Golden Goddess and not as heavily muscled, yet she carried the same air of power though it seemed younger and not as mature.

She paused before the group, bowing her head. Rosey was certain she could hear Alex screaming internally with jubilation, though he remained composed externally, eyes glistening emotionally.

"Welcome, Keeper, I am the Silver Goddess, the Golden Goddess's younger sister. I apologize for not being here sooner, but the Stealth Force doesn't pause for anyone." She looked at the silver rat creature. "I trust my attendant saw to you?"

Rosey bowed back. "Thank you for inviting me and yes, your attendant was very kind." She indicated the dagger. "And I want to thank you for Silver Knight. I've never seen a finer dagger."

The Goddess's eyes brightened. "You are very welcome. Silver Knight is not as amazing as Andraste I admit, but it is one of the finer pieces I've made." The Goddess began to bend down as if to be seated, but there was no chair. Rosey was about to say something when a silver crystalline throne materialized underneath the Goddess just as she sat down. Magic, she should have known.

"Please be seated," the Goddess insisted and they all settled back down. "I hope you've enjoyed the Caverns so far? With Gorons and Raptors about it's much safer to travel below ground, though I have no doubts about the skills of our guards." She inclined her head to Wolvereen and Nagura who beamed happily.

"I can honestly say, the Caverns are breathtaking...did you make them yourself? The crystal part of it, I mean?" Rosey asked.

She could practically hear Alex flinging mental questions her way. She was surprised he wasn't rattling off at the mouth already, though he looked a bit pale, perhaps he was too nervous to? *That would be a first!*

The Goddesses lips drew tight into an uncomfortable frown at the question. She took a deep breath before answering. "Yes...and no...it's difficult to explain. I maintain and keep these caverns in the state they're in and that's all I can really say," she answered awkwardly.

"With magic?" Alex managed to sputter out, making Rosey smile slightly.

The silver woman nodded as answer.

"I know the caves extend all throughout Hondan, but does the crystal part extend that far too? Or only in the area you're controlling?" Rochelle asked her. "I noticed on the way here that we were in a regular cave system before it became crystalline."

"My power reaches about a mile in either direction from myself, as such, the crystalline portion only extends that far," she explained.

Alex's mouth dropped open a bit. Rosey could tell his mind was calculating this information. "You must be unbelievably powerful to maintain the crystal at all times, for so long. Why do so and extend so much energy and use so much magic?" He managed to ask; whatever 'spell' he'd been under before broken.

"The crystal is linked to me and my senses. Through it, I can see, hear, feel, taste, and smell anything coming. It's a protective layer against intruders," The Goddess answered, again looking uncomfortable.

Why doesn't she like talking about her crystal? Rosey wondered, but decided better than to ask and thought perhaps they *all* needed to leave it alone.

Alex went to ask another question and Rosey quickly beat him to it saying, "I believe the Golden Goddess said you had some things to show us?"

"Of course, yes, I do!" The Goddess readily agreed, looking relieved. "The Stealth Force holds the largest archives in the world on the Gorons and Raptors. You might find it helpful. Want to see it?"

She cocked an eyebrow at her and Rosey heard Alex inhale excitedly, taking the bait.

Rosey nodded. "Very much so."

"I thought you would. Follow me," she said, rising elegantly from her throne, which disappeared as soon as she stood. "I'll take you to the archives, all are welcome."

Hearing this, everyone except Wolvereen and Nagura joined them.

Rosey expected to follow the Goddess through another series of twisting crystal tunnels but was surprised when she walked up to the crystal wall a few yards away, and without hesitation, walked right through the wall. Rosey stopped midstride startled. Noly made an "oooohhh" sound and yipped excitedly then plunged through the wall, following her.

Rosey cocked her head and Rochelle's brows furrowed. Alex passed them, not bothering to explain, and followed Noly through.

Rochelle huffed. "Well, I guess that's the only explanation we're getting." She followed him.

Rosey smirked and Hazel snickered from her shoulder perch. Taking a deep breath, Rosey walked into the wall and came out the other side, none the worse for wear. She was so surprised she stumbled and almost fell but a strong arm pulled her up right. She gazed at Alex thankfully then straightened and examined the wall behind her. Nothing seemed out of the ordinary, just a plain, smooth, crystal wall. She titled her head, perplexed but moved out of the way as the horses came last.

Noly raced up to Rosey and licked her hand. "What took you so long?"

Rosey patted her head. "Oh nothing...reality...physics...I don't know."

"It's a magical illusion," Alex explained. "They're fairly easy to cast and don't take a lot of magic to sustain."

"The door changes locations every now and then," the Goddess explained. She was standing a few feet away, waiting for them. "Only I and a select few ever know where it is at all times."

Rosey went still with apprehension. "Do the Raptors and Gorons *still* try getting into your caverns for the information?"

The Goddess's gaze grew distant as if she didn't want to answer. "Not anymore," she said finally.

Rosey swallowed, feeling more and more like a tourist rather than the Keeper. But the Goddess didn't pause for long. Turning she indicated the corridor before her and they followed suit. Every few intervals, a crystal shard hung from the seven-foot-tall ceiling casting a thin beam of blue light. The passage was only two yards across, so they had to walk single file. The 'clip clop' of the horse's hooves and the 'tat tat' of Noly's nails were the only sound echoing around them.

They came to a dead end but as before the Goddess kept walking and went right on through. Rosey flinched instinctively but made herself keep going. The room they entered looked like a giant library with hollowed holes in the wall for numerous books, documents, and artifacts, all labeled intricately and alphabetically categorized. The middle of the room hosted long skinny tubes filled with small compartments. A blue, purple, and turquoise glow hung about the room, casting light from glowing crystals.

"Now, feel free to explore and ask as many questions as you like. You can touch anything, it's all spelled against destruction and decay," the Goddess explained.

Alex's eyes wandered hungrily over the countless documents. He walked over to one and gingerly started flipping through the information. They separated, investigating different documents and artifacts. The Goddess followed them, explaining the various displays and answering any questions they had. She showed them how to identify Raptor and Goron prints and explained their various attacks and instincts. She even showed them the best way to outsmart, hide, or confront and attack them.

She placed a document on Raptor instincts back on its respective shelf. "Do you know what a Raptor and Goron looks like?" she asked.

They exchanged awkward glances and Rosey answered, "We've only ever seen images."

"I see," the Goddess said, not looking at all surprised. "Well, I have one of each for you to see. Dead, of course, but preserved in my crystal."

Alex's eyes grew wide and Rochelle gapped at her. Amazed, they followed the silver woman towards the back of the room. Drawing near they came to an abrupt halt, gasping. Frozen in a block of solid crystal was the very two beasts they'd heard so much about. Rosey gulped as she studied the immobile bodies. The Golden Goddess had shown them how to fight Raptors and Gorons just on the off chance they'd ever run into them, but seeing the real thing up close and personal left Rosey feeling suddenly very small.

The Horses joined her and Rosey gripped Sarabie's long mane, twisting the fine hairs around her fingers. She felt Hazel stiffen and her fur rose along her back. She patted the cat's head, her gaze taking in the Raptor. It looked just like all the images she'd seen, a slanted upright walking reptilian beast with humanoid-like arms and clawed hands. Its skin was a sleek greenish gray with sickly blue designs. The eyes were a milky violet, set against black markings making them look crazed and bloodshot. Its clawed feet had five toes, the big toe larger than the others with a wicked curved claw on it, three times the size of the other claws. Its most distinguishable feature, however, was the long line of spiky white hair that ran along its back from the forehead to the tip of the tail. The Blood Goron beside it was a black and red beast, standing at four feet tall with ten-foot-long spiked dragon-like wings as black as night. Its blood red eyes held a powerful intelligence, even in death, that Rosey feared more than its armored lizard-like body or spiked tail.

Her eyes flitted back to the Raptor. Wolvereen hadn't been lying, the Raptors were big! Its ten-foot-tall frame towered above them intimidatingly. *I'm going to be expected to face that?!* All of her training and preparation seemed so insignificant now that she was seeing the actual enemy. *Am I really...ready for this!?*

The Goddess turned to them. "I'm sure you're well aware that Raptors have acid glands in their mouths?" she asked, raising an eyebrow.

Rosey nodded and Rochelle shivered. The Raptor's vicious acid glands were at the top and bottom of their mouth along the teeth, just above the gums. Their bite would release a stream of acid, breaking down their prey so they could swallow chunks whole...or kill with one bite. Many warriors had returned home with missing limbs after suffering a Raptor's bite. The devilish brute's acid could eat through flesh and bone. The only way to stop it was to cut off the infected area.

"Is there still no way to counteract it?" Alex asked. He looked more intrigued than fearful, but Rosey knew better. He was just as concerned as they were, he just showed it differently.

"Unfortunately, no, we've yet to come up with anything that can counter their acid. Once bitten it eats away at all around it, though fire elementals have had luck in countering the damage by burning the infected area with their own fire. Still, it only works occasionally. Removal of the infected area is still the best treatment," the Goddess advised.

Alex squinted at her, amazed, then elbowed Rosey. "Remember that," he insisted and she nodded, knowing he was talking about the fire elemental trick. Still, if worse came to worse she might have to entertain the idea of cutting off her own limb...if she was lucky enough to get bitten on a limb and not somewhere else. She shuddered.

"Goddess, what of the assassin? Do you have anything on them?" Sarabie asked, making Rosey look to the Goddess both intrigued and fearful.

The Goddess took a deep breath. "I do," she admitted. "Follow me."

Reluctantly, Rosey followed behind the others to a black bound book, sitting in one of the wall shelves. She took it down and showed it to them. They each took turns looking it over. As the Golden Goddess said, there was very little. It was two eyewitness accounts, one from the Golden Goddess and the other from Addina, detailing thoroughly their encounters with the assassin. Rosey read over every word slowly, trying desperately to see or feel anything remotely important. Still, when the book was put up, she didn't feel like she'd learned anything new.

"That's all?" Filla asked, surprised.

"That's it," The Goddess agreed. "We've done lots of tests on the bodies infected by the poison, but have found nothing conclusive to assist in any way."

"Forgive me, but, *how* is that possible?" Hazel asked, bewildered. Rosey couldn't help but agree.

The Goddess sighed, looking slightly frustrated, not with them but with the lack of information that she could provide. "The problem is that the poison infected the victim and killed them *then* disappeared altogether. We can tell that the body was rotted from the inside out at a very rapid pace," Rosey grimaced, "but once the poison ate all the living cells, the poison *itself* simply vanished."

"So...all you had to study..." Alex said aloud.

"...was, essentially, an average corpse," the Goddess finished for him. "A rotted corpse, but no more different than any other. Besides the fact that the poison rots things, we have very little other information besides numerous theories."

"Theories are better than nothing...I guess," Rosey admitted. "Can you tell us what they are?"

"Of course," the silver woman replied.

After hear the numerous mindboggling and rather gruesome theories, they wandered about the archive a bit longer, asking as many questions as they could. By the time they were done they were thoroughly exhausted. Following the Goddess, they returned to the main chamber they'd been in before and found Nagura and Wolvereen talking hurriedly where they'd left them. They quieted as Rosey's group entered the living room.

"How was it?" Nagura asked. "Impressive huh? That's the whole life's work of the Stealth Force."

"Impressive....and intimidating," Rosey admitted. "I think we're all a bit overwhelmed."

"That's understandable, my Keeper," Wolvereen agreed. "There's a lot more to the Raptors and Gorons than one might think."

They were silent to that and the Goddess moved past them. "Well, I believe it's well past eight o'clock. Please, dine with me and stay for the night. It's certainly much safer here than above ground and I've got an amazing cook," she added with a smile.

Rosey's eyes brightened at the sound of food, her stomach rumbling. "Thanks, that sounds great. What do ya' say, guys?" She surveyed her friends.

"Sounds good to me," Alex agreed.

"I'll second that," Rochelle added, her arm draped around Filla's neck. "I'm starved!"

"We're all starved," Bronzo added. "Me especially...starved for something besides archives, books, and Gorons." He shivered, withers twitching.

"Indeed, let's eat," the Goddess agreed, exiting through the passageway she'd come from earlier and they followed behind her.

Rosey sighed, happy to be out of the archives, but the weight of her journey suddenly felt much heavier. Her chest tightened then and she bit her lip, smoothing her hand over her ribs. She took a deep breath but the feeling passed and she kept walking. Her hand sought the crystal and it grew warm.

Hazel patted her hand with a paw. "You okay?" she whispered concerned. Her whiskers twitched, tickling Rosey's face.

Rosey nodded. "Of course...it's nothing. Don't worry."

CHAPTER ELEVEN

A Night to Remember

Balra waited, impatience getting the better of her. Above the moon was a sliver in the sky, casting shadowed light over the clearing. For several days now she'd waited as the Gorons had gathered the nearest surviving Raptors. How long were they going to make her wait? She looked off in the direction of the Golden Palace, hidden behind tall pines and purple leafed deciduous trees. *Somewhere out there the Keeper sleeps, preparing to destroy the poison my Master and I worked so hard on! She must be stopped!*

A crackling met her ears and she turned sharply, her hand flying to the sword at her waist, but it was only a Goron, slithering through the woods to stand before her. His red eyes glowed mischievously. He'd *made* a sound so she'd know he was coming. Her gaze then brightened as she spied ten-foot-tall Raptors carefully approaching. Gorons slithered through the tree tops, keeping an eye on the fifty behemoths, working tirelessly to keep them quiet.

Balra looked at the outer wall of Neran a few hundred yards away. *If they knew their enemy was so close, I wonder if they'd sleep so soundly?* She turned her head away, quickly losing interest. Neran didn't matter, the Goddesses didn't matter. All that mattered was keeping the poison alive! It must remain rich and healthy so it could carry out its purpose. She shivered with excitement, the black stone on her chest throbbing comfortably with her happiness.

The Goron bowed his head to her. "As commanded, my lady." He indicated the tall Raptors. They clicked their teeth, large claws scoring the ground as white violet eyes settled on Balra. "Your army awaits. What do you command?"

Balra tensed drawing in a deep sigh. "Nothing yet," she said and the Goron cocked his head. "We need information first. We can't just go blindly barging in, do that and we put them on alert. We need to find out where Rosey is, what she's up to, and where she's going, then we can plan our attack." She paused, thinking. "For now, hide in the woods, remain as covert as you can and keep gathering the Raptors. Stay near the volcano." With it being so off limits to most citizens, it would be a good place to hide. *Also, Rosey might actually be going there, the first element is fire, after all.* "In the meantime, I'll get the information we lack. Understood?!"

The Goron dipped his head to her again. "Of course, we'll keep in touch."

He turned to leave but she gripped his horns, turning his head to her sharply.

"I didn't dismiss *you*, did I?" she asked menacingly.

The Goron shrunk under her gaze. "Apologies ma'am."

She smiled. "Good. For what I've got planned, I'm going to need a Goron's help. You remain, the others may go." She flicked her head signaling for the others to move.

Another Goron appeared and snickered at the one beside Balra before leaving, clicking orders to the Raptors. Her small scaled body flashed in the darkness before disappearing into the shadows. The Raptors cast Balra dumb looks, blind to anything but their orders, then ambled away.

She watched them go, waiting till their footfalls were lost to the wind, then turned away from Neran and headed quickly to the coast, the Goron following. There was someone she needed to apprehend. Like everyone in Neran, she knew about the Goddess's messenger, Argno who worked solely within Hondan's borders. He'd been flying back and forth recently between the docks and the Golden Palace. She was pretty sure why.

Rosey will eventually need transportation off Hondan. Argno's little trips to the docks had left Balra with little doubt they'd been arranging a ship for her. *So, Argno most likely knows where she is, what ship she'll be using, and when she'll be leaving. If I can get him, I can get her!* She licked her lips excitedly. After all her previous efforts had failed, this was the last opportunity Balra had left to find Rosey.

Despite the decree that the Golden palace was temporarily closed to visitors, Balra had tried approaching it as a regular citizen, asking for the Goddess's assistance. All she'd received was a Guard willing to help her and relay her needs to the Goddess should it be necessary, but Balra had still been denied entry to the palace and the Goddess herself. Balra cringed. *I knew there would be consequences for me showing myself sixteen years ago during the final battle, but I thought they'd have relaxed by now.* She had to give them credit though, the Goddess wasn't taking any risks with the new Keeper's safety. The Gorons Balra had had watching the palace twenty-four seven had reported no gaps in their defenses, not even a little. They *had* recently noticed an escort gathering with Rosey outside the palace, gearing up to leave, but the Gorons lost track of them after a powerful cloaking spell had been cast. *The Goddess has been teaching Rosey everything she needs to know about being the Keeper, and now she's ready, so she left. That much I can be certain of...so the new question is, where is she now?* Argno would be the key to finding that out.

Keeping pace, she ran as fast as she could, glancing through the trees to the sky above. She'd been studying Argno's path constantly for the past few days, watching him closely. She knew the routes he loved to take and so knew that he was close to the coast this very evening. Soon, he'd be within her sights.

As she approached the beach, the smell of salt water and sea life hit her. She came to a stop and crouched behind a rock. The Goron joined her silently, his red gaze flicking about.

"Soon, Argno, the Dragnagor messenger for the Goddesses, will appear," Balra explained, her eyes on the sky. "When he does, attack. He's a wizard level magikin, so keep it long range."

The Goron glanced at her, intrigued. Dragnagors weren't extremely powerful creatures. Despite their dragon heads, they couldn't breathe fire and their fighting ability was limited in the air. In Argno's case, his magic was adequate enough to be troublesome, but nothing that a skilled Goron couldn't face.

"Kill?" the Goron whispered, clenching clawed fists, fangs dripping saliva excitedly.

"No, you idiot!" she hissed in a low voice. "Bring him to me! I need to question him."

The Goron nodded, looking disappointed.

Suddenly she heard wings flapping and looked up. A Dragnagor's silhouette fell across the sky, winging its way towards the Golden Palace in the distance. Balra smiled and the Goron beside her clinched his fangs greedily, hungrily, but this time he waited for Balra's command. Inclining her head, she gave the signal and the Goron shot forward, fast as lighting. He wove through the trees silently, his small black body invisible against the night sky.

Approaching carefully, the Goron came in on Argno's blind side. With precision, he shot past Argno, clawing deep grooves in his delicate wings. Argno gave a startled cry and flipped in the air, angling away from the Goron who flapped away a few yards before making a quick turn. Diving, it sailed past Argno a second time, clawing his sides. Quickly Argno bent his torn wings and flipped his dragon's tail, slamming it into the Goron as it passed a third time. The Goron fell back and had to right itself as it lost its balance in the air.

Balra cursed, and kept pace with Argno as he began flying off. The Goron gave chase, using the tall pines below to hide in. When Argno turned his head away, the Goron launched from the shadows and attacked his underbelly, clawing his side and wing as he flew by. Argno cried out winging away and whispered a spell. The Goron flew above him now and plummeted down on Argno's delicate wings, but hit a weak shield that was now covering his body. The Goron screeched angrily and kept attacking, bombarding the spell till the shield broke into pieces. The Goron triumphantly dived in and raked its claws on Argno's sides and wings, quickly flying out of the way at the last minute before Argno could make a comeback. The Dragnagor cried out in pain and tried to avoid him, but the Goron's dark scales made him all but invisible in the darkness.

Balra smiled wickedly. *Perfect! Make him land! Get him to me!*

Argno dipped closer to the tree line, blood splattered the ground from his scratched body. Balra followed the blood trail, her gaze sharp as it traced him in the sky. The Goron let up his attack and herded Argno to the ground, commanding that he land. Argno had little choice with his wings in tatters. Still, he wasn't defeated yet. As he approached the ground, he defiantly began letting out long hollow barks into the night.

Balra clenched her fists angrily. *He's sending out a call for help! I've got to silence him.* But she knew it was too late. The Dragnagor's call could easily travel miles. Inevitably someone would hear him. Suddenly the Goron plummeted from the trees and gripped Argno's throat in a deadly grasp. Argno fell silent with a whimper, crumpling to the ground exhausted. His blood drenched wings beat helplessly as the Goron pinned him.

Balra pulled up sharply as she approached, but stayed out of Argno's sights. She didn't want him spilling the beans should he get away.

"Keep him pinned," she ordered. "This will only take a moment, then we're out of here."

Argno's ears twitched and he tried to turn his head to her, sputtering. "Who...who's...that?" he coughed, but the Goron cut him off, pushing down on his throat harder. He flailed but the loss of blood made him weak.

Approaching carefully, she placed her hand over his forehead. In an instant he went still beneath her touch. Acting fast she drew upon the black stone's power buried in her chest. Shoving through Argno's mind she looked for anything she could about Rosey. At the same time, she felt Argno's own mind starting to probe her's, but it was weakened by blood loss and pain. This was the only downside to using the black stone's power, mind-probing was a two-way street. If she could see into his mind, he could see into hers. It didn't matter though; he wouldn't be alive long enough to share his experience. Finally, triumphantly, she found what she needed and pulled away. The connection broke and Argno slumped to the ground, groaning.

"I have what I need. Kill him," she ordered, smiling.

The Goron snickered and raised a clawed hand, ready to slit Argno's throat, only to be flung away by a green vine twisting from the earth. It let out a shocked screech, black blood spattering the leaves as the vine slammed the Goron into the ground, leaving a deep groove.

Balra's gaze flickered to the shadows in time to see an Eglagor racing toward them, two Golden Guards followed suit. The Eglagor wasn't wearing any armor, was it a guard or a passerby!? She had no time to find out. Clenching her jaw, she pulled on the black stone's power to cloak her. It reacted swiftly, bathing her in a thick layer of concealment that even a mighty dragon would have trouble detecting. For it to fully work this close to the enemy, she had to remain perfectly still. Controlling her breathing, she bent in the leaves, watching the approaching Guards.

The leaves crackled and rustled as the Golden Guards raced to Argno's side. One of them was a large grey and white wolf. Her golden armor glinted, tail raised and ears alert with her nose to the sky, sniffing.

"I lost it!" she spat, angrily. "There was a Goron and...something else! But the scent of the other is gone now."

A human guard stopped beside her, giving her an incredulous look. "How? What do you mean?" he asked her.

"I don't know," she sputtered. "The scent was here and now it's...just...gone?" She put her nose to the ground, sniffing fervently.

The human guard cursed and swung his axe angrily, it missed Balra's concealed hiding spot by a fraction of an inch.

"Great, what now?!" He rounded on her. "How could *you* lose a scent!?"

She bared her teeth at him. "At least I *can* follow scents. You humans would have had to give up the chase long ago!"

"Okay, okay," he conceded, apologetically. "I'm sorry. Someone attacked Argno...I'm just angry!"

"We all are," another voice said, silencing the two guards.

Balra's gaze flickered to the speaker but she remained still. It was the Eglagor. Eglagors were a distant cousin to the Dragnagors. They had the body of a horse with eagle talons in the place of hooves, a horse's mane and tail, but the head of a dog with long pointed ears. Around the base of their necks was a puffy mane of fur. This one was a deep reddish roan color with a flaxen mane and tail. Golden eyes flashed in the night.

Was it his *earth element that stopped the Goron before?* Balra wondered.

"Lord Eglen," the male guard said, dipping his head respectfully and the wolf bowed.

"Please, there's no need to be formal," Eglen responded, smiling slightly. "I understand you're angry. One of your own was attacked and you want revenge, but blindly acting without thought will get you nowhere. Calm down. It's obvious our foe is gone...or well hidden."

His gaze raked the night and for a moment it settled on Balra's hidden location. She shuddered but didn't dare move. He then closed his eyes and concentrated. Balra felt the ground shift beneath her as the earth reacted to his call. *He's trying to find me with his earth element through vibrations!* She focused the power of her cloaking even more and the stone reacted in kind, thickening the defense. Cloaking was most effective from a distance, but up close was another matter, anything could give you away if you weren't careful. She had to remain calm. To do so, she studied the Eglagor before her, caught by a sudden flash of recognition. *I know this Eglagor! I've seen him before...but where? And when?*

Eglen's eyes suddenly flickered open. "Nothing," he reported, huffing with annoyance. He then nodded to Argno. "Come, it's more important to get Argno to safety than to chase shadows."

The two guards nodded firmly and went to Argno's side. Within minutes, Eglen used his earth element to weave a sleigh made of vines and branches from a nearby tree. He then used more vines to gently lift Argno into the sleigh. The wolf offered to pull it while the human and Eglen escorted them to safety. Before they left, Eglen hesitated for a moment, taking one last long look around them with brows furrowed. Huffing defiantly, he turned and signaled for them to move and they took off.

Balra waited for a few more moments, determined not to move till she was certain they were gone. When a good long hour had gone by and nothing stirred, she finally dropped the cover and got to her feet. Taking a deep breath, she walked over to the Goron who'd been with her. His body had been cut in half from snout to tail by one perfectly timed strike. Her brows furrowed, shocked by the ferocity and accuracy of the vine's attack. *Only an expert warrior elemental could pull off something like this! Just who is this Eglen?!*

Damn it! She cursed inwardly, keeping quiet just in case. *No doubt Argno will tell them everything that happened, and I'm sure that Eglen saw me...or suspects he saw me.* Not to mention the mind sharing, she had no idea what Argno had seen in her mind while they'd been connected. He may know who and what she was! *And if he didn't see it in my mind, he'll probably still be able to guess what species I am since I touched him.* She gazed at her hands. *There're not many creatures in this world with thumbs and four fingers.*

She turned and started walking towards Neran. Oh well, it didn't matter. He was hurt enough that it would take a while for him to recover and make a report. She had a small window of opportunity to make her move. She smiled, knowing exactly what to do.

The Silver Goddess was wide awake, staring blankly at the ceiling. Her bed was soft and welcoming, but tonight she found little rest. The Keeper's visit had caused her to wonder over old memories, keeping her from sleep. Some were welcome but others were hard, filling her with doubts. Her gaze wondered over the crystals lighting the walls of her bedroom. She didn't particularly like living underground and missed the Golden Palace and the comfort of its thick walls surrounding her with memories of her father, Roderick the Red.

She bit her lip as she thought of her father, feeling grief well in her heart. He'd been a huge man with fiery red hair and a short, well-trimmed beard. When he'd died from illness, she and her sister were left heartbroken and only just twenty. To honor him they'd taken on his namesake, becoming the Golden and Silver Goddesses. The ache in her heart thickened suddenly. Thinking of her father inevitably made her think of Castella the Purple, her mother. Castella had loved the color purple. She'd been gentle and kind with fine black hair and soft purple eyes. Her element, consequently, was ice and ice's color was purple. The Silver Goddess trembled at the memory because it was her birth that had killed Castella. Having a second child so close to the first had been too hard on her.

Castella had also been the one to name them. The Silver Goddess's real name was Hroevi and her sister's was Tlow. They'd never told anyone their true names since they were thirteen and anyone who knew kept the knowledge to themselves and for good reason. To honor their family's magical origins, Castella had named her daughters in the Fracture Language. The word 'Hroevi' was actually the word 'silver' and Tlow was the word for 'gold'. Unfortunately this had caused adverse effects for the sisters. Since their names were in the Fracture Language and magic responded to that language, calling them by their names not only enhanced their powers but caused their abilities to physically manifest *within* and around them. The signs were subtle: their golden and silver eyes, their golden and silver hair strands that Rosey had mistaken for decorative beads, their gold and silver eye shadow and lipstick that painted their faces, even the gold and silver plates of armor were molded into their bodies despite everyone's belief that they were armor. They had their clothes specially designed to make sure it looked that way too.

Hroevi ran her hand down the line of armor attached to her skin beneath her pajamas. It felt so natural. The ridges of the armor were almost soft like skin, but harder than any armor known to their world. Closing her eyes, the Goddess sighed. Though their names affected both of them, the Silver Goddess was affected more. For some reason her magic leaked from her very body, covering her surroundings in the very brilliant crystalline geode display that she'd carefully wrapped around Hondan's cave systems for years. Her powers had made everything from the chairs, to the lights, to the decorative walkways and passages. It had taken her years to learn to control it and those years had made her a master. She could even change its color or physical properties. She thoroughly enjoyed forcing it be any color *other* than silver, the color and metal that it wanted to be. Even during sleep, she could control the magic. Why *she* was leaking this tampered form of magic and her sister wasn't was still a mystery.

Maybe it's my mother's way of getting revenge for me taking her life? the Goddess thought sadly. *My sister is left to live somewhat normally while I'm cursed with this strange power?* If her sister knew she thought that, she'd never hear the end of it. She smiled, picturing Tlow's aggravated face glaring at her for thinking such thoughts. But it was bittersweet. The uniqueness of her situation meant she'd had to be secluded away from society, including away from her precious sister. After her powers had manifested at age thirteen, a masterful magikin, her mentor, had taken her to the underground caverns of Hondan to train her. Thanks to that exclusive training, Hroevi had mastered magic *and* her oddity, turning it to her favor and winning back her freedom...to some extent. Tlow had been a big part of that. She'd never fully stayed away from Hroevi, having always sent her letters and gifts, and dutifully scryed her with their father every day to talk. It was thanks to her that Hroevi's heart hadn't been hardened to crystal like the caverns she created.

Tlow really is amazing, she's never once let me think I'm anything other than her sister. And together, they made a terrifying team. Tlow's genius was in being able to utilize anyone around her with precision while at the same time staying respectful of their dignity and honor. Tlow had taken Hroevi's misfortunate situation and turned it to her advantage, making Hroevi the Leader of Hondan's Stealth Force and a vital part of Hondan's inner workings. Hroevi knew, if it hadn't been for her sister, she might have become a hidden prisoner, forever tied to the caverns of her own design. *I'm still trapped down here, but it doesn't* feel *that way.*

She griped the covers of her bed. Was their father proud of them? Roderick had been nothing but supportive with both his daughters, but he'd spent far more time with Tlow, preparing her to take over Hondan after him, thus leaving little time for Hroevi. Still, she didn't fault him for that as the demands of leadership were never ending. Heading the Stealth Force through the war had made Hroevi all too aware of that, so any former annoyance at her father for his lack of attention had very quickly dissipated. *Even Tlow found it hard to keep up with me on a familiar basis once the war started.*

Things had finally gotten back to a normal, comfortable peace. She and Tlow had reconnected and her days had been less stressful. And then this happened. The poison eating at their world, the appointing of a new Keeper, the continued attacks from remaining Raptors and Goron...Hroevi took a deep shuddering breath and cupped her hands around her face. She slapped her cheeks a bit, forcing life back into them. *I just have to keep moving forward. My sister needs me now more than ever!*

Suddenly a lite tapping at her door drew her from her thoughts. Her door opened and Nagura peeked in. The Goddess sat up startled. Blinking against the sudden light from the hallway's crystals, she beckoned the wolf in.

Nagura entered on silent paws and bowed. "Calra's reported a disturbance near the coast, ma'am," she said, quickly. "She's awaiting your orders."

"Is it Raptors?"

"We're not sure. Whatever it is, it's hiding itself pretty well."

"Great, that's all we need with Rosey here," Hroevi said, quickly throwing on her robe and leaving the comfort of her room, Nagura at her heels. "Whatever you do, be as quiet as possible. We don't want Rosey catching wind of this and getting any ideas."

Nagura laughed. "She's bold, that's for sure...and eager. But I believe she's starting to understand the gravity of her position. Slowly but surely."

Bursting into her office, Hroevi walked to her desk and sat down. Calra, another wolf guard, sat before her and bowed low as the Goddess settled herself. Calra was the largest wolf of the guards, standing at over seven feet tall with a red, tan, and black coat so elegantly speckled with vibrant designs that it was a shame to see it obscured by silver armor. Her golden eyes were piercing with firm power but they were also gentle and observant. She'd been the first guard Nagura ever trained and, because of her fierce loyalty, she'd quickly become Lieutenant of the Silver Guards under Nagura, their Commander.

"Calra," the Goddess spoke, her voice even but strong. "Report! What's going on?"

Calra bowed. "Ma'am. The guards were making their rounds as usual when they heard an animal give an alarm call, a call for help. It was loud, sounded like it came from..." she hesitated. "It sounded like it came from a Dragnagor."

Hroevi stiffened feeling her body grow cold. "Was it Argno?"

"I'm not sure, myself and my squadron heard the call but it was a long way off. All we can do now is wait for the patrol out by the coast to report back. Hopefully it should be soon. I sent reinforcements that way just in case, then came here to report to you."

She panted slightly and Hroevi realized she must be exhausted. She could see leaves clinging to her immaculate pelt beneath her armor and her claws were stained with dirt. *She must have run here.*

"Understood. You've done well," the Goddess praised. "I want you to take your best guards and scan the whole perimeter. Leave no rock unturned! Find whatever it is, even if you have to search all night!"

Calra nodded but Nagura growled, her armor clinking as if in protest. "Wait, my lady, I am the Commander, should I not lead the charge?" The Goddess gave her a warning stare and Nagura laid her ears flat. "Sorry, Goddess. I don't mean to challenge your authority."

The Goddess waved it away. "Are you sure you can fight? Has a healer cleared you for duty?" She hesitated, eyeing Nagura worriedly.

Calra cocked her head confused, eyes darting between the two of them.

Nagura eyed Hroevi with head held high. "I saw Master Healer, Reptani and she told me I have a good two weeks before I need to take leave. So yes, I'm more than capable to do my part."

The Silver Goddess looked her up and down but Nagura was unwavering. Eventually Hroevi sighed, there was no stopping Nagura. She was as stubborn as Wolvereen, if not more so. *Speaking of which, where is Wolvereen?* she thought, for the first time noticing he was missing. *He may be assigned to the Keeper but he still should have reported in.*

Turning to Calra the Goddess was about to give new orders when Eyasha came into the room. She was the Lieutenant of the Golden Goddess's Guards and had been away on a mission. Besides being Lieutenant, she also handled all the long-distance errands for the Goddesses. *She must have just gotten back.*

Hroevi's brows furrowed as Eyasha stopped before her, bowing low. She was a Capricosi, able to take on human or bird form at will. In bird form, she resembled an eight-foot-tall peregrine falcon. In human form, she was a tall, dark skinned woman with blonde hair. At present she was in her bird form with blue, golden, and black designs decorating her feathers. Beneath those feathers was a miniscule layer of scales acting as its own armor. Because of this, Eyahsa was the only one in the Guards that did not wear full body armor, however, the head and legs of a Capricosi were less scaled than the rest of them so she wore a golden helmet and golden gantlets on her long legs.

Turning into a human to better fit inside the office, she stood before them, her helmet and gauntlets adjusting to her human form. The scales along her body shifted into tan and black clothing, flowing over her as if alive. Despite her change, she still kept her giant wings, making her look like a large angel.

Eyasha turned her elegant magenta eyes to the Silver Goddess. "Sorry to barge in like this, but I have something I'd like to report, it's urgent," she explained quickly, her voice soft like the winds of spring. She had high cheekbones and full yellow lips.

The Goddess frowned. Eyasha was a strict soul who did as ordered without pause. For her to deviate from her mission and come see her was odd. "I see, give your report," she said, leaning forward.

"Ma'am!" Eyahsa responded proudly, straightening, "I was on my way back to the Golden Palace when I noticed a disturbance in the forest. Upon further inspection I discovered a large group of Raptors making their way across Hondan, they seem to be heading towards the Volcano."

At this, the Goddess frowned, brows furrowing. An immediate alarm went off in her head. First, a call for help from a Dragnagor and now a troop of Raptors near the Molt Volcano? Something ominous was brewing. The story Tlow told her about the assassin came to mind, making goosebumps rise along Hroevi's arms.

"Raptors?" Calra questioned, giving Eyasha a confused look. "That can't be. We've had no reports of Raptors anywhere near Neran or the volcano?"

"What I saw was real, Lieutenant," Eyasha insisted. She turned her gaze to the Goddess. "I thought it best to alert you before I returned to the Golden Goddess. Also, I believe I heard an alarm sounded in the night, but I was pretty high up when I heard it, I could have been mistaken."

"You have good ears, Lieutenant Eyahsa," Nagura commended. "You're correct, an alarm was sounded. We're attending to it now."

"Could Argno have been attacked by Raptors?" Calra wondered aloud, ears going back with anger.

"Argno?" Eyasha shot her a concerned look.

"The call was from a Dragnagor," Nagura explained. "It hasn't been confirmed as Argno, though."

Hroevi held up her hands. "All right, calm down. We will assume nothing till it has been confirmed. Good Work, Lieutenant Eyasha. You were right to come to me. Are you sure the Raptors didn't see you?"

"More than sure, my lady. I was flying very high. I always do so to avoid anyone from seeing my comings and goings. Normally, I'm above the clouds, but today the night was fairly clear. Good thing, or I would have missed the Raptors huddled near the volcano."

"What were they doing?" the Goddess asked, tapping a finger on her desk.

It was rhetorical but Eyasha answered faithfully. "I'm uncertain, but they didn't seem to be doing anything besides gathering. Perhaps they are preparing for winter, they do hate the cold."

"Whatever reason, it's not a good one," Nagura stated firmly. "My lady, may I lead a squadron to eradicate them as soon as possible?"

Hroevi thought carefully, the room silent, waiting for her orders. She looked up and met Nagura's gaze. "No, I want you to remain close to Rosey. For now, lead the squadron to investigate the Dragnagor's alarm." Her gaze then fell on Calra. "Calra, you will lead a squadron to eradicate the Raptors. Don't leave a single one alive."

Calra growled. "With pleasure, ma'am!" She rushed out of the office quickly on black paws, this time not pausing as Nagura growled angrily.

The white wolf faced the Goddess, tail twitching irritably. "I hope keeping me close to Rosey is the *only* reason you sent Calra instead of me."

Her icy gaze penetrated Hroevi but she just shrugged. "Of course." The Goddess then looked at Eyasha. "Lieutenant, I don't know what your mission is for the Golden Goddess, but would you be able to spare enough time to assist Calra and her squadron with the Raptors you saw?"

Eyasha bowed, her eyes glinting mischievously. "It would be my pleasure, ma'am." She rolled her shoulders as she left, her giant wings scrapping the floor and her scales glittering in the light. "It's been a while since my muscles tasted battle."

She left and Nagura followed. Hroevi watched them go, guilt pricking at her stomach. Typically, as leader, she'd have joined them, but her powers made it impossible for her to leave. If she left the caverns, her silver magic would leak out into the world, covering it in blue, purple, and white crystalized splendor. She had to remain in the caverns where her powers could be skillfully wrapped around the natural cave system. The Silver Guards knew this, sharing the precious truth with them was the only way to hold their loyalty, for most creatures would not want to serve someone cowardly enough to just stay behind and give orders. Still, she clenched her fists annoyed. It didn't matter what reason she had for staying behind, she still felt like an executioner sending her people to the slaughter.

She shook her head to clear her thoughts. She had to remain focused and calm. If she couldn't leave the caverns, then the least she could do was lead her warriors exceptionally. Often, that required sitting and waiting. Hours passed by. During that time, officers strode in and out of her office reporting what they found. She kept herself busy, finishing off paperwork and detailed reports to be taken to her sister later.

Eventually, Nagura returned, her face tight with solemn acceptance. Hroevi studied her carefully but didn't see any evidence that she'd been in a fight or gotten hurt in any way. She breathed a sigh of relief.

Nagura didn't waste time on formalities. "It was Argno," she said simply.

A knot twisted in the Silver Goddess's stomach. As a Dragnagor, Argno was not a very powerful creature, but they are renowned for their flying ability and stealth operations which was why he'd made a good messenger. Unfortunately, he wasn't the best fighter. *But my sister and I never thought he'd need to be since the war is over and he never leaves Hondan.* She gulped, the guilt clawing at her heart.

"Is he..." she started but Nagura shook her head.

"He's alive, my lady...but only just. He was clearly attacked and from the looks of it, it was a Goron."

Hroevi gazed at Nagura, surprised. "A Goron?" *Now Gorons are involved!*

"Argno's asleep, passed out form blood loss. The healers are treating him now, and they say he's exhausted..." she trailed off, her gaze confused. "Something seems off about his attack, my lady. From the looks of it, it was just one Goron, not a whole pack and normally they travel in groups....and why attack Argno? He's a messenger yes, but the Gorons have been doing so much to remain hidden all these years. A random attack on a messenger just seems..."

"...sloppy," the Goddess finished. She frowned. "No...its *purposeful.*" Her eyes widened. "Like it came from an order?"

Nagura's eyes widened. "But...from who?"

Their eyes locked, Hroevi could tell they were both having the same thought. *The assassin!*

Hroevi waved it off. "Let's not get ahead of ourselves. With Eyasha's report about the Raptors, it's possible the Gorons are trying to issue a challenge to myself and my sister, after all, we were the organizers of the war." She looked away. "But it's mighty coincidental that they'd act right now when Rosey is here."

The Goddess shivered apprehensively. Could the Gorons and Raptors really know about Rosey? Did the assassin?! They'd tried to keep it as secret as possible, but they knew better. The world's cities might have cast a spell that day to prevent Addina's announcement from being overheard outside the cities, but that wouldn't have been able to stop the citizens from gossiping about it once they'd left their city's borders. And eavesdropping was a simple way to gain information. *We knew the enemy would eventually find out, but I never imagined it would be so soon! She hasn't even left Hondan yet!* She took a breath to calm herself. *I can't jump to conclusions though, best to play it safe but smart.*

"We don't know if they're aware of Rosey yet and we shouldn't act like they do. For now, we take this attack as a challenge against us," the Goddess decided. "Argno has been the Goddess's messenger for years, since our father, Roderick the Red, was in power. He's a great friend and a longtime ally. For them to attack him is like an attack to us, personally." She gritted her teeth angrily. "Did you kill the Goron that did it?"

"I didn't...but *Eglen* did," Nagura answered, smiling.

Hroevi's eyes brightened. "Eglen's back? When did that happen?"

"He told me he just arrived. Apparently, he hitched a ride with Captain Marine and was on his way to see us when the alarm call was sounded. He assisted the patrol that responded." Nagura paused before saying, "He wants to join Rosey."

The Goddess tilted her head, amazed. "Really?"

"That's what he said," Nagura shrugged, just as surprised. "He's with Argno now, he wanted to be certain he saw to him first but he shouldn't be long."

"Indeed, I'm here now," Eglen announced, joining them. He pushed his way through the office doors, his sharp talons clicking on the crystalline floors. He bowed before her, touching his muzzle to his left leg, the formal Eglagor greeting. "My lady, it's been a while. You look well."

Hroevi looked him over warmly. "As do you, Eglen. Welcome home. If I knew you'd be joining a late-night fight, I would have sent you your armor."

Eglen smiled, fangs gleaming. "You know I would have refused. I'm not a Golden Guard anymore, my lady."

"I know, I know," she relented. "Have you changed your mind about that?"

She gave him a hopeful look but he shook his head. "No, I've only returned home to assist the new Keeper."

"That's what Nagura told me." Hroevi cocked her head at him questioningly and got up. So long siting made her stiff. She moved to lean against the front of her desk. "I admit, I'm a bit confused. I thought it was *because* of the Keeper that you left?"

Silence stretched between them and Nagura's gaze flickered between them, waiting. Eglen's gaze traced the bluish white floor of her office, crystals shinning bright light into the shadowed room.

"I left because she meant the world to me...." Eglen admitted finally. "And I wasn't there when she died..." He was still for a moment. "I'll be damned if I let that happen again!" He held his head high, firm determination lighting his eyes.

Hroevi sighed and shook her head. *He still blames himself for what happened to Esperanza.* Like Rosey, Esperanza had journeyed with a group of friends. Eglen had been one of them, and he'd been Esperanza's partner, much like Sarabie was to Rosey. Partnered warriors could come in many forms, depending on the relationship and the species involved, but steed and rider partnerships were the most common. Some said a steed and rider's connection ran as deep as the soul. When Esperanza had been brutally murdered by the assassin, it might as well have killed Eglen too. *If he'd been there that day, he might* have *died.* Eglen had been injured before the final battle, so he'd not been cleared to join the fight, instead he'd been forced to stay behind and recover while Esperanza rode Addina into battle. After hearing what happened, he'd blamed himself, then abandoned his position within the Golden Guards, leaving his armor behind. They hadn't heard from him since. *Now he's back to make amends to his beloved rider by seeing her daughter to the finish line. I can't say I blame him.*

"I and my sister have no right to stop you. You don't work with the guards anymore," she answered truthfully. "You're free to join Rosey if you wish...if she accepts you that is." She bowed her head to him. "I thank you for assisting Argno tonight, I shudder to think what might have happened had you not been there."

"Indeed," Nagura agreed. "It was *his* earth element that saved Argno's life. He did well, as always," she added smiling.

Hroevi looked to Nagura. "Was anyone else injured besides Argno?" she asked, scanning them for wounds.

Nagura shook her head. "Thankfully no, but...one of the guards reported scenting another individual in the attack, but once they arrived, the scent disappeared."

The Goddess's eyes widened, intrigued. "What kind of scent? What creature did it belong to?" she asked, apprehensively.

Nagura's eyes met hers. "She couldn't say specifically, it was muddled and rank like something that had gone rotten. But she said it most closely resembled a human's scent...a human corpse to be more precise."

Goosebumps rose on Hroevi's arms. The room was eerily silent. Eglen, along with a select few, were well aware of the assassin's existence.

"I'm sure I saw a human-like figure near Argno when I stopped the Goron," Eglen agreed, speaking softly. "But I was so focused on stopping it that I didn't get a good look at who or what the other individual was." He shook his head, ashamed. "I searched with my earth element, but located nothing...I suspect they may have been cloaking themselves."

Cloaking...just like Tlow thought. Her sister suspected the assassin was a master at disappearing or staying hidden. *A powerful cloaking ability fit the theory.* She couldn't deny it any longer, it had to be the assassin, or something close to it. She certainly couldn't ignore the possibility.

Hroevi raised her head. "We'll not let up till the way is made safe for Rosey. Whoever it was, we'll find them!" she declared boldly. "All right, that's enough for now. It's late, and I'm sure you're tired, Eglen. Please get some rest."

Eglen bowed to her thankfully. "Appreciated, my lady. I will see you both tomorrow." He nodded to Nagura before leaving.

Hroevi's gaze shifted to Nagura. "Why did Wolvereen not report in?"

Nagura's eyes grew wide and she looked away awkwardly. "Well...I felt there was no reason to wake him, considering all that he's doing for the Keeper. He'll need his rest if he's to stay in top condition," she admitted.

Hroevi gave her a sly look. "Really...or do you just want to avoid him nagging over you?"

"Possibly," Nagura agreed innocently, one claw tapping the crystalline floor.

The Goddess's gaze grew serious. "Are you certain you want him to go with Rosey, given the situation?"

Nagura gave her a quizzical look. "Are you kidding, I almost bit his head off when he told me he was going to stay with me and send Calra in his place. I didn't just train her, I trained *him* too before he became my mate, and it was *my* moves that made him the Commander of the Golden Goddess's Guards. There's no way anyone lower than a Commander is going with Rosey and if it can't be me than it's going to be him! We can't afford to let anything happen to Rosey. She's fairly defenseless right now without an element, even with her exceptional sword skills."

"I see, well as long as you're sure?" The Goddess's brows furrowed questioningly.

"Completely," Nagura proclaimed confidently, squaring her shoulders.

Just then, a small, brown, silver-armored wolf entered. He was young but strong with lean muscles and extensive stamina. Nagura studied him, confused. She didn't recognize him and she wouldn't. The Goddess had enlisted him while Nagura had been away visiting Wolvereen and put him under Calra as his mentor.

"Sorry ma'am," the brown scout said shyly, head lowered. "Cocoa reporting, my lady. The scouts have checked the perimeters and found it secure and quiet. What further orders do you have?"

The Goddess thought for a moment. "Continue the patrols throughout the night, and make absolutely sure nothing is there. Argno was attacked on our turf. That is unacceptable and will not happen again!" she said with force.

Cocoa nodded, firmly. "Yes, Lady Goddess!"

Nagura turned to the young wolf. "Well done, you'll make a fine guard yet. Keep up the good work," she praised, giving him a warm smile. "Go on, I'll be joining you soon."

The small wolf beamed as he gazed at his Commander in her striking silver armor. "Thank you, Commander. I'm honored."

He bowed to them both extensively before turning to leave. He was trying desperately to keep his tail from wagging, but the slight back and forth was unmistakable. Hroevi smiled to Nagura as they watched him go. Hroevi hoped there'd be a day where her and her sister's guards could finally rest easy.

Walking back to her room, the Silver Goddess bit back frustration. Despite all the patrols, they'd found little evidence of whatever it was the wolf guard had scented. If there had been a second attacker, they were long gone by now. She rolled her shoulders, feeling exhausted but at least Eyasha and Calra's patrol had returned unharmed. They'd managed to successfully kill a good portion of the Raptors near the coast though the rest had turned tail and run, disappearing into the night. Her guards were good, but the Raptors and Gorons were fast, very fast, and could easily outpace them.

They certainly didn't seem interested in fighting. For some reason that fact worried her. *Perhaps Eyasha was right, maybe they'd just been gathering because of the cold? Some survival instinct or something...*She doubted that. Taking a deep breath, she pushed the thoughts away, she was way too tired to think about it anymore. Nearing her room, she spotted Eglen a little way down walking towards her.

She greeted him with a smile. "Eglen, what are you doing up? I thought you'd turned in for the night?"

"With what happened, I found it hard to sleep," he admitted. His eyes looked drawn and baggy as if deep thoughts, not worries, had kept him up. "How'd it go? Is everything all right?"

"Yes, everyone's fine. Eyasha and Calra's squadron returned triumphant."

"That's good." He flicked an ear absently. "Well, goodnight, I hope you sleep well."

He was about to walk away but the Goddess quickly stopped him. "Eglen?"

He paused, cocking his head. "Yes, my lady?"

Taking a deep breath, she phrased what she was about to say carefully. "Are you going to tell Rosey about you and Esperanza?"

He tensed, withers twitching. Uncertainty flashed through his eyes for a moment and the mane of hair surrounding his shoulders bristled slightly before lying flat. When he spoke, he sounded normal, almost too normal.

"No, not yet."

"Why?" She leaned against the wall, watching him.

"Because...she has enough to deal with. Let her grasp the little stuff before she gets to the big stuff."

"I understand. Thank you."

He bowed and continued on his way.

Chapter Twelve

True Courage

Rosey jerked awake. She blinked, startled to find rough crystalline walls surrounding her with crystalline lights dimly illuminating the walls. She took a breath, remembering where she was and gazed about, dazed with sleep. The room wasn't as extravagant as the one she'd had at the Golden Palace. It was rather normal looking, with a simple dresser, mirror, bedside table, and bathroom suite. The strange iridescent lights were adjustable and on the lowest setting. Usually, Rosey slept in the dark but being underground with no windows made it a bit too dark, even for her.

She paused for a moment, half expecting her chest to tighten and pain to blaze through her lungs, but nothing happened. Everything was peacefully still, including her breathing. *No night terrors tonight...for now.* She yawned and looked at the locket her uncle had made for her, wrapped around her hand. For some reason, she couldn't separate herself from it, even at night. It comforted her and made her feel closer to the parents she never knew. She opened it and gazed at their faces, then looked at the bedside clock. It was too early to get up so she closed her eyes but couldn't fall back asleep.

I can't believe this is happening. She flipped onto her back and stared at the ceiling. *My friends and I always used to tease about leaving Neran, traveling the world hunting Gorons and Raptors, and valiantly rescuing fellow travelers along the way.* She bit her lip. *We even talked about the future; eventually settling down, marriage, families...maybe at a time when there were no Raptors or Gorons about?* She shivered and pulled the covers closer. *Now...everything's different. Sooooooo different...and I...*She shook her head. She couldn't think about this anymore, it was too much...too soon.

Glancing down, she gazed at the sleeping forms of Noly and Hazel curled at the foot of her bed. Years of sleeping with them had made her an expert at moving around without disturbing them. For some reason watching them sleep made her feel tired. She snuggled into the pillows, pulled her parent's locket close to her heart, and happily fell into a peaceful slumber.

When she next woke it was 8:00 a.m. She jumped up feeling rejuvenated, took off her pajamas, put her hair up, then took up Andraste and Silver Knight. For the next hour, she trained with both weapons till a comfortable sweat layered her body. She didn't do anything drastic, just practiced a few sword forms, working on her stance and footing. It had been a while since she'd trained in the nude. It wasn't something she did often, mostly due to the fact that she was rarely alone when training, but it was a valuable practice that helped forge the bond between mind and body. Without armor or clothing, the body was truly exposed making the warrior more aware of their surroundings.

As she moved, Rosey's mind inevitably went back to the time she'd first heard of this training form. Two years ago, she'd been sparring with a young human warrior who'd been traveling through Neran. Afterward, they'd talked for a bit and gotten into a debate about which training techniques were the best or most difficult and he'd told her about nude training.

At first, she'd made fun of it, laughing it off as ridiculous, but the man had smiled saying, "You laugh, but try it yourself and *then* see if you can make fun of it. Nothing will make you more uncomfortable then being naked to the world. And if you're uncomfortable, you're vulnerable. Nude training isn't really about training the body, it's about training the *mind.*"

Despite her disbelief, she couldn't ignore the challenge so she'd given it a try one morning. She'd locked and barred her door to make sure no one would interrupt or see her. She'd closed her window shutters, stripped down to the flesh and was shocked at how incredibly awkward her stance and footing became as a result. She still remembered the look of utter distaste and embarrassment on her face as she watched herself in her bedroom mirror, seeing just how sloppy her form was. Only then did she truly realize what the young warrior had meant. Ever since then, she'd been determined to train herself in the nude...sparingly, and only when she was certain no one would see her. *But that in itself is another issue I must overcome. To be a truly exceptional warrior, my skills shouldn't be limited based on my clothing or if someone sees me without them.* Still, she wasn't sure how she'd move past the human awkwardness surrounding nudity. Oddly, she wasn't at all uncomfortable undressing around Hazel and Noly, who'd always made fun at the humanoid need to wear clothes in the first place, so they'd been her only witnesses to this kind of training.

After finishing her last form, she showered and brushed her teeth, then got dressed. Lastly, she strapped on Silver Knight and Andraste. She'd cleaned them and their sheaths to perfection the night before, the multi-colored lights of the room gleamed off them now.

"Come on you two," she said, swatting the bed where Noly and Hazel still slept. "Let's go! Don't want to be late or we'll eat everything and all you'll have is scraps."

Noly's ears perked and she jerked awake, accidentally kicking Hazel off the bed.

Hazel huffed, writhing on the floor. "NOLY!" she sputtered, tail whipping from side to side threateningly.

"Whoops, sorry," Noly murmured innocently, gazing at her with tired eyes.

The ploy seemed to work for Hazel left it alone, mumbling under her breath about letting Wolvereen take a bite out of her. The cat hopped up onto the bed beside Rosey as she strapped on her black riding boots.

"You're getting better at the whole nude training thing," Hazel stated, purring while licking a paw.

Rosey looked at her from the corner of her eye. "You saw?"

Hazel bobbed her head. "There's not much you can hide from me. From Noly, you can hide everything...except food...but me, not much."

Rosey smiled and scratched her head. "Well, I'm happy to know I'm improving." Though she wasn't certain how well Hazel's judgment was when it came to humanoid fighting forms.

Hazel gave her a pointed stare. "How did you sleep?"

Rosey looked away then said, "Admittedly, I tossed and turned a bit, but at least I didn't wake up with my chest tightening around my heart, that was a nice change." She'd meant it as a joke but neither Hazel nor Noly laughed. Rosey coughed, awkwardly. "It's nothing, all right. I slept fine and the night terrors are less frequent...at least for now." She finished fastening the last strap of her boots and stood up, tapping her foot to test the feel. When she was satisfied, she titled her head to the door. "You ready or do I need to give *someone* a bath?"

Her eyes rested on Noly and the dog sprang to her paws. "Let's go, what you waiting for?" she yipped, pausing by the door.

Hazel and Rosey exchanged amused glances before Hazel leaped to Rosey's shoulders as she stood up. They exited the room and followed the beautifully carved corridors of glistening crystal to the dining room. Inside Rosey spotted Alex, Rochell, Wolvereen, Nagura, and the horses already eating breakfast. The Silver Goddess wasn't present. After taking her seat in-between Alex and Rochell she inquired after the silver woman.

"She was up late last night with some security details so she might be sleeping in," Nagura answered, giving her a warm smile.

Rosey returned her smile but felt curiosity poking her sides. She had half a mind to ask about what the 'security details' included but thought better of it. It was obviously something she didn't need to worry about, otherwise they would tell her. Besides, if it was something related to Neran's Stealth Operations, then she had no business being involved.

A few minutes later, the Goddess came in looking well rested but also distracted as if whatever had happened the night before still occupied her mind. She apologized for her lateness but didn't elaborate more. Her silver robes swooshed as she took her seat but Rosey's eyes grew wide to see the Eglagor following her.

The Goddess turned to him, extending her arm. "Everyone, I'd like you to meet Eglen. He's a former member of the Golden Goddess's Guards and has asked to join you on your journey, Rosey."

Rosey's brows rose, amazed. She'd never met an Eglagor before...of course, there were a lot of species she hadn't met thanks to her confinement behind Neran's walls. The only creatures she got to see where the ones that visited Neran and they were usually all humanoids, only rarely were they animals. She bowed her head to him, intrigued.

"Nice to meet you, Eglen," she said politely. "May I inquire as to why you wish to join me, besides the obvious?" She wasn't sure how else to ask but felt it was a fair question.

Eglen bowed to her elegantly, touching his snout to his left leg. "I'm afraid the 'obvious' answer is the only one, my keeper. I simply wish to provide you with whatever protection and guidance I can."

"Eglen is very knowledgeable, Rosey. He fought in the war and has killed many Gorons and Raptors. Without a doubt, he'll be very helpful. He's also a talented earth elemental," the Goddess explained.

Eglen snorted. "I wouldn't go that far," he said, amused. "Really, my elemental powers are not nearly as refined as I'm sure your friend's is." He inclined his head to Rochelle politely. "But I will do my best, I promise."

Rosey smiled. "Well, I certainly have no right to say no. Welcome aboard, we're glad to have you."

Alex nodded while Noly and Hazel bobbed their heads. But no one made more of a ruckus than Wolvereen. The giant beast stood up suddenly, his gaze hard, settling on Eglen like red daggers.

"You're back..." Wolvereen breathed out, his tail erect. Nagura looked away, as if she felt the same but wasn't quite as open about it.

Eglen stared at him, neither surprised by Wolvereen's outburst nor challenging it. "I am," he agreed softly, as if issuing some promise.

Silence stretched out and Rosey looked back and forth between them, unnerved.

"Ahem, well...yes, he *is* back, Wolvereen," the Silver Goddess said, breaking the awkward stillness. She gave Wolvereen a hard stare. "Eglen returned to help Rosey. He heard about her and wanted to offer his assistance. That is all."

Wolvereen's gaze rested on her, then went back to Eglen. Eglen tilted his head, something in his eyes was pleading with Wolvereen and Rosey stiffened. *What's going on?*

Wolvereen's eyes softened and he sat back down. Nagura licked his cheek gently. "Yes, welcome to the group, Eglen. It's nice to *finally* see you again," Wolvereen said, dipping his head.

Something about his tone made Rosey feel like it was the last thing Wolvereen wanted to say. The black beast looked ready to spring at Eglen and claw his face off, but why was beyond Rosey. *What happened between them?*

"Please, let me ride you later?!" Rochelle blurted and everyone shot her a look. Rochelle slunk in her seat at Eglen's flabbergasted expression. "Sorry...I've just...*really* wanted to see an Eglagor for a *really* long time..." she trailed off, looking away.

Eglen laughed. "No offense taken, I'll tell you what," he turned to her, "you teach me how to be a better elemental and I'll let you take a spin, eh?" He flicked his dog head to his back and Rochelle smiled.

Rosey and Alex exchanged amused glances. She'd almost forgotten how much Rochelle loved Eglagors, the girl had images of them plastered all over her room back in Neran. They were the one species she knew more about than any other. *She's also a great teacher. If Eglen is an elemental, she'll do wonders for his technique. I only wish I could be so lucky...*She shook her head of the thought and began piling her plate with food as Eglen joined them. She glanced at Wolvereen from the corner of her eye. *And what in the world was all that about?*

After the delicious meal, everyone gathered to leave. Rosey, Alex, and Rochelle checked their travel bags, while Nagura, Wolvereen, and Eglen discussed their course with a few Silver Guards. She eyed the trio wondering if they'd start bickering again, but whatever was between them seemed to be gone. To make it even odder, they worked remarkably well together, organizing the Guards and debating the best routes like they'd been doing it their whole lives. Most likely they had. *The Goddess said Eglen was a former member of the Golden Guards. Perhaps I should have asked why he left? But that might have been too intrusive.* It was too late now; she'd already accepted him and the Goddess wouldn't have recommended him if he wasn't trustworthy. *Whatever happened was personal, so there's no reason for* me *to get involved unless Eglen choses to share it with me.*

Finally, they were ready to leave. Rosey felt bad to eat and run, but each moment they wasted was another moment the poison grew in power so, after saying their farewells, they resumed following Nagura through the crystal covered tunnels. After thirty minutes, the caverns opened into the natural cave system again and the world was suddenly filled with grey, black, red, and brown cave formations. The only odd part about it was the lighting. The path was lit by equally-spaced, magically lit, crystal orbs that cast a low glowing light.

At lunch time, they took a break while Nagura and Wolvereen scouted ahead, talking with various Silver Guards who came and went from the shadows. To Rosey's disappointment, the reports included Raptor sightings nearby which meant Rosey's group would definitely be sticking to the caves all the way to the volcano. Rosey sighed exasperated, after hours of walking in the brown nothingness she was ready for some sunshine.

As the afternoon wore on, they approached the end of the caverns. Suddenly, Rosey heard a strange rumbling above ground. They all stopped, but no one offered any explanation. Noly whined apprehensively and Hazel tucked her body against Rosey's neck, whiskers twitching.

Wolvereen's harsh growl silenced them. "Hush now, and don't move. Something's not right..." he put his scarred snout to the air and sniffed, ears swirling for the slightest sound. Nagura growled beside Rosey before suddenly rushing forward and positioning herself protectively before her. Someone or something was coming.

Rochelle and Alex were beside Rosey in a heartbeat. Hazel lashed her tail from her perch on Rosey's shoulders. Noly took a defensive stance in front of Rosey while the horses ringed them in, pawing at the ground. Nagura did not sound any alarm, only stood powerful and strong in her gleaming armor. All the while the ground kept rumbling, a few powerful blasts went off above their heads and dust fell from the ceiling. Rosey didn't know what to do, her heart pounded in her chest and sweat beaded her forehead as the ground above them seemed to tremble. What was going on!? She had the sudden urge to run but held it back. The lights illuminating the path flickered as the rumbling got worse.

"What in the world is happening up there?!" Alex said, using a tone Rosey had never heard from him before, probably because it sounded panicked. He was staring at the ceiling; eyes wide.

Despite the tension Wolvereen and Nagura remained calm, Eglen too, though he looked shaken. Alex whipped out his wand and was about to utter a spell when Cocoa, the tiny brown armored wolf Rosey had seen here and there, came running from the passage before them screaming at the top of his lungs.

"RUN, NOW! RAPTORS ARE COLLAPSING THE CAVES! FOLLOW ME!" He commanded before turning and taking off.

That was all it took and they were suddenly in hot pursuit. Rosey barely saw or comprehended anything after that. She was vaguely aware of Rochelle and Alex grabbing each of her arms, pulling her along with them as they started running. Noly was in front, beside Cocoa, her eyes wide with fear. She saw flashes of Nagura's white pelt to her left and Wolvereen's golden armor to her right, but the others were lost amongst chaos.

The world became a sudden confusion of sounds and lights. The hard paced pounding of the horse's hooves and scrapping of Eglen's claws sounded behind, around, and in front of Rosey even though she was sure they remained behind. Mounting them would have made for greater speed, but there was no time. A roaring boom resonated throughout the entire cave spurring on their adrenaline rush. It was so loud Rosey's ears rang. The lights began flickering, bathing them in random darkness. All she could see was the walkway in front of her and the backs of Cocoa and Noly. She knew Alex couldn't risk trying a spell, he could fall, mess it up, or worse. Not to mention a shield wasn't always capable of holding up against certain extreme weights and the gigantic rocks of the cave ceiling probably exceeded that weight limit.

Cold air and dust suddenly billowed at the back of Rosey's feet, making her run faster. The dust cloud caught up with them and Rosey quickly covered her face as stray bits of grit flew into her eyes. Hazel hung on for dear life and Rosey grabbed her leg to make sure she didn't fall. She knew she was squeezing too tight, but it was better than losing her grip. She'd long ago lost the sounds of Eglen and the horses and she couldn't see Nagura or Wolvereen anymore. She prayed they were all right.

Tiny bits of debris hit Rosey's back and small pieces flung past her face, if one hit her leg or foot just right, she'd be done for. Hazel hissed and turned around, yanking her front leg free but presenting Rosey with a back leg. Rosey gripped it and realized the tiny cat was batting away small rocks. If Rosey weren't panicked, she might have asked if Hazel could see the others, but she couldn't speak, too afraid to stop her steady flow of breath. *In and out. In and out. In and out.* She said it over and over again as she ran, determined not to falter. The exit was almost there, just around the corner, maybe the next. Almost! Almost! Her muscles screamed at her, but sheer will power and years of training kept her going.

After what seemed like hours, Rosey saw light. Her hopes rose and she felt a burst of energy shoot through her, numbing whatever pain remained in her muscles, that is, until she got outside. With no other possible rout of escape or time for strategic planning they burst out into the open and right into a full-on battle. Rosey was hit immediately with the freezing air of winter, but her heated body barely noticed. She tried to reach for her sword but her friends slammed her to the ground as a giant creature, Rosey wasn't sure what, flew over their heads screaming in pain. Alex's wand was out and he cast a powerful spell in another direction. Rosey couldn't see what he aimed for, but she heard the spell make contact and a scream split the air. Alex muttered what she thought was a protection spell and saw a pink, shimmering bubble start to surround her. She was now safe, but everyone else wasn't and she couldn't do anything to help them! Shields were stationary and didn't move unless constructed to. If Rosey moved outside the shield, it wouldn't follow her and her friends weren't planning on letting her go anywhere any time soon.

Rochelle lifted her arm and air swished around the three of them as it plowed into the chest of a giant creature on two massive legs bearing down on them, jaws agape. Rosey gasped at the power in Rochelle's attack. It was so strong that it immediately threw the giant beast backwards and into the winter thriving bushes it had emerged from. It took a moment for Rosey's brain to register that the giant beasts they were fighting were Raptors.

Rochelle and Alex kept her pinned against the ground, shielding her with their bodies. Hazel managed to make it out from under her neck and stood at Rosey's side hissing defiantly. Andraste pushed into Rosey's back so there was no way she could unsheathe it and she couldn't get to Silver Knight either. She fought the urge to shout at her friends angrily. *They're just keeping me safe!* she reasoned, but the sting of their protection scored her pride and she bit her lip. The only thing she could do was pull her legs in close so nothing could go for them.

Her eyes searched for the others but they were lost in the chaos. A black mane and tail flickered at the edge of her vision; it was Sarabie. She watched in horror as something large slammed into the giant horse, knocking her back. Sarabie screamed but disappeared from view. Raw rage flared in Rosey's chest.

"DON'T TOUCH MY PARTNER!" she screamed, trying to burst from Rochelle and Alex's cocooned protection. Her adrenaline rush almost knocked them off but their grip tightened in unison and slammed her back down.

"Rosey, stay down!" Rochelle ordered, flinging an arm full of whirling air at the trees nearby.

It was the last thing Rosey wanted to do, but then another black figure soared over her and she recognized Wolvereen. He went in the direction Sarabie had been knocked and she breathed a sigh of relief but the sight of him reminded her of Noly. Where was she and the others!? Fear crept into her heart and she trembled.

"Rochelle, the dust!" Alex said, nodding toward a billowing cloud of debris from the collapsed cave.

Rochelle nodded and in unison they hoisted Rosey between them, half-dragging, half -guiding her into it for cover. Rosey coughed and lifted her shirt over her face. She grabbed Hazel as she sneezed, shoving her under her shirt. Suddenly the air cleared as Rochelle set up a swirling mass of air about them, encasing them in the middle of a miniature dust tornado with a core of breathable air. Hazel poked her head out of Rosey's collar but Rosey held her close, her tiny frame shivering, but safe. It was the only solace in the whirlwind of emotions flowing through her.

She sank to the ground and closed her eyes. Without any element and only a sword and dagger to help her, she was essentially *useless*. She couldn't risk getting in the way of the people desperately trying to protect her. She grasped the crystal and in an instant the world seemed to slow to a crawl. Rosey looked up and started. Standing before her was the see-through shape of a tall woman with long black hair staring at her, a smile on her face. *Am I hallucinating!* Hazel didn't seem to see it, but the figure was there, hiding in the folds of the whirlwind surrounding her. She didn't say or do anything, just smiled.

Rosey felt herself relaxing and she reached for the mystery woman, only to see her disappear as a solid sheet of blue, pink, and purple crystal surrounded them. Turning to the cave exit, Rosey saw tendrils of bluish liquid leaking from the cracks and rocks of the collapsed cave, forming around her and her friends. Other branches of the strange liquid swerved off in other directions. Her gaze followed it, intrigued. She had no doubt it was coming from the Silver Goddess; it had the same flawless design as her Crystal Caverns. She'd sent it to protect them!

Suddenly, Alex and Rochelle gasped as a vortex of swirling purple energy appeared a few yards away, sending out a buffeting shock wave over the clearing. To their amazement, a blue unicorn come charging out, whinnying a war cry. The giant embedded her horn into an advancing Raptor, tossing the body aside like a rag doll before the Silver Goddess's crystal covering extended over Rosey's head, encasing her, Alex, Rochelle, and Hazel into a wide crystal dome.

Rochelle quickly dropped the protective tornado and fell to her knees, eyes wide. Alex joined them, a hand resting gently on Rosey's back. She saw their lips moving but could barely hear what they were saying. Her mind zoomed with everything that had happened and she was mute for a few moments before Alex and Rochell's voices started to make sense.

"Was that...was that a unicorn!?" Rochelle stammered between breaths.

Rosey stared at her friend, a dusty coating covered her from head to toe, her pony tail loose and crooked.

Alex met her gaze. "I believe it was." He looked just as ragged and wiped a bead of sweat from his forehead.

"My eyes are better than both of yours," Hazel stammered. "It was most definitely a unicorn!" She was still shivering, Rosey held her tighter.

"What in the world....who..." Alex paused. "Addina..." he whispered softly under his breath.

Rosey shot him a glance, still too numb to speak.

"You think she sent her?" Rochelle asked, nodding towards where they'd seen the blue beast.

"Who else?" He titled his head questioningly and Rochelle nodded. "Remember, the Goddess told us she'd be sending someone to protect Rosey. And just in time."

Rosey looked between them but neither mentioned anything about seeing an ethereal floating woman. She sighed. *So I was the only one who saw her! What and who was she?* At least they'd all seen the unicorn, after seeing the woman she'd seriously started to doubt her sanity. The unicorn dug up a whole plethora of questions Rosey knew no one could answer but the unicorn herself. *Did Addina really send you? Are you coming with us? Do unicorns really live in the Settled Valley with Addina? Are you as mysterious and powerful as the legends say? Are your horns really made up of every metal and rock known to the universe?* She could go on and on but right now she just wanted to take a nap.

It was then Rosey noticed the dome was soundproof. She couldn't hear a single sound besides their unified breathing. Beyond the blue dome a battle raged and she was safe and sound. She bit her lip, wiping away sweat and grit.

Her voice, cracked and dry, finally came through. "What's going on?"

Alex shook his head. "I don't know. Seems to me the Raptors either found out you were in the caves or knew about them and wanted to destroy them anyway. We're safe now, the Silver Goddess's crystal barriers are impenetrable by most regular means."

Rosey stared at him, flabbergasted. "They weren't supposed to even *know* I existed!" She stammered angrily, her helplessness making her angry. "That was the whole point of the caves, wasn't it?!" She looked between them but they were silent. They had nothing good to offer her.

"Rosey," Hazel squeaked from her shirt. "It's like the Goddesses said. They knew eventually the Raptors and Gorons would find out about you. It was never meant to last forever..." She licked Rosey's hand comfortingly but Rosey looked away.

"I thought I'd...we'd have....more time..."

The words hung between them. Silence followed and Alex sighed, leaning against the crystal wall. He fingered a small cut just below his cheek and licked his lips, grimacing at the dust. Taking some water from his pack he washed his face. Rochelle copied him mindlessly. Rosey touched her own face, tracing a line through the grit and reached for her water pack. Hazel wriggled free and started licking herself. The chaotic world just moments before had now been reduced to a quiet sanctuary and quickly replaced by worry. Was Noly okay? Maybe Sarabie was out there whinnying in the dirt as she bled to death? Rosey closed her eyes against the image, heart hammering in her chest.

Her muscles ached, her back was bruised from Andraste poking into it, and her lungs burned. She could only imagine what was going through her friend's minds; probably how in the world the Raptors had learned about them, but all Rosey could think about was how ridiculously useless she was. This was the first real time their lives had been in danger and she'd been unable to do a thing. *Mostly cause I was being squished to death. Just how long will others have to fight my battles for me?!* She took a deep breath and swallowed her pride, shoving it as far down as possible. There was no room for that on the battlefield.

"So, we just stay here?" she asked shakily.

"That's all we can do," Rochelle agreed, leaning towards her. She didn't seem in the least bit phased. Her now clean but wet face, beamed at Rosey happily. She flicked her hand and a gust of powerful wind blew across her face drying it immediately. She flung some at Rosey and her wet skin dried without drying out. Rosey nodded her thanks.

"Thank the Almighty One this place had adequate magic, I wouldn't have wanted to dive into the magic I have stored up," Alex commented, giving his wand a glance as he sheathed it.

Rosey nodded agreement. While at the Golden Palace, Alex had taken some time to store magic in his wand just in case they'd enter a magical dead-zone. It had taken him five hours of careful meditation to completely fill his wand.

Seeing her quiet demeanor, Rochelle and Alex gave her a smile and Rochelle blew air in Alex's direction to dry his face. "I'm surprised the Silver Goddess can do this," he said, tilting his head at the crystal structure surrounding them. "She must have a lot of magic stored up for something like this...and when we're so far away from her."

He rose and started to examine the gleaming walls making Rosey smile. That was Alex, finding something to analyze even in the face of danger. *It must be his way of coping.*

"I want to apologize," Rosey said suddenly, drawing her friend's attention. "I should have been more...helpful."

They gave her startled looks and Rochelle placed her hand on Rosey's shoulder squeezing reassuringly. "You've got nothing to be sorry for Rosey. You don't have an element yet, remember? Until you do, staying out of the battle is the best thing you *can* do. You stuck with us and you didn't overreact." She inclined her head to her. "You did well."

Rosey didn't feel like she'd done well. All she'd done was hide and cower behind her friends like a coward.

"Ow!"

She gave Hazel a flabbergasted expression. The cat had pressed her extended claws into Rosey's left leg.

"I'm sorry, Rosey," she stated firmly, "but I've known you long enough to know what you're thinking." She tilted her little chin defiantly. "And it's not true! Running head first into a battle and waving your sword above your head is *not* courageous! It's easy to fight...it takes *courage* not to."

Rosey felt warmth flood her cheeks and swallowed a lump in her throat. For some reason, hot tears tickled the corners of her eyes and she quickly wiped them away.

"Well damn, cat. Shit just got real!" Rochelle giggled, suddenly.

Rosey shot her a wide-mouthed grin. "Rochelle?!"

The brunette shrugged and they all started laughing.

Chapter Thirteen

A Chance Encounter

Balra crouched high up in a tall purple coned pine, gripping its bark angrily as she watched the blue crystal substance seek out Rosey's group, covering them in a protective shield. She cursed and banged her fist on the trunk, then turned to a Goron beside her, hidden as she was in the thick canopy.

"Organize the Raptors into another attack position, make sure they don't get caught by that stuff!" She indicated the glowing crystal and the Goron bobbed her head, beady red eyes flashing maliciously as she scurried off into the shadows.

Great! Do they know how long it took me to whip up a Time Release Spell that would blow that cave sky high! She quickly ducked back into the canopy and jumped from the tree, landing gently on the forest floor. She quickly rolled behind a few scraggly bushes for cover as Raptors battled around her. She had to stay hidden or her cover would be blown, as it was, she shouldn't even be this close but with Rosey a few feet away she had to take this chance. *I might not ever be this close again! Better to kill her now!*

She'd spent hours working on the bomb that blew up the cave, only to have Rosey and her friends still make it out alive! Of course, the Goddesses were mostly to blame, their damned guards had been doing their jobs splendidly over the past few days. First, they'd managed to spot her Raptors the other night and send a Capricosi-led squadron to attack, almost decimating them, and now they'd noticed her Raptor squadron carrying the spell she'd made and rushed out to meet them. *If I hadn't of picked off a few guards here and there, they'd have never made it to the caves in the first place!* She gritted her teeth. And now the Goddesses were ruining yet another plan. Her eyes glowered on the crystal encompassing Rosey and her two friends. Inside that dome was the source of her Master's demise!

Her gaze flickered about her, uneasily, pulling on the black stone's cloaking ability to hide her. Still, at the moment, everyone's focus was on the ten-foot-tall Raptors. All manner of species encased in golden and silver armor battled the ferocious beasts, plowing over vegetation and spattering blood over every leaf. Cries of alarm, pain, and horror rang through the trees. Balra's gaze shot to the canopy where she knew Gorons flitted from branch to branch issuing silent commands to the Raptors, trying to keep them organized and doing their own killings. *Their* orders, in turn, came from her. *They have to stay hidden, and they especially can't let anyone know I'm the one calling the shots!*

Balra kept herself low, trying desperately to avoid the guard's eyes. Her cloaking ability would make her appear as a shadow in the day, but she could still be spotted or sensed this close to the enemy. If they did detect her, well...she'd just have to be the last thing they ever saw. Passing as quickly and as unnoticed as possible she drew close to the dome where Rosey hid. She gripped the black stone at her chest and it beat between her fingers, pulsating as if it knew the new Keeper was close. Her brows furrowed at the weight the stone suddenly exerted on her, pain lacing her chest, but she shook it off and grabbed the blade hanging by her side. Casting a quick glance around and finding the coast clear, she drew the blade quickly across the crystalline surface. It rang against her sword, making far more noise than she wanted, but the crystal dome held.

Balra cursed and drew on the power in the stone, feeling it react swiftly. It covered her sword in a glowing purplish black energy that made the blade hum. Doing this came with a price, the stone could no longer power the cloaking spell covering her. She was now visible for all to see, so she'd need to work fast. Balra smiled wickedly then hacked at the dome again, this time scoring deep black marks into the surface. Still, it held, defiantly strong in the wake of her Master's power. Balra wanted to scream, but she feared attracting any more attention. Instead, she banged her fist into the crystalline surface, then hacked at it again, sending more power from the stone into her blade. As she worked, she continued to glance around her, hoping no one would notice her assault but that's exactly what happened.

"Citizen!" someone shouted behind her, making her pause, the blade lifted above her head to strike.

She licked her lips, tasting sweat. It beaded her forehead and the stone in her chest hummed as if panicking. She lowered the blade and turned to see a man wearing golden armor standing a few feet away. He looked human with dark hair and green eyes, his arms were coated in thick layers of earth, hard pointed stones poking out at the ends. *He's an earth elemental!* she gauged quickly. A dead Raptor was at his feet, the chest pummeled in and dark crimson blood bathing the ground. The ends of the guard's arms were covered in Raptor blood and it was splattered on his face and clothes. She shivered. *He's good!*

He took a step toward her, brows furrowed. "Citizen, what are you doing here?" He looked massively confused and she knew why. "It's not safe and..." he looked behind her, "...what are you doing?"

She didn't answer, thankfully he still thought she was a regular 'citizen', she needed to keep it that way. She softened her features slightly, trying to look innocent and lowered her sword.

"I...I don't know what's happening!" she stammered, trying to sound panicked. It wasn't hard given that she was indeed panicky. "I just...went for a walk and suddenly...." She looked around and hugged her arms to her sides, trying desperately to look confused and scared.

The man came closer and it took all her strength not to back away. "It's okay," he said comfortingly. "I'm with the Golden Guards as you can see," he tapped his golden armor smugly, making her want to punch him. "Come on, stick close and I'll escort you to safety." He turned his back to her. "By the way, that crystal you're attacking is the Silver Goddess's Crystal, so there's no reason to be..."

He stopped midsentence as her sword pierced through his chest from behind, slicing through the Golden armor and his heart like butter. The purple-black tip hummed drawing on her stone's power. He coughed up blood and sputtered, confusion rippling across his face as his skin slowly turned black. He turned as she yanked her sword free and he fell to the ground, reaching out to her. She took a step forward, his blood dripping down her blade and bent close to his ear.

"Such a good Guard, too bad your efforts were in vain," she whispered before severing his head.

The head rolled a few feet away before coming to a rest in some bushes. She turned back to the crystal dome, the black marks she'd left were repairing themselves, disappearing as if they'd never been made. She cursed again. *If my Master's power is useless, I can only imagine how useless my magic would be!* She shook her head and cleaned her blade before sheathing it. *I cannot win here!* Not to mention she was exposed. With a guard dead, it wouldn't be too long before someone came looking or noticed her again. Rosey had escaped, for now.

She bent low in the bushes and touched the stone on her chest, summoning a Goron with her mind. One slithered from the trees, bending close to her.

"Make this body look like it was killed by a Raptor," she ordered indicating the Guard at her feet, his skin had started to sink in on itself as her poison continued to eat him from the inside out.

The Goron chuckled, licking her lips before descending on the Guard, ripping the blackened body limb from limb, knowing the poison wouldn't hurt her.

Balra moved through the battle, taking to the trees with one solid leap, covering herself in the cloaking power again, and flicking from limb to limb alongside the hidden Gorons issuing orders. She passed over the blood-stained world below, numb to the violence and the dead bodies littering the ground, most of them Raptors. Away from the commotion she paused for a moment, taking deep breaths.

I can't do this on my own anymore! She thought suddenly. The realization scored her heart. Using the Raptors and Gorons was one thing, but she needed more than that. She needed someone to take the fall for her, someone to take all the risk but who was just as smart and capable of leading her Master's army! *Of course, they won't come willingly.* Even she had had doubts before the Master convinced her otherwise. Her hand traced over the stone in her chest. *I'll need more... but am I good enough to copy my Master's creation?*

Suddenly she heard something slithering toward her, quickly she turned to see a crystalline shape bobbing through the trees. The Silver Goddess's crystal defense was still active! And coming straight for her! Panic flared through her chest. More than likely, it was blindly seeking out anyone who wasn't a Raptor, Goron, or Guard. She should have been more careful approaching it! She didn't know much about the Goddesses' individual powers but the Silver Goddess's power seemed much more animated and independent. *If it catches me, that's it! I'll be trapped!* If she'd been unable to break into it, she doubted she'd be able to break *out* of it.

Turning she took off, zigzagging through the foliage as fast as she could. Quickly she put up her hood and covered her face, hoping the crystal didn't also allow the Goddess to *see* through it. If so, the Goddess would now know there was a human amongst the battle. Of course, she might just assume, as the Guard had, that she was a hapless citizen who'd happened upon the situation, but she didn't want to take that risk. If she fell into the enemy's hands, her Master's poison would be done for! Fear blazed through her chest. *What if it saw what I did and is coming to stop me!?* The new possibility spurred her on.

Moving quickly, she took a complicated route through the trees, moving faster than should be possible. She glanced behind her and sighed, relieved to see the crystal was suddenly missing, thinking she must have outmaneuvered it, or was out of the Goddess's range, but as she rounded a tree, there it was. She swung into it so hard, it caught her in the chest and she fell back out of the tree, but at the same time it touched the stone in her chest. A zing of purple black energy shot through the crystal and the crystal crackled, screaming as it started popping suddenly, melting into a black liquid at the touch. Balra didn't stick around to see what happened next, she took off again, weaving through the greenery as fast as she could.

Hroevi shrieked and fell backwards as the purplish black energy shot through her crystal and straight to her. The nearest guards surrounding her rushed to her side as she writhed on the ground. Pain sliced through her nerves as if she'd been stung a thousand times. Her nerves fired on end and heat scorched her body from head to toe. People shouted around her but she couldn't make sense of them.

She gasped at the pain. It took all her might to keep her still existing crystalline structures from cracking on the battlefield. *I can't falter, or Rosey's done for!* Already she'd sensed stress on the crystal protecting Rosey, most likely from some Raptor, but Hroevi had been too distracted with seeking out the others to figure out what exactly had attacked Rosey's dome. She could only focus her sight through the crystals in one place at a time and the crystal holding Rosey was impenetrable, so she hadn't much worried about it. She gritted her teeth against the muscle spasms but, eventually, the energy, whatever it was, dissipated. She sighed and gasped for air, trying to remain calm.

What the hell was that!? One moment she'd had her sight crystal following some random woman she'd spied through the trees as the battle died down, trying to catch up to them, and the next she was hit in the face with a powerful energy she'd never felt before. *Who was that? Did* they *do that to me?* She'd been certain it was just some unlucky citizen, caught in the fray, but doubt filled her mind now. The black cloak, the way she'd moved, trying to avoid the battle below...it's like she knew. Hroevi's mind screamed the word 'assassin' at her over and over again. Her odd powers allowed her to feel and understand many things that the crystal came into contact with, but she'd never felt anything like that before...it was dark, twisted, and malicious! *Could it really be...was* that *the assassin my sister saw sixteen years ago?!*

Someone was holding her to their chest, a glowing green hand running up and down her body inspecting her for wounds. It was one of her healers, a woman called Reptani. She was a Warf from the floating cities and one of the Elemental Humans. Like all Warfs she was an air elemental but she was also gifted with healing ability, one she'd honed splendidly in the Silver

Guards. She had the Warf's pale white skin, straight silver hair, and light grey eyes. They flashed with relief as Hroevi awoke.

"Oh, thank the Almighty One you're okay," Reptani gasped with a slight accent, relieved. "Take it easy, my lady. What happened?"

Hroevi righted herself, wiping away the sweat on her forehead. "My crystal located...a human woman in the battle and I went to protect her with my crystal. She ran and my power pursued her, but when it touched her....it recoiled. Something felt like...it attacked me? Some kind of energy?"

Reptani's bows furrowed. "That's odd. What was a random citizen doing out there?"

"There *shouldn't* have been *anyone* out there. We've been doing countless perimeter checks these past few days since the Raptors were spotted near the volcano," a guard said nearby, sounding confused. Hroevi couldn't see him. "My lady, what you felt was most likely a magic spell the woman had for defense, after all, most citizens don't know of your crystal power."

A fact she was all too aware of. Hroevi turned to him, it was Treybain, a black and white dappled horse from her guard. He'd always been rash which made for a fearless warrior but a reckless one which was why she'd chosen to keep him out of this particular skirmish.

She nodded to him. "I believe you might be right, Treybain. Still, I've never known magic so much stronger than mine? It's unsettling...and it didn't feel at all welcoming. It felt dark...like a terrible poison..."

Neither Treybain or Reptani added to that. For now, Hroevi kept her true guess to herself, the knowledge of the assassin wasn't one the World Leaders shared with just anyone and she couldn't be certain that that's who this person was. Still, she'd need to share her encounter with Tlow as soon as possible. Hroevi got to her feet with Reptani's help.

"You're not injured physically, my lady," she reported dutifully. "But you need to rest, I sense great weariness in you from today's efforts."

Hroevi smiled as she righted herself. "Thank you, Reptani. Today has been *very* strenuous," she agreed. "But the battle is not over yet. I can still hold out."

If it hadn't been for Hroevi's crystal holding up the structure of her part of the caves, they'd all have been crushed by now. The spell that had been used to collapse the caves had been strong and far too close to Rosey's location for comfort...as if they'd *known* where she was. *But how could that be?* Her mind suddenly flashed to Argno and the attack he'd suffered. Had something or someone gotten information out of him? Perhaps...Rosey's location? But the Raptors and Gorons had no such powers! How would they have gotten it from him? Perhaps through torture, after all he *was* pretty banged up. She shook her head, *Argno would never talk, he'd die first...which might have happened had Eglen not showed up.* There were also mental forms of torture but, once again, the Raptors and Gorons had no such powers. *Perhaps it was a lucky guess?* But Hroevi's experience told her otherwise. This attack had been carefully planned and Rosey had been the target.

The thought was unsettling enough that her legs almost buckled beneath her again, but sheer will power kept her standing. Now was not the time, *now* she had to focus on keeping the defenses in place while her warriors battled on. *Without me there to lead them...*a small part of her mind said and she gritted her teeth.

Reptani sighed, putting her hands on her hips exasperated as Hroevi's legs wobbled. "Then let me give you an energy boost, at least," she insisted and Hroevi offered her her hand.

Reptani took it and held it between her own green glowing hands. Gently, like a soft spring breeze, Hroevi felt the energy transferring from Reptani into her own body, filling her to the brim and bringing color back to her cheeks. She sighed with relief, her body rejuvenated, and thanked Reptani who bowed to her before stepping back, looking tired all of a sudden. *She shared more energy with me than she should of,* Hroevi realized, sighing.

Reptani and Treybain stood by, watching her closely as she sank back into meditation, mentally connecting herself to the crystal flowing from her. She checked everyone, glad to see they were all still comfortably safe and protected, then started surveying the battle, pleased to see they were winning. But a nagging fear throbbed at the back of her head. The woman she'd seen, was she just a random citizen or something more?

Put the pieces together Hroevi, her mind screamed at her and she took a shuddering breath. The attack on Argno, where Eglen had reported seeing a cloaked humanoid figure that had suddenly disappeared. Then, a powerful spell, created by a masterful magikin, being used by Raptors to bring down the caves. And now, a black cloaked, random woman in the middle of a place she shouldn't be and had suspected magical powers that had assaulted Hroevi's own. *I can't deny this...not anymore.*

Her mind honed in on the scene her sister had shared with her years ago. During the sorrowful aftermath of the final battle at Scorched Mountain, Hroevi had never seen Tlow so battered and defeated despite the successful exorcism of the demon from their world. Tlow had shared what she'd seen that day with all the World Leaders...the assassin...a thin humanoid figure, covered in a black cloak, hood up and with their back to Tlow on the battlefield. They'd slowly turned to look at Tlow from a shadowed hood, face hidden within and surrounded by black corpses, before suddenly disappearing. Hroevi compared her sister's memory to the memory of the woman Hroevi had just chased through the woods: the same hood, the same black cloak.

Suddenly, a golden armored, blood-spattered Eyasha burst into the room. In her arms was the sunken and blackened body of another guard, this one wearing golden armor. She placed the body gently on the ground as Reptani went to inspect it. Hroevi's eyes grew wide as she studied the black corpse, remembering the image in Tlow's memory of all the bodies turned black by poison, lying at the foot of the assassin. She gulped, barely hearing Eyasha as she reported finding the body mangled and destroyed in the bushes, but the head had clearly been cut off by a sword and he'd been pierced through the chest by the same weapon. Hroevi clenched her fists. *There can no longer be any doubt...I've just seen the assassin! And she's a human magikin!*

Chapter Fourteen

The Protector and the Protected

Rosey wasn't sure how long the barrier stayed up, nor did she know anything about Balra's attack, but it must have been about an hour. When the crystal finally came down, she expected to see dead bodies and blood but the only traces were scuffed footprints and rocky debris from the collapsed cave. She didn't really care about that so much as for the figures in front of her. Everyone was safe! Noly came running, yipping and barking, talking so fast that Rosey didn't understand her. It was something about biting the leg of a 'giant, upright walking, mutated reptile' which Rosey took to be a Raptor.

Her eyes located Sarabie and she rushed over and threw her arms around her neck. Rochelle and Alex following to Bronzo and Filla. Sarabie pushed her muzzle into Rosey's back, holding her close.

"Thank the Almighty One you're all okay, thank you, thank you!" Rosey whispered it over and over again into Sarabie's thick neck, shaking with relief.

Sarabie inhaled deeply, taking in her scent. "Oh, little one. I'll be running with you for a long time yet." She nibbled at Rosey's hair and nuzzled her fondly. Hazel purred from Rosey's shoulders and rubbed her cheek along Sarabie's snout.

Rosey quickly flitted from person to person, exchanging hugs. She even managed to get a hold of Wolvereen, hugging his giant neck as he cringed...but only slightly. She didn't care, she was just thankful no one had suffered any horrible injures beyond a small scratch or bruise. Even Sarabie, who had indeed been attacked by a Raptor, had escaped terrible injury when she nailed the beast in the head with a well-aimed kick before Wolvereen bit its head off.

Her gaze rested on the collapsed tunnel. "What about the Goddess and the other guards?!" She turned to Wolvereen worriedly. "Are they all right? Did all the caves collapse!?"

"Rosey, relax," Wolvereen asserted sternly, but gently. "The same crystal that protected your friends is also draped around every inch of most of the Goddess's caverns, remember? No bomb of any kind can break or dislodge that stuff. Only the natural part of the caves fell, I assure you." He dipped his head to her reassuringly and she sighed with relief.

"Indeed, I doubt even a unicorn such as myself would be able to break through that crystal. Then again, we unicorns *are* very powerful."

As one they turned to the horned horse who respectfully stood a few feet away. She must have measured twenty-five hands high and had blood spattered over an immaculate blue body. Rosey gasped as the blood slowly started to disappear, melting into the creature's flesh. Her horn gave off a low blue tinted light and then settled as the last of the blood disappeared. *She removed it with magic!*

The giant equine was the most beautiful color Rosey had ever seen. Her main body was white with light blue and dark blue highlights, but the highlights were...moving. They fluxed in various waves, disappearing and reappearing in an array of designs, almost as if her skin was a constantly moving image. Her spiraling horn had a blue swirl running through it and her elliptical hooves were a silvery grey with a light blue lining their edges. Her mane and tail were turquoise with white cream highlights. Large sapphire blue eyes regarded them, holding an unreachable intelligence and missing the iris and pupil. A slight glow radiated from her, but it didn't hurt to look at her, the light only tickled the eyes, like a ghost.

After a few seconds Rosey found it hard to keep eye contact with her. She had no idea if it was due to respect or their startling power. Trying hard not to look too intimidated, she walked up to the unicorn and bowed her head. She was about to speak but the unicorn beat her to it.

"I apologize for not being here sooner, my Keeper. I was finishing up some things for Addina concerning the spell they're working on for the Scorched Mountain. Just left from there. Thankfully, it seems I arrived just in time."

Rosey heard Rochelle and Alex gasp. *She* was *sent by Addina! And she knows about what my uncle is doing?!*

"Addina sent you? She did say she'd be sending a friend to assist; we just didn't know who," Rosey explained.

"I see, Addina can be a bit...indecisive at times, though I can see how she'd be unsure on who *exactly* to send," the unicorn answered, seeming to think about something before going on. "With so much riding on your success, she was very careful in *who* she sent to assist you and *I* was the final decision." She dipped her head politely. "It's good to meet you, Rosey Mystic, daughter of Esperanza Mystic and Mathew Kingsley. I am Ysandir, Addina's most trusted advisor and dear friend. I'm the main correspondence between Addina and the people. I run errands for her, deal in confidential matters, and handle her affairs." The unicorn's voice wasn't harsh, but Rosey could tell she was someone who was used to being respected and expected it. She went on. "To make sure you have every possible protection, I've been assigned to advise and guide you throughout your journey. I can also ensure your safety." She raised her head proudly. "I'll be joining you, however, I can't always be around. During the more... uneventful parts of your journey, I'll be attending to other duties. I hope this doesn't worry you though. Rest assured, even if I'm not around I'll always be able to sense your presence and well-being."

Rosey's brows furrowed. "How?"

Ysandir shook her mane. "Addina. She has a mental link with all the unicorns and pegasi of this world, including me, and she can track your health through the necklace she gave you. If you befall any trouble, Addina can relay it to me if I happen to be away, though, I wouldn't be away from you if you were in a dangerous situation to begin with."

Rosey squirmed under her gaze. Given the reputations of the unicorns and pegasi, a part of her was thrilled to have one escorting her on her journey, but she couldn't help feeling like Ysandir's help was the halfhearted gift an absentee parent gives you after returning home from a year long trip.

"Not that I'm not ecstatic to have you helping us," Rochelle said, "but shouldn't you stay with Rosey *every* moment of the way? There's a...*you know what* out there." She said this last under her breath...eyes darting around suspiciously.

The members of their group were all well aware of the assassin, Wolvereen had assured her that even Eglen knew about the mysterious brute. But it wasn't general knowledge to be spoken of lightly, thankfully the rest of the Gold and Silver Guards escorting them were off tending to the collapsed tunnels and scouting the perimeter right now, so the group was alone in the clearing with Ysandir. Still, better to be safe than sorry.

Ysandir had the same thought. She drew close and whipped her horn around while whispering a few words under her breath. The tip of her horn gave off a slight glow and a glowing blue shield suddenly surrounded them. As an added bonus, it also kept out some of the cold, trapping their warmth inside.

"We're now in a protected sound barrier so we can speak freely," she explained. "I'm well aware of the assassin, Rochelle. I can assure you if the assassin comes close to Rosey, hidden or not, I will know. That I can promise," she proclaimed. She then stepped closer, her pupil-less and iris-less eyes staring straight into Rosey's. "Why do you think I came here so quickly?" she whispered and everyone went deadly silent.

Rosey's eyes widened and her mouth fell open slightly. Slowly, her body grew cold and she started to shiver, suddenly alert for the black cloaked, humanoid figure that was the assassin. Her hand went for the crystal and it grew warm at her touch, soothing the sudden panic shooting through her. A thousand questions shot through her mind all at once...thankfully, her breathing remained calm and she settled on one.

"How did you know," she managed to choke out.

"Addina, myself, and many others have studied the poison infecting this world ever since she found it. There's a sort of scent and other..." she paused, searching for the right word, "...aspects we've managed to identify. Not enough for us to use a tracking spell to find the assassin, but enough that if they come close to you, we can pick up on it, or identify it if we ourselves happen upon them. Addina sensed it drawing near to Rosey and alerted me, so here I am," she explained, raising her head proudly.

"Care to share the scent with us?" Wolvereen asked and the other animals of their group nodded eagerly.

Ysandir put her ears back, looking apologetic. "We've shared what we've found with every other grown unicorn and pegasus in the Settled Valley...but, unfortunately it's too species specific for any other creature besides a unicorn or pegasus to identify." Wolvereen huffed disbelievingly at this. "But, trust me, when I leave Rosey's side it's for good reason. I'll be on the hunt, along with every other one of my Settled Valley companions."

There was absolute silence at this, the mind-numbing reality of Ysandir's words hit Rosey like a ton of bricks. *Addina hasn't just been laying around doing nothing, no one has!* The Silver Goddess' words about the poison came back to Rosey then. *Now that they have the actual poison, they can study it. And that's exactly what they've been doing! I'm such a child...*She bit her lip.

"Did you see them then?" Rosey asked softly, and everyone tensed, waiting for the answer. The unicorn had come running, supposedly because the assassin had shown up, so it stood to reason that the unicorn had crossed paths with them.

Rosey held her breath as Ysandir answered, "I did not. I saw that you were well protected inside the Goddess's crystal, so I leaped into the battle. I could sense the assassin was nearby, but I couldn't find them. There were too many Raptors and Gorons getting in my way, I believe on purpose, trying to keep me distracted. I still enjoyed killing them though," she admitting raising her head and stomping her right hoof.

Wolvereen cursed, ears back. "Are you serious! You have the scent, or whatever it is, so how could you have *not* found them?!"

Ysandir turned to him, looking not in the least bit intimidated, "Really...losing a 'scent' amongst the blood, guts, gore, and stench of Gorons and Raptors about...in the heat of a battle, how strange indeed?" she stated, sarcastically. Rosey could almost see her eyes rolling. "My goal was to be sure Rosey was safe, and she was, all the rest is just extra. Though, I admit," she said, turning now to Rosey, "I regret deeply that I couldn't find them and kill them for you, my Keeper." She bowed her head then.

Wolvereen's ears went parallel with the ground, embarrassed. "Yes, well...happens to us all," he admitted, shamefaced.

Rosey nodded, sobering up. "It's okay, I understand. I appreciate Addina sending you, and...so much more. Please thank her for me when you see her next?"

Ysandir stared at her for a bit before saying, "I will. But for now, I'll remain by your side. It's obvious from today's battle that the enemy is now aware of your presence, so we no longer have the safety of secrecy. There's far too much Raptor activity going on for comfort and the assassin may come back to finish the job, though I don't sense them anymore." Her blue gaze flicked about them, as if seeing and looking for things Rosey couldn't. Rosey's eyes followed hers, but she saw no evidence of the struggle that had taken place. "I only wish I'd gotten here sooner, but it's a bit hard to compete with a collapsing cave system."

"Agreed, but I have to ask...where's all the...." Rosey asked, eyes flitting about the clearing.

"Blood and guts?" Ysandir finished for her and Rosey nodded. Ysandir flicked her tail absentmindedly. "I cleaned up a bit. Those nasty brute's carcasses shouldn't be rotting all over the nice scenery."

Rosey shivered at the image but didn't doubt Ysandir's words. She was a unicorn, cleaning up dead bodies was probably child's play for her magic.

"How did they find out about me? Do the Goddesses know?" Rosey asked, turning to Wolvereen and Nagura. They'd no doubt gone to see the Silver Goddess by now, or heard from her or the Golden Goddess in some way?

"I didn't report to the Goddesses after the battle, too busy helping the other guards. Nagura did though," Wolvereen said, turning to his mate.

Nagura sighed and stepped forward. "We have something to tell you, Rosey," she admitted, catching everyone's attention. "Ysandir's report has helped add fire to a theory the Silver Goddess has. She's asked me to share it with you and bring everyone up to date on everything."

Wolvereen's ears pricked, looking startled. "Everything?" he asked.

"Everything," Nagura agreed, sighing again. "Let me begin by saying that Argno was attacked last night."

They gaped at her, shocked.

"Wait, Nagura. Please, let me explain," Eglen insisted, speaking up. Rosey glanced at him, surprised.

"No, Eglen," Nagura said. "Let us *both* explain."

Rosey looked between them amazed while Noly leaned into her legs for comfort. Rosey felt cold...and it had nothing to do with the terribly cold wind blowing through the clearing. The group quieted down and listened as Nagura, Wolvereen, and Eglen explained what had happened the night before with Argno. As they spoke, Rosey felt anger threading her veins from head to toe. She hadn't known the Dragnagor long, but he was a friend of the Goddesses and a respected messenger, the assault was personal.

"Argno is out cold, so we haven't been able to question him," Nagura explained. "It seems pretty likely that the attacker got something out of him, perhaps Rosey's location in the caves? Until he wakes up, we really don't know."

"Does the Goddess think the attacker was the assassin?" Rosey asked bluntly. Anger had replaced the cold in her heart, though the two went hand in hand. Nagura nodded so Rosey asked next, "Why was I not told about this?"

Nagura's ears went parallel with the ground, ashamed. "The Goddess didn't want you to worry about something that she and the guards *thought* they could take care of," she explained. "I admit, we were wrong."

Rosey sighed, rubbing her head. *So that's what was worrying the Goddess this morning.* This was getting out of hand. An attack had happened and only *now* was she hearing about it! If she was going to be the Keeper, this was the kind of stuff she needed to know about. But lecturing them on that wouldn't help.

"That's not all," Nagura went on. She took a deep breath and then explained what had happened with the Goddess and the woman her powers had confronted. "She believes *that* woman was the assassin *and* that she was behind it all. That she's the one who's been dictating the Raptor and Goron movements, that she attacked Argno, *and* that she tried to approach Rosey on the battlefield today, trying to get to her. Ysandir has now confirmed that last, at least." The wolf even divulged how they'd found a blackened body of a golden guard, one who's head had been cut off and been stabbed through the chest by a sword, a humanoid weapon.

If any of them had doubted Ysandir's senses concerning the assassin before, it was now thoroughly gone. There was stunned silence all around, imagining just how close Rosey had come to being within the enemy's hands. If it hadn't been for the Goddess's crystal, things might have been very different. Though, she doubted Ysandir would have let the assassin get near her.

Noly whined. "Is it safe here anymore, should we stay?"

"Do you really think we'd be here *talking* if it wasn't safe, dog? There are guards scouting ahead as we speak," Wolvereen explained, looking annoyed. "And with a unicorn here, I'm sure any remaining Raptors or Gorons have turned tail and fled...the assassin obviously has." His gaze rested on Ysandir who silently nodded. "I thought Eyasha took care of the Raptors?" He whispered to Nagura questioningly.

"Obviously there were more," Nagura answered, unsure.

"Anything else we should know?" Rosey asked, hoping there wasn't.

"One last thing," Nagura said. "From her crystal's interaction with the assassin, and the collapse of the caves, the Goddess now believes that the assassin is a human magikin."

"What? Why's that?" Rosey asked, confused. "What exactly happened today? How *did* the Raptors collapse the tunnels?"

"Cocoa reported a Raptor was carrying a Time Release Spell," Nagura explained.

At this, Alex cursed and threw up his hands.

Rosey frowned. "What's that?"

"The same thing as a time bomb, but with pressurized energy instead of explosives," Alex explained and Rosey's eyes widened. "The magikin condenses a massive amount of explosive pressure into a sphere and covers it in a barrier that will dissipate at a certain rate, adjusted based on the time the magikin needs. Once the barrier dissipates, the pressure is released all at once as an energy bomb."

"A Raptor started digging right above the caves and the others surrounded it, protecting it, then boom, the spell went off," Nagura finished.

"Wait...so you're saying there was fighting going on up here *while* we were down there?" Rosey asked, cocking her head.

Nagura looked away, confirming her suspicions. "We had Cocoa running back and forth with information just in case."

"Good thing too, or their plan might have worked," Wolvereen huffed.

They all shot him a look and he scuffed a paw in the ground.

Nagura bowed her head to Rosey. "I apologize, my Keeper. We should have told you, but we didn't want you to worry when there was nothing you could have done."

Rosey shook her head, too amazed to speak. There were a million things zooming through her mind, but nothing felt right to say out loud so she stayed quiet.

"Well, how about no more secrets from now on?" Hazel stated firmly from Rosey's shoulders, almost giving Rosey a heart attack. She'd been so quiet till now that Rosey had almost forgotten she was there. "We're in danger here as much as you are," her little eyes looked the six-foot-tall wolves up and down, "so keeping the truth from us is only going to hurt us more, not help us."

The wolves were moved to silence and Rochelle and Alex exchanged glances. The horses kept flicking looks back and forth between Ysandir and the others, nervously fidgeting so close to a unicorn.

"So...how did the Raptors get a Time Release Spell?" Bronzo asked, snorting.

Filla's ears flicked. "Yeah, aren't Raptors and Gorons supposed to be powerless? At least in terms of magic and elements?"

"The assassin gave it to them, that's why the Goddess believes she's a magikin?" Sarabie deduced, ears flicking forward. Her gaze rested on Rosey like a mother protectively eyeing her foal.

Nagura nodded, confirming their suspicions. A shudder passed through them at the idea and Rosey could tell a bunch of them were about to start talking all at once. She closed her eyes, her mind really wasn't interested in sorting out all of the possibilities and theories they were about to voice, but Ysandir's loud whinny hushed them.

"Just because she has a humanoid form doesn't mean she's an actual human. Remember, a demon can detach pieces of itself and those pieces can take on the shape of anything they want. And just because the Raptors used a Time Release Spell doesn't mean *they* now have magical powers, either. Or that the assassin is a magikin. The assassin could have *forced* a magikin to make the spell *for* her." She turned to Nagura. "The assassin being a human magikin is a plausible theory, I admit, but until we are able to apprehend the assassin or meet them face to face, we know nothing for certain."

Nagura opened her mouth to argue, but Rosey stepped between them, holding up her hands to quiet them. "I agree with Ysandir," she said. "There's no sense driving ourselves crazy with things we don't completely know." She hoped she sounded convincing. "Still, I appreciate everything you've told us Nagura. It's more information than we had before and that's better than nothing" The wolf nodded. "We obviously can't use the tunnels anymore and it's getting late." She looked to the sky where the sun was dipping below the tree line. The afternoon was way behind them now and Rosey didn't want to travel at night. "We're definitely not going to make it to the Volcano before nightfall. Wolvereen." He stood to attention. "I believe I read somewhere that this path has a Travelers Stop on it? Right?"

Wolvereen dipped his head, eyes glowing proudly. "Indeed, my Keeper. It's down the path a bit, but not far."

"Good, that's our destination. Let's get going."

Traveler Stops were safe locations where travelers could make camp for the night while going from place to place. They were built with powerful magic and elemental techniques to ward off Raptors and Gorons. There were many different kinds and designs depending on the one who'd made it. Rosey remembered reading that this path's particular Traveler's Spot had been made with Big Thorn Bristle Weed. It was a thick vine-like weed that produced poisonous thorns as large as a human head and smelled horrible to Raptors and Gorons. To them it was disorienting, annoying, and itchy; the equivalent of having that sneezing feeling without sneezing.

Ysandir stepped toward Rosey. "I'll scout the road ahead and check back in occasionally. Never fear, I'll be watching."

Before Rosey could say anything, the barrier around them dissipated and Ysandir turned tail and leaped through the woods, disappearing through the winter greenery as if a part of the landscape.

Rosey gawked at where she'd been standing, amazed, then turned to Nagura and Wolvereen.

"Don't tell me you know her, too?" Her gaze flicked to Eglen and he shook his head.

Nagura answered. "No, we've never seen or met a unicorn before, but the Goddesses have mentioned getting visits from Addina's advisors every now and then...though they never mentioned who or what they were." Her blue gaze rested on where Ysandir had been standing.

"Really?" Alex said, eyes wide. "Addina sends unicorns and pegasi to talk with people on her behalf?"

Wolvereen nodded. "Sometimes...especially if she can't do it herself. I hear her advisors drop in and out of places all the time, often with Raptor and Goron reports. They're kind of like Addina's messengers." He flicked an ear. "They're also very secretive, rarely ever letting anyone but a World Leader see them face to face." He grimaced as if the idea made his stomach turn. "I never liked that about them..."

Rosey considered for a moment. "I guess we should just be happy Addina sent one to help. We're certainly much safer with her than without her." They all nodded agreement.

Quickly composing themselves, they fished out their winter gear from their travel bags. Without the cave's constant temperature or Ysandir's barrier, the cold was quickly nipping at their hands and feet. When they were ready Nagura took the lead, assuring everyone the way was clear and thoroughly checked. Ysandir concurred when she randomly appeared from some nearby bushes, startling them all to death before, just as quickly, disappearing again. After what had happened, it seemed hard to believe the way was safe but staying put was out of the question. Without any more delays they got on their way, Wolvereen bringing up the rear.

It's too bad we can't use those handy vortexes unicorns and pegasi make! Rosey thought with annoyance as they rode. For some reason only unicorns, pegasi, and magikins could use their vortexes to instantly travel from place to place. The limitations obviously had something to do with magic, but it thoroughly made sure that Rosey's travel methods were limited to the usual ones.

After about thirty minutes' walk, they arrived at a clearing surrounded by an impenetrable dome of Big Thorn Bristle Weed. Walking up to the dome Wolvereen spoke into it and the vines moved forming an entrance. Inside, Rosey spied a round fire pit at the center, soft mulch underfoot, and a single oculus above letting in light. When they'd all entered, the vines fell back into place as if the opening had never existed. The woven vines were thick enough to make getting in impossible but unwound enough to let in light and the thorns pointed outward away from the interior.

For a moment, they all paused and took a deep breath. They'd traveled all the way with nerves firing on end, now they could relax. Rosey quickly helped set up camp, removing Sarabie's gear and getting out her bed roll. She positioned herself close to the fire Alex started in the pit. He took up a place beside her and Rochelle took the other side. They prepared dinner and ate in relative silence, weariness dragging them down. Wolvereen hunted, bringing back two non-sentient wild deer for himself, Eglen, and Nagura to share. They ate outside the dome so as not to make a bloodied mess.

Ysandir checked in, literally phasing through the Big Thorn Bristle Weed wall like it wasn't there, and again scaring the hell out of everyone gathered. Still, she dutifully reported that all was silent and that the assassin, Raptors, and Gorons had indeed gone. They could rest assured she'd keep up a constant watch all night. Wolvereen and Nagura were adamant that the guards were also keeping a tight patrol. Despite their assurances, Rosey couldn't help but wonder what other tricks the enemy had up their sleeve.

As Rosey was walking back from the outhouse, she heard Wolvereen and Nagura talking through the wall of their dome. Something about Wolvereen's tone made her pause and listen.

"Nagura, please...don't you think you should be more careful? That was a close call back there. There could be another Raptor attack and..."

He was cut off by Nagura's sudden growl. "And if they do attack, I'll kill them as I did today. Won't I?!"

Wolvereen relented. "Of course, dear," he said without further remark.

Rosey shivered, feeling guilty for eavesdropping and quickly moved on, but found their conversation odd. After the battle, she could understand Wolvereen being a little on edge for his mate's wellbeing but it was strange to hear Nagura react so harshly? She'd have expected Nagura to express worry for *Wolvereen's* safety as well, not snap at him? She shook her head; their relationship was none of her business.

After dinner they sat and talked. Eglen quickly became the center of attention; he was a born story teller and had everyone watching him as he told tales from his travels. Wolvereen, sitting side by side with his mate and showing none of the unrest Rosey had heard earlier, listened intently as if Eglen were divulging secrets.

A few hours later, everyone began to settle down and doze off, but Rosey found herself wide awake. Looking up from her bed roll she gazed through the oculus in the ceiling at the stars and found the gryphon constellation Alex had showed her a few days ago. The sudden image of the see-through woman she'd seen during the battle came rushing back. Had it been real, or the product of her panic? She didn't want to think about it.

Alex rolled over in his bed roll and noticed the constellation. He smiled and was about to open his mouth but afraid he'd launch into a long lecture, she put a finger to his lips before he could say anything.

"Don't..." she said with a smile.

He smiled back. "Wouldn't dream of it."

CHAPTER FIFTEEN

A Nagging Feeling

Everyone woke at dawn, eager to get moving. After eating a simple breakfast, Eglen, Nagura, Wolvereen, and Ysandir checked their surroundings with the other guards while the others packed up camp. When the wolves and Eglen returned they didn't come alone. Calra, the lieutenant of the Silver Guards came with them. She bowed to Rosey.

"The guards have thoroughly checked the perimeter, my Keeper. Your way is secure." Her gaze flicked between Rosey and Ysandir, amazement in her exquisite eyes.

Rosey hid a laugh. "Thank you, Lieutenant. Please let the Goddesses know that Ysandir," she indicated the unicorn, "has joined me. She's the promised friend Addina sent to assist me."

Ysandir stepped forward saying, "The Golden and Silver Guards have my and Addina's thanks for your exemplary work all of these long weeks. Please know that I will be sure Rosey gets to her ship safely from here, if a larger escort is needed, we will contact you."

Calra nodded curtly. "Of course. May your journey be swift and safe." She bowed again before turning to leave.

Not wasting any time, they mounted and set off along the trail, Wolvereen bringing up the rear. As they rode, Rosey took in the crisp winter scents of early morning. It smelled so normal as if there wasn't some sickly poison eating away at the planet's very core. A gentle snow started up and she stuck her tongue out, catching a snowflake. She was suddenly reminded of long winter days growing up in Neran and playing in the snow with Rochelle and Alex. She sighed, her breath billowing on cold air.

Two hours later they arrived at the volcano unscathed and in one piece. The group sighed with relief as they examined the rocky landscape. The volcano was a sure sign of safety but an inevitable sign of farewell. Rosey tried not to think about it but Nagura was already turning to their group with a look of sadness.

"Well, it's time for me to return," she said softly.

Rosey dismounted and came to her. Without pause she hugged the wolf's thick furred neck, feeling hot tears burning her eyes. The sudden emotion surprised Rosey.

She pulled away, wiping her eyes. "Are you sure you won't stay?" she asked.

Nagura was completely intent on returning to her duties as Commander and Rosey had no right to ask her to do otherwise. Still, Rosey couldn't help but think it was odd. Why bring her to the volcano only to turn back now? Why not escort her to the ship? Her mind flashed to what she'd heard between Wolvereen and Nagura last night. Could it have something to do with that?

Nagura shook her head. "I'm sorry Rosey, but I've got some very important...business to return to. I can't stay with you." Her gaze rested on Wolvereen for a second and something passed between them. His ears went parallel with the ground, eyes softening. "Just know that I'll be rooting for you all the way. I expect to see you back here as soon as you're done, you hear?"

Rosey nodded and hugged her close again. "Thanks for everything."

"Of course, it's the least I could do." Her blue gaze settled on Rosey suddenly. "Be a good Keeper."

Rosey nodded firmly. "I intend to."

Nagura smiled and licked her face then said goodbye to the others. When she faced Wolvereen they rubbed faces affectionately, licking each other methodically as if memorizing each other's scents. To finish, they touched foreheads, standing still for a few moments. A cold wind stirred their fur but neither moved. After a few moments they backed away.

"Protect Rosey at all costs," Nagura said firmly to the gathered team and they nodded. Her gaze rested on Rosey. "She's our last hope."

With a nod to Ysandir as she passed, Nagura turned and ran back the way she'd come, silver armor flashing in the morning light. Rosey watched her go and suddenly her heart lurched. It was the same feeling she'd had when her uncle had stayed behind. *They're hiding something…both of them. Secrets and plans they just won't share.*

Alex patted her back comfortingly. "We should get moving, Rosey," he said gently.

She sniffed, realizing she'd been standing there, watching the undergrowth were Nagura had been. She never realized how much she'd meant to her.

Taking a deep breath, Rosey indicated the Volcano. "Let's survey the area. Alex is right, we need to find a place to make camp. After all, there's no telling how long collecting the element might take."

The others gave the volcano hesitant looks. Though Rosey had never seen a volcano up close before, she was sure it wasn't supposed to look like this. A normal volcano wouldn't be radiating an area of heat around itself to keep it a constant, tropical temperature when everything else was covered in snow.

"Wow," Alex said, gazing upward. "It really does keep it warm all year around, doesn't it?"

For some reason, the two-mile radius of magic-filled land around the volcano also kept it warm all year long. It might be easy to blame the Elemental Well for the anomaly, but Rosey and her friends knew better. The Molt Volcano had always had this power. *It must be fueled by one of the wild spells Alex said are always active,* she thought remembering what he'd said. However, those same spells were also what made it one of the safest destinations on the planet. Not a single Raptor or Blood Goron could approach it this close. Many had tried in the past, but they were immediately melted from the inside out upon entry. All others could come and go as they pleased. There were a lot of theories about this oddity.

Some said it was completely random, like all the other wild spells here, while others insisted that the anomaly was a direct result of the Goron and Raptor's actions on the planet. The volcano was literally exacting vengeance and retribution against the beasts that had killed innocents and ravaged the land. Rosey didn't have any real opinion about it, she was just happy the volcano's protection meant they could rest easy while they were here.

As they approached, Rosey paused as she suddenly felt something touch her consciousness. She touched her forehead, taken aback as a nagging feeling blossomed in her temple. It was weird but also good, like heat, fire, and lava were calling to her all at once. Without a doubt she knew it was the element. Excitement bubbled through her. *The element! I'm actually sensing the element! Could this really be happening?* She wanted to squeal with delight but remained calm and decided to hold off saying anything till they were settled. Besides, it felt...private, like something only she should know.

Looking ahead, Rosey saw a line where the snow ended and warmth began. It was like being at the border of two countries and having one foot on either side. Only, one side was twenty degrees and the other was seventy. They all paused unsure. From the looks on their faces, they were all thinking about the stories they'd heard.

Hazel sniffed and jumped from Rosey's shoulders to Sarabie's back, perching on the riding gear. "You think we'll melt if we enter?" she asked spookily, flicking her tail. Noly whined slightly.

"Only if you're a Raptor or Goron, kitten," Wolvereen said, joining Rosey's side. His giant head was level with Hazel's.

She flicked an ear at him. "You never know. I could be?" She grinned at him and he huffed.

Rosey smiled at them, but then saw Ysandir from the corner of her eye. The giant unicorn continued walking, passing harmlessly into the Volcanos' perimeter. She turned and gave them quizzical looks as if just noticing they'd stopped. Self-consciously, the group hurried through without incident and sighed at the sudden warmth, pausing long enough for Rosey, Rochelle, and Alex to remove their winter gear before moving on.

They took their time, careful of the large piles of fallen rocks that covered most of the barren land. Small patches of long grasses were dispersed here and there and several large divots jotted the ground with awkward and random holes, hiding behind immense boulders and scraggly bushes.

As they walked Noly ran along Rosey's side. "So, you see anything that looks like an Elemental Well anywhere?"

They all cast anxious glances about them, unsure. They were just as new to this as Rosey was and, admittedly, had no idea what they were looking for. Their eyes eventually settled on Rosey, but she had nothing beside the nagging in her head.

"Hey, Ysandir, maybe you could give us a clue?" Rochelle asked tentatively. "You know, point us in the right direction?" She held her arms out to the side in invitation but the unicorn shook her head.

"I'm sorry young ones, but I'm unable to offer assistance outside of Rosey's protection," Ysandir answered. "Everything else is up to her."

She offered nothing else and the others exchanged glances. Even Wolvereen looked disappointed by the unicorn's confession. With no leads and no apparent direction, they continued on.

Eglen trotted up to Rosey's side. "Shall we split up? We'll cover more ground that way?" he suggested and Rosey nodded.

"Sounds good to me."

With the threat of Gorons and Raptors gone, there was no reason not to search on their own. There was a brief conversation about the assassin and if the volcano's protection would include her or not, but Ysandir assured them that she'd be able to sense the assassin if she got within a hundred feet of Rosey, and the fiend was nowhere near this location. Still, to be safe, Ysandir would stick close to Rosey. That was good enough for them so they split into groups. Wolvereen, Noly, Hazel, and Rochelle went off in one, the horses and Eglen in another, and Rosey, Ysandir, and Alex in the last.

Rosey and Alex scrambled over random rock falls, Ysandir behind them. They walked for a few minutes then stopped to catch their breath. All the while, the nagging feeling was growing stronger. Rosey ignored it as it pounded at her, drawing her closer to the Volcano. She needed to get her team settled at a camp first before she could try doing anything drastic about the element.

After finding nothing suitable for a campsite Rosey's group returned to their rendezvous spot. Once there, Wolvereen's group led them to a place they'd found hidden in a grassy spot bordered by large rocks. They set up camp and prepared lunch while Noly, Hazel, Wolvereen, and Eglen left to hunt. While Rochelle got a fire going, Alex and Rosey took off the horse's gear and brushed them down. They whinnied their thanks then left to graze. Ysandir joined them and, to Rosey's amazement, she rolled in the dirt with the others, kicking up her hooves happily. *Once a horse, always a horse.* Noly and Hazel returned triumphantly, Hazel with two mice and Noly with a squirrel, followed soon by Wolvereen and Eglen who brought a wild boar. They offered Rosey, Rochell, and Alex a section of meat and they accepted.

After everyone had eaten, Rosey stood up and paced away from the fire a few yards. She needed to stretch her legs, and the nagging feeling was really starting to drive her crazy. It beat at her forehead, pummeling her like a bad headache without the pain. It was like someone was repeating the same phrase over and over again in her head. It felt uncomfortable and she was certain it was coming from inside the volcano. She rubbed her temples and tried to relax.

Alex and Rochelle came up and stood beside her, studying the cliffs. Hazel and Noly sniffed at their heels curiously.

"Is everything all right?" Alex asked gently. "You've been fidgeting all day. Don't think we haven't noticed." He tapped his finger on his leg, drawing closer to her. "Is it the element?"

"Yeah," she answered simply. She smiled suddenly, overcome with joy. "I didn't think...being a non-elemental, I half expected nothing to happen." She paused, studying the volcano as if in a trance. "But I can feel something! I'm actually *feeling* it!"

Rochelle smiled slightly as if she understood the feeling.

"Okay," Alex said firmly, glancing at Rochelle. "Let's do something about it. What do you feel? Where do you need to go?"

Rochelle joined her on the other side. "Tell us, it's all you at this point."

"She's right, Rosey," Hazel added. "We got you here, but you have to do the rest."

She nodded as she turned to them. "I know. This is going to sound strange but...I want Alex and Rochelle to come with me *into* the volcano. I don't want all of us trying to scale it at once so I think we should stick with a small group."

Alex's brows furrowed, but his voice was calm. "You're sure? You know where to go?"

"Yeah, I have this...feeling that I need to get in there. There's something pulling me. The element, it's calling to me. At least that's what I believe is going on...I don't know..." She knew she sounded a little strange but the nagging was getting worse and she could barely think straight. She gripped the crystal at her neck and it seemed to pulse, sending waves through her as if supporting her assumption.

"How's your chest?" Rochelle asked.

If Rosey's head wasn't aching so badly she'd probably have come up with some clever retort, but she was too distracted for that.

"It's fine. For a change it's my head that's bothering me, not my chest." She rubbed it and Alex and Rochelle exchanged worried glances. "Let's just get going, okay?"

Alex gripped her shoulder. "Sure thing. We'll do this together, but safely. Let us grab some gear."

"I'm coming..." Noly began but Rosey cut her off.

"You'll do no such thing!" she snapped and Noly's eyes glistened sadly. Rosey sighed; her headache was getting worse. She went over to Noly and bent down to gently rub her head, softening her voice. "You can't come with me this time, okay. I need you here to look after the others." Her gaze flickered to Hazel, sitting nearby. "And you too, missy. Please."

Dog and cat exchanged glances and Hazel bowed her head to Noly, indicating she agreed. Noly whined and placed her head in Rosey's underarm.

"Okay, but you better come back!" she panted sternly.

Rosey smiled and combed her hand through her fur. "Of course, you daft fur ball! Of course!"

Alex took a deep breath and let it out slowly, Rosey's words running through his head. It wasn't normal for her to be so jittery, but Alex could tell the time had come. She was sensing the element. *It's finally happening, everything Rochelle and I talked about is happening!* he thought, his mind racing. Though it should have been good news, it was only painful for Alex.

Rosey was truly taking her first steps as the Keeper and that scared him. He'd always looked to her and Rochelle for fun, a distraction from the horrors beyond Neran's walls. Now, everything was different. Now, she was looking to him for support and he felt both excited and unnerved by her strength. Alex couldn't imagine trying to cope as she had. How would he feel knowing his parents had been some powerful heroes that saved the world? *Only to be brutally murdered by a terrifying assassin?* An image of his mother came to mind, her bloodied body lying dead at his feet, joined by his lifeless father.

Alex shuddered and pushed the images away. He knew better, his parents were safe at their secret hideout, living happily with Rochelle's parents. He fingered the letter they'd written him, hidden in his pant leg pocket as if its physical presence was proof they were all right. The Golden Goddess had given both him and Rochelle a letter from their parents and assured them that any correspondence between their parents and them in the future would be secured by herself if needed.

Despite the ache of separation he and Rochelle felt being apart from their families, they both knew it was for good reason. They'd feared disrupting the friendship between Rosey and their children. Their presence might distract Alex and Rochelle from keeping Rosey safe if they were worried about their parent's safety and vice versa on their part. Still, Alex wished his mother was here with him, chasing away all his fears like she used to when he was a child, except this time it wasn't a ghost but the fear that something would happen to Rosey. She was one of his closest friends and he didn't want to lose her.

They left Rosey to continue staring at the volcano with Noly and Hazel while they returned to camp to get some gear. Nearing the camp, Alex drew close to Rochelle and grabbed her arm, gently pulling her away from the others. They ducked out of sight behind one of the large stones that were surrounding the clearing. Casting a glance around to be sure no one saw them, he looked at Rochelle, his face a mask of confusion.

Rochelle eyed him worriedly. "What is it? What's wrong?"

"I'm not ready for this," he said suddenly, taking a shaky breath.

She regarded him knowingly. "Alex, we knew this day was coming when Rosey was chosen. She's not just Rosey anymore. She's the Keeper now!" She smiled but he could tell she didn't believe her own words.

"I know, it's just…I wish I was more prepared. I didn't…I didn't think it would make me feel this way. I'm…I'm afraid that…."

"…that she'll die like Esperanza did?" Rochelle's voice was flat and clear. It was obvious she had the same fears.

Alex nodded; eyes glossy. He was prepared for this, wasn't he? He'd known things were going to change when she'd been chosen, but it all seemed so surreal now. How could she just go from being the Rosey of Neran to their Keeper? It was different, more different than he'd realized.

"The battle yesterday…I," he stuttered, looking down. "It got to me…I…I don't understand why I'm feeling this now all of a sudden."

He shook his head but Rochelle laughed slightly and his gaze met hers. She flashed him that brilliant wide grin. "I did the same thing…back at the Golden Goddess's castle." He blinked shocked and she went on, "She'd just given me my parent's letter and I was reading it in the common room…" she trailed of, her eyes downcast. "It hit me then…that overwhelming sense of change…that things were never going to be the same. That all our years of fun were gone and my friend's lives would now be in danger. I started crying…and I couldn't stop." She took a deep breath. "John came into the room to read and found me. He comforted me. He told me the same thing had happened to him when Esperanza was chosen, but not until she'd already collected three of her elements. One day, he'd just sat down in his room and started crying."

They were silent for a moment and Rochelle sniffed, "John said that we will need to be Rosey's rock, her foundation, and her support. But we will also have to support each other. And…it doesn't matter if or when we break down and cry a little, it only matters what we do the rest of the time." Rochelle held him at arm's length, meeting his gaze, eyes focused. "We're here to make sure that what happened to Esperanza doesn't happen to Rosey. Are you with me?"

Alex's mouth hung open, shaken by his sudden emotion. He took a swig of water from his water skin then hung it back on his belt. For a few seconds his mind skipped through all the days he'd spent training with Rosey, running through Neran, playing games on warm summer days, and sleepovers under the stars. Her history as the daughter of the planet's most powerful warriors had never stopped him from seeing her as his friend. He couldn't let it affect him now. He nodded firmly, suddenly feeling much better.

"Bring it on," he said, finding strength in the milky cream depths of Rochelle's eyes.

"Good, now let's do this!"

"You better," came a gruff voice from behind Alex.

Both of them jumped, letting out startled yelps, but it was only Wolvereen. His giant head peered at them from around the boulder, red eyes flashing in the low light of day.

"Sorry for eavesdropping," he said, "but did you honestly think I didn't see you two duck behind here? I wanted to be sure everything was okay."

He came the rest of the way around the boulder and sat down, looking the two of them up and down. He'd taken off his armor for a change and the difference was startling, he was the same fluffy furred wolf, but his midnight black pelt made him seem more like a shadow than a solid form.

Alex gulped, but straightened his posture, refusing to be intimidated.

The giant wolf sighed. "The Battle of Rustle Rock," he said suddenly.

Alex blinked and exchanged a confused glance with Rochelle. There'd been a lot of battles during the war and Alex had read about pretty much all of them or had had a lecture on it from school. He searched his brain for the Battle of Rustle Rock and managed to remember a small Raptor skirmish near Neran's southern coast where Rustle Rock was, a giant cliff overhanging the sea that was periodically chipped away by the ocean every year.

"What about it?" Rochelle asked curiously, leaning against the boulder.

"That's where *I* broke down," the wolf confessed in a low voice, surprising them.

"You? No way...really?" Rochelle asked, flabbergasted.

Wolvereen nodded. "I almost went over the edge, but I managed to knock the Raptor off instead. That was the first time I'd come close to death...and Nagura and I..." he stopped, closing his eyes suddenly, looking away. He huffed and got to his feet stretching, then said. "Do what you gotta' do...but I want you two to know that, for your first battle, you did really well. Be proud."

The three of them smiled at each other with respect. Then Noly's head suddenly popped out from between Wolvereen's legs.

"What's going on," she whispered curiously.

Wolvereen made a sound they never thought they'd hear from him. He squealed...but in such a low whistly way that it was almost silent. He jumped in the air about two feet and bounded away form Noly, fur suddenly fluffed up and tail raised high.

"DOG! Don't you ever do that again!" He snarled at her, showing his fangs.

"Do what?" she asked, cocking her head innocently, though Alex was certain from the gleam in her eye that she knew exactly what he meant.

"How long are you all going to talk, Rosey's getting antsy," Hazel asked from Noly's back. She then turned to Wolvereen, "And wolf, you stink. You might want to...lick yourself clean." She then proceeded to slowly lick her paw condescendingly.

Wolvereen glowered at her. "I'm gonna eat you both," he murmured softly, eyes wide.

"I think you three need to get back to the fire so Alex and Rochelle can get going," Ysandir said.

Alex blinked, looking around confused. Where was the unicorn? Rochelle tapped his shoulder and pointed up. His gaze followed hers to stare, dumbfounded at the huge unicorn who was balanced perfectly on the top of the giant boulder.

Rochelle whispered, "How'd she get up there?"

Alex shrugged.

Wolvereen sighed and straightened, then lumbered back towards the camp. "Come on now or Rosey will worry," he ordered, disappearing behind the boulder.

Ysandir turned and expertly jumped to another boulder from her perch, flicking her tail as she went.

Alex smiled, as he followed Noly back to camp with Rochelle. He gathered the rest of the gear, then stared at Wolvereen laying down by the fire, chastising Hazel and Noly for starting to play with one another too close to the fire. Ysandir watched them amused from another perch on a nearby boulder while the horses asked what all the fuss was about. His heart warmed and he had a funny feeling that Rosey would be okay no matter what was to come.

CHAPTER SIXTEEN

A Fiery Guard

Alex and Rochelle joined Rosey who paced from foot to foot anxiously. The others wished them luck as they set off. Following the pull Rosey felt, she led them around the volcano's base to its other side. What had before been a land of mystery was laid out on a silver platter as if she'd been there her whole life. Within minutes she led them straight to a long staircase leading up to a small hole in the side of the volcano that had been missing before. Wordlessly and without hesitation she began climbing, Alex followed with Rochelle bringing up the rear.

"You sure you don't want me to levitate us up there?" Rochelle huffed as they climbed, looking winded. As a queen level elemental, she could easily float all three of them to the top.

Rosey spoke as she climbed, "No, based off what Alex told me, this place is unpredictable. We don't want things to go wrong, elementally or magically."

If she'd been watching them, she'd have seen them exchange aggravated but understanding glances. It made sense after all, but Rosey was focused on only one thing: stopping the pounding nuisance in her head! She didn't feel the sweat beading her temples or tickling her eyes, she just felt the rough stone beneath her hands as she climbed and the steep steps beneath her feet, muscles straining. After a good ten minutes they reached the opening. Inside they took a few moments to catch their breath.

Alex would have put up a protective shield to guard from any smoke and heat but Rosey's earlier warning still applied and they couldn't take any risks. They entered the tunnel cautiously, Rochelle going first, Rosey next, then Alex. The walls were dry patchy black earth and everything smelled of smoke and ash. Rosey squinted but couldn't see any source of light, yet the tunnel was bright enough to see in. Perhaps it was a lingering type of magic?

They hurriedly followed the tunnel, taking turn after turn as if in a maze. Whenever they came to a dead end with multiple tunnels to choose from, Rosey would carefully pace between them, listening to the nagging feeling in her head. When she passed a tunnel that intensified the feeling she'd stop and plunge down the corridor, the others in hot pursuit. They didn't ask questions, trusting that Rosey knew which way to go.

After a while the tunnel they were currently in opened into a large magma crossing where a long and narrow rock bridge stretched over a field of magma flowing down into the earth. Its heat rose in billowing waves, making Rosey's hair dance but far enough away to be bearable.

Rochelle gasped when she saw it and paused, eyes wide, holding out her hands to stop the others. Rosey halted, for the first time doubting the nagging feeling that had led her so far. She and Rochelle exchanged looks but the brunette set her chin and walked across smoothly. Rosey gulped but followed. Going too fast she missed a step and fell against Alex in surprise. He held her steady until she'd regained her balance. She smiled her thanks and turned back to the bridge, walking carefully this time. She trembled, imagining what it would be like to die by lava. She steadied her racing heart and focused on Rochelle's back, not daring to look down.

Finally reaching the other side, she almost lunged for the platform that extended a few feet from the wall. Sweat beaded her forehead, whether from the heat or her terror, she didn't know. She wiped it away, feeling as if she'd been played.

"Where is this *Mother* anyway? I want to slap her!" Rosey said.

Rochelle nodded. "I'll hold her, you aim," she agreed, raising a fist and flashing a wicked grin.

Alex patted their backs and chuckled. "Come on now, the Mother will appear when she thinks it's best. Remember she's still got to test Rosey first, for all we know, this little field trip is a part of that."

They glanced down at the lava and Rosey swallowed. She didn't like that answer but there was little else they could do. They were in the Mother's territory now. It was all up to her and none of them had any idea what an Elemental Well was or wasn't supposed to be and Esperanza hadn't recorded or told anyone about her tests. Apparently, that information was confidential. Not even the Goddesses knew. Had her mother walked across the same pit of lava? Had her tests been the same or were they different? She'd never known.

Suddenly Rosey gripped her head as the nagging feeling raged to life. It was calling to her now, like a distant echo. The noise was so strong her head throbbed. Alex's brows furrowed as he saw her and she quickly straightened not wanting to worry him.

"Let's go, the element's not going to get itself," she said as steadily as she could.

"Wouldn't that be nice," Rochelle muttered, following her. "Wait Rosey, let me go first, okay?"

Rosey stopped and let Rochelle pass before her, then followed, Alex close behind. They continued swiftly, the patchy dirt tunnel suddenly turned into hard, black, rock as they got deeper. Or what they thought was deeper. They'd made so many turns and twists that they could easily be *above* where they'd started. For all she knew they'd gone in circles.

They walked for what must have been an hour until the tunnel opened into a large domed room. Rosey gawked as she spied magma falling down the walls on either side. The heat hit her like an explosion and she reeled back. They immediately backtracked into the hallway and stood, fanning themselves.

"Well, there's no way we're getting through there without some protection," Rochelle said, wiping sweat from her brow.

Rosey nodded. "Okay, magic is out of the question, but Rochelle, maybe you could do something?"

She looked at her friend hopefully but she shook her head, pony tail swishing. "Sorry Rosey, all that would do is make the hot air blow around us as a hot-air tornado." She chuckled slightly at the idea. "I'd have to pull in cold air from the atmosphere and right now, we don't have any...all we have is that." She pointed to the interior of the smoldering room.

Rosey closed her eyes, afraid she'd say that. "Well then, magic it is." She fixed Alex with a cautious eye. "What do you think?"

She was by no means an expert and if he really thought they shouldn't use magic then she'd never force him to. He was the magikin, not her. Both girls waited for him to answer. He studied the ground for a few moments, lost in thought. Finally, he licked his lips and looked up.

"I'll try and cast a protective shield. Once we cross, I'll take it down." He took a breath. "I can't guarantee the magic will work...or even respond...hell, I can't guarantee anything..."

Rosey's brows furrowed; it was the first time she'd heard him sound so unsure about magic.

His gaze rested on her and he set his chin firmly. "But I'm gonna try. Step back."

Rochelle and Rosey followed his advice willingly, stepping a few feet back. Magic spells gone awry were never anything good, literally anything could happen and that was cause for great concern, but they had little choice. They certainly couldn't make it across without something to lessen the heat.

Alex took his wand from its scabbard, quickly uttered the spell, and a pinkish shield surrounded them. The girls released a sigh of relief, the spell had worked. Suddenly, as fast as it had settled the spell phased out making both her and Rochelle jump.

Alex lifted his wand and paused for a moment, eyes closed, brows furrowed, then cursed under his breath. Rosey gave him a surprised look.

"This area is magically dead!" he exclaimed, putting his wand away.

Rosey shook her head. "How can that be? This volcano is supposed to be magic central!?"

Alex nodded. "Yeah, but magic doesn't always spread evenly. This area is what you might call a Magic Black Hole, it's an area that's magically void even though the rest of the area around it is magically charged. They do happen sometimes though no one knows why. We can't go that way, Rosey, I can't protect us from the heat." He slumped against the wall, looking defeated.

Rosey swallowed and licked her dry lips, feeling the heat piercing her face from the room. "That's just great! We *have* to go that way, that's where the feeling is leading me! Couldn't you use the extra magic stored in your wand to work the spell?"

"No, it wouldn't work. Magic Black Holes don't allow *any* magical action, no matter what. That's why they're called black holes. They swallow all the magic that gets near them."

Rosey shook her head angrily. There's no way they could've known about a Magic Black Hole, but that didn't stop her from feeling partly responsible for not being fully prepared. She hadn't thought this through, but the nagging had made it almost impossible for her to think.

She rubbed her head. "There's got to be a way to...maybe...oh!" Suddenly she grabbed her water container hanging from her belt. "Let's pour our water over ourselves and make a run for it. We should be fine as long as we're fast. The heat's not *that* bad."

Alex cocked his head, thinking it over. "I guess we have little option."

Rochelle smiled. "It could work. Let's do it. If worse comes to worse, I can keep a slight breeze going and that with the water should keep us cooler."

The brunette grabbed her own water bottle and together they wet their heads and clothes, leaving a little for consumption.

Rochelle took a step behind Rosey. "Keepers first," she said, indicating the doorway on the other side of the domed room.

Rosey shot her a bemused glance, but knew her friend was still thinking of her. They wanted to be sure she got across in one piece. *Two sets of eyes are better than one.* She had little doubt they'd sacrifice themselves to get her to the other side should something go wrong. The thought dampened her amusement.

Facing the room, she prepared herself and, taking a deep breath, she set off. The heat hit her like a stifling cloud of ugly gas. She coughed and sputtered, but charged ahead, putting her wet hand to her mouth to act as a filter. They were only halfway across when Rosey started to feel completely dry. Though she felt a slight breeze from Rochelle's power, the heat was almost unbearable. The running wasn't helping either but she pushed on. To her utter horror, the doorway before them suddenly drew shut.

They came to a halt, eyeing the doorway with confusion. Almost in unison, they turned around to head the other way, their instincts taking over. They were just about to make it when that door also shut, a wall of magma flowing over it. Alex grabbed Rosey and yanked her backwards to stop her from running into it. This was bad. They were now trapped, but why? For what purpose?

A sudden gurgling sound came from behind them. They turned to see a giant bubble of magma stretching out from the magma waterfall along the walls. It condensed slowly, turning and falling over and over again forming a shape. Rosey drew Andraste, sweat beading her forehead. The room's heat was stifling but she'd just have to push through it. Alex reached for his long dagger, a weapon he only used when magic wasn't an option. Its golden hilt gleamed while the red jewel decorating the pummel reflected the magma. It had been a gift from his mother but Rosey never thought she'd see the day he'd have to use it. Rochelle drew her blade, its pristine blue-studded hilt glimmering. Pink designs etched its pummel, the color of her element. Around her left hand, hot air started to swirl and condense into a fast-spinning mass. Suddenly, hot wind blew around them in fast sprints, cooling their sweating frames just enough to keep them from collapsing. Without Rochelle's power, Rosey knew they'd most likely have fainted by now.

Rosey held Andraste ready and fixed her gaze on the magma-beast before them. It took on the shape of a human covered in multiple layers of hardened lava-armor. As it finished forming, it turned its head and gave her a deadly stare through two glowing eyes that looked like golden holes in its head. Its entire body pulsated magma while hardened armor set over top of it like floating islands. Rosey felt a bead of sweat trickle down her cheek and gritted her teeth. *What in the world is this thing!?*

The armored humanoid took a step towards them and raised its right arm, in it a sword began to form. Around its left arm a lava shield hardened, jutting spikes decorating its rim. With a sickening feeling, Rosey knew what the creature was here for. It wanted a battle. Was this her test? She hadn't expected something this extreme for her first test but there was no turning back, literally. She was trapped, and the only way to move on was to go through the circling giant magma man before her.

Rosey kept a firm stance as she began to circle the beast, Alex and Rochelle by her side, keeping a good distance from the creature. Suddenly a wave of magma reached up from the wall and slammed down in front of Alex and Rochelle, separating them from her. Rosey gasped, shocked. That answered her question. Her friends were okay she was sure, but something had purposefully separated them from one another. This had to be her test. Why else would she be drawn to a spot that just so happened to be a Magic Black Hole? The nagging was humming in her head, telling her to move but Rosey had to block it out and focus on the fight she knew was coming.

With Rochelle trapped, Rosey expected her hot breeze to dissipate. The wind wavered slightly but to her surprise it kept going, giving Rosey just enough breathing room to stay up right. *Rochelle's still keeping it up!* How, was beyond her, but she didn't care, she was just thankful. Still, the heat fell over her like a heavy blanket and she groaned, her breath ragged. Fear and adrenaline buzzed through her limbs and she straightened Andraste. She refused to be beaten!

She gritted her teeth and gave the magma warrior a glaring look. The creature stepped cautiously and Rosey mimicked it, carefully evaluating her opponent as she'd been taught. Finally, the giant made its move and came at her with finesse. She dodged and danced behind it. Swinging her sword, she knocked it off of its feet and used its forward momentum to send it flying head first. The creature flipped and landed on its feet, squatting. It turned and examined her with deadly eyes. *That was a move to simply evaluate my skills,* Rosey thought, moving back into a new stance.

She waited patiently; sweat drenching her shirt and chest, running down her forehead. She wiped her head carefully without breaking eye contact or stance. The thing came at her again in the same manner and Rosey once again dodged around it, but the humanoid placed its feet firmly and brought its sword around, thinking she wasn't able to block, but Rosey had seen this coming. She blocked and used the momentum to gain some distance before neatly landing away from her attacker. The lava humanoid turned to face her again, its blank eyes narrowed. It cocked its head as if impressed. Rosey simply took up another stance. She knew she could not remain on the defensive for long, but she had to wait for the opportune moment and conserve her energy against the searing heat or she'd tire. This fight was all about patience and careful observation.

The humanoid then did something she wasn't expecting. It lifted its arm with the shield towards the air. The shield become gelatinous and reformed itself into a crossbow before aiming at her. Rosey felt her heart race, and she cursed as the creature released an arrow in her direction. *Great!* She thought as she dodged the arrows. *The damn thing can change its weapons!* It wasn't too hard to believe given it hadn't had a sword or a shield the first time it formed. But what else could it do? Could it conjure up monster lava dogs to sic on her? *Nope, I better not tempt fate.* She quickly dodged again, doing her best to avoid the arrows. There was no cover so she was reduced to running away and was feeling pretty happy that her friends couldn't see her right now. Dodging arrows wasn't as graceful as a sword fight.

Rosey eyed the crossbow. It was going to be difficult to take down and she only had one weapon! No, wait, she had two. She remembered Silver Knight and smiled, knowing what to do. She switched Andraste to her left hand and turned her body away from the magma beast so it wouldn't see her grasp Silver Knight then started running around the warrior. Normally, she wouldn't do this until her attacker ran out of arrows but the giant seemed to have an endless supply forming from its lava body so she'd have to wait for an opening. Till then, she kept dodging, all the while keeping her left arm, holding Andraste, pointed at the humanoid deflecting arrows.

She waited patiently...wait for it...wait...finally there was a lull in time between the arrows firing. It was a small second, but it was all Rosey needed. She immediately pulled Silver Knight from its sheath, sending the small dagger hurtling toward the lava creature with expert precision, ironic given her terrible aim as an archer. It was so distracted by the crossbow's malfunction that it didn't notice the dagger before it was too late. The blade, however, hadn't been for the humanoid, only for its crossbow. The dagger imbedded perfectly in the crossbow and tipped the humanoid off balance, distracting it. As fast as lightning, Rosey jumped forward and kicked the warrior off its feet and onto its back. Expertly, she had Andraste hovering at the creature's neck as it propped itself up. The battle was over, Rosey had won.

She backed away as the humanoid reabsorbed the crossbow and its sword back into its body, yielding. Silver Knight clattered to the ground and the humanoid picked it up. It bent on one knee and extended the dagger, hilt first, to her. Rosey reached out and took it, sheathing it. The creature then stepped backwards and into the flowing magma-covered walls, reabsorbing back into its surface. The doorways were suddenly flung open and the way forward was once again clear.

Rosey turned and saw the wall surrounding Alex and Rochelle disappear. They stepped toward her, weapons' still drawn, covered in sweat but looking none the worse for wear. They looked around but when they saw Rosey and her calm demeanor, they sheathed their weapons.

"What happened? You know what, hold that thought. Let's get out of here first!" Alex said, extending his arms to the open doors.

No one argued and they quickly rushed out of the boiling room, pausing a few feet down the much cooler corridor to rest and recover. Rochelle twirled more air about them, the relatively warm breeze was far cooler than it had been inside the room and Rosey sighed.

She smiled, finally able to answer Alex after downing the last of her water. "Well guys, I think I just won my first test."

Alex grinned, wiping sweat from his face. "Really," then his face fell, "and I missed it, man...I would have liked to have cheered you on!"

"You and I both," Rochelle added looking just as disappointed. She looked far more exhausted than Alex and no wonder given she had managed to keep the air going during the battle.

"Don't worry," Rosey soothed. "I'm kinda happy you didn't see what happened." They gave her startled looks but didn't ask her to elaborate. "By the way, thanks for the air, Rochelle. How did you manage to keep it up?"

Rochelle grinned. "Not easily, I had to meditate and ask the air where you were. Then I *also* had to keep it going for myself and Alex."

Rosey blinked, amazed. She'd heard how elementals could communicate with their element. The mental link was random and had nothing to do with their level. An apparition level might be able to hold whole conversations with their element while a queen level might barely be able to speak to it. The link could also come and go as different forms. For some people it manifested as a ghostly spirit, for others it was a simple thought in one's head. She licked dry lips. *That's got to be what this nagging feeling is right?* Though the fight had been a good distraction, the nagging was back, calling out to her with even more persistence than before.

She fidgeted, eager to keep going and wiped sweat from her brow. She nodded towards the hallway. "Are we ready? I've got an element to collect!"

She didn't wait for them to agree but ran on ahead, sheathing Andraste as she went, the others following.

CHAPTER SEVENTEEN

The First Element

To Rosey's utter horror, they spent almost another hour following her nagging feeling through intricate passageways. They stayed alert as they went but didn't come across anymore chambers filled with magma humanoids looking for a fight. After a few more turns and bridges over flowing magma, they entered a gigantic room and halted on a small platform suspended about twenty yards above the bottom. Exhausted from their long trek, they grabbed the railing and surveyed their surroundings.

Looming about a mile above them was the gaping hole of the crater. Evening light poured in from above, casting dim but sufficient light, and the air was cool and still like the inside of a cave. Below, the crater's bottom was a wide black circular floor. There, a single flame flickered at the center, waiting for them.

Rochelle nodded to it. "What do you want to bet we've come to the end of the road?"

Alex and Rosey nodded. Her words sent shivers up Rosey's spine with its irony, but Rochelle didn't seem to notice. She looked to her left and saw stairs leading down to the ground.

"Let's not keep it waiting," she said and quickly pushed onward. She hated to rush, but the throbbing in her head was starting to really get to her.

Rosey slowed as the stairs steepened and she gripped the railing with one hand, using the other for balance. In her peripheral vision she saw Alex and Rochelle doing the same. She'd rather get there safely then end up as an omelet on the ground. Besides, she'd waited this long, she could wait a little longer. But that was getting harder to do, the nagging was horrendous, its call almost like a scream in her head. It took all her strength to stop herself from holding her head in pain. And, as if that wasn't enough, even her sword Andraste was beginning to vibrate in its sheath as if excited, or in rebellion, or...something.

Finally, they reached the bottom, casting their gaze across the wide crater. Blinding light penetrated the darkness, making her squint. The towering walls intensified the light into a ball shape, like the sun at its brightest during the day. It hurt her eyes and put pressure on her already throbbing head, so, instead, she looked down. The circular black floor covered the entire crater's circumference. Rosey squinted, making out grooves in the rich black rock. She bent to examine them and noticed they corresponded to one another in intricate patterns. They weren't natural, they were *made*. Alex joined her, smoothing his hand over the ridges. Rosey did the same but it didn't feel any different than what she thought hardened lava would feel like. That's what it looked like anyway: hardened lava.

Nearby Rochelle danced from foot to foot, her gaze locked on the floating flame at the center of the room.

"Well, this certainly isn't' what I pictured when I imagined an Elemental Well," she remarked, giving the flame a sideways glance.

Rosey straightened and she and Alex joined the brunette. She looked the free-floating flame up and down. From afar, it had resembled a small flame no larger than the length of her arm. She'd been mistaken. It was very clearly as big as she was, reaching up towards the crater as if a giant candle was lit beneath it. For a moment, Rosey found herself looking for a wick and chuckled at the thought.

"No, this definitely isn't what I pictured either," Alex agreed. He looked at Rosey. "What do you say? Is this it?"

He inclined his head to the flame and she shrugged. "I don't know." She put a hand to her forehead, the throbbing was coming so hard it was getting difficult to ignore. "All I know...is that my head is killing me..."

She couldn't say much more and Alex and Rochelle exchanged concerned looks. They started talking but Rosey could barely hear them anymore behind the throbbing. Something was calling to her, something sharp and strong. It wasn't coming from her chest, so it had to be the element. She paced forward suddenly and started running; drawn by inner instincts she didn't understand. Rochelle and Alex gave off startled cries as she moved but Rosey didn't wait for them. It was as if she was no longer in control of herself. Quickly and without hesitation she thrust herself into the dancing flames.

Power rushed through Rosey's body, more intense than anything she'd felt before, like a whip cracking across her brain. Very quickly the throbbing in her head dissipated as if it had never been, instead she was filled with brilliant warmth. Suddenly the cracks in the floor lit up as real lava flowed in-between the grooves, seemingly fed from the dancing fire that surrounded her. At her chest, the Shanobie Crystal began to shine a bright orange light, pulsating with energy.

Rosey glanced at herself, expecting to see her flesh burning, but she was unharmed, cradled in the flames like a mother holding its child. Heat rushed over her skin but didn't harm her, the billowing hot air filled her lungs but it didn't hurt to breathe. She gasped at the sensation. Why had she entered the flame so willingly? Shouldn't she have been scared? But without any thought for herself she'd boldly taken the plunge. *What was I thinking?*

"What indeed?" a gentle feminine voice asked from no place in particular.

Rosey glanced around, still caught in the flames' grasp, but saw nothing to suggest anyone had spoken and the voice had very clearly not been from Rochelle or Alex. The two were looking around, their eyes wide and confused. At least they'd heard it too. Who was it? She didn't have to wait long to get her answer.

A gush of exploding fire burst from the magma under the hardened lava floor forming an arch and landing in a swirling mass of crackling energy before them, the floor repairing itself in its wake. Swathed in flames the magma formed into an orange and gold pegasus. Beautiful red, orange, and golden wings, their plumes blazing with liquid fire, folded along her back elegantly. Long tendrils of crackling fire made up her mane and tail. A line of flames danced down her back connecting them like a dorsal fin. Twisting fiery plumes enveloped her forelegs and flame extended from her shoulders, blowing back towards her flanks. Her glowing red streaked body gave the impression of flowing lava. Her golden eyes glowed as if an ember lit them from within. She was huge, at twenty-five hands, as large as Ysandir and just as majestically powerful.

The pegasus regarded her. "Not many would have entered that flame so willingly, little Keeper." Her voice was intrigued, not mocking. She cocked her head at Rosey, as if confused. "Why, even Esperanza took a few moments to realize what I wanted...but you..." She paused, pursing horse lips. "You're different?"

Was it a question? Rosey didn't quite know. Her mind was starting to feel muddled.

Rochelle and Alex were stunned into silence, their eyes bright and amazed at the same time, locked on the Mother in silent awe. She paid them no mind and approached Rosey cautiously, her body as beautiful as it was intimidating. Her massive wings arched over her, making her look much bigger than she was.

"Well, no matter. You've passed my tests," the Mother said, her voice matter-of-fact. "You've earned your reward."

She paced forward and reached her giant head unflinchingly into the flames. Without explanation she placed her forehead to Rosey's. Rosey gasped as heat sizzled up and down her body, nerves tingling. Despite the strangeness, she felt oddly relaxed, it was like a list of instructions were filling her head suddenly. In a heartbeat, something took over and she was in a stupor. The only thing that seemed to matter was the pegasus and what she bore inside her. Rosey could almost see it, there, turning inside. The element was suddenly the center of her world, the thing she needed above all others, and the Mother had it with her!

Her eyes flashed and Rosey smiled, overtaken with a need she did not quite understand. She could hear the element pulsating inside the Mother's body, beating with her heart. The Mother smiled and long red tendrils of energy began to pulse from her body, surrounding Rosey in a heated cocoon. The Mother neighed slightly, but didn't move. Suddenly the element surged from her body, releasing waves of cascading energy. The ground shook and the crater rumbled as the fiery power beared down on Rosey becoming a menacing fireball. It struck her straight on and consumed her in massive fiery torrents.

Rosey gasped as her body was filled with an inexplicable heat. Startled, she fought it at first, but some deep instinct set in and she relaxed into its fiery grip. She was ready for this. Somewhere inside she'd always been ready. The heat overwhelmed her and she cried hot tears of...happiness. They felt so strange yet so perfect. Pure joy filled her heart, but it wasn't coming from her, it was coming from the element. It was singing with joy, burning with jubilation and crackling over her skin excitedly. Rosey had no other way to describe it. The element's joy coursed through her, so filled with purpose it screamed through her consciousness. It was like the element was welcoming her, talking to her, soothing her. Then Rosey heard it, a sound like distant thunder, calling something. Her name? It *was* her name.

Slowly she opened her eyes. At first the strange heat and exploding emotional power made her flinch. The element sensed her pain and backed off, but flickered as close as it could without hurting her. Rosey focused and tried to make out what it was saying. A strange form appeared before her swathed in flame. All she could make out were two yellow eyes burning with intense heat. Finally, she could hear it, echoing all around her. The voice sounded like the crackling of a fire in a warm hearth and though the words echoed around her they were also in her mind, making her start when the creature spoke. It gasped and wisped, drawing out the s's on its words.

"Oh Rosssssey, Rosssssey, Rosssssey! My chosen one, my Master, my Keeper! It is so good to sssssee you again, ssssso good to be one

**with you after we've been sssssseparated for ssssso long. I love you
with all my fiery passssssion. My Rosey, my child, my flower. Take me
and do with me as you see fit!"**

Rosey's brows furrowed. *Again? What does it mean by again?* But she
couldn't answer or even cry out for at that moment the fire exploded
around her like a thousand fireworks. She wanted to scream, not in pain,
but in jubilation. The stinging of the heat was exciting, exhilarating, racing
across her body and setting her blood on fire.

She couldn't see the Mother backing away, exhausted, nor her friends
taking a step back, eyes wide with awe. All she could see was the fire.
Around them the crater rumbled and giant rocks tumbled from the walls.
She was numb to it all but the gentle stirring of power as the element forged
with her, its real master, its real mother! She was the one it belonged to, the
one it hungered for. She let it come, welcoming a new part of herself. She
felt a little more complete in that moment as if a small void inside her had
been filled. She was the Keeper, this was *her* element!

As the element filled her, the last dregs of power settled into simmering
control. The nagging sensations thundering through her head faded away,
replaced by new strength. She opened her eyes and cupped the power in her
palms. Feeling the love that beat there, she let it encircle and change her.
Her hair and eyes changed to a deep orange with red and yellow streaks.
Her outfit burst into flames and a new orange one blossomed across her
body. There was a powerful jerk as the fire encircled her again and she
suddenly started falling. She felt a twisted pain as something hard grew
near her shoulders. Wings! She had wings! Not knowing she'd been lifted
into the air in the first place she instinctively unfolded her fiery wings and
flapped, lifting into the air effortlessly. It took a while to get used to the
movement and the new muscles in her back but finally she got the hang
of it, the knowledge coming naturally somehow. Maybe it came with the
element? At that moment she didn't care. She flew around the crater's
circumference laughing joyously, looping and soaring all the while trailing
miniature fires from her plumes in her wake.

Looking down she saw Alex and Rochelle jumping up and down
whooping and cheering her on. Her gaze rested on the Mother, who ex-

amined her with something like surprise but Rosey didn't care, she was just so happy. Landing, she folded her giant wings neatly behind her, the thick flaming plumage trailing the ground. Alex stared at her in wonder and Rochelle smiled.

"YOU'VE GOT WINGS!" Rochelle shouted. She danced around Rosey cautiously, instinctual fears making her weary of Rosey's flames.

Rosey laughed. "I KNOW!" she screamed back before prancing around excitedly like a child.

The heavy wings unbalanced her and she almost toppled to the floor on top of them but caught herself in time, her wings flailing to balance herself. She laughed giddily and Rochelle giggled nearby.

"Careful now," Alex said as he approached. He ducked as she turned to him, almost winging him in the head.

She gasped but smiled again despite herself. "Sorry, these wings are going to take some getting used to."

"Hell yeah!" Rochelle agreed, looking them over. She bit her lip. "Can I touch one?"

Rosey glanced at the Mother. "Can she?" The brilliant wings *were* covered in dancing flames after all.

The Mother nodded and neither girl waited. Rosey quickly stretched out one of her wings toward Rochelle who backed away slightly. It was easily over twelve feet long. Rochelle gently ran her hand over the superheated feathers.

"It's like a soft feathery pillow!" she squealed excitedly.

Alex joined her and ran his hand along the wing, eyes wide with awe.

Curiously, Rosey reached out and touched them, surprised by how soft they were. Like air and smooth cotton, warm but not scalding. Rosey felt breathless, overcome with joy. She tested the muscles, feeling the way her second arm bent, moving the wing as if she needed to be certain they really existed. She beat them and flapped them, loving the fiery tendrils that swirled off of their heavy plumage.

This was the stuff of legends and it was happening to her, her! She'd never imagined this in a million years, and yet it all felt so perfect and so...right. She couldn't quiet the raging storm inside her: the power, the strength. It was like drinking a fizzy drink and enjoying the feel of carbonated liquid running down your throat.

It was then she noticed her clothes had changed. Looking down, she gawked. She was now wearing a sleeveless, orange, midriff top, cut below her breasts down the middle, the lose sides tied in place across her stomach through her belt. A red, metal plate, decorated in golden designs, covered her breasts in an 'm' shape. Long red metal strips encircled her arms. Looking closely, she saw they were shaped like dragon scales. Her matching orange pants were covered in crimson knee-high boots, also designed to look like dragon scales. A gold head band with orange ambers rested gently on her forehead. But her fiery armor wasn't the only change, at Rosey's shoulders were two masses of fire, blowing outward. They were not in the least bit hot near her face. She shrugged and watched as the billows responded, moving in rhythm. They were there to stay.

Glancing at her arms, she whistled, astonished. The muscles had doubled in size, and she flexed them admiringly, imagining what she could crush with them. She was also a lot taller than she remembered. Her head was almost as tall as the Mother's was and Alex and Rochelle's heads only came up to her chest. She felt like a titan or a queen. She was bigger, badder, stronger, and a hell of a lot more powerful. She could feel the fire running through her veins and the heat falling off her in waves. It was exhilarating and strange at the same time. She felt complete, perfect, as if she'd found something she'd been missing. It was...the perfect feeling.

She gave the Mother an awestruck look. "You didn't tell me I'd have wings. This is awesome!"

The Mother tossed her head. "I...didn't know!" she admitted, amused as she watched Rosey heft the wings. "I don't think Esperanza had wings."

"She most certainly did not," Alex confirmed. "If she had, the stories of her power would be far more thrilling than they already are." He squinted as he examined Rosey's armor. "Though, I believe there was some mention of a 'transformation' of some kind. The armor must take on a different form for each Keeper," he reasoned.

Rochelle elbowed him. "Leave it to you to analyze it, Alex! Rosey, in other words, you look...stunning!"

"Thanks," she said turning a complete 360 to show off her fiery self.

Alex smiled and glanced away embarrassedly. He seemed unsure around her suddenly and she frowned. She'd been his friend for so long, she could only imagine what it must be like to look upon her when she was so different. Still, she was just too happy to give it much more thought, she finally had an element! The Shanobie crystal glowed a brilliant orange as if in confirmation. It felt like holding an inferno inside her heart. She could hear faint whispers in the flickering flames surging through her. Patterns of orange, yellow and red colored her vision. She sighed and breathed deeply, as if feeding the oxygen to the fire instead of her lungs. Her whole body radiated.

Suddenly Rosey fidgeted as she felt Andraste hum against her back in a way she hadn't felt before. She pulled it from its sheath and the blade exploded into flames. Alex and Rochelle jumped back as Rosey brought the burning blade in front of her. It looked exactly the same except the blade had turned a bright whitish orange, as if heated in a forge. Flames licked at its edges pulsating with heat. Studying it for a few moments, she finally sheathed it. As the blade entered the leather sheath, the flames snuffed out. *So, it's only like this when I'm in this form,* she thought eyeing her new look. She smiled, impressed then glanced down at Silver Knight. Curiously she pulled the dagger free, but it didn't transform or even glow. Rosey sheathed it, a little disappointed but not daunted.

"This is amazing! I can't wait to see what the other elements feel like!" she said giddily, bursting with energy.

"In such a hurry to leave Mercury, Rosey?" the Mother asked, amused.

Rosey spun around, surprised. In all her excitement she'd almost forgotten the pegasus. She smiled sheepishly. The Mother's voice was distinctly feminine though not as sophisticated sounding as Ysandir's. It had more of a homey feeling, like she'd known Rosey her whole life.

Rosey rubbed her head apologetically. "Sorry about that. Mercury...is that your name?"

"Yes it is," Mercury said, drawing closer. Her hooves silent on the dirt floor.

Her fiery power had died down now, calmer than before. Rosey noticed the flames that had originally created her mane, tail, wings, and feathered legs were gone, replaced instead with regular hair and feathers. Her mane and tail were bright red with golden flecks while her skin was a sharp orange with red designs at her flank looking much like an appaloosa. Her hooves were pure black like coal and her large wings were red with yellow and black highlights. She was just as large as she was before but since Rosey was almost as large as she was now, she was not as intimidating.

"You now have the power of Fire, Rosey. Use it wisely for it can be very wild as well as tame. You must find the balance between them and use it to your advantage. This is your first element; thus, your tests were very simple."

Rosey wanted to protest, but Mercury's words made Rosey go still. If those tests were easy, then what else would she have to face with the other elements?

Mercury continued. "Normally the first test would challenge your control of your birth element but, because you lack an element...well..." Rosey felt herself go cold despite the heat. She didn't question how Mercury knew; she'd actually be more surprised if she *hadn't* known. The Mother's withers twitched embarrassedly at having brought up the touchy subject but went on. "So...given the circumstances, I rearranged my test. It consisted of two parts: the first was for you to find me on your own. Which you did...rather quickly," she said under her breath as if surprised. "Your task was simple, track the element and let it lead you to it. I admit I intensified things a bit..."

"You made me feel all those things before? That nagging feeling?" Rosey asked incredulously. It had felt so natural and yet so rampant.

"Yes and no, I simply intensified something that was already there. When you draw close to the element, you'll begin to sense it. It helps you find it, otherwise you could be running around it and never know the difference and we don't want that."

Rosey shook her head. "No, I wouldn't think so." Still did it have to be so painful?

Mercury paused before her. "The ability to sense the elements comes naturally to the Keeper, so don't be surprised when you next feel it, but what *I* did was far more powerful than what you should normally feel. It was a way for me to help establish *and* test the bond between you." She leaned in closer. "There is no greater bond than the one forged between you and the elements. It's that bond that led you to me. You did splendidly; better than I thought you'd do for your first time." Rosey felt her cheeks flush with pride, but it could have also been heat for all she knew. "The second part was a physical test. I wanted to see how well you'd do under harsh conditions, which is why it was fairly hot, and I also wanted to see how you'd react to a one-on-one fight. You also passed these tests with flying colors and far more skill than I expected for someone of your age. You've had extensive training prior to being chosen, haven't you?"

Rosey smiled. "Yes, my uncle taught me the basics and my friends were my sparring partners. Not to mention I've picked up a thing or two from various refugees and travelers in Neran." She turned her gaze away. The mention of her uncle opened up a can of worms she didn't like getting into. It still held a hard edge for Rosey, even though she understood the circumstances.

Mercury tossed her now normal mane. "As he should, he knew you were special and did the best he could...it shows. Though I doubt he imagined you'd have to face real danger." She paused before moving on. "You were exquisite in the fight, that's the fastest anyone's ever won against my magma golem."

Rosey recognized the word golem. A golem was a creature that could be made of any material substance but had no mind or soul of its own. It was created simply for the purpose of carrying out its creator's will. Most golems were made from earth or rocks but they could be formed using any material except gases like air.

Rosey looked at her sharply. "The magma golem I fought one on one? I was the fastest? Really?"

She nodded. "Yes, Esperanza was a great warrior but my golem is made to find your weaknesses and use them against you. Esperanza was far too passive and was shot down at least three times before she finally got smart." Mercury snickered and pawed the ground.

Rosey gave her a surprised look. "Wait, what do you mean she was shot down three times!? Are you telling me those arrows wouldn't have hurt me?" She gestured back in the direction of the stairs leading out the way they came. Alex and Rochelle gave Mercury a questioning look.

Mercury laughed, once again pawing the ground. "Of course not, dear! None of the Mothers would ever make a challenge you could actually *die* from! If you'd been hit by an arrow or the sword, you'd just feel the pain as if it *had* hurt you. It wouldn't have actually done you any damage. We're not *evil*. If you fail a test, it won't end in your death, only the knowledge that you...you know...failed."

Rosey knew all too well what that meant. The Golden Goddess had been very specific. If she failed even one test, she'd not earn the element. There were no second chances. Rosey thought this was a bit unfair; after all, everyone made mistakes, but the Goddess had insisted these challenges weren't lessons to be learned but rather proof that you were worthy of the element's power. Failing meant you weren't ready. It was as simple as that. Though the Shanobie Crystal was good at choosing the right person, it was ultimately up to the individual to prove their worth. Rosey had to be very certain she took every test seriously, still, it was nice to know her life would never be in danger.

Mercury spoke again, pulling Rosey from her thoughts. "But other tests will not be so kind, Keeper." Her voice became stiff and she eyed Rosey intensely. "These tests may be the worst things you fight or the best. They could challenge your beliefs, your understanding of life, and even your perception of reality. Always be brave and ready for anything."

Rosey nodded, feeling like the mother had given her a promise instead of a warning. Turning to gaze at the walls of the volcano, Rosey's brows furrowed. "Um... what happened to the volcano, if you don't mind me asking?"

She cast her gaze about her puzzled. The chamber's charcoal black bottom with its odd grooves had been replaced by regular old dirt with small clumps of greenery here and there. The fiery power that had flowed before was no longer there as if it had never existed. It felt suddenly dead and lifeless, despite the greenery. It was like they were now in an extinct volcano. What had happened? Had the Elemental Well suddenly run dry thanks to Rosey's success? No, it was as if the *very being* of the volcano had shifted suddenly and changed.

Rosey swallowed, sudden understanding making her sweat. Did *she* do something to it? Had it been zapped of its own fiery power! With a sinking feeling, she wondered if the exchange of the element between herself and the Mother had caused it, but why? The natural magma of the volcano wasn't fed by the element but the mantle, like any other. It had to have been an external source that caused it...right?

She looked to the mother expectantly. The large pegasus regarded their surroundings. "I'm not sure," she answered, brows furrowing with shock. "I believe my elemental presence may have aggravated it, and then, for some reason, once you collected the element it...died. Almost as if the power keeping it going was sucked out." She stared at one spot on the wall, taken by her thoughts. Rosey wasn't sure what to say or do. Finally, Mercury huffed as if it was nothing. "Oh well, this volcano has a habit of doing whatever it wants. I believe the magical barrier around the volcano is still in place, though, so you shouldn't have to fear any attacks."

"But...what about the Well?" Alex asked, looking around. "Isn't the volcano *still* the Well of Fire?"

Mercury bobbed her head. "Yes and no. What makes a Well is *not* that the element is using it. There are Wells all over the world, places where the Energy Flows touch the surface of our world. The elements simply use these Wells to disperse their power to the people, allowing them to be elementals." She then nodded to Rosey. "To make sure people can still use their elemental power, *Rosey* essentially becomes a *replacement* Well so fire can continue being used by the world's fire elementals. Otherwise, people would lose the ability to work the element once Rosey collected it."

There was stunned silence at this. The three friends exchanged amazed and shocked looks.

"No one told me that," Rosey stuttered, feeling slightly queasy.

"Of course not," Mercury snorted. "That is information only the Mothers, Addina, and the Keeper knows." She glanced at Rochelle and Alex. "And the Keeper's direct friends, and it's imperative that you keep it that way. Even Esperanza didn't speak of this information to anyone and neither should you."

Rosey had learned a lot from the Goddesses and the guards, but not even her uncle had mentioned this little situation. He *must have not known either...or was keeping the secret as he'd promised.* Though, with Rosey being the next Keeper there'd be little reason to. Rosey's hand went to the crystal and it grew warm at her touch, but that warmth now held a lot more meaning than it did before.

"Could I have..." she asked hesitantly, "...been the reason behind the volcano's...?" She didn't want to say death, but it felt like that and a little fear filled her heart at the idea. Her friends exchanged quick glances; their expressions unreadable.

"I'm not sure, could have been, but..." The pegasus shook her head as she saw Rosey's face become stricken with surprise. "It's not important. There's no reason to fear. If it was you, then it was, and that's nothing to be afraid of. If my presence affected it than I'd hope yours would too, since you are the Keeper and your power far outweighs my own. Please Keeper, do not worry," she insisted.

Her voice was reassuring but Rosey didn't feel better. How powerful was she to be able to affect something as strong as the famous Molt Volcano?

The Mother suddenly cleared her throat, drawing their attention. "I must take my leave, Keeper. Without the Well to bind me to this place, I am free to scatter my fiery influence. That means flying around Hondan to try and take on any Raptors, Gorons, or *slippery assassins* that might be about." Rosey and friends exchanged looks. "Farewell! And rest easy tonight, but the sooner you're back on the road the better, I'm afraid. You may use this shortcut to get outside if you like." Mercury waved her head to a separate passageway a few feet from where they stood, heading back the way they'd come.

Rosey regarded her, surprised by her abrupt end to their meeting, but she understood. She didn't have time to waste here. *Especially if she's going to be patrolling Hondan for my sake!* Rosey and friends thanked her with deep bows, Rosey's wings folding out at the sides. When she rose her leather outfit was back and her wings and shoulder fires were gone. She hadn't really noticed the fire power receding but it felt almost natural as if she'd been doing it her whole life.

For a few moments Mercury stared at her with something like curiosity and intrigue in her bright eyes, but before Rosey could ask what was wrong, the pegasus returned Rosey's bow and turned away. She watched in awe as the fiery pegasus lifted into the air with massive beats of her giant wings before flying up and out of the crater.

Rosey blinked away the sight, then turned and hugged Alex and Rochelle again, her doubts forgotten in the excitement of the moment. She'd finally taken the first real step to saving the world! She expected to feel tired or something but instead she felt powerful and strong, like she could handle a whole group of Raptors! Her heart beat fast as she thought about the fiery power within her and wondered what it would feel like using it in combat! Finally, she'd feel like a true warrior and elemental! Like she belonged.

She sighed. Had her mother felt this way about the elements? Did she have the same need to be with them? And what about what the element had said to her, that it was happy to be with her *again*? She might never know but that didn't matter. She couldn't let anything get in the way of her goal. She pulled away from Alex and Rochelle then, with a sly smile, took off quickly down the passageway.

"Race ya back!" she called over her shoulder with a laugh.

"No fair, you always play dirty!" Alex shouted taking off after her once he'd recovered from his open-mouthed shock.

Rochelle raced to catch up. They laughed all the way out of the volcano and into the dying sunlight.

Chapter Eighteen

Aftermath

When Rosey, Alex, and Rochelle returned to camp, the others stood to attention, the burning question of her success reflected in their eyes and Rosey wasted no time. Smiling, she changed, igniting the fire element through her body and flying above their heads. Everyone gapped at her with awe before clapping and cheering.

Rosey returned to the ground and her regular form before gathering around the fire talking hurriedly. They moved in close, captivated by her tale. When she explained how the volcano died, everyone became silent. She asked if they knew what could have happened but no one had an answer. She still had a feeling she'd caused it but there was nothing she could do about it now.

"Okay, I admit, I've been saving this for just this moment!" Rochelle said, smiling broadly as she bent over her travel bags, rummaging through them till she took out a hidden bottle of Wineswallow.

Rosey's eyes brightened and Wolvereen licked his chops. "Ooooo, you've been holding out on us wind-child," he said, smiling.

Rosey would have to concur, Wineswallow was a finely crafted drink that tasted like grape juice but had a warm almost intoxicating affect, making you feel giddy but not ridiculous and was completely harmless to the body. It was hard to get ahold of and most production had stalled since the Raptors and Gorons made keeping large vineyards almost impossible. Necessity had overtaken common delicacies.

She marveled at Rochelle. "Where have you been hiding that?"

She shrugged. "It was a present from my parents. They'd been holding onto it for years and well...when they heard about you, they figured you could use the pick-me-up," she explained as she served the drink.

Rosey accepted her cup thankfully, inhaling the sweet fragrance wafting from the purple liquid. It was like violets mixed with honey. She smiled, closing her eyes with bliss. She'd had it before when her uncle had surprised her with a bottle for her sixteenth birthday. The thought of him made her heart ache slightly, she knew he'd be so proud of her.

Alex raised his cup when everyone was served. "To Rosey and the quest!" His gaze locked with hers. "May we be successful and the world be safe once again!"

They cheered and tipped back the drink, letting out loose giddy exhales at the bubbly taste. Afterward, Rochelle and Alex made a feast from the supplies, cutting away chunks of meat from a kill Wolvereen had brought down while they'd been in the volcano and roasting it with vegetables they'd foraged. Combined with the Wineswallow, it was the best thing Rosey had ever eaten. The party lasted for two hours as they told stories, their laughter ringing through the night air. Wolvereen was even persuaded to tell them one of his many battle stories from the war. Eglen launched into storytelling mode, putting in details that Wolvereen left out.

Through all the excitement, the team managed to discuss their next plan and Wolvereen, ever the serious one, suggested they stay put. Even though the volcano now seemed lifeless, it was still providing a barrier from Gorons and Raptors, the Mother herself had confirmed this. Leaving would be irrational since they had no idea where they'd be heading next. Not to mention that it provided a more agreeable climate for camping.

"What about the ship? It's waiting for us at dock, isn't it?" Rochelle asked, frowning.

"The ship will be fine, as well as its crew," Wolvereen assured them. "Their orders are to wait until we arrive, however long that may be. And don't fear for its safety. Captain Marine is the best and the Golden Goddess has trusted him with her transportation for a while now. Believe me, he can handle himself." His gaze locked with Rosey's. "Until the White Witch gives you the next destination, we'd be sailing out blindly. We need to wait."

Rosey nodded. "Agreed, let's hope the Witch comes sooner rather than later."

A round of agreement went up from the team before they started celebrating again and pouring more Winsewallow. Eventually, night beckoned and they all settled down for sleep, the humans snuggling in their bed rolls, exhausted from the day's events. The sooner Rosey was asleep the sooner she might see the Witch. Despite this, she lay awake, excitement and possibly Wineswallow keeping her up. Examining the night sky, she determined it was probably around eleven o'clock. She wanted to sleep but her mind was still a buzz. Judging by the hushed whispers the others were just as awake but remained silent, unwilling to disturb each other.

Rosey heard Noly's soft snores next to her bedroll and Hazel pushed herself into Rosey's pillow by her head. Everything was so peaceful. Who would have thought she'd do something this amazing!? All the things she'd heard and learned was all real! The idea shook her to the core but excited her as well. Maybe she *was* cut out for this after all? Still, being the Keeper wasn't going to be easy and Rosey knew that. Collecting the elements guaranteed she'd be in constant danger, especially now that it seemed like the assassin, Raptors, and Gorons had caught onto her. She might have gained power, but she'd adopted a responsibility that was bigger than herself. Looking around, her eyes ran over the sleeping figures of her friends. They all depended on her. They weren't just there for a road trip. They were there to make sure she made it through alive.

A sudden image flashed through her head. The woman she thought she'd seen when the Raptors collapsed the caves. Had it been...her mother? She knew it was impossible, her mother was dead. Yet, she was certain the figure had resembled her. Rosey closed her eyes against the memory, feeling restless. She'd kept what she'd seen to herself, afraid of what her friends might say. Still, was it that impossible to think she might have hallucinated her mother's image in her time of need? Some might have even called it normal.

Sighing, Rosey pushed it out of her mind. She couldn't let it bother her. She'd made a promise. An oath to give everything she had to this journey and she didn't intend to quit or turn back no matter the perils...or the hallucinations.

Taking her parent's locket from her pocket she examined her uncle's face, then flipped it to her parents, her gaze resting on her mother. "I won't fail you...mom," she whispered, breathlessly. The crystal warmed at her chest and she fell into a deep sleep, her mind a comfortable twist of fire and flames.

Before they settled down to sleep, Alex and Rochell took a few moments to sneak away. Alex needed to tell Rochelle something important and the look he'd given her let her know it was serious. They successfully managed to sneak off without drawing any questions and once again found themselves behind one of the large boulders that surrounded the camp.

Taking a deep breath Alex said, "Remember when Rosey was flying around the volcano cavern after receiving the element?"

Rochell nodded, brows furrowing.

"Well," he said, framing his words carefully, "Mercury... the Mother...I was watching her closely. She looked...confused? It was like Rosey was...doing something *wrong*?"

Rochelle stared at him and tried to remember, but she hadn't been paying very close attention to Mercury with Rosey flying around. She crossed her arms, and shifted her weight to her right leg. Alex recognized it as the position she took whenever she was considering something. It was the same thing her mother did.

"But, why would she do that? Was she surprised or something...I mean Rosey's *supposed* to collect the elements, right?"

"I asked Mercury that same thing and she told me not to worry about it, but she was staring at Rosey as if concerned! She had this look on her face...as if seeing something she didn't quite believe." He considered for a few moments, finger tapping on the boulder. "But...you remember when

Rosey stepped into that fire! She didn't even blink? It was like she was hypnotized."

"And when Mercury came, it was even weirder," Rochelle added, brows furrowing at the memory. "The Mother burst into flames and these red tendrils began running off her and into Rosey. It looked like Rosey was *sucking* the element right out of her!" She shook her head. "Rosey didn't look anything like her usual self. Her eyes were so blue they were shining and her hair looked like it was alive."

Alex shrugged. "I thought it was the way things were supposed to be. I mean, how would I know the difference? But then...the Mother looked far too surprised. I don't know what's happening but, whatever it is; Rosey's not doing what's expected. Something's *different* and I don't know if that's a good thing or a bad thing."

Neither of them spoke for a while after that, lost in their own thoughts.

Alex looked at Rochelle's worried expression. "That's not all. I don't understand why the volcano died," he added shaking his head. "That volcano has never been dormant. Do you think it's really possible Rosey 'zapped' the fire from it, causing it to die?"

Rochell shrugged, she'd noticed something was off as soon as Rosey transformed. The once lively volcano was suddenly, inexplicably, dormant and dead, as though suffocated. No one had dared cast negativity on it and squash Rosey's success but Rochelle had seen their surprise and restlessness.

Rochelle took a deep breath. "Listen there's nothing we can do about it and it's not like this volcano has ever been normal, right?" Alex nodded. "So...let's just let Addina worry about the rest."

"Yeah, I know. I just can't help but worry," Alex said.

Rochelle smiled. "Me either, but that's how it's going to be. Being there for her...it's the only thing we can do." She smiled and reached over to Alex, grasping his shoulders. "But hey, I'm just amazed and honored that I was able to witness all this. I mean, come on! Our best friend is the new Keeper? Did you ever think that would *ever* happen again?" Alex smiled, shaking his head and Rochelle went on. "We've always said we'd stick together. Even when Rosey told us she was powerless and only had her sword and fists to fight. Well...now *she's* the one leading the charge, and I couldn't be prouder. So what if she's a bit different? Maybe that's a good thing. Maybe that's the key that will finally end all this!?" She threw her arms out, taking in the world. She paced a few feet away before turning back to him, her face growing somber suddenly. "The only thing that worries me now...is protecting her from that assassin. She's still out there, somewhere...and what happened to Esperanza could happen again."

Alex gulped feeling himself go numb. It was true. After all this time, the assassin was still at large and no one had been able to find her. *At least Ysandir, the pegasi, and the unicorns can sense the assassin's presence now...but only if she comes close to them or Rosey...and that might not be enough.* If it hadn't been for the Goddess's crystal protection earlier...he shuddered. What if the same thing *were* to happen again? To himself, Wolvereen...anyone. They were all in danger from this secret enemy. *But who could it possibly be? Someone* was still out there who was willing and powerful enough to carry on the Raptor Demon's will. *Powers like mine...magic.* Alex thought, remembering the collapsed cave. His hand curled into a fist as anger replaced the worry.

"We know more than we did before about the assassin," he said. "We know, or at least believe, she's a female humanoid magikin. That puts us at an advantage we didn't have before."

"Yeah...but her being a magikin makes me even more worried. There are limitations to elemental power," Rochelle said, conjuring a breeze around her hands, rippling her hair. "But magic...yes I know it has limitations too," she said quickly as he was about to start listing them off, "*but* magic allows you to do things that my air can't, like conjure something, or create a shield...or take control of someone's mind..."

They both stared at each other. Alex fidgeted, becoming nervous and worrisome, thinking now of all the ways that the assassin could use her magical ability to hurt them.

Swallowing, he stood up straighter. "You're right, Rochelle. There's a very real chance something like that could happen. So, we have to be very careful. Not just you and me, everyone! We can't and won't let anything bad happen to Rosey!"

Rochelle faced him. "And you have to promise me, if the assassin does try to take control of my mind," she gave him a hard look, "then you...have to promise to take me out, you hear?"

Alex blinked, taking a step back. He took a deep breath and nodded. "I promise. And the same goes for me, too. Don't let me hurt her."

"I promise," she agreed quietly, her gaze more serious than it had ever been before.

After a few brief moments, they walked back to camp.

What they didn't know was that Wolvereen had heard them from the shadows. He watched them with a newfound respect and felt the weight of their words echo through his soul.

"I promise," he whispered, determinedly.

Balra watched the Molt Volcano from afar, eyes narrowed. She clenched her fists, anger flaring through her. Rosey was right there for the taking, it was as simple as walking up to her, but there was no chance of that. The volcano's defenses were strong and she knew without a doubt that it's protection would also bar her entry.

She'd really messed up. The thought sliced through her, but it was true. There was no denying it. She'd taken a huge risk when she'd approached Rosey during that battle. Revealing herself to the world like that. *And the unicorn, why in the world did it appear all of a sudden? It couldn't have been a coincidence that it appeared right when I got close to Rosey! How did it know?* Her mind fired off the possibilities, but the only reasonable explanation was that the unicorn had somehow sensed Balra approaching. *But that can't be...how? I made sure the poison was untraceable.* She sighed, exasperated. *It had to have just been unfortunate timing,* she told herself, but that explanation sounded very empty and desperate.

I shouldn't have approached; I shouldn't have revealed myself without a clear shot at Rosey. But how could she have resisted? Rosey had been so close! And yet, it had all been for nothing. Rosey was alive and well and had successfully collected the first element, Fire. Balra resisted the urge to scream, to pound her fists into the ground, to unleash the horrid poison coursing through her, it would do nothing to change what had happened. Instead, she took a deep breath and calmed her mind. *I need to focus and move past this.* She had to admit it. She needed help. She couldn't keep doing this on her own. *But how...how can I get the help I need!*

She rubbed the black stone on her chest and it hummed against her flesh, searing red suddenly, painfully, and she snatched her fingers away. She glanced at it sharply. That was the first time it had done that. Was something wrong? She glanced back at the volcano and wondered if, in some way, her Master was still aware of her struggles and was disappointed in her. Was that why it harmed her? Because she'd failed? It's not like she hadn't tried! The Goddesses were strong and their defenses made things difficult. And the unicorn had certainly thrown them for a loop, Balra doubted she'd have made it out alive if the Raptors and Gorons hadn't have kept the horned beast busy. There was little she could do against such odds, and the Guards had gone on to successfully hunt down most of the remaining Gorons and Raptors. Her army was disappearing!

The black stone seemed to sting again, slicing through her chest suddenly and she took a knee, bending under the sudden pain lacing her nerves. She gripped the tree she'd been hiding behind and yanked back the hood of her black robe so she could breathe better. She was still quite shaken from her encounter with the Silver Goddess's crystal, maybe the stone's activity had something to do with that?

The stone seared again and she moaned holding her head. What was going on?! Quite suddenly her mind filled with images, flashing across her vision so fast she barely saw them. She made out a location nestled far from here...the Scorched Mountain perhaps? The searing increased and she coughed. No, not the Mountain, another place...colder, more inhospitable....where was it? The images raced and she tried to keep up.

Like a fire igniting, something revealed itself to her. She gasped and gripped the tree's trunk suddenly overwhelmed at the information filling her mind. She sputtered and the tree beside her began to quake under her fingers, its bark crisping as it burned from the inside out. All around her, red and black leaves began to fall, littering the floor as the tree died.

Tears from pain and sheer joy rolled down her face and she smiled, almost laughing but managing to stay silent.

My Master's secrets, all its plans...things it did...things I wished I could have done! It's chosen to share them with me! She wiped the tears away, suddenly filled with giddy happiness. Her Master, whatever remained of it, had shared information with her she'd only dreamed of. Things she'd tried again and again to recreate but had always failed. There'd always been something missing but now she knew just what to do! All those holes in her knowledge had finally been filled! She wanted to shout for joy, but the Goddess' Guards might still be on patrol, so she stayed quiet, overcome by her happiness.

With this I can finally take charge and continue what my Master left behind. Finish what it started! She rubbed her hands together excitedly, thinking of all the things she could do. *What other things could I create? What affects would they in turn cause?* Her mind raced with the possibilities, adding, subtracting, and formulating equations in her mind.

Blindly she trudged forward, making her way through the trees, leaving the dead one behind. Already it was turning black, the ground tinted a slight purple as liquid poison wafted from the earth. The Raptor Demon's touch was devastating indeed but she barely noticed, she was too taken by what she now knew. *There's so much potential, more than before...so much more.* It's not just Rosey her Master wanted....it was everything! She shuddered with the ferocity of her Master's emotions. It could sense a deep danger from Rosey, a threat that wasn't there before and more powerful than Esperanza's had been. She'd felt it too, especially when, quite suddenly, the legendary Molt Volcano had been reduced to a dormant rock. A rock with a protective covering, but a rock nonetheless. With the new information she held, she'd change all that. She'd stop Rosey and any other who sought to undo her Master's creation!

Smiling, Balra rubbed the stone, now as cold as ice. On cue, a Goron joined her, stealthily landing beside her as if it had always been there.

"What do you command, my lady?" she asked, her crisp voice low, beady eyes regarding her.

"We've got some work to do and I'm going to need a few things. Get your best Gorons ready, we're going on a little scavenger hunt," she responded, her dark purple eyes alight with crazed passion.

John gazed out the window of the common room in the Golden Palace, watching the area where Rosey had left days before. He sighed against the odd little emptiness in his chest that had opened up when she'd left and closed his eyes against hot angry tears. He'd hated letting her go without him. Hated it more than anything, but the call to the Scorched Mountain was far too important to ignore. He took a deep breath, trying desperately to ease the ache, it was immediately soothed by the gentle voice that greeted him.

"Am I always to find you like this?" The Goddesses words were gentle and teasing. "You've been looking at the same spot for days now."

He turned to her, his chest now tightening with a new feeling, one he'd kept subdued for years now. One that Rosey had called him out on.

He smiled at the Goddess as she joined him. "I know, I just...hope she'll be all right," he admitted.

The Goddess's smile chased away his worry in seconds. "We have trained her well, John. Trust in her to use it wisely." She gripped his hands in hers, squeezing tightly.

He nodded asking, "Is there word yet from the Scorched Mountain Team? Are they ready?"

"Yes," she said with a sad smile, "they're finally ready for the team to arrive. They send their apologies for the unexpected delay."

John had expected to leave the Golden Palace shortly after Rosey's own departure, but the team's arrival had been delayed. Apparently, all of the most powerful unicorns and pegasi had been gathered at the Scorched Mountain with Addina, working on something important. She'd been trying to attach a scent to the poison that the unicorns and pegasi could detect, thus allowing them to identify the assassin that created it. They'd been at it ever since Addina first found the poison months ago and to get it right they'd needed to be free of all other distractions and scents, including the ones the team would have inevitably brought with them. So, the Mountain had been off limits till they finished. Success had come just two days ago, and Addina had the unicorns and pegasi leave the Scorched Mountain to seek out the assassin on their own.

"So, they can really scent out the assassin now?" John asked, incredulously.

"Seems so, but only if they come close to it."

"Shame they can't share the scent with other species."

"Agreed, it would make it easier." They stood silently for a moment, then the Goddess took a breath. "I don't want you to go. I'll miss you so much. It's been so nice having you here," her voice was low and breathless as she looked at him.

He couldn't look away from her, he felt his face flush as their gaze locked. "Tlow," he said softly, then immediately regretted it. He knew better than anyone how forbidden it was to say her name aloud. The power it held could harm her.

She shook her head. "I want you to say my name more than anyone else," she admitted, placing his hands on her chest and holding them there. She brought her right hand up to his left cheek, her palm warm against his pale skin. She leaned in close to him.

"I'll be leaving soon..." he whispered, a last pitiful attempt to stop what he knew was happening.

"I don't care," she whispered back before titling her face close to his, hoovering a few inches from his lips.

Rosey's words echoed back at him and the image of his sister and Matthew inside the locket flashed before him. It was time to stop being so stubborn! He closed the gap between them, pressing his lips into hers. Years of subdued passion erupted forth in moments and their kiss became more passionate, he wanted so much more and that shared desire drowned out the sound of the vortex that was opening nearby.

An awkward whinny finally broke the spell, but only slightly. Tlow stepped back a bit, but kept her arms around him, not willing to let him go after finally getting him. He couldn't blame her; he was just as unwilling to release her. Together, they turned their gaze to the newcomer, a giant green unicorn.

"You think you could come back in like…an hour," Tlow asked it, her voice slick like she'd had too much Wineswallow.

The unicorn's ears went parallel with the ground. "Sorry Golden Goddess, truly I am, but we need to get started as soon as possible. We've already been delayed enough as it is," he said with a deep voice. His pupil-less and iris-less eyes focused on John. "Magikin Master, John Mystic, I am Zeyzeen, leader of the Scorched Mountain Team, here to escort you there."

The unicorn bowed deeply, his green mane and tail were woven with vines and the crystal horn on his head had a green strip flowing through it. His hide was white with green dancing designs, moving about his large 25 hands tall form. His large green hooves were a darker green then the rest of him and his eyes seemed to glow with a slight greenish hue. It wasn't the first time John had seen a unicorn, he'd seen many of them, as well as pegasi, when he'd journeyed with Esperanza. Still, their sheer size and brilliance always amazed him no matter how many times he'd seen them.

"Ugggggh!" Tlow sighed, leaning back exaggeratedly with obvious annoyance.

John obligingly held onto her as she leaned backwards, supporting her full weight. He smiled as she righted herself and gazed into his eyes. He kissed her a few more times, drawing out the last kiss longingly, hugging her close. He then stepped away slightly, placing his forehead against hers.

"You come back to me and to Rosey, you hear," she whispered to him.

He nodded and kissed her forehead. "I will *not* keep you waiting again," he promised.

"Never you mind that, we were both a bit foolish and stubborn there," she admitted. "I will scry you often. Once I get word that Rosey is on the *Silent Marine*, I will let you know so you can scry her, too."

"Thank you, my Goddess," he said, kissing her hands.

She blinked back tears, and he did the same. It felt horribly wrong to leave her now, but there was no way to avoid the duty he'd been assigned and their planet relied on it.

"I love you, Tlow," he said, not caring what it might bring to say her name. He had to say it this way, at least once.

"And I love you, John," she responded, smiling. "Now go on, Zeyzeen is starting to get fidgety."

John glanced back to the unicorn surprised to see him awkwardly shifting his weight from hoof to hoof, looking anywhere but at the two of them. He smiled and with one last kiss, he left Tlow to go and get his things.

The ten minutes it took him to get back to his room, grab his things, which he'd pre-packed, and rejoin Zeyzeen and the Goddess seemed to fly by. She kissed him one last time as he followed the giant unicorn through its vortex, her left hand resting on his cheek as he passed through. The last thing he felt before the vortex carried him away from her, was the gentle touch of her hand on his.

The next thing he knew, he was stepping into the shadow of a giant blackened mountain, towering several miles above him. He'd refused to turn away from Tlow, so he was still facing away from the horrifying mountain, but no amount of will power would whisk him back to the woman he'd loved for so long. Taking a deep breath, he turned a determined gaze onto the place where his sister had made her last stand.

The mountain was huge, stretching in either direction like a terrifying black scar on the land. Sixteen years hadn't done anything to heal that scar, it was still as lifeless as it had been all that time ago. Nothing but black earth and charred debris remained. Memories came rushing back to John and the pain of loss and sorrow raced through him from head to toe. Cold wind froze the tears in his eyes and he pulled his winter jacket tighter about him. So many had died here, so many had fought here, and shed their blood. He thought time would have healed whatever tremors his war days had scored into him; he was very wrong. For a few moments, he couldn't move. He once again saw the land dotted with warriors screaming, crying, and jostling about. Raptors and Gorons slammed into them, teeth tearing, claws ripping, blood spurting. The air ran with the cries of the dying, and the clang of weapons, the sky was dotted with winged warriors caught in their own battles. He might not have partaken in the Battle of Scorched

Mountain, but he'd fought in plenty of other battles, and the stain it left in the land couldn't be forgotten or removed.

He swallowed back the bile rising in his throat and wiped the sweat at his temple. The healers had long ago diagnosed him with post-traumatic stress disorder. Most warriors who'd seen such battle as he had suffered from it, thankfully his case wasn't nearly as bad as others were. Still, he could feel his left hand shaking, his dominant arm, the one he cast spells with. As if it could sense his unease, his wand seemed to vibrate in its sheath on his right hip. He patted it thankfully and took long deep breaths to calm his racing heart.

You're safe, there's no battle here, he told himself over and over again. *Not yet anyway.*

He then noticed something odd about the mountain, there were pockets of color here and there, moving about. John squinted and realized they were unicorns and pegasi dotting the mountain in various locations, flitting about as they did their work. Whatever it was.

He joined Zayzeen's side. The giant had waited for him, no doubt he knew about John's disorder and was being patient with him for which John appreciated. The two of them made their way to a series of brown wooden structures nearby. It was clear that they'd been grown by an earth elemental and would serve as the temporary base camp for the team members while they were here. John wasn't so sure how he felt about being this close to the mountain where so many had died, but he wasn't about to complain. He had a job to do.

Approaching the largest structure, Zeyzeen and John suddenly came to a halt as a giant magenta and pink colored pegasus flew towards them from the tip of the mountain. It landed nearby, her wings sending air currents gusting about the two of them.

The pegasus nodded to them, "Zeyzeen, Master John, please hurry, there's something the two of you need to see," she insisted, her voice sharp and regal.

Zeyzeen exchanged glances with John then nodded to the pegasus. The tip of his horn glowed slightly and another vortex opened before them. The pegasi took to the air again while John hurriedly followed Zeyzeen through the swirling purplish mass. When he stepped into the light of day again, he was standing at the top of the mountain. For a moment, he was stunned by the sheer beauty of the world stretched out before him, but it was short lived as he immediately found it hard to breathe. He took out his wand and uttered a small spell, stabilizing his body and oxygen levels with the extreme elevation change. The pegasus joined them moments later, air currents twirling about her.

The three of them joined a group of people starring down into a huge crater inside the mountain top. They were deadly silent, eyes wide. John didn't examine the people for long, for his gaze was immediately consumed by the giant oval shaped object resting at the center of the blackened crater. It was surrounded by a swirling black and purple liquid-like substance. John swallowed apprehensively, shuddering with a terrifying dread like he'd never felt before.